J. J. Halcombe

The Emigrant and the Heathen

Or Sketches of Missionary Life

J. J. Halcombe

The Emigrant and the Heathen
Or Sketches of Missionary Life

ISBN/EAN: 9783743420977

Manufactured in Europe, USA, Canada, Australia, Japa

Cover: Foto ©Andreas Hilbeck / pixelio.de

Manufactured and distributed by brebook publishing software (www.brebook.com)

J. J. Halcombe

The Emigrant and the Heathen

THE

EMIGRANT AND THE HEATHEN;

' OR,

Sketches of Missionary Life.

EDITED BY

THE REV. J. J. HALCOMBE, M.A.

Rector of Balsham, Linton, Cambridgeshire.

PUBLISHED UNDER THE DIRECTION OF THE
TRACT COMMITTEE.

LONDON:
SOCIETY FOR PROMOTING CHRISTIAN KNOWLEDGE,
SOLD AT THE DEPOSITORIES:
77, GREAT QUEEN STREET, LINCOLN'S INN FIELDS;
4, ROYAL EXCHANGE; 48, PICCADILLY;
AND BY ALL BOOKSELLERS.

NEW YORK: POTT, YOUNG & CO.

CONTENTS.

SKETCHES FROM NEW ZEALAND.

SKETCHES FROM INDIA.

EMIGRANT AND THE HEATHEN.

Recollections of Ministerial Work in the Diocese of Newcastle, New South Wales.

CHAPTER I.

FIRST IMPRESSIONS.

IT was a bright Sunday morning, on the 16th of January, 1848, when the ship "Medway" entered the heads of Port Jackson, having on board the Right Rev. William Tyrrell, the first Bishop of Newcastle.

His party consisted of two clergymen, seven candidates for the ministry, a schoolmaster and mistress, and some servants from the Bishop's Hampshire parish of Beaulieu.

Our voyage had been a long one, 120 days from Gravesend, but the delay had not been unprofitable. A sudden change from English to Australian work would have been like an abrupt transition from a dense to a rare atmosphere. The mental and spiritual constitution would not have been fitted for it. The pause gave time to prepare for the change; and the opportunity thus afforded of reviewing our past work in England, and considering the duties which were awaiting us in our new sphere, full as they were to be of untried and novel circumstances, helped us, by God's grace, to enter upon our mission with greater

B

calmness and circumspection, and not, I trust, with less determination, than if we could have passed suddenly from the one part of Christ's vineyard to the other.

The two daily services, the Sunday congregations on the main-deck or in the cuddy, and the monthly celebrations of the Holy Eucharist—begun as soon as the sea-sickness was over, and continued down the Atlantic, across the Southern Ocean, and up the Pacific—had joined us in imagination, as they kept us united in soul and spirit, with our blessed English Mother Church.

The tedium of our ocean-life had been relieved by the regularity of our daily lectures to the candidates for the ministry, and our own studies; as well as by the various little incidents of catching sharks in a calm, and dolphins in a breeze; watching an occasional whale, or the shoals of flying-fish in the tropics, as they sprang glistening out of the water, and, after their few hundred yards' flight, darted again, like a discharge of rifle-balls, into their proper element.

Our first view of Australia had been at Cape Otway, near Port Philip, the chief inlet to the rapidly growing colony of Victoria.

I need not say with what interest we had scanned it, nor how eagerly, after passing Ninety-mile Beach on the south, and doubling Cape Howe, we had asked the name of each bay, or hill, or green spot, as we sailed up the eastern coast.

Contrary winds had retarded us almost to the last; but at length, having passed the heads of Botany Bay, and having, a few miles further north, taken the pilot on board, we passed between those tall stern cliffs of sand-stone which look down upon the chafing waters of the Pacific, and guard the entrance of one of the most lovely harbours in the world.

A long, disastrous drought had lately been relieved by abundance of rain, and the headlands and islands which rested on the blue waters were looking bright with fresh green.

Seven miles up the harbour lay Sydney, with her beautiful wooded promontories and sand-fringed coves, basking in the early sun. And as we glided up towards our anchorage on that calm summer morning, and saw the tall spire of St. James's Church rising out of the buildings that were each minute growing more distinct, we felt that the dearest part of old England—her Church—made even a strange land home.

About 9 A.M., the last bit of canvas was taken in, the anchor let go, and the ship at rest.

What a feeling of security passes over you at that moment, as you find yourself fast by the ground, after four long months of perpetual motion ; and how near seems the realisation of all the hopes, trials, and, if God please, successes, to which the heart has long been looking forward !

The venerable Bishop Broughton, whose body now sleeps under the shadow of Canterbury Cathedral, was, at the time of our arrival, absent from Sydney on a visitation; but one of his clergy came on board to greet us. Under his guidance, the Bishop, with some of our party, landed, and proceeded to the temporary Cathedral of St. Andrew, while I was conducted with the rest to St. James's Church.

We publicly returned thanks for the mercies of our safe voyage, and received our first Communion with our Australian brethren.

It was a happy thing to kneel once more within the walls of a church; and I might have believed myself in old England, but for the shrill noise of the tettigonia or locust, whose continuous *whirr*, like that of a scissor-grinder's wheel driven by strong steam power, seemed to fill the whole air during the hot hours of the day.

In the evening, the mosquitoes awoke with their hum at

the top of the room; and a few skirmishers attacked our
hands and faces before making their descent upon us in
force.

I can never forget the open-hearted hospitality with
which we were received by our Sydney brethren. Australian hospitality is not confined to new arrivals from
England; through the whole of a sojourn of thirteen years
I found it unvarying. But it is especially cheering when
you land upon a strange shore, and have everything to
learn as to the details of living, to be received, as you are,
like an old friend, with liberty to go in and out as you
please, and every one ready to help you.

The new diocese having, up to this time, been a part of
Bishop Broughton's vast see, we learnt from his secretary
what cures especially needed filling up.

There were three to begin with:—Morpeth, twenty miles
up the Hunter, where the navigable part of the river ends;
Singleton, thirty-five miles further up; and Muswell Brook,
thirty miles further inland on the same river, beyond
which, toward the west, there was no clergyman, but sheep
without a shepherd.

The Bishop himself determined to go to Morpeth, to
live at first in the parsonage, and to take the duties until
he could ordain one of the candidates, and place him there
under his own eye. He kindly gave me my choice of the
other two, and I fixed upon Muswell Brook. My dear
friend the Rev. H. O. Irwin took Singleton as his work;
each of us having candidates for the ministry to reside
with us.

The first movement was to despatch Mr. Irwin in charge
of some of the candidates and all the servants to Morpeth,
to await the Bishop's arrival, it being an object to remove
them from the port and to give them something to do.

The Bishop wished me to remain with him, to see the
Bishop of Sydney, our Metropolitan, as soon as he should
return, and to have the benefit of his advice.

I enjoyed this privilege in a few days, and then, with my pupils, followed the first detachment to the Hunter, leaving the two Bishops in consultation.

Newcastle, at the mouth of the Hunter, is sixty miles to the north of the heads of Port Jackson. Its situation on the side of a hill is good; and it looks inland up the river, over a broad valley filled with wood, and bounded on the south-west by the Wollombi range, and on the north-east by the hills of the Paterson and the Williams. At that time its railway was not thought of, nor its harbour secured by a breakwater, or so well filled with shipping as it now is. The Sydney steamers touched there to land passengers and cargo for the place, and then proceeded with their chief freight up to Morpeth.

For the first few miles up the river the banks are low and sandy; but by degrees they show some ten feet, increasing as you advance to twenty feet or twenty-five feet of rich alluvial soil above the water. In the midst of tall dead gum-trees—which had been purposely barked all round for some inches in width, and whose gaunt white trunks and branches had formerly a thick scrub and tangled festoons of creepers beneath them—were growing rich crops of maize, and lucerne to be cut for hay; and, in some places, tall-growing wheat.

In the midst of these you might see stumps of large trees, about two feet and a-half in height, where, after the crops of former years had been gathered in, the settler's cross-cut saw had thinned some of the dead forest giants, leaving the rest to be cut, and afterwards grubbed up at leisure.

Here and there were scattered the slab-built and bark-covered huts of the owners or renters of these lands; and near them, occasionally, a small planked stage would run out on posts into the river, to enable the people to get their bags of wheat and maize, or their trusses of hay, on board the steamer on her way to Sydney; while a boat, tied to the little pier, heaved up and down in the waves made by the passing vessel.

On our right, a few villas at long intervals, with their verandahs, tasteful gardens, vines and orange-trees, showed a higher kind of civilisation.

After passing on the same side the "townships" or villages of Raymond Terrace at the mouth of the Williams River, and Hinton at the mouth of the Paterson, we rejoiced to find ourselves at last alongside the wharf at Morpeth, and some of our party waiting for us, ready to escort us to the parsonage.

CHAPTER II.

MORPETH, or, as it was originally called, "The Green Hills," lies along a sandstone ridge, which rises from the south bank of the Hunter, and runs in a westerly direction two miles to the town of East Maitland.

On the opposite side of the river stretches a fertile flat about a mile in width, extending many miles up and down the river : where English, Scotch, and Irish settlers exhibit their respective national characteristics and differences of religion.

In most places a furrow alone divides one farm from another; but here and there a small piece of land is enclosed by a post and rail fence for the milch cows, or for the working bullocks which plough the land, carry off the produce, and fetch the supplies.

Around most of the wooden houses of the settlers are a few young standard peach and nectarine trees, bending about Christmas time under the abundance of their delicious fruit. Melons and pumpkins spread in wild luxuriance over the ground. And, along the verandahs of some of the more careful and industrious, vines keep off the fierceness of the summer heat, or, tied to stakes, like raspberries in England, bear grapes, which in our English climate could only be produced in a hot-house.

Beyond these rich lowlands, hills of moderate elevation bound the view towards the north, rising to a bold outline, where the River Paterson cleaves them, and opens up a vista, along which ridge rises above ridge distinct and clear, under a sky exquisitely blue; and among these picturesque hills lie the little townships of Paterson and Gresford.

Only twenty-seven years before the arrival of the Bishop's party at Morpeth, this neighbourhood showed no sign of civilisation.

Not a human habitation had been built; not a spade, or plough, or implement, however rough, had ever broken the surface of the forest-covered ground. Not a herb, or tree, or seed, had ever been grown, which did not spring of itself.

The poor black natives, who had roamed over the country and fished the waters from times unknown, had left absolutely no memorial to show that social reasoning beings had ever shared the land with the opossum and the kangaroo.

In the twenty-seven years before 1848 a great stride had been made in fulfilment of the command to "replenish the earth and subdue it."

The valley had been cleared, and brought into luxuriant cultivation. Two wharves received the imports from the Sydney steamers for the inland towns and settlers, and shipped off, not merely the agricultural produce of the neighbouring farms, but the still more valuable cargoes of wool, tallow, and hides, sent down from the large grazing districts, which were being taken up into the interior.

Three long lines of straggling streets had grown up on the eastern end of "The Green Hills," containing a population of some 700 persons; among whom were found the ordinary elements of a rising colonial town.

Edward C. Close, Esq., the father and founder of this little community, who was only lately called to his rest, full of years, was one of those men who are so valuable among the heterogeneous elements of a young colony. Firm enough in Christian principle to stand alone in doing right, and to give those who are weaker an example to follow, without any censoriousness or self-assertion, but ever ready to do good to all classes; he was a considerate Christian gentleman, and a sincere Churchman.

In early life he had served under the Duke of Wellington in India and in the Peninsula.

At one of the seven engagements in Spain named on the seven clasps of his medal, while lying down with his regiment under heavy fire—himself untouched among his dead or wounded comrades—he had made a promise to God that, if spared, he would build a church as soon as he should have the means of doing so.

In the year 1817 Mr. Close arrived in New South Wales with his regiment—the 48th.

A contemporary of his, himself a valuable and highly respected Churchman, mentioned to me a few years ago how remarkable Mr. Close was for steadiness and Christian principle from his first years in the colony, when considerable licence was the too general rule, and holy laymen were scarce indeed.

He would often withdraw from the carousing of the mess-room to enjoy a quiet evening with his steady-minded friend; and on Sundays the two young men would not unfrequently read the Holy Scriptures together, and thus strengthen those high principles, of which Mr. Close to the end of his life, and his friend to the present day, have been eminent examples.

In the year 1821, at the time of his marriage, Mr. Close received from the Government a grant of land, which he had selected on and about the present site of Morpeth.

He had not forgotten his vow made in the hour of his danger on the other side of the world. Whether for good or for evil, it is still true, "*Cœlum, non animum mutant, qui trans mare currunt.*"

For a while he had not the means necessary for building

a church without assistance. But he was not idle in Christ's service; there was plenty of preparatory work to be done. There was not a clergyman in the whole Hunter district.*

In his own service, and all around him, were convicts, or, as they were called, "*assigned servants*," working out their sentences. He did much to humanise these men by the kindness, as well as by the justice and firmness, with which he treated them.

The importance of keeping large numbers of men, who had already broken through the laws, from insubordination and rebellion, made it necessary to arm their masters, who were generally magistrates, with very summary powers. A great amount of restraint, which could easily be made very oppressive and irritating, was left to their discretion. And although masters could not at their own will order their servants to be flogged, it was easy for brother magistrates, sitting on the bench together, to order the flogging of each other's servants on insufficient grounds or with undue severity. There is no reasonable doubt that this was not unfrequently done in the early times. And if anything was likely to turn transportation from a reformatory punishment into a means of completing the hardening of a man's heart, it was such absence of fellow-feeling and perversion of justice under cloak of legal power.

Mr. Close was too conscientious a man ever to be unjust, and too sincere a Christian to be harsh and tyrannical to those who were in his power. As a magistrate he held the balance justly between masters and their convict servants. As a master and a neighbour he acted with consideration, always ready to encourage those who showed signs of im-

---

* The first clergyman appointed to the Hunter was the Rev. C. P. N. Wilton, who was placed at Newcastle in 1831. He remained single-handed for three years, riding sometimes, as he has told me, to Murrurundi, 180 miles inland. In 1834 the Rev. G. K. Rusden arrived from England, and was sent to East Maitland.

proving habits. And when there was no medical man near, which was long the case, he was constantly found at the bedside of the convict or of the free settler, acting as the doctor and Christian friend, where both body and mind wanted relief.

But he did more. Before any clergyman visited the district, he used to call around him his convict labou...'s, and any others who would come, for prayers on Sunday, using, as far as a layman could do so, the Book of Common Prayer, and reading a printed sermon to the people assembled. And this he continued to do for years, whenever a clergyman was unable to be present.

He opened also a Sunday-school, as the increasing population caused the need of one, and taught in it, with the members of his family.

It need hardly be said that Bishop Broughton warmly approved and seconded one, who so truly " laboured much in the Lord."

Of his character as a Christian host the Bishop of Newcastle says, in a sermon preached on the Sunday after his funeral, " Those who have traversed all parts of this northern district of the colony, as I have done, have often heard the squatter and the settler living hundreds of miles from hence, describe with grateful feelings how, years ago, they rested for the night under that roof, when not only every want was supplied and every comfort provided for the body, but they had felt years afterwards it was *good for them* as men and *as Christians* to have enjoyed the hospitality of that home."

In the earlier days of the colony, when churches were required, the Government not only gave the site, but met the contributions of the subscribers with an equal sum for the building of the church.

Mr. Close might have availed himself of this assistance, but he would not allow himself thus to be deprived of rendering the full tribute which he had vowed.

Having given the land for the church and parsonage, with garden and paddock attached, he built a substantial stone church with a tower; which, though not up to our present improved knowledge of church architecture, was in every way vastly superior to anything which the colony could then show. The colonial architect of that day turned out such sorry specimens of churches, that it was well that Mr. Close drew his own plan, and himself superintended its erection. He was also the means of getting the parsonage built, which is one of the best and most convenient in the diocese.

Thus had this good layman prepared the way for the work which was to follow.

Up to the time of the arrival of the Bishop of Newcastle, good Bishop Broughton, having the enormous area of the whole of Australia to provide for, had been unable to supply a separate clergyman to Morpeth. But from this date, not only were its spiritual wants supplied by the occupant of its own parsonage, but it became the centre of the diocese, and the source from which the chief Church movements proceeded.

Bishop Tyrrell, having obtained from the Bishop of Sydney such information as would enable him to enter upon the work before him, proceeded to Newcastle; and in Christ Church, of which the Rev. C. P. N. Wilton was incumbent, he was formally installed as Bishop of the diocese, on Sunday, January 30, a fortnight after his landing in the colony.

The less said about the architecture of that beautifully-placed church the better. It was built in the early days of the colony, on the hill above the town, looking from its east end, where the low tower stands, down upon the broad blue Pacific; and from the west, where the apse strangely projects, upon the river and the wooded inland flats and hills.

As this is the cathedral of the diocese, and as many

essential Church works have already been accomplished, it is earnestly to be hoped that a building more worthy of bearing the name it does, may be raised on that beautiful site—erected, not by the Churchmen of Newcastle alone, but by the united efforts of the diocese. And may I express one fervent hope besides,—that the daily sacrifice of prayer and praise may there be offered, and aid the growing religious life of the Hunter River district?

But we must move up again to Morpeth. The Bishop was soon there, settled in the parsonage, with the two senior candidates for the ministry, whom he purposed to ordain on the second Sunday in Lent. He set himself vigorously to work as parish priest of Morpeth, having under his charge the little hamlet of Hinton, one mile off, across the river, and a considerable district around.

Even when he had ordained one of these candidates as deacon, to minister in Morpeth and its district, he himself discharged the priestly, and shared to a large extent the other ministerial duties of the parish, besides often aiding the clergy of East and West Maitland, and of the parishes within a radius of some fifteen miles.

Settlers had located themselves, not in reference to the proximity of a church, but according as the land was better suited for agriculture, or more accessible to means of transport. Hence, even in the Hunter Valley, little clusters of slab-built houses were often built six or eight miles from the nearest church; and, unless they were to be left uncared for on a Sunday, the clergyman of the district was obliged to leave his larger congregations for their sakes.

To meet these wants, the Bishop, whom no fatigue or heat withheld from work, was ubiquitous: now at Morpeth, or in some portion of its district; now taking the ordinary service for one or other of the neighbouring clergy, that they might gather in some school-room or settler's hut

those who were too distant to come in to the church, and
at other times taking his own turn in ministering to those
small outlying congregations.

I remember, on one occasion, when I had come down
the country to Morpeth for an ordination, riding over with
the Bishop to Miller's Forest, some six miles off, for such
a service.   Our route, not road, lay sometimes among tall
dead trees, with rich crops of maize growing among them;
sometimes through a bit of swamp, which let our horses in
to the knees; and then over rough log bridges covered
with loose saplings, from which much of the earth had
been washed or worn off, and care was needed to avoid
getting your horse's leg into some awkward hole, where
the sapling had been broken or thrust aside.

The population, with the exception of some Irish Roman
Catholics or Scotch Presbyterians, consisted chiefly of
Wesleyans, or "Primitive Methodists."   But they assembled, filling the little building as full as it could hold, and
were reverently attentive during the service, and grateful
for it afterwards.

For the first few months after his arrival, the Bishop
was uncertain where he should buy or build a house for
his permanent residence.   It was not an unimportant
matter; for a place badly chosen would have greatly
interfered with the usefulness of the Bishop and his
successors.   Obviously the great desiderata were, that he
should be at the place most easily accessible to clergy or
others coming from the different parts of his enormous
diocese, and where the post from these and from Sydney
was most regular and frequent.

Morpeth possessed nearly all the requirements of the
centre of the diocese.   Placed at the head of the navigable
part of the Hunter, it was easily reached by sea from all
the northern parts of the colony.   With Sydney, the seat
of government, from which it is distant about ninety miles,
the communication was daily; and for travellers or letters

from the interior, it was almost as convenient as Maitland, and far more so than Newcastle.

The only drawback was, that it was not, nor hitherto has it become, populous enough to develop, under the Bishop's eye, those diocesan institutions which need numbers in order to make them successful. This, however, is of minor importance. Whatever institutions are started at West Maitland or at Newcastle, the distance of four miles in the one case, and twenty-two by rail in the other, is not enough to interfere with the Bishop's complete *supervision*. That he himself should *work* them would, of course, be out of the question anywhere.

At first, there was no available house at Morpeth, and the Bishop had some thoughts of buying a large unfinished place beyond Maitland, ambitiously begun in earlier days of unhealthy speculation, and never made habitable. But this idea was soon rejected. Besides requiring too large an outlay to finish it, the capital objection to Aberglaslyn was, that it was too much out of the way for ready communication with the Bishop.

Mr. Close solved this difficulty by selling his own house as the Bishop's residence. For this it was very well adapted. It is placed on some of the highest ground at the west end of Morpeth, and within two hundred yards of the church and parsonage.

Since changing its owner, that house has witnessed many an anxious consultation for the good of the diocese, prolonged far into the night. It has welcomed the clergy and schoolmasters on their first arrival from England, for which it is particularly convenient, being distant but five minutes' walk from the wharf. It has been the centre to which the wants, difficulties, and troubles of the various districts have found their way, and from which has flowed out comfort, or advice, or help, or, it may be, needed monition. Thither hard-worked clergy have ridden, to pour all their plans, their successes, into a sympathising ear; and, if they were worth anything, they have gone away refreshed and inspirited, and nerved for fresh exertion by the example of the untiring energy which they had witnessed in their Bishop,—at once an indefatigable worker and a diligent student. Sometimes those who were staying with him, or had dropped in from some neighbouring parsonage, would be asked to join him in his favourite walk up and down the path between his garden gate and that which opens into the road opposite to the church tower. And, as the last phase of the Education question was discussed (for Mr. Lowe was in the Parliament of New South Wales), or the Synod question, or the means of supporting the clergy, or some special parish matters, needed a few more words, the pace became quicker, and the dinner hour was forgotten, to the no small displeasure of the good old housekeeper, whose cap might be seen from time to time peering impatiently between the pillars of the Bishop's verandah.

Often has the large paddock in which the house and garden stand resounded with the merry voices of the school children, on their annual feast day. And at the garden gate the Bishop would stand with large baskets of oranges, from the orangery at the back of the house, to scramble them among the children, or with barrows full of grapes from the vineyard, to give each child a bunch or two before the end of the day's pleasure.

The school, with master's house attached, was built by the Bishop in 1849, on a block of land separated by a road from the church enclosure. Since then the Bishop built on the south, or left side of the school, an infant school, a dwelling for the mistress, and a room for the use of the clergy; and a well-designed and well-built chancel has been added to the church by a relative of the venerable founder.

Mr. Close retired for a while, after selling his house, to a large, wood-built bungalow, which he had built when he first fixed at Morpeth, but, after a little time, began building on a piece of land immediately adjoining that which he had sold to the Bishop; and there he spent the last years of his useful life, genial and warm-hearted as ever, and taking part, almost to the last, in the working of the Church.

CHAPTER III.

ENTERING ON WORK.

WHATEVER traits of old England may be found in her
colonies, yet the circumstances of the young progeny differ
so materially from those of the parent kingdom—rich,
populous, and fettered as well as adorned by the labours
and precedents of centuries—that a fresh immigrant has
much to learn before he can act vigorously and effectively
in his new country.

Hence every sensible settler, however many improvements he may have in his brain, follows the routine which
he finds around him for a while, until he has become
accustomed to the peculiarities of the climate and soil, the
value of labour, and the means of transit. A self-willed
theorist soon finds himself losing his capital, instead of
gaining interest for it.

The same holds good with Church work. The Catholic
faith and the essential principles of the Church are the
same everywhere; but a bishop or clergyman, transplanted
from English to Australian soil, finds the *circumstances* of
the Church to which he is introduced very different from
those to which he has been accustomed in the old country;
and time is required to enable him to understand what
things he may hope to reproduce after a while, what he
must be content to let go altogether, and what new modes
of working he must adopt in order to meet the new state
of things in which he finds himself.

In the meantime there is abundance of important work
on which he may zealously begin, and through which he

becomes acquainted with the people and they with him; and when he has learnt to understand the nature of the material on which he has to work, he may, under God's blessing, apply his former experience with good effect.

It was, therefore, resolved that we should begin to work with things as we found them, learning by observation the existing needs, supplying them as we were able, introducing improvements in detail as our experience increased, and so preparing ourselves and the people for any new plans and more general efforts.

The first scheme postponed was that which we had cherished in England and talked of on the voyage—the commencement of a theological college for training candidates for the ministry; and this has continued in abeyance up to the present moment. Neither at the time of our arrival nor since has there appeared the prospect of a sufficient number of candidates to make it worth while to establish and keep up a separate college for their training.

Instead of establishing a distinct clerical college, which would have been weak from paucity of pupils, those who were candidates for the ministry were placed by the Bishop under some clergyman, from whom they received assistance in their reading; and by working in his school and visiting in the parish under his direction they gained experience of parochial work. When he was absent at some of his many places of service, they read the prayers and a sermon appointed by him to any congregation to which he sent them.

This is, no doubt, a state of things far from satisfactory. A hard-worked parish priest has not time, and scarcely strength, to devote to keeping up in himself and imparting to his pupils a thorough knowledge of theology; and the beneficial training which numbers give to each other is wanting. But we were obliged to adopt it as the best course which the circumstances admitted. Some very good and useful men, who have now for some years been ordained to the priesthood, have been trained in this way. As to the lay services, the congregations had by this means the opportunity afforded them of hallowing the Lord's day; and while they were habituated to the regularity of assembling for prayer, praise, and teaching, they never confounded the office of the lay assistant with that of the ordained clergyman.

At the time of our arrival, there was nothing like any regular offering from the people towards the maintenance of their ministers. The English Churchman, accustomed at that day more than now to see his clergyman in the old country maintained, without his aid, by tithes or pew-rents, or living on his own private means, or on the profits of pupils, with a mere nominal income from his parish, carried to the colony, almost as a part of his Churchmanship, the idea that the voluntary support of the pastor by his flock was a burden to the flock and a degradation to the pastor; and seeing that the ancient offering of tithes had been enforced by the law of the land, he looked to the Government to provide for his clergyman from the public funds; and where the sum provided by the State was insufficient, the Church societies of the mother country were expected to come to the aid of the colonial Church.

In the early days of the colony, when the convicts were many and the free settlers thinly scattered over the country, such extraneous aid was necessary. But the more the free population increased in numbers and in wealth, and the more largely the powers of self-government were conceded to the colony, the more evident it became that the Church must look for her maintenance and growth to her own inherent vitality,—in full accordance with the apostolic rule, "*Let him that is taught in the Word communicate unto him that teacheth in all good things.*" *

The necessity of ceasing to rely on the Government and

* Gal. vi. 6.

on the English societies was but dimly before the minds of
the Bishop and clergy at first : the laity of the Church had
no better perception of it.   It was therefore resolved that
working among and for the people, under the existing state
of things, must precede any organised attempt to obtain
from them support for the maintenance or extension of the
Church's work.

But though the principle of the support of the ministry
by the offerings of the laity was not rightly understood,
pecuniary aid for any Church work was expected through
the medium of the Bishop. A bishop, as being in connection
with the Church societies at home, and as an influential
person with the members of the colonial Government, was
apt to be looked on as an inexhaustible source of revenue.
Hence the Bishop of Newcastle, soon after his arrival, had
requests poured in upon him on every side for aid in
building new churches, schools, and parsonages.

He had, no doubt, some means at his disposal.   But a
little inquiry soon revealed the fact that many of the
existing Church buildings were considerably in debt, and
that the churchwardens and trustees were contentedly
acquiescing in this state of things, paying from year to
year out of that miserable source of income, pew-rents,
the interest due on the debts, but making no endeavour to
wipe out the principal by fresh subscriptions.   Only a few
days after his arrival at Morpeth, I received a letter from
him, dated Feb. 5, 1848, in which he says, " Certainly the
state of our church is most unsatisfactory.   Every church
and building belonging to the Church down here is en-
cumbered with debt."   The Bishop therefore preferred
the less showy course of getting the existing debts cleared
off, to the more pleasant one of at once beginning new
buildings.

I believe I am correct in saying that he in no case paid
off all the debt for the people, but that he promised them
a certain amount of aid, on condition that they raised the

rest, either at once or within a specified reasonable period.
A little persuasion, backed by a conditional promise of £10,
£30, or £50, inspirited many who had for some time been
sitting down hopelessly under their burdens.   Fresh subscription lists were opened, and within a short time the
Church buildings were free.

It is but fair to say that many of these debts had been
contracted during the times of prosperity, and that the
sudden and deep reverses which the colony had suffered,
and from which it was only slowly emerging when we
arrived, had prevented many who had put down their
names for large sums from fulfilling their promises.   In
the meantime many had been forced to sell their properties
at a great sacrifice, and to make a fresh start on a more
humble scale in some other part of the wide unoccupied
territory.   Some had migrated to California, in order to
retrieve their fortunes, little thinking that the feet of many
Australian flocks and herds were wandering over mines of
gold, which, in three years more, would attract shiploads
of energetic men from Europe, and give a vast impetus to
the prosperity of the country.

The coming outburst of such prosperity was at that time
hidden from us; and I remember the Bishop expressing
to me his disappointment that he could not use the means
at his disposal in forwarding new works, which he saw
were urgently needed.   But he rightly considered it most
important to begin with the humbler work of honesty
for the past.   And he was content to *seem* to be doing
little, and to bide his time, until he could begin fresh
works on a clear foundation.   His was a species of self-
denial little known and not much appreciated, but very
genuine.

The pressure of business which came upon the Bishop's
shoulders on his first arrival at Morpeth may be imagined
by those who consider what the arrival of one who was
both head of a large party and Bishop of a new see implies.

I had started for my cure at Muswell Brook within a few days after my arrival at Morpeth, as my predecessor had left the parish a fortnight before we landed. Mr. Irwin went up to Singleton the week after the Bishop came from Sydney. The Bishop therefore kindly undertook the small details of receiving all our goods from the ship, as well as his own, and forwarding them to us. At the same time he was settling himself and his household in the parsonage at Morpeth, looking after carpenters and other workmen, and seeing clergy, churchwardens, or settlers who desired to pay their respects to the new Bishop, and to make known to him their wants. Letters began to come in upon him from distant parts of his diocese, so that it is not to be wondered at that in his first letter to me from Morpeth he says, "I am here in a perfect whirl of business, with scarcely a moment free from intruders.". Two days later, Feb. 7, he wrote, "My head is nearly splitting, from the number of things I have to think of. It will be a great treat to me to pay you a visit."

The same letter mentions that one of his episcopal troubles found him out on the threshold of his work in the loss of one of his clergy, and the need of supplying his place by another. The important district of Moreton Bay, which has since grown up into the colony of Queensland and the bishopric of Brisbane, stretching northward from about the 28th parallel of latitude, had but one clergyman in its whole extent. Of this he writes, "There is another district now vacant, Moreton Bay, the Rev. Mr. Gregor having been unfortunately drowned last week while bathing."

The Bishop had never seen him, nor had there been time as yet even to communicate with him by letter. This loss could not therefore be felt as that of a friend; but in our little band, which we desired to stretch as widely as possible to tend Christ's scattered flock, it made a perceptible gap. The death of one clergyman in an English diocese,.

unless he be a man of great eminence, is not felt beyond
the sphere of his own parish and personal friends, but in
an Australian diocese one loss is felt through the whole.
The whole number of clergy whom the Bishop, on his
arrival, found in his vast see was but twelve.* His two
new clergy were at once needed for two vacant cures,
and now one of the most extensive and distant districts,
which had no neighbouring clergyman to bestow on its
people even an occasional service, was suddenly left
destitute.

To meet this great need the Bishop was obliged to arrange
with the clergyman who was vacating Singleton, and had
intended to leave the diocese, to go up to Moreton Bay.
He was only too thankful to be able in any way to
supply so serious a vacancy. The arrangement was but
temporary, yet, by God's blessing, the present need
was met, and the Bishop turned to work vigorously upon
the duties which, thick and increasing, were claiming his
energies.

I have seen Bishop Tyrrell, during the thirteen years I
enjoyed the privilege of working with him, under many
heavy trials and disappointments. He has sometimes
written to me, mentioning how sharply for the moment he
has felt the seeming blighting of some cherished scheme
for the Church's good. But he has a happy disposition,
or rather a clear faith and buoyant hope, which enable
him quickly to perceive God's overruling wisdom in such
crosses; and he has set himself cheerfully to the task of
repairing the loss, and of doing the work next before him,
instead of fretting over the vanished hope, or fearing idly

---

* The cures which Bishop Tyrrell found provided with clergy were,
on the coast line, Newcastle, Port Stephens, Port Macquarie, Moreton
Bay; on the Hunter River, Raymond Terrace, Hexham, Paterson, East
Maitland, West Maitland, Jerry's Plains; above it, Scone and Armidale. But the clergyman of Port Macquarie was, from the infirmities
of age, able to do very little duty. And before long the Bishop ordained
a clergyman to take the great work of the district.

for the future. He has seemed to have learned the lesson which our Keble puts so beautifully :—

> " Live for to-day ! to-morrow's light
> To-morrow's cares shall bring to sight.
> Go sleep like closing flowers at night,
> And Heaven thy morn will bless."*

In the midst of these busy weeks, which claimed his attention and care on every side, he was preparing for the solemn time of his first ordination. The letter is before me in which he announced that it was to be on the second Sunday in Lent, March 19. And the dates at three different parts of the letter, with several days' interval between them, will illustrate his words in it : " I really am incessantly occupied. Last night I was writing till 1.30, and was up again at six this morning;"—not an unusual event, I may remark, when work was pressing him, only that sometimes the hours of rest on the narrow iron bedstead were still fewer.

That first ordination, like all the subsequent ones, was held at Morpeth, and the church was crowded with those who came from the neighbourhood to be present at the service. Mr. Irwin said the morning prayer; it was my duty to present the candidates ; and the Bishop preached a sermon, of which I have now no record, but can only remember that it was an earnest and valuable one, addressed to the congregation as well as to the candidates.

With what thankful hearts and solemn hopes did we leave St. James's Church that morning ! Who can foresee at such a time the mighty possibilities of success in Christ's service, which open out before him ? Who can forecast the enemies and battles, and alas ! perhaps the failures, that lie before those who then have girded their armour on ?

One of these deacons, since made priests, was sent before

---

* *Christian Year.* 15th Sunday after Trinity.

long to the Darling Downs, in what is now the diocese of
Brisbane : where, in spite of weak health, he has laboured
on faithfully, and has been made archdeacon by the Bishop
of Brisbane.   The other was placed at Morpeth, where he
remained for about two years, and then returned to England.   The duties of Morpeth being thus provided for, the
Bishop was enabled to assist the clergy in the neighbouring
districts of the Hunter Valley ; and so to work toward the
object which he had proposed in a letter written some
weeks previously, in which he said, " It is my purpose to
work well this line of country, that all may see in some
degree what our Church is when fairly and efficiently
carried out into practice."

In the course of this first year a second ordination was
held in September, at which three deacons were ordained.
Two of them candidates brought with us from England,
and one who had been for many years residing in the
colony.

On looking back to that first year it seems marvellous
how much of his diocese the Bishop was enabled to visit,
holding confirmations whenever he found candidates prepared for him ; and gaining that general view of the wants,
and acquaintance with the chief inhabitants of the diocese,
which would enable him to lay his plans for the future.

The Lent ordination, and Lenten work in and around
Morpeth, occupied him well through March, and nearly to
the end of April.

About the middle of May he went through the district
of the Upper Hunter for about eighty miles, visiting
Singleton, Muswell Brook, Scone, and Jerry's Plains,
where clergy were stationed, as well as the smaller intermediate townships.

In June he went by sea to Brisbane, and visited the
distant northern portion of his diocese, where settlers had
gone out, and clergymen were greatly needed to follow
them.   This visitation occupied about a month.

In September he rode down almost, if not quite, to the southern extremity of the diocese: and visited Brisbane Water * and its beautiful neighbourhood, where the population chiefly consists of sawyers, and those connected with the timber trade. Tall thick forests cover the hill-sides, and in the deep valleys the dense glossy foliage, the festoons of creepers, and the cabbage-tree palms, with occasionally a tall ant-hill, three or four feet high, give a semi-tropical character to the shady tracks through which you ride.

Soon after the ordination in September, the Bishop passed up the Hunter to the rich western grazing districts of Merriwa and Cassilis, and, having visited these, rode northward across the Liverpool range to the towns of Tamworth and Armidale. Thence he worked his way eastward down the rugged hills, which fall from the table-land of New England towards the coast line; returning by Port Macquarie and Port Stephens to Morpeth.

I am not aware that he had visited the districts of the Clarence and the Richmond rivers; but by the end of his first year far the larger portion of his huge diocese could be realised in his own study at Morpeth. Besides these long journeyings, he was continually riding to places ten, fifteen, or twenty miles off, to give those who were remote from their clergyman opportunities of Divine service.

Of course, plenty of work awaited his return, and his correspondence grew in proportion to the places he had visited. But in the midst of this, his reading was never forgotten. He wrote, shortly after his return from his last long visitation: " I have just been under severe discipline, not of illness, thank the Lord, but self-discipline, changing the habit of ten hours' daily riding to the same period of daily reading and writing."

---

* Brisbane Water in the south must not be confounded with Brisbane in the north. They are separated by some six degrees of latitude, or rather more than 400 miles.

There are always dark shades in every picture, and some of these appeared in the midst of our first year's work.

Two out of the candidates for the ministry were instances of what is too often found,—men who from their own hypocrisy, or the carelessness of those who professed to know them, obtained recommendations which they did not deserve, and whom it was found impossible to make anything of. It was so far well that partly on the voyage, and partly soon after their arrival, their entire unfitness was discovered. The passage of both was paid to England; and one, the least unfit, sailed. Of the other, who had been intrusted to me, and had for some time caused me deep anxiety, I can say no more than that to my bitter sorrow I followed him to his grave in Sydney four months after our landing.

One more, a gentle, holy-spirited youth, who doubtless would have done good work had he been spared, was diseased in the lungs when he sailed, and he only drooped and died. In the September of our first year, I received the following account from the Bishop: "Poor Mr. Ison was released most easily and happily on Monday evening, and I followed him to the grave as chief mourner yesterday. It was a melancholy scene."

Such was our beginning—"*Toiling, rejoicing, sorrowing.*"

CHAPTER IV.

WHAT strikes most new-comers, when they really get up into the Australian "Bush," is the unfenced and apparently unappropriated land through which they travel. And I may add that those who return to England, after a long familiarity with Australian scenery, are equally struck by the entire enclosing and minute subdivisions of far the greatest part of the old country. In New South Wales the feeling is, as a gentleman once said to me, suiting the action to the word, "Here 's a land where one has plenty of elbow-room." In England you have hedge-bordered roads, and paths to which you are confined, however circuitous they may be. In the Australian Bush you leave or follow the track at pleasure; and no one complains of your riding or driving over his grass for a few furlongs, or for twenty miles.

When I started on my first journey to my appointed district of Muswell Brook, taking with me two candidates for the ministry, and two servants, there was very little fencing to be seen after the first two miles above West Maitland. I had engaged the whole of the mail—a two-wheeled car, carrying one on the box with the driver, and four behind, with a modicum of luggage for each—and in a short time we came upon parts of the road where the ground was so saturated with water, or the ruts in the native soil so deep and wide, from the heavy rains, that our driver would frequently strike off among the trees, and, after many a winding, bring us back again into the worn and beaten track.

Our journey that day was but thirty miles, from Maitland to Singleton. The greater part of it was through tall gum*and iron-bark trees, growing thickly together, with but little underwood or scrub; but occasionally we came to a place where the timber was thinner, and the appearance not unlike that of an extensive park.

Along the whole route there was but one apology for a bridge, consisting of some trees thrown across the little creek, one over another, and covered with earth; and bad enough it was. At all the other "creeks"—as the brooks or water-courses are called—the banks were cut down, sometimes to the depth of twenty feet; and we drove down one side, through the bed of the creek, and up the opposite side. Probably in the one exception, at Anvil Creek, the creek bed may have been too soft to bear wheels at all. As might be expected, traffic was often stopped after heavy rains. Impatient horsemen might swim across;

---

* The trees which are most common in New South Wales are known by the names of white gum, blue gum, spotted gum, red gum, apple-tree, box, stringy bark, and iron bark. They differ very little in the colour or shape of their foliage. In common with nearly all the trees of the country, they are evergreens, of a dull bluish green. The leaves are shaped like the willow, but are so thick that the ribs and fibres neither project on one side, nor are indented on the other, as in English leaves. They hang on their stems, not with their face, but their edge, turned to the sky; and being few in number, and high up, they cast but little shade. On one occasion, being exhausted and unwell, in an intensely hot day, I wished to get into shade; and, though riding through thinly timbered country, was obliged to sit against the stem of the tree on the shady side; the leaves afforded no shade. The iron bark and red gum are the hardest of the woods mentioned. The former is so heavy that I have seen a block of it used to sink the slack of a punt rope. The stringy bark is the best for sawing into flooring boards. The hard woods work well, when fresh; but if long dried, turn or break the edge of an axe, break a gimlet, and will not admit a nail. Several of these trees shed the outer skin of their bark periodically; and you may see strips hanging from them twelve feet or fifteen feet long, and from one to three inches wide, and as thick as brown paper. These thin strips of bark, and the dry leaves, are of service to the bushman who wants to light a fire to boil his "pot o' tea," but they add to the readiness with which a bush fire often sets miles of country in flames.

but vehicles were detained until the water had run off. The traveller of the present day would find not only a wide road with bridges over most of the creeks, but a railroad *in use* as far as Singleton, and nearly finished to Muswell Brook. On our way, we passed through the two small townships or villages of Lochinvar and Black Creek; distant from Maitland seven and fifteen miles. At the former there was no outward mark of worship; at the latter there was a small Roman Catholic chapel, to which a priest came at intervals. Soon after the arrival of the Bishop, a wooden church was built at Black Creek; and after a while at Lochinvar a church and parsonage were built, and a clergyman settled there.

Singleton, which had then a population of about five hundred, now more than doubled, is built on the banks of the Hunter, on a wide alluvial flat called Patrick's Plains, from which most of the forest trees had been cleared; and good crops of wheat, barley, or maize were raised on the rich lands. It is in itself singularly devoid of beauty, as it is built on a dead level. But hills rise all around; and, to the north, Mount Royal stands well among the broken ridges, from which the Paterson, Fallbrook, and the Rouchel flow. The little town had a brick parsonage, and a school used as a church; but in about a year from the time we first saw it, the foundation of a stone church was laid, which has since been considerably enlarged, and the windows have been enriched with stained glass.

We were detained here one day, as the mail, which started on the following morning, had not room for us. And as it at that time went on to Muswell Brook only two days in the week, we must have remained until the week following, had not the proprietor sent down especially to fetch us. The river being unfordable, we were put across in a boat; and found the vehicle awaiting us at the other side.

We had hardly started, when, after pulling through some

heavy black soil, we came to a shallow gully crossing our
road, into which we sank with a bump; and one of the
horses refused to pull us out of it. He looked the very
picture of sulks and obstinacy, and probably remembered
that soon after the gully a long stiff hill awaited him. The
driver gave him a little time, and then tried him again.
The other horse was willing, but could not move us by
himself; and, when the whip was applied, the only indica-
tion our sulky friend gave of movement was to crop his
ears, and show signs of resenting with his heels any further
use of the whip. Fortunately, I had a piece of bread in
my hand, the remains of my breakfast; so I jumped out,
and after patting and talking to the rebel a little, held the
bread to his nose. The sulks were still strong upon him;
but at length his ears came forward, he began to sniff at
the bread, lifted his upper lip once or twice, and then fairly
took the bait. The victory was nearly won: a few pats on
the neck, and rubbing the nose, completed it. I took his
head with my right hand, and still patted him with my
left. The driver started the near horse; both took the
collar; and with a good jump, that nearly shook the three
inside passengers into each other's laps, the wheels got out
of the hollow, and we were off again. I ran on, holding
the rein for a short distance, till I saw that all was right,
and then jumped into my place.

Much of our drive was through tall white-stemmed gum-
trees, which shut in our view, and enabled us to appreciate to the full the badness of the road, as we bumped
sometimes into a deep rut, sometimes over a large fallen
bough; occasionally passing the carcase of a dead working
bullock, which told of the severity of the late drought,
when the ground, which was now covered with bright green
grass, had been bare as the road itself. Pleasanter and
more amusing sights were frequently afforded us, as from
time to time flights of the lowry, or rosella, or ground parrots,
with their gorgeous crimson, green, and blue plumage,

Page 32.

rushed screaming over our heads ; or that solemn-looking kingfisher, the great " *laughing jackass*," made the wood ring with his merry peals of laughter; or a black and yellow iguana, three or four feet long, waddled along the ground, made for the first tree, and scrambled up out of reach.

The road was more hilly than before we reached Singleton ; and sometimes from the top of a hill we obtained a fine view of valleys and hills in endless undulations, clothed universally with forest. At the several creeks which we passed, the view was more open, the grass more abundant ; and the graceful casuarina, with its rich dark foliage and tapering branches, kept up a pleasant whispering sound over the streams or pools which it shaded.

On our way we had passed but one small township, called Camberwell, nine miles from Singleton, on the banks of Fallbrook. It consisted of a few wood-built houses, and a brick inn ; but represented a district, in which a few years before there were several establishments of considerable size. On the opposite side of the brook was an unfinished stone church, with three lancet lights at the east end, and single-pointed windows at the sides. Bishop Broughton, who laid the first stone, said that several among those present on that occasion could easily have provided the whole expense. Soon afterwards the reverses which overtook the colony so impoverished the principal men of the district, that most of them were scattered to distant places, and the work was stopped. The church remained roofless until about the year 1856 ; when it was so far finished that the Bishop of Newcastle consecrated it. But the original design, which included a tower, has not yet been carried out.

From Fallbrook to Muswell Brook the drive was more pleasant, but in that twenty miles we passed but two dwellings—one being a good stone-built inn in an open space, crossed by a watercourse, which had given it the

D

name of "The Chain-of-Ponds Inn;" the other a shepherd's hut, one of the humble-looking sources of the
wealth of the country. To our right and left there were,
no doubt, huts or larger houses a mile or two off the
track; but they were out of our sight, and scattered very
widely from each other.

We were now fairly reaching the sheep-farming part of
the country. And it may be as well to describe the dwellings of the shepherds at once. The simplest kind is the
bark hut; which is thus made. A framework of posts and
saplings is first fixed in the ground, and to this sheets of
bark from the eucalyptus, three or four feet wide, half-an-
inch thick, and from four to seven feet long, are tied
strips of undressed bullock-hide, usually called " ῃ
hide." The ridge piece is dried in a curve, laid over the
top, and weighted down by heavy saplings slung across.
with green hides. The door and window-shutters, for there
is no glass, are often of bark fastened to frames of wood ;
and the tables and bedsteads are not unfrequently made in
the same manner. The floor is the native earth; and
inside the bark chimney boulders from the creeks are piled
up, to prevent the fire from setting all in a blaze. Sometimes there is a skillen at the back of the hut ; and now
and then some sheets of bark in front form a verandah,
and add much to the comfort of the inmates.

Slab huts are built much on the same plan ; only that
slabs, split from the gum or iron-bark, set into the ground
and nailed to the wall-plates, form the sides and ends
instead of bark.

A watch-box is often used when lambing is going on,
or when the native dogs are troublesome; and the
shepherd or hut-keeper has to lie near the sheep-yard,
to be ready to render any help that may be needed
through the night. It is a kind of barrow-frame, long
enough for a man to lie in, and covered with bark, as a
protection against cold and rain.

There are usually two flocks, of a thousand each, at a sheep station, with a shepherd to each flock, who leads them out to feed by day; and there is a hut-keeper, whose duties are to clean the sheep-yards, take care of the hut, and act as cook. If there is a family at the station, the wife acts as hut-keeper; and if there is a boy big enough, he takes charge, under his father's direction, of the second flock.

On our way up the country, we had seen something of another class of men. Many drays had met us, carrying down wool, tallow, or hides to the coast; others we had passed on their way up the country, loaded with supplies of all sorts for the establishments of the large sheep and cattle masters, for the "stores" in the inland towns, or for the publicans. One dray, which we passed the first day, was bringing up the furniture which I had purchased at Maitland. The drays are large two-wheeled carts, very strongly built, with low sides, and made to open, if necessary, before and behind. Those drawn by horses have shafts, and carry from twelve to fifteen hundred-weight. The bullock-drays, which are drawn by eight or ten oxen, carry two tons. They have a strong pole, to which the yokes of the pole-bullocks, and the chain of the leaders, are fastened. Each night a halt is made, near water, if possible; the horses are unharnessed, and the bullocks unyoked, and turned to feed in the bush, with hobbles on their fetlocks. This being done, a fire is made of the dead wood, which is lying about in all directions. The quart tin pots are put on to boil, ready for the tea to be thrown in; and the salt beef and "damper," which is made of flour, water, and salt, kneaded on a sheet of bark, and baked in hot ashes, are drawn out of their bag for the evening meal. If several drays camp together, the men usually sit talking over their camp-fire until it is time to turn in for the night. They commonly carry a piece of sacking stuffed with dry grass; this they lay under their dray and lie on it, wrapped in a blanket or in a rug made of opossum skins.

If the stopping-place is near a township or one of the inns which are scattered along the chief lines of road, the evening is too often spent in the tap-room, and rum takes the place of tea, to the mischief of the poor fellows, who are very apt to drink. A few of the draymen, however, entirely avoid this temptation, and stick to their tea.

A midday halt is also necessary to refresh both man and beast.

These draymen are a considerable class, and need special treatment, if the pastor will really try to perform the duties imposed on him at his ordination, and will "seek for Christ's flock that are dispersed abroad." * They spend most of their time on the road, seldom remaining at their homes longer than to rest their horses or bullocks; and many live in the bush, far from any place of Divine service. A few, but few indeed, take their best clothes with them, so as to be able to go to church, if they stop at a town on Sunday. Therefore, if one does not minister to them on chance occasions, they probably go almost without any ministrations at all.

I soon felt it to be my duty to walk by their side, if not pressed for time, and to converse with them; and if I found any encamped at midday or in the evening, having my Bible and Prayer-book strapped in a kind of ecclesiastical holster before me, I offered to read and pray with them, and never found my offer rejected. As they were such complete wanderers, I did not consider myself to be trenching upon any brother clergyman's sphere of duty by offering them such a short service, when I fell in with them by the road-side, even out of my own district.

On one occasion, as I was riding down to Morpeth for an ordination, I came upon some six or seven encamped among the tall gum-trees, five miles short of Singleton.

* Service for the Ordering of Priests.

It had been dark some time, and they were sitting on fallen trees round their fire before turning in for the night.

I rode up to them, and said, "My friends, I am a clergyman riding down the country; and as I am accustomed to have prayers with my household when at home, I shall be glad, if you like, to read you a chapter of Holy Scripture and pray with you before I go on." They assented at once, took my horse, and tied him to one of their dray-wheels, and threw on some fresh wood to enable me to read. I was rather too tired to stand, so they set an empty water-keg on end, and, putting their cabbage-tree hats beside them, listened attentively to a chapter from one of the Gospels, and to my comments upon it. We then knelt down on the ground, and prayed from the Book of Common Prayer. And as I left them with a "God bless you, my friends," they thanked me with apparent heartiness, and I rode on in the delicious air of the calm starry night.

I can still see that crackling bush-fire, with its curling smoke leaping up into the darkness, and the bent figures of my brethren, the tall white stems of the gum-trees rising around, and the dim shapes of the loaded drays in the background. Probably we never saw each other again. The effect of that night may have been transient or not, God knows; but a bush clergyman who would do his Master's work must thus continually cast his bread on the waters, and leave the seed to be nurtured by Him to Whom it belongs.

But we must return to the conclusion of our first journey up the country.

After toiling over some very bad road, we reached the top of a high ridge, with the ground sloping down before us, and more thinly timbered than we had seen for many miles. And there, to our delight, the driver pointed out the snug little village of Muswell Brook. It lay below us about two miles off. We could not see much of the buildings; but the general view from the hill was very fine, and we longed for some of our dear English friends to share it with us. There was no lack of hill and valley, covered with wood as usual; except where, along the courses of the brook and the River Hunter, which here we saw again for the first time since leaving Singleton, man's hand had made clearings for the town, and for small patches of cultivation on the alluvial soil.

To the north, some thirty-five miles distant, stood the bold rugged outline of the Murulla, a portion of the Liverpool range, with its attendant crags. And these were followed, all round to the right, by lower ridges, varying in elevation; while, about five miles east of the little town, a fine abrupt hill, called Bell's Mountain, lifted himself head and shoulders above his neighbours, as if looking patronisingly down on the civilisation that, after so many centuries, was beginning to spring up around him, and exchanging glances with his cone-shaped brother Mount Warrendie, usually called *Mount Dangar*, who, thirty miles to the south-west, stands over the River Goulbourn, which winds round his feet, in the midst of the sandstone cliffs and peaks which fill that part of the picture.

I could not but feel thankful that my lot had fallen in a part of the country where God's hand had made the objects around so pleasant to look at.

We were now rapidly approaching our destination. But before we reached the wooden houses of the white-skins, we were reminded in whose land we were, by seeing some dozen of those houseless, homeless children of the bush,. the black natives, who had happened to camp close to the township, and were lying or squatting on the ground, with their curly heads uncovered; the elders with a blanket skewered at the neck by a piece of sharpened stick, or with merely a small girdle round their loins. Two or three little children were playing round them, clothed simply in

their own black skins, which, by the way, even in the case
of adults, is almost of itself a clothing, and takes away the
idea of nudity. They had evidently passed the night there,
as there were several sheets of bark resting with one edge
on the ground, and propped up in a slanting direction, so
as to make a slight shelter from the windward. Some
smouldering ashes, the remains of last night's fire, were
before them; and under one piece of bark an old grey-
haired aboriginal was lying on his blankets asleep. They
turned to look at us; but we were passing on, and at about
two o'clock we entered the south part of the town, for it is
divided into two parts by the deep creek from which it
derives its name; and, driving over a very substantially-
built wooden bridge, we drew up in a few minutes at the
Royal Hotel. Nine years before this had been the only
building in the place, a mere bush inn, surrounded by
forest. And, in spite of its name, it was only a weather-
board cottage, with the royal arms standing, not very
conspicuously, against the front, and containing two
sitting-rooms and two small bedrooms, entered from the
verandah, besides those commonly used by the publican's
family.

The first business of hungry travellers, who had break-
fasted more than seven hours before, and had had a long
bush-drive since, was to get something to eat. And then,
as the Royal Arms could only accommodate two, I left the
candidates for the ministry in possession, and went with
the servants to the next small inn, about two hundred
yards farther on.

Having thus fixed our abode till the furniture should
arrive, we went down to look over the empty parsonage
and the church. They were both within one fence, and
the school about a bow-shot beyond. I found the sexton
preparing the church, for it was Saturday, and it was
known that we should arrive that day. From him I heard
of one poor woman who was drawing near her end; so,

having set my boy to begin upon the weeds, which in the last few weeks had nearly overrun the garden, and were choking the vines, I began my ministrations by the bedside of poor Mrs. Wilde, whom I saw twice, and promised to administer the Holy Communion to her on the next day.

The rest of that first afternoon was spent in learning what I could about the parish from the schoolmaster and my host, and in preparing for the services of the morrow.

" Oh, dream no more of quiet life :
Care finds the careless out ; more wise to vow
Thine heart entire to Faith's pure strife ;
So peace will come, thou knowest not when or how."

KEBLE *in Lyra Apostolica.*
" *The Watch by Night.*"

CHAPTER V.

THE township of Muswell Brook, which was to be my head-quarters, is situated on the north-western road leading from Morpeth and Maitland to the great squatting districts of the Liverpool Plains and New England. The southern road to Sydney, surveyed by Sir Thomas Mitchell, joins the mainland road here. But while the north-western road is the great line of traffic to the coast from Tamworth and Armidale and the surrounding country, the southern road is unused, except for some small intermediate townships, as Jerry's Plains and Wollombi. The formidable ranges, which have to be crossed near the River Hawkesbury, have always been a barrier to dray traffic; and even horsemen prefer riding to Morpeth, and taking the steamer to Sydney, instead of toiling along the rugged and weary southern line.

In 1848 Muswell Brook had a population of about 300, including a doctor and a clerk of petty sessions. There were four or five storekeepers—most useful men in a colonial town—who kept in stock nearly every article you could need, except books; and five publicans, largely supported by travellers, draymen, and shepherds from the neigh-bourhood, as well as by some of the residents in the town. At one end there was a steam flour-mill, with machinery attached to it, which has at times been used in a small way for making cloth. And at the other end was a "boiling-down establishment," where, before the influx of the population caused by the gold discovery, the surplus fat stock of the settlers was killed, and reduced to tallow for export. Blacksmiths, wheelwrights, rough bush-carpenters, joiners, masons, bricklayers, and the other small tradesmen and labourers necessary to supply the wants of their neighbours, some six or eight carriers, and the police force, consisting of a chief and three constables, were the elements of the little community.

Like all young colonial townships, it was laid out in good broad streets, which bore their names on the Government chart, but, except in the best situations, were scantily built over. Here and there, in the middle of the roadways, might still be seen the stumps of the old forest trees standing, as the cross-cut saw of the first clearing had left them, obliging all drivers to keep their eyes about them for fear of an overturn.

Of the houses only about twenty were built of brick; the rest, including the little, low, four-roomed cottage, dignified by the name of " the court-house," were built of slabs split from the surrounding trees, or of weatherboards. On the hill to the east of the town stood a Presbyterian kirk, served at intervals from Singleton, and on a twin hill were the foundations of a Roman Catholic chapel.

Almost in the centre of the township there was an allotment of two acres, on which had been built, only a few years before, a brick school, with a master's dwelling, a parsonage, and a church, consisting of a nave, with a somewhat pretentious porch and vestry, built transeptwise, and a small tower at the west end. There was no chancel, but in the east end were three qu' '-lancet lights, each with a thin stone moulding over it, and glazed with square panes in wooden sashes, *Gothicised* at the top. Within were high pews of red cedar, the top moulding of which came well up to the back of the head of the sitter; and when the congregation was kneeling the church seemed

to be empty. In my journal I have recorded that I was
" *disappointed*" at the first view. But this was perhaps
unreasonable, as mine was the westernmost church in the
new diocese. Not a building for any kind of worship was
to be found between it and Western Australia. Besides,
there was something in the central position and grouping
of the buildings which gave the idea that the Church had
rooted itself among the people, and offered to be their
true mother in God. When, in about eighteen months
after, a chancel was added, with a triple lancet in stone,
and two of the nave windows were replaced by stone-worked
and mullioned lights ! and after a while the seats became
low and open, the general view, with all its faults, brought
to mind "the old country," to which all colonists look back
with affection.

The history of that little church is characteristic of the
colony in those days. Before a resident clergyman was
appointed, subscriptions had been raised, and Government
money promised for the building. A captain in the army,
then a settler, living about four miles off, took the contract for building the nave, with the porch and vestry.
The plan was *said* to have been drawn from the sketch of
a chapel in Barbados, given in a quarterly report of the
S. P. G. But whatever was the original of the plan, its
execution was intrusted to a *convict* overseer, and convict
labourers. These men, acting upon a well-known principle of convict morality, no sooner saw the master off to
Sydney than they neglected their work, for which, as convicts, they would receive no payment, and worked for any
one who would employ them, spending their earnings in
drink. At length they heard that their master was shortly
coming up the country, and, knocking off their extra jobs,
which might have brought them under the lash, they
turned to their neglected task. But, in the meantime,
there had been heavy rains, and the trench was half-filled
with water. Some of this was dipped up ; at one corner

the foundation was solidly built, the rest was thrown in with careless haste—the stones, small and large, alike unsquared, being left, as I was told, to bed themselves; and over all a cut base-course was placed, and the brick-work carried up above. In due time a surveyor was sent to inspect the work, in order to report whether it was executed in such a way as to entitle the trustees to the payment of the Government grant. On the day of inspection the overseer contrived to open that corner of the foundations which he had built up well. The fraud answered, and the money was paid. But before Bishop Broughton came up for the consecration, the faulty foundation had betrayed itself, and the walls were so cracked that the whole building was nearly coming down again. With much trouble the walls were secured; and the Rev. W. T. Gore, who had a little before that time been appointed to the parish, got the tower built at the west end, which both improved the look of the church externally, and acted as a buttress to keep it up.

It was discovered, however, by painful experience, that even good building, with well-laid foundations, would not stand. The foundations of the tower and of the chancel, which was afterwards built, were laid four feet deep on what seemed a dry, impenetrable soil; but the drought and heat penetrated so deeply during the fierce summer months that they have cracked them and other buildings, in all directions. And a noble stone church, which is now being built in place of the smaller one of brick, through the exertions, and mainly by the friends, of the present clergyman, the Rev. W. E. White, and his family, from plans by Gilbert Scott, of London, is, by order of the architect, placed on a thick bed of concrete, as the only safe foundation.

The day after our arrival being the fourth Sunday after the Epiphany, the gospel for the day furnished the morning sermon from Matt. viii. 28—32, on the power and readiness of Jesus to cast out evil, and to restore Satan's thrall to his right mind: a message with which I was thankful to be able to begin my ministry in a land where, by the confession of all, Satan had held terrible sway. In the evening the words of Isaiah lviii. 13, 14, at the end of the first lesson, were a not inappropriate text, where, in the absence of clergymen, many a Christian man had realised at his "station," and on his sheep and cattle "run," the sad but expressive saying, "*There's no Sunday in the bush.*"

Two days afterwards I had an instance of that change of customs which a change to a hot climate necessitates. My poor sick parishioner died on Monday morning, and on Tuesday afternoon we laid her in the grave. A funeral thirty-three hours after death would in England be revolting to the feelings of the friends. In New South Wales it is sometimes necessary to bury within twenty-four hours; indeed, in an extreme case, I have buried a corpse within twelve. In the case of this poor woman, I was glad that I had reached the parish in time to administer the Holy Communion to her while, though in extreme weakness, her mind was perfectly clear.

What was at that time considered the extent of my parish, and the Church services in it, I learned from a memorandum left by my predecessor. There were three places at which Divine service was held: St. Alban's Church, Muswell Brook, of which I have spoken; the little wooden court-house at Merton, a small township of about thirty people, eleven miles down the Hunter Valley; and a room *in a public-house* at Merriwa, a township with a population of sixty or seventy people, across the ranges to the west, forty-five miles off. Around these townships, at distances varying from two to nine miles, a few gentlemen settlers were living,—the owners of sheep and cattle, who had a few dependants close to them, besides their households. These could assemble at the places where

Divine service was held, and were always considered parts
of the congregation.

At Muswell Brook there were two services on one
Sunday and one on the next, which allowed one Sunday
service a-fortnight at Merton. Merriwa had but one
service a-quarter, held on a week-day. Holy Communion
was celebrated at Muswell Brook only four times in the
year; and a glass tumbler, and a common plate, not
appropriated to the purpose, had been used as a chalice
and paten.

The good-will of the people was immediately tested for
the supply of the last-mentioned want. They readily responded to the call, and within a few weeks a set of silver
Communion vessels and a linen cloth for the altar were
procured from Sydney, and we began monthly Com-
munions. The Bishop having auth----ed the candidates
for the ministry to read the service in my absence, I was
enabled to give two services each Sunday at Muswell
Brook, keeping to the Sunday service once a-week at
Merton. On the alternate Sundays I sent one of the
candidates over to have prayers, and to read a printed
sermon selected by me. And I myself went every other
Friday for a service, and to teach the children for an hour
before the service began.

We were not well off for music, but within three weeks
several of the mechanics and a storekeeper in Muswell
Brook expressed a wish to join a weekly practice of Church
music. And though our attempts were of a very humble
description, they improved the singing; and by the kind
aid of Mr. John Cox and his wife, whose house was two
miles off, we advanced to a piano, and thence eventually
to an organ. Our English friends may smile at a piano,
but they will not smile at the loving zeal which, in the
bush, did the best it could, giving such an instrument as
was at hand, and bringing over a fully occupied mother to
play at the weekly practice, as well as on Sunday. We

all know Who it was that commended an offering with the words, " *She hath done what she could.*"

Ash-Wednesday came that year on the 8th of March, and on Monday the 6th I had the privilege of beginning the daily service. Foreseeing that the distant parts of my district and other duties would often call me away, I gave notice that when I was at home the service would be regular, but that when the bell did not ring it might be understood that I was absent. We began with prayers twice a-day, at seven A.M. and at five P.M. But after Lent, by the advice of the Bishop, we only had *daily morning* service, a service with a sermon at seven P.M. every Wednesday, and two services with a sermon during Holy Week, and on all holy days. It was so often necessary to ride out five or twelve miles to visit sheep stations, that the daily evening prayer would have been frequently interrupted; but, except when I was absent on long journeys, the daily morning prayer could be regularly said. To the present day those services are still continued, and with fewer interruptions than I found possible.

Merriwa I first visited on March 14th, and spent part of two days there, visiting all the houses, and having a service in the evening of the first day and the morning of the second. From that time their service was always once a-month at least.

I will at present speak of a part of the country, not so far off as Merriwa, where, before long, I established a monthly service, and usually passed the night. The River Goulbourn, which must not be confounded with the town and diocese of that name, far to the south, rises on the eastern slope of the dividing range of the colony, which is of volcanic formation, but almost immediately enters sandstone ranges, and, flowing through a narrow winding valley for sixty or seventy miles, empties itself into the Hunter fifteen miles below Muswell Brook.

It is a lovely ride up the Goulbourn, and has delighted

me on many a weary journey. In some parts bold rocks
stand up perpendicularly from their base ; in others the
face of the precipice is broken by grassy slopes, which
throw back the summits as if buttressed from below; and
as you look up you may see the little rock wallaby, about
the size of a hare, and the form of a kangaroo, bounding
from ledge to ledge, or jumping in and out of the small
caves in the face of the rock above your head.   Sometimes the rocks close in almost to the river's bank; in
other parts they sweep away, leaving between their base
and the casuarinas that shade the river, a quarter or half-
a-mile of alluvial soil, mixed with a large proportion
of sand, moderately timbered, and covered with long
grass.

In many parts the rocks are exchanged for steep hills,
some of them cone-shaped, clothed with trees and grass,
through which large fragments of rock peep out.   Their
tops are generally crowned with small pines; down their
sides grow various kinds of the gum-tree and the *banksia*,
or bottle-brush ; and interspersed with these may be seen
the grass-tree, with its dark crooked stem and long grassy
crown, surmounted by what looks not unlike a large
bulrush, its brown head dotted over with little white star-
shaped flowers, each glistening with a drop of clear honey.
At the base of the hills, here and there, are clumps of
arbor vitæ, the pretty wattle or *acacia* bush, with its long
delicate leaves and sweet yellow blossoms, like little balls
of floss silk ; and various small flowering shrubs, which
give a civilised look to what in parts is quite a natural
pleasure-garden.

It is indeed a pretty neighbourhood, and the soil grows
good fruit and vegetables around the homesteads.   But
the grasses are not so nutritious on the soil of the sandstone as they are on the black soil of the volcanic
formation, some few miles to the north. And it is
surprising to see, as I have seen from the top of the high

hills, how many miles of country are so rugged as to be unavailable for pasturage. Hence it has not been taken up by the large sheep-masters, with their thousands of sheep; but a few men of small capital have fixed themselves by the banks of the river and its tributary creeks, mostly keeping cattle, which can travel farther for their food, and need no protection, as sheep do, from the native dogs.

Most of the settlers make cheese; and a wooden building beyond the dwelling-house is usually a dairy and cheese-room, in which, besides other means adopted for keeping it cool, nearly the whole of the interior is sunk several feet below the surface.

I had been at Muswell Brook several months before I heard of the Goulbourn. It is situated off the direct track to Merriwa, from which in most parts rocky ridges separate it. The Church was at that time only feeling its way into the country from the coast; and this valley had never seen a clergyman, and the poor people were living without any attempt at Divine service or teaching. When I was first told of them, and said I should look after them, the reply was that the trouble might be spared, for they would never attend to a parson; and some rather severe things which might have been true of some were applied to them generally. Of course this was no check to my duty, so I rode up and visited each house. I was most civilly received everywhere; at each place I had a short service, though my coming was unexpected, and I left them, having appointed a day and hour for the next service.

On my next visit, at the appointed time, I found in each case that I was not expected, and that no preparation had been made. At one house they thought my appointed day was in the week following; at another, they had quite forgotten what day it was; at a third, they supposed that some heavy rain, and the threat of a thunderstorm, would have

E

prevented my starting. However, ready or not ready, I induced them to assemble, and left them something to think about and some books to read. For several months it seemed as if with most of them the time would never be remembered, and the discouraging prophecy would come true. But at length, on riding up to the several verandahs, I used to find that the work had been arranged, and preparations made for service; and I have good reason to believe that those times were looked forward to with pleasure.

The nearest of the houses, called Richmond Grove, was seventeen miles from me, where the Wybong Creek joins the sandy bed of the Goulbourn. And there I have often found some green wheat cut ready for my horse to eat, while we were engaged in the service. One good effect of my visits was that, after a time, several of the family would find out when was the Sunday service at Merton, which was about six miles from them, and, horses being plentiful, would ride over to it.

The next house, called Mount Dangar Farm, was eight miles higher up the river, and was situated about a mile from Mount Warrendie, generally called, from a surveyor, Mount Dangar. Between this and the farm the river ran. Immediately behind the house was a productive vineyard, and on the opposite bank of the river stood another small settler's house, with its well-stocked fruit-garden, containing oranges, grapes, figs, and mulberries. Past this, to the right of Mount Warrendie, was a pleasant ride through a narrow valley, bounded by high rocks, to the Merriwa road, six miles distant. In front of the farm there were two houses, two and four miles off, up a tributary creek; and before long another house was built up the Goulbourn in the same direction.

It took some time to find out these outlying families, and to gather them into one congregation. My whole district, of which this was but a corner, was so large—

more than 2,500 square miles—that, coming from an English parish of about 1,800 acres, I could not for a while lay out my plans clearly to visit it all with the least amount of waste. At first I used to ride out one month by the Goulbourn, which was on the south of the district; and, after going to Merriwa to the western extremity, work homeward under the Liverpool range on the north side; and the next month I used to ride in the contrary direction. But after gaining a knowledge of the whole work, I found it best to keep the same direction always, and then I took Mount Dangar first. Either way, I generally slept there; and by degrees all the families within four miles came regularly to the service; and sometimes the Richmond Grove people came up and joined. We assembled in the sitting-room, into which the left of the two front doors opened, and which was lighted by an unglazed window on the left of the door. Often the room has been as full of fathers, mothers, and children as it could hold; and at times we had baptisms and churchings during the service. After which the outlying families found their way through the bush-tracks by starlight, some of them having to cross the river several times. Three different families in succession occupied Mount Dangar Farm while I ministered there, and from all of them I received a cordial welcome. Occasionally I stopped at the house of a Mr. Hungerford, on a creek four miles off; but Mount Dangar, being the most central, suited the congregation best.

Several of those adventures, common to a clergyman's bush experience, are connected with my recollections of this place. On one occasion, after working my way down the country, I had stopped for a service at a wayside inn, at that part of the Merriwa road lately mentioned. I delayed some time after the service to give instruction to a very nice family of children, whose circumstances required all the spiritual help I could give them. By the time I was in the saddle, twilight, which only lasts half-an-hour, was nearly gone, and heavy black clouds were arching over the narrow valley. Before I had gone a mile the inky black clouds had shut out every ray of light, and were pouring down a steady and very heavy rain, without a flash of lightning to show me the way. Though I had good *night sight*, I could not see anything, and rode on only by the sound, listening when my horse stepped off the narrow track on the grass or sticks at the side. After two miles, when we had just passed through a narrow gorge in the rocks, my horse lost his track; and after some wanderings, in which he was more disposed to pick the grass than to find the way, he brought me up among some acacia-trees, at the foot of a bluff rock. I could not afford to wander on carelessly, for at my right was a deep creek, into which it would be most unpleasant to fall, but through which, at two different crossing-places, the track lay. The pouring rain quite prevented any idea of " camping out," if it could be avoided ; so by taking my direction from the rock, and feeling the ground, sometimes with hands, sometimes with feet, I found the track at last; and in time, after several other losings and findings, reached Mount Dangar Farm, where the good people had given me up.

On another occasion, when a confirmation was approaching, there were candidates at Richmond Grove, Mount Dangar, and at the inn just mentioned. I had too much to do at home to be absent longer than duty rendered necessary. I therefore started at daybreak, took each class in its order, spending between one and two hours with each, and reached home at ten P.M., after a ride of sixty miles, which, I must confess, tired me ; but I was all right the next day.

Towards the end of the first year, I had, in this part, one of those misfortunes which horsemen must always be prepared for. I left home on a fine, handsome iron-grey horse, which I had lately purchased, and seemed to be in perfect health. During the service at Richmond Grove he was enjoying some green rye, which the good people had given him. I fear he had eaten rather greedily, as during the eight miles' ride between that place and Mount Dangar Farm he became very sluggish, and on arriving we found him suffering from a bad attack of colic. We did all we could for him; but as after some hours he became much worse, I determined to go to the inn I have before spoken of, six miles off, where better remedies could be procured. The son of my host, whose name was Hewitt, kindly lent me a horse, and, riding another, led my poor grey. He could but walk, and that with increasing slowness; and after passing four miles up the creek by Mount Warrendie, came to a stop at the narrow pass in the rocks before-mentioned, and could go no further. Young Hewitt galloped on to the inn to get something for his benefit, and I stood by the poor animal, who was by this time bathed in a cold sweat, and trembling all over. The sun had set, and the twilight had faded, but there was a glorious moon overhead, and the stars were shining, as only in such a clear, dry atmosphere they can shine. I kept rubbing my poor horse, and talking to him, but he was failing fast, and found it difficult to keep on his legs. At length he languidly pricked up his ears—for he heard, before I did, the hoofs of the returning horse—and gave a feeble neigh. It was his last, for the exertion seemed too much for him, and he staggered and fell. He tried to rise, but could not; and by the time Hewitt had reached us, his head was flat on the ground. A vein was opened to no purpose, and in a few minutes all was over.

Two months afterwards, as I rode through the same pass, I saw the bones of my poor steed picked clean. The eagles, hawks, crows, and ants had done their part to help the more voracious jaws of the native dogs, and in a few months more no two bones were left together. But eight years later, when I drove my wife up there, I showed her the skull.

I cannot help adding that this loss gave occasion for
one of the many kind acts by which the Bishop lightened
the difficulties of the clergy and others.   Just after
Christmas, 1848, I received a kind letter, in which, after
expressing his sorrow for the loss of my grey, he made
the value of him a New Year's gift, accompanied with his
blessing.

One service, which I held at Mount Dangar Farm, I
shall not easily forget, from the painful sense of weariness
which oppressed me.   I had left Cassilis, the westernmost
town in my district, early one morning—had visited, as I
rode, eight shepherds and hut-keepers, the former on their
"runs," the latter in their huts—and had had a short service
with each.   At Merriwa, through which I passed, I had
presided for an hour at the last meeting before giving the
contract for building a church there; and at the meeting
there were not a few difficulties to get over.   In the evening, at the end of a fifty miles' ride, I dismounted at the
verandah of Mount Dangar Farm.   It was just service
time, and the people were assembled.   I had therefore
time for nothing more than to wash my hands and face,
drink a refreshing glass of milk, and, after putting on my
surplice, come out of my room and begin the service.   The
feeling of sleepiness from sheer bodily exhaustion was over-
powering, and I earnestly hope that, if the sense of shame
at the exertions I was obliged to make to keep myself
awake was distressing to me, the service may not have
been unprofitable to the congregation.

One of my last acts before leaving the colony, early
in 1861, was to draw for Mr. Hungerford, at his
request, a plan for a wooden church, which I have since
heard has been built on a piece of land close to Mount
Dangar Farm.   The Rev. W. E. White, the present
clergyman, has informed me that a few fresh settlers
have added to the population of that neighbourhood; and
he sent me an interesting account of the opening of the

little church, and of his celebrating, for the first time, the Holy Communion within its walls.

O Lord—

> " Wherever meets Thy lowliest band
>   In praise and prayer,
> There is Thy presence, there Thy holy land—
>   Thou, Thou art there."
>
> *From the Author of the " Three Wakings."*

I have previously mentioned that, when appointed to the district of Muswell Brook, my farthest limit to the west was the little township of Merriwa, forty-five miles distant. But after a few months our eyes opened to the country beyond, and the Bishop gave into my charge Cassilis, another small town twenty-five miles still farther towards the west. This place had, before the formation of the diocese of Newcastle, been served by Mr. Gunther, the clergyman of Mudgee ; but Mudgee being now in the diocese of Sydney, Mr. Gunther only continued his services at Cassilis until the Bishop of Newcastle provided for it.

In colonial Church work one step generally leads to another in the endeavour to supply urgent wants which lie around you on every side. And thus, the district having no definite limits, I soon heard of some stations beyond Cassilis, some of them with large families of children ; and occasionally extended my rides to the stations of Uarbry, on the Talbragar, and Coolah, on the Coola-burragundy, lying on different lines, fourteen and twenty miles off towards the west.

The necessity of attending with regularity to the larger population of Muswell Brook and its neighbourhood, and reading as steadily as I could with the candidates for the ministry, determined me not to increase my district farther to the westward. Thus it was, before long, roughly defined ·in *breadth* by the line of the Liverpool

range to the north, and the Goulbourn River to the south,
where they run parallel to each other, about thirty-five
miles apart; and, in *length*, from Muswell Brook at the
east to Uarbry or Coolah at the west end, eighty-four or
ninety miles: not to mention some twelve miles of country
east of Muswell Brook, where shepherds' huts were dotted
on the sides of the bold hills, and near the bottom of deep
narrow valleys, which seemed to close in on every side.
I have before roughly estimated the area of the district as "more than 2,500 square miles;" it was really
about 8,000; or, to compare it with English measurements,
about the size of the counties of Somerset and Wilts
together, which are respectively 1,642 and 1,895 square
miles.

The *geological* characteristics of the district are remarkable, even to one who, like myself, can make no pretence
to geological accuracy.

The Liverpool range, which divides the waters which
flow to the Pacific from those which join the Darling, and
empty themselves through South Australia, is entirely
volcanic. Its outline is broken by bold cones and bluffs,
and it descends to the low lands by the successive steps
which mark the "trap" formation. The hills through
which the Goulbourn flows, as already mentioned, are
sandstone, and show many a precipitous face of rock
along the lines of the valleys. Six main *creeks* or
rivulets, known by the names of the Wybong, Hall's
Creek, Smith's Rivulet, Bow Creek, Krui Creek, and the
Munmurra, rise on the southern slope of the Liverpool
range, and empty themselves into the Goulbourn; besides
others, with which we are not now concerned, which flow
into the upper part of the Hunter. And between these
creeks lie, in succession, large undulating hills, with their
spurs and smaller valleys. These, for the greater portion
of their length, follow the volcanic formation of the parent
range, from which they spring like ribs from some

gigantic backbone.   But as they approach the Goulbourn,
in some cases for the last ten or fifteen miles, the sandstone cliffs succeed the volcanic hills.   In one part of a
range, called the Dartbrook range, the trap may be seen
overlapping the sandstone.   In some of the ranges con-
glomerate rocks appear.

In some places the road is deep with sand, in others it
is a dry hard gravel; while the decomposed "*trap*" makes
a rich black soil, which in wet weather is most tenacious.
About twelve miles east of Merriwa there is a deep sand,
which was the very plague of the draymen, and within a
hundred yards of it is a treeless or *bald* hill, from which a
large fragment has been torn by some convulsion.   The
two portions are about five yards apart; and as you walk
down the small watercourse which divides them, you see
the ends of pentagonal basaltic columns on each side,
lying at about an angle of fifteen degrees.*   Within a
mile and a half from this hill is the only pool fed by its
own springs which I have met with in any part of the
country which I have visited.   Bubbles are constantly
rising to the surface, and the water, though usually fouled
by cattle, is strongly mineral.   The pool is known by the
name of the *Gingerbeer Springs*.

In several parts there is a great deal of fossil wood, not
imbedded in stone, but in loose earth or clay.   It occurs
near the surface, and appears where the heavy rains have
washed off the soil.   I have found several trunks of fos-
silised trees nearly whole, besides considerable quantities
of fragments.   In the neighbourhood of Muswell Brook,
in a clayey soil, they are largely impregnated with iron.
About ten miles from Merriwa, near the division of the
volcanic and the sandstone formations, I have seen several
large pieces almost white, and very hard.   Some are in

---

* I give these particulars from memory, having no record of observations made at the time, but I believe that what I have said above is
substantially correct.

part crystallised, and others, by their different colours,
show very distinctly the rings of the wood.

When speaking of the district of the Goulbourn River I
mentioned some of the varieties of ornamental and flowering shrubs, which make the sandstone country, though
poor in soil, so picturesque. The volcanic districts have
not the same variety. The timber most prevalent on that
soil is a small kind of eucalyptus, popularly called the box-
tree, from the colour and grain of the wood; and the chief
variety in the foliage is made by the currajong, which, in
bark, and in the colour and shape of its leaves, is very like
the pear-tree. The black soil is thinly timbered; but
what it loses in shrub and tree, it much more than gains
in the richness and abundance of its grasses, which make
it admirably adapted to the support of large flocks of
sheep and herds of cattle and horses. On this soil there
are three principal grasses, popularly called barley grass,
kangaroo grass, and oaten grass; and the last, unlike
most of the things in the colony which have a popular
name, really bears an oat, as it professes to do, in a rich
brown sheath. All these grasses grow in tufts, like small
specimens of the Pampas grass, and from their centre the
seed-stems spring. The former two grow about two feet
six inches in height; but the oaten grass, in favourable
seasons, throws up a seed-stem from six to eight feet long.

In the midst of these rich pasture grounds a few large
flock-masters had taken up their stations. And their
families, the few men employed about their head stations,
and the shepherds and hut-keepers belonging to them,
scattered thinly over the face of the country, claimed the
especial attention of the clergyman of a pastoral district.

Among the owners of these bush establishments men
of good family are often found, and some who have
graduated with honours at Oxford or Cambridge. Many
of their men, when I first knew the colony, and some of
the inhabitants of the small townships, were old convicts,

the terms of whose sentences had expired, or who were still holding tickets of leave. There were, particularly among the cattle-stations, some natives of the colony, born of British parents; and there was also a considerable element of the emigrant class, which year by year increased, while the convict class, not being replenished by fresh arrivals from England, steadily diminished.

The religious condition of the district assigned to me, with some most pleasing exceptions, was, generally speaking, very low. Could it have been expected to be otherwise, when the deteriorating influences at work, and the scarcity of good ones, are considered? In the first place, the colony was founded upon England's convicts, with a few men who came out to make money by their labour. The former brought with them habits of evil, often deeply ingrained, and a good many of the latter were men who would rather live below a high Christian standard, even if it were customary around them, than strive to raise the standard in the midst of surrounding difficulties. From time to time not a few wild sons, whom their friends could make nothing of at home, were sent out to try their fortune. Many of the emigrants of the labouring classes were badly selected, and some of the unthrifty and useless in various English parishes were encouraged to go out, not because they were adapted by their habits and characters to help the new country, but because they could not get on in the old one, and to be rid of them was a benefit to the employers of labour and to the ratepayers. Even to some who had been steady while they were surrounded by the opinion and advice of friends and the regularity of Church services, their entire uprooting from all accustomed influences, and the unsettling idleness of a long voyage, proved too great a trial of their faith. Habits of prayer and reading Holy Scripture had been broken in upon; and the excitement of settling in a new country, new faces, and new circumstances, and the want of any one near them who cared how they lived, often made sad havoc of what had been good in them.

In the townships there were frequent examples among all classes of impurity and drunkenness, not sufficiently branded by any public opinion, which acts as so useful a police on the outskirts of morality. And in the shepherds' huts, where three men usually lived together, the constant companionship, night and morning, of one corrupt "*mate*," if only one, exerted a very deteriorating influence upon the one or two who might have been of a better mind. There was some compensating power in the long solitude of the day, when each shepherd was following his flock under the brilliant blue sky, and the hut-keeper was left at home to do the easy duties of preparing the hut and the sheep-yards. Each had then abundant time for reflection, and for any teaching of good in past days to rise up in the mind. But the ever-recurring unchaining of the tongue, when evening and morning brought the *hut-mates* together again, gave the bad a terrible power of suggesting thoughts of evil, which were only too ready to germinate.

Add to this the grievous deficiency of clergy, and the consequent impossibility of meeting evil, or strengthening weakness, by a sufficiency of holy influences ; and it is not to be wondered at, though it is most distressing, that many Christian men never said a prayer, and had no thought for anything but self and sin, and that even among the more decent there were so few who had any idea of earnestness in following God.

The shepherds were especially destitute. Services held in the small townships were useless to them. The residents might attend, and even the stockmen, who looked after the cattle and horses, might easily find time to ride in from the bush to join. But the shepherd must lead his sheep out of the sheep-yard early on each of the seven mornings of the week, remain with them all the day, while they were feeding or lying down, lest the native dog should fall upon them, and lead them back to the yard again only a little before sundown. Even a service held in the evening would, in most cases, be quite unavailable to the shepherd; for the greater number of huts were many miles away from the nearest place where a small congregation could be assembled. And yet all these, wanderers though they may have been, were Christ's sheep, for whom He shed His Blood.

The problem of ministering to men scattered over so wide an area was a very difficult one. They were scattered, one here, and another three or four miles off, along the banks of the "creeks," and near hollows on the higher lands, where wells might be sunk; from the Liverpool range to the Goulbourn, and from Muswell Brook to Coolah. And yet, as soon as I saw the district, I saw that some visitation of these poor fellows must be attempted. If the manner of doing it were ever so imperfect, it would be better than leaving them quite uncared for.

It took me some months to feel my way along, and to learn the different features of so large a district, and where each little obscure hut was placed. But by information afforded by the proprietors as to their huts; by the kindness of an overseer now and then conducting me; by following the tracks of the ration carts, which each week took the supplies for the men; and sometimes by stumbling on a remote hut by chance, as I might be riding across the country without a track, I gradually became acquainted with by far the greater number of the huts.

Soon after the whole district, which I have mentioned, was assigned to me, I was enabled to lay out a general plan of the work, with the object of spreading Church ministrations over as large a surface as possible. Every fourth week, including a Sunday, I was absent from Muswell Brook, leaving one of the candidates for the ministry to read the prayers and a sermon which I had selected. When at any time no candidate was with me, the Bishop authorised John H. Cox, Esq.—a thoroughly conscientious and zealous Churchman, who was in very many ways "a comfort to me"—to keep the congregation together in the same manner. That Sunday I spent at Merriwa or Cassilis on alternate months, having a morning and afternoon service, teaching the children, and, between the evenings of Saturday and Monday mornings, visiting the houses in the township. Whichever had not the Sunday services had one service, or sometimes two, on a week-day; and the rest of the day was spent with the children, and in the houses. On each other night during the week's journey I stopped at some station, which had previous notice of my coming. In some cases as many as twenty people assembled, in others only five or six. Each morning, before leaving, I had prayers, and spent the time from nine till sunset in making my way to the next halt for the night. During the day I took sometimes one line of country, sometimes another, so as to visit in turn all the huts which I had been able to discover.

But this would not do the work that was needed; for the hut-keepers were the only persons to be found at home during the day. To get at the shepherds it was necessary to find them on their *runs*. A sharp look-out would often detect a flock in the distance, or perhaps a few of the sheep just appearing above a ridge; they might be a mile to the right or left of the direct route, but with them was a shepherd, and he must be sought. On reaching him, the rein was thrown over the horse's head, and he was left, nothing loth, to rest and feed among the rich grass. A little ordinary conversation followed, often about the old country, which both of us remembered with affection; and then, upon the offer to read to him and join in prayer, he sent his dog round to bring closer the scattering sheep, and to sit on the farther side to watch them, while we drew under the best shade we could find—generally little enough; and, without answering for others, I often felt how lovingly our Lord had provided for our wants, by promising His Presence "in the midst," "where *two*," as well as "three," should be "gathered together." Some part of Holy Scripture was read; such teaching given as appeared most suitable; and then we knelt side by side, and prayed in the words of the Confession, or part of the Litany, and some of the collects of the Book of Common Prayer.

On one such occasion I had fallen in with a weather-beaten shepherd, who had been a soldier. It was by the side of the *old* Cassilis track, three miles from Merriwa. When our short service was over, and I was shaking him by the hand, before riding on my way, the poor fellow, who had been very attentive throughout, said, with tears in his eyes, "Thank you, sir: you are the first clergyman I've seen for *sixteen* years." For so long had this poor fellow been without the help of any service. And his was no uncommon case. For some time after I began my bush work, I frequently found men, and sometimes women too, to whom the sight of a clergyman, or any approach to a service, were events of long-past years.

Not a few of the men whom I met were Roman Catholics; and some were Presbyterians: to all I offered reading and prayer; and in very few instances was the offer declined. Most persons accepted it gratefully, and looked out for the next visit. This was especially the case where there were children. The mothers would gladly sit and listen, while the little ones were being taught: glad that their children should receive instruction, and welcoming the old, simple teaching, which in some form or other they had themselves received in their early days. I generally found that, though the short teaching which such a visit allowed hardly elicited an answer, and the little things at first seemed shy and inattentive, what was said was remembered afterwards.

With young and old there was this advantage to balance
their many disadvantages, that whatever was said or done
was impressed on them by the rare circumstance of a
clergyman's visit to their bush home.   And there were
not, as in our towns and villages, a number of persons
and events rapidly succeeding each other, to efface impressions which the teaching had left upon their minds.

Before leaving, I nearly always drew from my saddle-
bags some book or tract to be kept till the next visit.   And
as the visits were repeated from time to time, the number
of Bibles and Prayer-books, which my bush people asked
me to bring up for them to purchase, increased.

One thing which I always endeavour to impress upon
them, was to do their best to hallow the Lord's Day by
especial prayer and reading, joining with each other in
the services of the day, if they could find those with them
willing to do so, with the especial view of maintaining
their union with the body of Christ's Church, into which
they had been ingrafted.   I found it often useful, when I
met a man in the bush, to connect our prayer with the
Church's hours, the third, sixth, or ninth, as it might be,
and with the Divine acts which had hallowed those hours.
There was this great advantage in this practice, that it
hallowed something definitely.   One of the great difficulties of religion in the bush is, that there is nothing
externally hallowed : no church, nothing outward to *remind* the people that God has a claim upon this world,
and that He bestows His blessing where His claim is duly
acknowledged.   But wherever shepherds may be, they
know by the height of the sun what is the hour; and to
make them feel that certain hours are consecrated by
particular acts of God's mercy to man, and to teach them
how to put up a short prayer from time to time under the
" shadow " of those " great rocks in a weary land," was
one means of reminding them that even in the wild bush
God's own sun continually witnessed to His Presence and

gracious acts. If they had no recognised *places*, where the springs of living waters gushed forth, the Church's " *hours*," if they would use them faithfully, seemed to bring to them, as to Israel in the wilderness, the " Spiritual Rock " following them, from which they might drink.

No doubt a good deal of seed was sown " by the wayside," or " among thorns ; " and apparently came to nothing. And the very extent of the surface over which the work had to be done, hardly allowed it to be deep. But in the famine of the Word of God it seemed better to labour to give a small portion to all, if possi' 'e, rather than to leave the scattered ones, who could not help themselves, to starve, while providing fully for those who could be gathered together.

Thank God! better times have dawned since then ; the district has been divided, and two hard-working clergymen, the Rev. W. E. White and the Rev. W. S. Wilson, are zealously and lovingly labouring there ; the former fixed at Muswell Brook, the latter at Cassilis. But there is still need of more labourers to do that work aright.

Work among sheep and cattle stations is for the most part a simple work of faith—casting " bread upon the waters"—for not only is it impossible to watch growth, as in a parish where you may see your people frequently, but shepherds and stockmen are very apt to migrate. They generally engage with a master for a year, and when their time is up many leave, and either go to another part of the country, or turn to some other employment. Yet some appeared to do their best with the opportunities they had.

There was a cattle-station twenty miles from Muswell Brook, on the Wybong Creek, where, at one time, I used, every alternate month, to stop for the first night on my journeys. The stockman was the chief man at the station, and with him was a hut-keeper, besides two or three occasional helpers. A few hundred yards off, on

F

the opposite side of the creek, was a sheep-hut belonging to another owner, with its three inmates.

When the work of the day was done, and the supper at about six o'clock over, the shepherds came across, and we had service, in which most of the men took their part and made the responses. Service ended, we used to sit round, and talk on various subjects till we went to bed.

On the first evening, during our conversation, I asked, "What do you do, my friends, to try to keep Sunday?" "Oh, nothing, sir," was the reply. "What can we do? You know we have neither church nor clergyman nearer than the Brook." "I know your wants too well," said I, "and am sorry for them. Still, even as you are, you could do more than you think." I then pointed out that although they could not enjoy the peculiar blessings which Christ's minister could impart to them, they might at all events, as Christian men, enjoy the blessings of united prayer and praise in the words of the Prayer-book; and the stockman, being the chief man there, might read the lessons and the epistle and gospel to the rest. And I suggested that the men from the opposite hut might well come over and join with them.

"There are," I said, "two reasons which might prevent men from doing this. First, they may fancy that he who took the lead was assuming the office of Christ's ministers, like the teachers of the sects. But this is not the case. You could not come to the church on Sunday if you wished to do so, and, in taking the lead in the prayers, would be doing no more than any parents might do, if obliged to stay from church with some of their family that were sick, or than every good captain of a merchantman does every Sunday, when he is at sea, if he has no clergyman on board. Any Christians may thus pray and read together most profitably, and without doing anything but what is strictly right. The other difficulty which men may feel is, that it would be hypocrisy to join in prayer

together, and then to go out and swear and drink together.·
It comes, then, to this, that either the drinking and swear-
ing, or the praying and reading Holy Scripture, must be
given up. Which would be your greatest loss ? Don't wait
until you have overcome your evil habits before you begin
the prayers. If you desire to overcome them, your
prayers and reading together, with that desire, will not be
hypocrisy, and will help your endeavours."

After removing what I thought their chief obstacles, I
did not attempt ʻo bind them to any promise, nor did I
urge them. We then went off to bed. The men had
listened very attentively; but I cannot say that I felt very
sanguine, as I rode away the next morning, that they
would follow my counsel. But I wronged them.

Two months later, as we were sitting round after our
evening service, I said, with some misgiving, " Well,
John, what have you tried to do about the Sunday
prayers ? " " Why, sir," said John, " we thought what
you said was nothing but reasonable, and the men were
agreeable, and so we began the next Sunday evening, and
Cox's men came over, and we've gone on with it ever
since." And they continued as they had begun.

In about nine months after this, John, the stockman,.
was out of his time of service; and, to my great regret, went
off to Moreton Bay, and I have never heard of him since.
The next month after his departure I met the hut-keeper
getting water at the creek, and asked him, " What have
you done about the Sunday prayers since John left you ? "
" O sir," he answered, " we all liked them, so when the
new stockman came, we told him what John used to do,
and he fell in with it ; so it goes on as before."

This was indeed good news to me ; but in a year after
this all the men left, and a Roman Catholic and his wife
came to the place, and these, though civil enough, would
not be guided by me. However, after another year or
two, a married Churchman succeeded, and the Church's

prayers were again used by the inmates of the hut, when
they could not, like their more fortunate brethren, be
present at a service.

Many a time, in hot weary days, I rejoiced to be among
those poor destitute brethren in the bush, for it is a happy
thing to be able to bring a cup to parched lips ; and often,
thank God! I was enabled to suggest some help for their
souls, which seemed very obvious, but had not occurred
to them, simply from want of a suggestion.

Within sight of the shepherd's hut just mentioned, is
a fine gap in sandstone cliffs, through which the road goes
towards Muswell Brook.   Will the reader forgive me if I
introduce here a few stanzas which I wrote one day on
horseback after passing it, when the sweet yellow acacias
which studded it, and were relieved by a background of
cypress, were out in full beauty ?—

DUTY'S BLESSINGS.

Sept. 14, 1852.

There are flowers round beauty's pathway,
  Where'er we toil along :
And the perfumed air is vocal
  With the bell-bird's liquid song.

The viewless breezes whisper
  To the tall trees as they go,
And fan the wanderer's weary cheek
  With their balmy breath below.

And standing round, on either side,
  The tall cliffs' giant forms
Bend their calm grey heads, which have braved
    the wrath
  Of a thousand lightning-storms.

They speak of bygone ages,
  Of the days when Earth was young,
And upheaving Nature's tossing throes
  On her Maker's accents hung.

And oh ! the clear blue heaven,
  With its fathomless abyss !
Its still calmness seems to tell us
  Of the realms beyond of bliss.

From our Father's hand, on every side,
  There are blessings strewn around :
Duty's path still leads our footsteps
  O'er hallowed Eden-ground.

Yet seek them not, these joyous things,—
  They wither as we gaze,
And leave us still, with a yearning heart,
  To tread deserted ways.

To cheer thee on thy pilgrim path,
  From thy Father's love they 're given :
To gladden, not to stay thy steps,
  On thy forward road to Heaven.

Seek the kingdom of thy God : 'tis found
  Through meek and lowly ways ;
Where calm-cheek'd duty guides thee far
  From the siren voice of praise.

Cheer the lonely, soothe the broken heart :
  And, where the earth-turn'd eye
Is dazzled by sin's flickering glare,
  Point to Heaven's pure joys on high.

See a brother in each human form ;
  And thy toil will gladness be :
E'en the Cross itself is a blessed thing,
  Since thy Saviour died for thee.

Seek duty thus : along its course
  Thy Lord will joys provide ;
And in thy sorrows thou shalt find
  Thy Saviour by thy side.

Bless His mercy for all gifts of love :
  Yet on this world's mouldering clod,
One only fills thy craving soul,—
  Thy Saviour and thy God.

Church work in a remote bush township has much to
contend with, where a clergyman's visits are few and far
between.

From one week's end to another the inhabitants meet each other without anything occurring to remind them that they are united by any other tie than those of neighbourhood, or business, or subjection to the same laws. That they are Christian brethren is kept out of sight, not only by the petty squabbles and contending interests which are always rife in small communities left much to themselves, but by that powerful engine of evil, religious division. A tolerably strong infusion of Irish Roman Catholics is generally found among them; there are a few Irish or Scotch Presbyterians, and usually a small sprinkling of followers of some of the sects which flourish on English soil. These altogether make about one-half of the community, the other half being members of the Church of England.

Separated from each other by differing ideas of religion, they usually ignore the subject of religion in their intercourse with each other; and thus, at each short period of his visits, the clergyman has to lift up the hearts that have been turned to the world during week-days and Sundays since the last time of service. It is not, therefore, to be wondered at if the seed sown on soil so unprepared for it brings forth little fruit.

Still, the alternative of *neglecting* to do what one can do, because it is impossible to do more, is not to be thought of. People are better for having even infrequent ministrations than for being left almost absolutely without any; and Christ's truths, even when rarely heard, leave a blessing behind them, and prepare the way for happier times. In all ministerial working—but especially in places where the services are unavoidably rare—the only way to prevent throwing all up in disappointment, or going on in cold formality, is to labour carefully, *because Christ has sent us* to take disappointments as part of our allotted cross; and to leave the issue to Him Who, when hope seemed extinguished, rose from the dead in triumph.

"One soweth, and another reapeth," and so our faith is tried. The people are Christ's, the work is His; it will prosper, if we do not mar it by our unfaithfulness and mismanagement. And the anxious burden of a weight beyond our strength, and the sight of Christian souls, who *need* the Church's work if they do not desire it, stir up the fervent prayers of many a toiling bush clergyman, that "the Lord of the harvest would *send forth more labourers into His harvest.*"

It was up-hill work for some time at Merriwa, with only thirteen visits in the year that could be paid to it, supplemented by occasional letter-writing. The great want was the presence of some earnest layman, who would in some way make his influence felt for good during the absence of the clergyman; and several years elapsed before one was raised up.

It has been mentioned before that the place where Divine Service was first held was a room in a public-house. One of my first endeavours was to procure another place. At each fresh visit I felt a greater repugnance to assemble the congregation at a house where, at almost all other times, there were scenes of gross drunkenness. The publican was very accommodating. He took what care he could to prevent drinking at the bar during the time of service, even on a week-day; and if I slept at his house, which on some occasions I did, I could rarely induce him to take any payment for either my bed or meals. But his civility could not reconcile me to use a place, surrounded by such associations, for the holy rites of Christ's faith; and I chafed to see that, when each man could get up a building for his own use, as a dwelling or an improvement to his establishment, we could not all join together to erect a building, however humble, for the worship of God.

There were certainly legitimate hindrances to undertaking anything very costly at that time—the pressure of pecuniary difficulties, which has already been mentioned, and the small number of inhabitants in the township, not a few of whom were Roman Catholics. But there were means sufficient, had faith been clearer and love warmer, to erect a small, simple church, which would have rescued the services of Christ's holy Church from the loathsome associations of a public-house. Had the chief settlers consented to do their part, every poorer Churchman in the district was prepared to follow; and it was always found that when any district took up its burden their brethren in other districts helped them. We found this the case afterwards; but *then* there was an indisposition to move, which nothing apparently could overcome; and my infrequent visits could not stir the *vis inertiæ*. One alternative which was proposed to me was to erect a room to be used in turn by the *ministers of all denominations*, as each might require it—a proposal which was urged upon me some years afterwards, when I resided at Morpeth, and was endeavouring—and, thank God! successfully—to get a small stone church built at Seaham, on the Williams River.

It need hardly be said that I could not accept this solution of the difficulty; and we still assembled at the public-house, though several of the congregation felt the incongruity of our using such a place. The early Christians could worship among the dead in the Catacombs, for fear of persecution. At Philippi,* St. Paul could go out " by a river-side, where prayer was wont to be made." Even in the rhetorical " school of one Tyrannus,"† St. Paul disputed daily with the Ephesians, to lead them to the faith of Christ. But when, though ministering among Christians, who were not badly off, we were driven by sheer necessity to the room of an inn, we were forced to feel humbled, and to remember that Jesus, Who sat at meat

* Acts xvi. 12, 13.   † Acts xix. 9.

with sinners, could be with us, and rescue from sin those
of His flock who were living in the midst of it. I may
mention with thankfulness that I have lately heard from
the clergyman of that district, that the publican's step-
children, whom I have catechised in that house, and who
are now grown up, are active and earnest Sunday-school
teachers.

After a few years, I was, thank God! enabled to get up
a wooden church, but I was to be exercised by many a
disappointment first. Doubtless it was well, in the very
low state of Christian faith and practice then prevailing,
that we should have many a check, and that the cross,
which was eventually reared on the little hill that over-
looks the town, should in its measure be like Him for Whose
sheep it was erected, " *a root out of a dry ground,*" stunted
in growth, for want of the moisture which the worldly
means which God gave ought to have supplied.

Failing during our early days to get aid for a church,
I tried to induce those who were able to join me in
subscribing for a school. The Bishop would have provided
a master ; and at his request, the " Denominational Board
of Education" had appropriated a salary to supplement the
payments of the parents. In this school we should have
held our services until the time came for building a church.
After some delays, the manager of one of the sheep
establishments agreed to assist in raising a subscription
for the school-house ; and on my next visit we were to
meet, and set the plan at work. The next month, on my
arrival, I found that, in concert with others, he had already
made application to the *secular* board of education, which
at the end of 1848 was formed by the Colonial Government. That board had promised a master, and the school
was to be built forthwith. One of the regulations of the
secular board, miscalled the *National Board of Education,*
provided that the school should never be used for religious
services. Thus my hope was again frustrated ; and the

sound moral and religious progress of the poor little township was indefinitely retarded by the exclusion of a school, in which the training and discipline should be founded upon God's truth.

There is no need of dwelling at length upon the various obstacles in the way of building the church. The endeavour was often repeated, and as often resulted in nothing. However, we left the public-house.

Small as the houses in the township were, being little better than huts, some of them roofed with bark, and with earth floors, we met sometimes in the little room of the widow who kept the post-office; sometimes in the huts of two or three others, as it was convenient for them to receive us; for a while, in a wool-shed belonging to a sheep establishment a mile above the township; and for a few times at a new, untenanted hut, from which we were fairly driven by fleas and bugs, which in that warm climate always swarm in such places. This wandering was, however, productive of good: the discomfort it caused enforced my arguments for building a church.

Towards the end of 1849 I had, with one of the townspeople, selected a piece of land; and the Government, upon application being made in the usual form, granted the allotment to the Church.

It was on a rising ground composed of sandstone, about thirty feet above the black trap soil, on which the greater portion of the little town was built. As you stood on it looking towards the town, the ground rose gently behind you moderately covered with trees. To the west, on your left hand, it sloped down towards Smith's Rivulet, which ran over its rocky bed between deep black banks; and beyond this rose, step after step, the high line of hills over which lay several tracks to Cassilis, and thence into the interior. Towards the north, the eye looked over the little town to another low hill, half sandstone, half trap, which bounded it on that side. And over this, and up the valley that stretched away on the left of it, the fine bold outline of the Liverpool range, twenty miles distant as the crow flies, bounded the view. But that fine range of hills was not dim and hazy, as it would be at such a distance in our English climate, but clear and distinct, marking well the lights and shadows on its rugged sides. If you could climb to the top of that range and look down on the other side, you would see the vast treeless level of the Liverpool Plains extended before you as far as the eye could reach, rich with luxuriant grass, a perfect ocean of pasturage. And you would be standing on the line that divides what is, at the time when I am writing, the newly-formed diocese of Grafton and Armidale, from the parent see of Newcastle.

From different parts of this range issued four small creeks, which, uniting three miles above the township, flowed past it to the Goulbourn in one channel, which bore the names of Smith's Rivulet and Gummum, corrupted into *Gammon*, Creek.

Having secured a beautiful site for the church, I was desirous of putting up the most temporary building, which would cost only the labour. I proposed merely a sapling frame, with a bark covering, and subscribing month by month until we had enough to build a stone church. This, I am convinced, might have been accomplished, if the people had agreed to the plan ; but it is necessary to work with the means at one's disposal, and several of our small number had not patience to wait for this : if anything was to be done, they must see it at once, so it was agreed about May, 1850, to put up as good a slab building as possible for £60. Even that was thought by a few an unattainable sum. To save expense, I drew out the plan, as much like Early English as I could in wood ; the timber being of stout iron-bark. One gentleman gave the hauling, small subscriptions were collected in the township, and on October 17th, 1850, in the presence of Mr. Thomas Perry (who gave the hauling), and twenty of the people, I laid the first iron-bark sleeper of Holy Trinity Church. I undertook the collection and management of the small fund. About £10 more than the whole sum voted was expended on the shell of the building, which was thirty-two feet long by sixteen feet broad, with a vestry attached.

Little by little subscriptions trickled in. We got in the windows, and then, with what benches and boards we could procure, began at once using it for Divine service in very primitive form. Soon, as there was a prospect of raising a little more, some open seats of red cedar were ordered down the country, and the Holy Table. An accident characteristic of the bush befell the latter. It was being brought up on the top of a loaded dray; and, at some peculiarly bad part of the road, the bullock-driver turned aside into the bush, when the limb of a tree, under which he was passing, caught two of the legs, and they were torn off with about as much ease as you would snap a twig.

When our seats came up, we were still for some time longer without flooring, and sometimes, as I stood at the altar, I sank into the sand up to my ankles.

By this time a gentleman had been appointed to super-intend one of the sheep establishments, who was heartily desirous to aid in Church work. Wishing to have some-thing permanent among so much wood, we had the floor paved with stone, with steps up to the altar; and my good friend Mr. Marlay presented a harmonium to the church, which he played himself.

At length, when in 1855 all was as far prepared as our small means would allow, the Bishop crowned the work by consecration. A notice appeared in one of the colonial newspapers at the time, from which the following is an extract:—

" On Monday, March 19th, the Lord Bishop of Newcastle visited this township, for the double purpose of consecrating the church and holding a confirmation, and nearly every member of the Church of England in the town and its neighbourhood came to take part in the service. About five years ago an effort was made to commence a church. It was found impossible to erect one of stone or brick at that time, but the best was done in the way of a slab building which the material admitted. It has simply a nave and vestry attached ; the roof is high-pitched, with a small bell turret at the west end. There are three lancet windows in the east end, and two in the west, with two single lancet lights in each side, and one in the vestry. The woodwork inside is relieved by a stone floor ; and the interior and exterior of the building, with the fittings-up, though simple, have a church-like appearance, which may lead some minds to think that what we do, even in a humble way, to the honour of God, ought to be taken pains with."

In a letter I have lately received from the present clergyman, he says that it will be necessary to enlarge the church, as there is no longer room for the congregation which assembles in it.

I can never think of that church without calling to mind him who gave me the first subscription towards it— a poor man, and a shepherd. It is now some years since I heard that he had been called to his rest. His name was Robert Baird, and I first found him at a remote station, eight miles above the town, towards the Liverpool range.

His hut was at the foot of a high ridge, near Coulson's Creek, one of the small tributaries of Smith's Rivulet. A few yards before his door was a small bit of ground, enclosed, in the roughest bush fashion, by whole trees and large limbs, heaped one upon another, with the lighter wood thrust in at intervals to stop up gaps. Within this garden the rich black soil bore an abundance of pumpkins and water-melons, which scrambled luxuriantly over the ground, or climbed up and hung over the rude fence ; and on the parts of the enclosure which they did not occupy

were cabbages, quickly grown and excellent when the
season was wet, but in dry hot weather hanging exhausted
and flaccid, and in colour and toughness like " *blue cotton
umbrellas,*" as a friend used to call them. Not far off were
a couple of cows ; for where the master encourages the
men, calves are cheaply bought, and easily reared. In a
small log pigsty, under the shade of a leafy kind of eucalyptus, called the *apple-tree,* were two or three pigs, or
sometimes a litter. A few fowls were foraging about,
picking up grass-seeds, and running after grasshoppers
and insects of various kinds that swarmed everywhere.

Baird appeared to be thirty-five or forty years old, and
had a wife and several young children—three boys and, I
think, two girls. I had heard at Merriwa that there were
sheep-stations up Coulson's Creek ; and, while hunting
them up, fell in with Baird and his family in their retired
nook, about eighteen months before there was any prospect
of building a church.

They had never before been visited by a clergyman, as,
indeed, was the case with all the stations on that creek ;
and they seemed genuinely grateful for anything approaching to Christian worship and Christian teaching. From
this time I made a point of going round by that line of
country as often as possible ; taking it on my way between
the upper part of the Wybong Creek and Merriwa. Sometimes I visited it for several months in succession. Sometimes, when I took another line of stations, there was an
interval between my visits of two or three months.

One thing that distressed me was that, when the good
woman knew I was coming, there was always a fowl or
something dressed especially for me. All my entreaties
that she would spare herself this trouble were unheeded.
Gudewives in all ranks, all the world over, will have their
way ; so, although I should have much preferred riding on
to the next station as soon as my work was finished, taking
perhaps a bit of *damper* and some tea or milk, I could not

decline to take what she had so thoughtfully provided for
my refreshment.

We always had a short service : some of the prayers
and collects of the Prayer-book, a psalm or two (generally
those for the day) ; and some short part of Holy Scripture
was read and explained.　Before leaving them I always
gave the little ones some especial teaching.　Little, gentle,
shy things they were—those children of the bush—very
respectful in manner ; but for many a month not a word
could I get out of them.　Sometimes I told them Bible
stories, with the youngest standing between my knees ;
sometimes I asked them questions, and answered them
myself ; and when I had patted them on the head and
blessed them, they would run out, and leave me to say my
last words to their parents.　And as I mounted my horse,
I could see them clinging together, and peeping round the
end of the hut at me with timid, roguish smiles, coming
out from their shelter and having a good stare at me as I
rode away.

Their mother told me that, when she questioned them
afterwards, they remembered much of what I had said to
them ; but she could not get them to give their attention
to the simple books in monosyllables which I left for their
use.　The first book which seemed really to get into their
minds was "First Steps to the Catechism."　That gave
them the end of the clue, and they gradually got out of
what had appeared to them an insuperable difficulty.　On
my next visit after leaving the book, their mother said that
they were beginning to try to read their letters, as well as
to learn the answers to the questions in the little book.

A year or two after this, when they had really begun to
make some progress with the teaching which their father
gave them in the evening, Baird told me that he was
anxious to remove to some place where he could send
them to school.　He could not put his plan into effect
immediately ; and in the meantime heard of our intention

of building a church at Merriwa. He did not wait to be
asked, and did not hesitate from the knowledge that he
should need his money when he moved. He came forward
before any subscription list was opened, and begged me to
take charge of 10s. for the church, to which, some time
after, he added another 10s.

Does not this poor man's ready and unsolicited offering
to the service of God, which he would seldom be able to
attend, shame many Christians, who, having the *talent* of
abundance, spend it readily upon some self-indulgence,
some showy dinner-party or ball, some jewelry or dress;
and become suddenly fearful of expense when an appeal is
made to their charity? They who have squandered money
by tens, or it may be by hundreds, give some poor pound
or half-a-crown at a collection, and often evade giving at
all in the aid of the work of Christ at home or abroad.

That poor man's offering always made me look on the
little church at Merriwa with hope. I cannot but trust
that God's eye will be over that house of His, towards
which He moved His humble servant's love to contribute
so readily out of the little that he had.

Baird sold off his cattle, took his wife and family to
Maitland, and while he put his children to school his wife
endeavoured to make their small savings last longer by
keeping a little shop, while he earned money in any way
he could.

The shop was not successful, for bush-life had not made
his wife a good shopkeeper. And after two years he came
back to his old employer as a shepherd; and now his two
oldest boys were able to take turns with a second flock of
sheep. I had lost sight of him most of the time when he
was in Maitland, and for some months was not aware that
he had returned to my district. He had been sent to a
station some few miles off, which I had never heard of.

At length, to my surprise and pleasure, I saw him one
Sunday in the church at Merriwa. He had left his own

flock for a few hours in charge of one of his sons, while
the second son was tending the other flock. After service
we were mutually glad to meet; and he told me he had
been wondering, poor man, at my not having found him
out. He described where his station was, on a creek
called Middle Creek; and the next month I rode up from
Merriwa to look after him and his family.

After some six or seven miles' riding, keeping a good
look-out, I caught sight in the distance of some sheep;
and looking carefully, soon made out the figure of a man
sitting down at the foot of a tree by the bank of the creek.
As it was about midday, I thought he might be taking his
dinner, but soon saw a boy by his side; and when I
reached him, I found that he was hearing one of his sons
read in the New Testament. I heard the boy read, and
questioned him, and found him much improved by his
schooling.

Baird then told me that, besides keeping school at home
every evening, with much better success than in former
days, he made it his practice to take one of his boys with
him each day in turn, to read, while one of the others
tended the second flock.

He continued to come down to the service at the church
while I ministered in the district. A few years after,
when I was at Morpeth, I heard that his work on earth
was ended.

> "Go, to the world return, nor fear to cast
> Thy bread upon the waters, sure at last
>   In joy to find it after many days.
> The work be thine, the fruit thy children's part:
> Choose to believe, not see; sight tempts the heart
>   From sober walking in true Gospel ways."
> KEBLE'S *Christian Year.* Ninth Sunday after Trinity.

CHAPTER VI.

THE westernmost township in my district, as has been already mentioned, was Cassilis. It was seventy miles from my residence at Muswell Brook, and twenty-five miles beyond Merriwa. Its Scotch name betokened the love of its founder for the " land of the mountain and the flood." Two miles above it was a place called Llangollen, so that Scotch and Welsh memories came close together.

I must say that, in a new country, I prefer using the native names, which, as in North America, are often very euphonious, and serve to keep in memory the old and, alas! rapidly fading races which have preceded the white man. Still, it is a pardonable attachment to old associations, which makes a colonist give to his new home a name that reminds him of his native village or county. A Government surveyor is hardly so pardonable when he fixes on some old-world name, taken without reference to any connection. To a stranger the jumble of old associations is sometimes a little perplexing; and makes him think he has got hold of a dissected map, the pieces of which have been shaken up and spread out at hap-hazard.

I had a good illustration of this when, in 1857, being ordered off by my doctor for coolness and rest, I paid a very pleasant visit of a month to Tasmania. On a stage-coach journey across the island from Hobart Town I crossed the River Jordan *running into the Derwent*, and passed in succession Bridgewater, Brighton, Bagdad, and Jerusalem Plains. Jericho, York Plains, Tunbridge, Ross, and Campbell Town followed *in the county of Somerset;* and in a few miles I got off the coach at Porth, being only a short distance from Longford, Launceston, Hadspen, and Westbury.

However, such has been the fashion of colonists all the world over. Portuguese and Dutch have given way to it in some degree; but British settlers, whether in North America or in Australasia, have sowed the seeds of old names broadcast; and a name once given is soon fixed by use, and is rarely changed.

The creek on which Cassilis lies keeps its native name, the Munmurra: it is the last creek deserving a name which flows from the Liverpool range to the Goulbourn, and so on to the Pacific. About eight miles further towards the west, the range, which has been growing less bold in outline, turns sharply round, and, becoming a ridge of moderate elevation, stretches towards the south: continuing to be here, as it is in its more mountainous form, the division between the eastern and western waters.

The valley of the Munmurra is much narrower than that on which Merriwa lies; and, not having a bold broken outline to head it, is less picturesque. But Cassilis is not without its pleasing views, and the richness of the pasturage makes it and its neighbourhood of great value to the flock and herd-master.

It was early in October, 1848, when I first visited it. As I reached the brow of the hill which looks down upon it the sun was nearly touching the ridge on the opposite side. Without a cloud, without any softening haze, it sank glowing to the last of that more than warm spring day: and the more distant hills were already becoming purpled, as though the olive-coloured gum-trees which clothed them had been changed to purple-flowered heather. The road turned to the right, and began a long slope of nearly a mile down the side of the hill; at the end of which, on the other side of the creek, the little township was beginning to enjoy the first cool shadows thrown by the black hill behind it.

This part of the valley was almost free from trees; and, being surrounded by wooded hills, had much the appearance of a piece of park land. On the near side of the creek the first building which met the eye was the residence of the mounted police, commonly called the " Police Barracks : " and a few hundred yards further, also on the bank of the creek, stood a strong slab-built cottage, called the Court House, containing a room about eighteen feet by ten feet, which was the justice-room, lighted by a small window. At the end of the room, on the left as you entered, a small platform, raised about a foot above the floor, with a table and three common chairs, was the bench: and facing the presiding magistrate a door opened into a small windowless room, strongly slabbed all round, ceiling and all, the lock-up of the township; so that it was but a step from judgment to punishment. Cassilis was fortunate in having well-educated men in the commission of the peace, two of them representatives of the honour schools of Oxford and Cambridge. Hence the decisions of that bench were generally well considered, and were relied upon as just and impartial, and free from the pettinesses and vulgarity which in some parts deprived the courts of their due respect.

After riding through two large enclosures called paddocks, about three-quarters of a mile square, fenced with the ordinary post and rail fence, I reached the house of Mr. Busby, a large flock-master, whose breed of horses was known far and near. A hospitable welcome awaited me there : and I was agreeably surprised to find a well-chosen library of standard authors so far up in the bush, and the taste that could appreciate them. The tide of lady-society had not flowed up so far from the coast : but the habits and conversation were such as would have been enjoyed in a well-educated household in England.

That evening my good host had asked to meet me his
nearest neighbour, a brother of the late Bishop Denison, of
Salisbury, who had ridden down from Llangollen: and in
him I recognised a man with whom, ten years before, I had
passed through the class schools at Oxford. Such links to
the old country are not infrequently found at the other side
of the world; and they make a man feel almost at home
again in the midst of the land of cattle and sheep stations.
Old scenes, old friends, old events, are talked over, until
imagination does the work of reality, and the emigrant can
hardly believe that 16,000 miles of ocean roll between him
and the things that stand up so clearly before his mind's
eye.

I was sanguine enough to hope that the better-educated
men who had come out from England would settle permanently in the country from whose abundant resources they
were accumulating wealth; and would therefore take an interest in improving the social condition and moral tone of those
around them. There are some *few* who do so; and it is
worthy the ambition of a Christian patriot so to labour to
mould the character of a young colony, which is growing
up into a nation. But, to my disappointment, I found
after a while that the majority of those who made money
withdrew, one after another, to spend it in England: and
thus, even while residing in the colony, they felt too much
in the condition of sojourners to exert themselves with full
heartiness to improve the state of things among which
their lot was cast.

The personal security in which one lived was remarkable; when it is considered how recently the colony had
been freed from the annual importation of England's convicts, and that many of the shepherds and labourers were
still but ticket-of-leave men. The little bedroom in which
I slept then, and on most of my subsequent visits, had no
fastening of any kind: and within twelve inches of it one
of the outer doors of the house was either unbolted, or, far

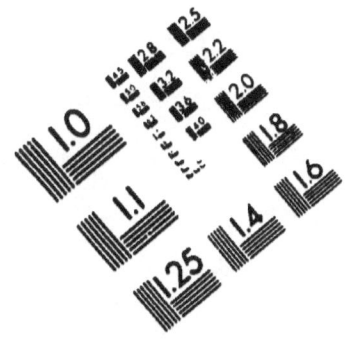

**IMAGE EVALUATION
TEST TARGET (MT-3)**

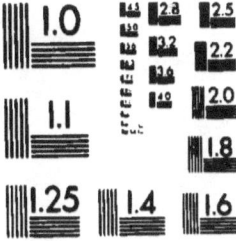

o

more frequently, stood wide open ; so that any one might
have walked in at his pleasure at any time during the
night, and taken purse or clothes, or, if so disposed, life.
It was even more surprising to see with what perfect freedom from apprehension my good host would often on a
summer's night leave the silver candlesticks on the table
of his sitting-room, when we went to bed ; and set the
windows, which opened to the ground, wide open, that the
night air might draw in and cool the room before morning.

The same immunity from robbery and violence prevailed
throughout the greater part of the colony in respect of
" *bushranging*," as it is called, or, in English language,
highway robbery. In the thirteen years that I lived in
New South Wales I rode more than 86,000 miles, by night
and by day, in all kinds of places, and never had grounds
for the slightest apprehension. There seemed a sort of
lull in crimes of violence. Since that time bushrangers
have occasionally infested parts of the country ; and a
few years before I came their depredations were frequent.
Desperadoes lived in remote places, and would make
descents upon travellers, or rifle houses. In the very
house where I have slept so securely I have been told that
it was a common and necessary precaution for each person
at the dinner-table to have a brace of loaded pistols by his
side : for the bushrangers often made their attack when
the masters of the house were within, being pretty sure
that the assigned servants would not come to the rescue
when their master's eye was not upon them ; and the
masters, if unarmed, might be kept quiet by one or two
men with pistols, while the rest took anything which could
be found in the house.

The lock-up attached to the Court House, which has
just been spoken of, was, during those troublous days,
connected with a singular scene of violence. Two assigned
servants were about to be made use of as witnesses against
some evil doers : and to keep them safely they were

lodged in the lock-up, under care of a constable. Some of the gang, who were at large, declared that they should never give evidence against them. Very early one morning, before daylight, the constable ran up to Mr. Busby's house, and told him that the lock-up had just been broken open, and the men carried off. Mr. Busby waited until there was light enough to see tracks; and then started with a mounted party in search of the bushrangers. They had taken the way towards the interior, in the direction of Tongoy; and the pursuers followed, with their eyes on the ground, watching the newly made track. Presently it was found that the bushrangers, thinking to leave less track, had left the dusty road, and taken to the grass. But what they thought would have baulked their pursuers really gave them the greatest help.

The sun was hardly up, and therefore the dew, generally very heavy, was thick upon the grass. The fugitives, as they went, had therefore made through the dew a track far more clearly visible than they would have left on the road: and Mr. Busby and his party were enabled to follow them at full gallop.

After about eight or nine miles, on reaching the top of the dividing range, they found the body of one of the witnesses, whom the miscreants had shot to prevent his giving evidence. The other had by some means escaped from their hands; and though shots were fired after him, he got safely off. Leaving a constable to watch the body, Mr. Busby galloped on with the rest of his party; and followed the dew-track up to the hut of some shepherds, where the murderers had gone in to get their breakfast. Their capture was at once effected, and they were taken down the country. The surviving witness, who had so narrowly escaped with his life, filled up the very clear evidence against them: and, like too many of the desperate characters of those days, they ended their lives upon the scaffold.

My first visit to Cassilis was so timed that I preceded the Bishop by a few days. He was on his first visitation to this part of his diocese: and he thence proceeded to the northern districts of Liverpool Plains and New England.

He had arranged that I should ride up first; and, besides visiting the people, and having services, that I should search out those at Merriwa and Cassilis, who were so far fit for confirmation that a short preparation would be sufficient for them. These, as might be supposed, were not many in number; but there were a few, both adults and young people, who, even upon so short a notice, desired to avail themselves of this opportunity. And I was glad to begin with them, on my first visit, those intimate relations, into which a preparation for confirmation brings the pastor and his flock. The day or two, which was all I had to devote to the work, was not spent in teaching and examining *classes*. The shortness of the notice and the smallness of the population made me take each candidate separately; and thus the teaching was more personal and searching than would have been possible if several had been taken together.

My work of preparation being finished, as well as time allowed, I rode back to meet the Bishop, and to accompany him to Merriwa and Cassilis. Starting after my day's work at the latter place, I went by appointment to the house of Mr. Hamilton, at Collaroy, eleven miles off: and had service in the evening with him and his family, and the people living around his store and woolshed, about a quarter of a mile off. Collaroy is finely situated, looking northward from the brow of an abrupt hill, that rises in the valley of the Krui Creek. Below it is a rich flat, threaded by a winding line of casuarinas; which, except at one reach half-a-mile up, conceal the waters of the creek. Hills rise on all sides, not over-thickly timbered; and, twenty miles off, the landscape is backed up by one

of the finest views of the Liverpool range. As you stand
in the verandah the eye takes in at one glance the East
Bluff, the Moon Rock, and, if my memory serves me
rightly, Oxley's Peak. The ride up to the house from the
Cassilis side is remarkably beautiful. A hill not far up
the valley breaks the line of the range ; and as you pass
on, the features of the bold background successively
emerge, or are concealed behind it.

The next morning, after a ride of twenty-eight miles, I
met the Bishop, followed by his groom, not far from the
Gingerbeer Springs, and turned back towards Merriwa.
Such meetings and rides were generally times of much
refreshing conversation : and past and future work were
well talked over. On that ride the Bishop kindly rescued
me from a little difficulty.

My first horse having become very much jaded by some
months of hard work, I was looking out for a second ;
and had taken one that morning on trial from a station
near Merriwa. It was a fine young animal, with plenty of
spirit, not long broken in from his bush freedom. After
riding some few miles with the Bishop, and having reached
the top of a high ridge called the Wapingi, we were overtaken by a shower—one of those short, *decided* showers,
which come down in a hot climate, when every drop
makes itself felt. The Bishop put on his macintosh, and I
proceeded unguardedly to do the same, as if I were on my
own quiet Dobbin. My steed did not fancy the unstrap-
ping and unfolding ; but when, holding him hard with my
left hand, I had got the right hand into the sleeve, off he
dashed ; and as I was then unable to get the macintosh
on or off, its flapping against his shoulder in the strong
wind that had sprung up made him still worse. Of course,
he did not keep to the dray track ; and, my right hand
being entangled, I had the greatest difficulty in keeping
him clear from trees with low branches, which would have
struck me off.

In this emergency the Bishop called out to me, " Stop till I come to you ! " Stop—why, that was the very thing I wanted to do, but could not effect. However, I did my best to moderate the speed of my frightened horse, guided him clear of trees, and dodged the branches as well as I could. The Bishop pushed on his horse to my side, and caught my flapping macintosh. I loosed my right hand from the bridle for a moment, and with one good jerk the Bishop relieved me and my horse of the offending garment. Of course a wild, frightened dash followed the movement; but two hands soon guided the terrified animal clear of dangers, and before long brought him under control: and we finished our ride without any further adventure. We rode to Mr. Perry's, at Terragong, four miles up the creek from Merriwa : and after a ride of forty-seven miles, thirty-two of them on a very uneasy horse, I was not sorry to rest.

The next day, October 5th, 1848, the Bishop held his first confirmation in that district at a private house, one mile above Merriwa ; and one of the candidates was my good friend the tenant of Mount Dangar Farm, who had ridden up twenty-one miles to be confirmed. The next day the Bishop called with me on most of the people of Merriwa ; and we then rode on to Collaroy.

On the 8th the Bishop confirmed in the Court House at Cassilis ; and the next day, after a good deal of talk with him and the gentry there, about future operations for the good of the district, I left the Bishop to proceed on his northern visitation, and myself returned to Muswell Brook.

The visitation of an Australian Bishop is not like that which bears the name in England. It is a hand-to-hand and heart-to-heart visit to each clergyman, and to his people with him. The Bishop of Newcastle's *first* visits were necessarily for the sake of gaining a personal knowledge of the districts, and of the chief laymen in them.

In many places there was no clergyman; and, besides holding services wherever he went, the Bishop had to discover where clergymen and schoolmasters were most wanted; and to form some kind of idea what must be the area of which each must at first take charge.

In a year or two, when matters had become more settled, in writing to each clergyman to arrange his visit, he would ask how he could best help him in his work: by services in different parts of his district, with or without meetings; by visiting any of his people, especially any with whom a misunderstanding might have arisen, or who, from any cause, were difficult to be dealt with; by examining schools; by helping forward some disheartened, or stimulating some sluggish building committee. In fact, wherever a clergyman needed a helping hand in his work, he found a ready sympathiser in his Bishop, and one who would throw himself heartily into his plans, or improve them if necessary.

On his first visit to Cassilis it was considered that a school was the desideratum. The Bishop promised to provide a master and books; and to procure a salary from the "Denominational Board" of Education. And the gentry agreed, on behalf of themselves and the district, that a school should be erected by subscription, which might also be used when needed for Divine service, until the time arrived for building a church; which appeared to be in very distant perspective. The beginning seemed hopeful: but in colonial Church work pre-eminently those whose hearts are in it must learn to labour on under disappointment and delay—only too happy if, by God's blessing, their plans are permitted to take effect after a season.

Within the next month one of the principal settlers wrote to the Bishop, saying that he was informed that if such a school were established as had been contemplated, the Roman Catholic children would not be sent to it: and

that so many difficulties had arisen, that he should throw
his weight into a plan for a *secular* school, according to
the scheme of Government, which was newly set on foot.
He would not break his promise made to the Bishop, if he
still held him to it; but to rear a Church school under
such circumstances would be against his judgment. One
such defection in so small a community made the other
settlers hopeless of building a Church school : and the
Bishop, with much regret, released the now unwilling
promise; and it seemed as if the hope of daily Church
education had vanished.

Meanwhile, we were enabled to establish a Sunday-
school, with the aid of a well-disposed woman, the wife of
the chief constable : and on each visit I found a little
flock of children assembled to be catechised.   Our
progress was very small, for want of the day-school to
carry on the Sunday's work; but it was better than
nothing.

The establishment of a secular school in such a place is
an almost irremediable evil ; until, as is earnestly to be
desired rather than hoped, the whole system crumbles,
and is discarded.   In a *large* population, if there are some
who unhappily think that their children are better taught
without the influence of Christ's Church, and the full
truth, which her Lord has committed to her charge, there
is still room for schools in which the children of the
Church enjoy their full inheritance of clear Christian
training.   But in a *small* population, where a single school
could embrace all the adult residents, as well as the
children, there is no place for a second.

The Church, no doubt, must always struggle through difficulties for the good of God's children. Should the pecuniary
resources and worldly power wielded by the State flood
her, where she is weak, with the creedless system of *teaching*, miscalled education, she must not simply throw up
her hands and sink.   She must arouse herself, and in the

strength of her great commission, "*Feed My lambs,*" she must by more diligent catechising, not only through her clergy, but through her devout laity also, supply the deficiencies of the schools. But we are not theorising; we are only speaking from *many* happy examples, when we say that the most beneficial education, which makes itself felt through the whole population brought into contact with it, is that of a school under a master who is thoroughly imbued with the doctrines of the Church, and works intelligently under her. In such cases the intellect is provided for, and all its powers drawn out; but all is subordinated, as it ought to be, to Him Who created, redeemed, and sanctifies us, and has given us life *in* His Church.

Poor Cassilis! it seemed as if, as soon as the living form of Christian education was offered, it was withdrawn, and the dry bones of a worldly system substituted in its place.

The two gentlemen who lived nearest to Cassilis, though they would much have preferred the original proposal, despaired of a Church school, and allowed themselves to be made "local patrons" of the new "Board of Education." But the wheels of the new institution in Sydney moved slowly. Month after month nothing was done. The year 1849 slipped away, and 1850 was advancing; and all concerned had had abundance of time to think over the whole question. I had found out, and told the "patrons," what they had learnt from other sources, that they had been mistaken in supposing that the Roman Catholics would not allow their children to attend a Church school. They would have been quite willing that they should have attended, provided they had been permitted, which we always conceded, to sit apart at certain portions of the religious teaching. And the Roman Catholics especially were not at all in love with the secular system, in spite of its being sometimes called the *Irish* "National System."

The people, therefore, had long felt that it would have been better had they accepted the proposal first made to them, and the "local patrons" were good Churchmen enough to appreciate the benefit of having their clergyman really working for their school, and with them. However, the step had been taken; and it seemed as though they must lie on the bed they had made for themselves.

About the middle of the year 1850 a master was sent up by the so-called "*National Board.*" No school was yet built; but he was to have a room in one of the houses of the township where there was space for all the scholars who would come. On the first or second day one of the "local patrons" went to visit him; and, on his knocking at the door, it was opened to him by the master himself in an unmistakable state of intoxication. He at once turned away in disgust, went home, and wrote to his colleague to come to him. The "patrons" consulted; and after writing one letter to the board at Sydney, in their official capacity, announcing that they had dismissed the new master as unfit to be entrusted with the education of the children of the township, they sent a second, in which they resigned their office, and stated that they should throw all their weight into the scale of the "Denominational Board," which, only through misrepresentation of the facts of the case, they had been induced to desert.

Within a few days after this had been done, I arrived for my monthly visit, and they communicated to me the change in the aspect of affairs. We agreed not to say anything in the township, that we might not raise expectations before we could see our way to do something effectual: this was on the 25th of July. After the services I rode to Pembroke, a station about twelve miles distant. There are two roads, starting from different points at Cassilis, diverging gradually to a distance of seven or eight miles, and meeting again at Merriwa. On

one of these roads lies Collaroy; on the other, to the
north, up the Krui, the small germ of a township called
Cockrabel, consisting of four or five huts.* Two miles off
the road from this is Pembroke. Here, after evening
service, and before I turned into bed at two o'clock in the
morning, I wrote a letter to the Bishop, informing him of
the change which had taken place at Cassilis, asking if he
could provide a master, and saying that I should ride
down to Morpeth soon, to consult him about the whole
business. When I did so on the 1st of August, he kindly
promised to look out for a master at once, and send him
up as soon as possible, and to see that a salary was
forthcoming for him.

On the 22nd of August I was again at Cassilis, and
after returning to Mr. Busby's from the afternoon service,
found a letter from the Bishop, saying that the bearer was
a very good and earnest man, lately arrived from England,
and that he had sent him up to supply our want of a
master. In fact, Mr. H—— was then in the township, and
had sent up the Bishop's letter with one from himself.
Our good fortune, long pent up, had come upon us with
a burst, before we were ready for it, and we felt a little
perplexed. There are seldom any spare houses in small
bush townships, and we did not at that moment know
where to house the new master, still less where he might
assemble the scholars. The people were still in profound
ignorance that any Church schoolmaster was to be sent
to them.

That evening I rode up to Llangollen, and it was
arranged that Mr. Denison, Mr. Busby, and I, should go
early the next day to the township, to find some place for

---

* A year or two after the time of which I am writing, a carrier who
owned one of these huts, finding Merriwa a more convenient place for
his work, bought an allotment there; knocked his hut to pieces, carried
it and its contents in several dray-loads to his newly purchased bit of
land, and put it up there.

our new acquisition. Mr. Denison most kindly showed him Australian hospitality in his own house until his whereabouts was settled. The next morning we tried the most likely houses for a spare room, but without success. At last Mr. Busby came to the rescue. He bethought him of a house he had two miles off, on a retired creek ; and though it was too far off for the schoolmaster, he promised it to the clerk of petty sessions, who rented a house in the township, if he would give up to him that which he occupied. There was no difficulty on his part, and the landlord agreed to the transfer of the tenancy, Mr. Busby paying the rent. So our first difficulty was overcome.

The next point was to announce the arrival of the master to the people, ascertain what children would be sent, and what fees would be paid for each ; for it was customary to have different rates of payment, according to the ability of the parents to pay. Not a single parent refused. Whether they were Roman Catholics, Presbyterians, or Church people, all rejoiced in the prospect of a school; and after two or three hours all the preliminaries were settled. I had a good long talk with the master, who proved to be the very man for the place. There have since been several masters, but, with varying success, the school has continued until this day, and is now in better condition than ever, having a clergyman resident in a newly built parsonage-house just below the township.

After the school had been a few years in the cottage, I drew a plan for a school with a master's house attached, and saw it nearly up, but was obliged, from a break-down of health, to leave the district of Muswell Brook and Cassilis before its completion.

It was Friday evening when my work of preparing for Mr. H——'s establishment in the school was done. I started a little after sunset, intending to ride twenty-five miles to Merriwa, that I might reach home for my Sunday duties. On reaching the inn at Merriwa, I found that the only bed was occupied. It was a glorious night, with the full moon shining as no English moon ever did shine; so I took a cup of tea and pressed on. By the time I reached the next inn, sixteen miles further on, it was nearly two o'clock, and I knew my horse would receive little care from the sleepy ostler if I succeeded in getting him out of his bed, so I jogged on, dismounting occasionally, and lying down for a few minutes to rest myself and my horse; and about an hour after sunrise I pulled up at my own gate, after a ride of seventy miles.

I have to confess that both my horse and I were sufficiently tired; but I had the thankful feeling which he, poor old fellow, had not, that the cloud was removed from Cassilis, and the Church school established there.

> "How couldst thou hang upon the cross,
> To whom a weary hour is loss?
> Or how the thorns and scourging brook,
> Who shrinkest from a scornful look?
>
> "Yet e'er thy craven spirit faints,
> Hear thine own King, the King of saints;
> Though thou wert toiling in the grave,
> 'Tis He can cheer thee, He can save."

KEBLE's *Christian Year.* Tuesday in Whitsun Week

CHAPTER VII.

BUSH LABOUR AND BUSH FOLK.

Since returning to England, it has occasionally been my
duty to search for, and aid my brother commissary in
selecting, clergy for the diocese of Newcastle. In the
search I have fallen in with two very different classes of
minds: each of which forms a very erroneous idea of the
work of a colonial clergyman.

The first of these two classes is a high Christian type of
mind: one which yearns to give up something for its
Saviour: which longs to sacrifice home and ease, and to
toil for Him Who shed His blood for us. For such hearts
unknown difficulties have a special attraction. They look
with satisfaction at the ninety and nine sheep safe in the
fold; but they *yearn* for the wanderer. They would
gladly embrace weariness, painfulness, lone hours and
sleepless nights, and think them gain, that so Christ might
grant them to bring in the lost one, or to rear in the desolate places of the earth slips and shoots of His Holy
Church.

Not a few of these overlook colonial work, as though it
did not afford them a fit field for their exertions. Africa,
India, and China, or the Melanesian Islands, they think,
can alone furnish what they yearn for.

Now, I am very far from wishing to draw such spirits
from any call they may have to bear the standard of the
cross to idolatrous or Mohammedan countries; but such
spirits are wanted for our colonies also. The most enterprising can find souls enough in them, which, without his

labours, would be untended : he may exhaust both body and mind, and yet find wants lying beyond the powers of the present small band of clergy. In the bush towns, and in the outlying stations, there are poor wanderers who cannot find their way back without aid, and have no one to aid them. And there are not a few, who, when sought, resist at first ; yet, under God's blessing, are caught and brought in by persevering endeavour.

To carry to each of these scattered ones their portion in turn, requires careful economy of time, activity, bodily endurance, and determination. And to perceive, during the short occasional visit, what is most needed, and to administer it to the best advantage, often to the unwilling, taxes a man's penetration and resources, and, many a time, his self-command over the exhaustion of a wearied body, and, consequently, a flagging mind.

In the larger towns there is abundance of scope for all the powers which God has bestowed on him, to lay solidly the foundations of Christ's Church in the midst of a population swept together from all parts, and imbued with very different shades of opinion and faith.

And if he looks, as he will, beyond his own parish, to his clerical brethren and their flocks, he may be sure that the steady, intelligent working out of the Church's system, with such *measured advance* as will enable his people *to understand* and follow him, will prove the greatest strength and help to the whole diocese. I have remarked before, that, for good or for evil, the various clergy and districts in a colonial diocese, though many miles apart from each other, affect their brethren far more perceptibly than is the case in the denser population of old countries.

There are also many vital questions connected with the constitution and the government of the colonial Churches, and their intercommunion with each other and with the Church Catholic ; which, I am persuaded, must be solved, *on their part*, by their internal powers exhibited in their

H 2

synodical action, and, *on the part of the English* mother, by her obtaining freedom of action in spiritual things, which at present she lacks or cannot see her way to grasp. The contradictory judgments of the English law courts, each claiming a *quasi infallibility*, cannot be the support on which the Church in the colonies rests.

Whether, therefore, the energetic spirits of whom I have spoken desire to succour the spiritually destitute, to enter upon a laborious work, to mould elements somewhat chaotic into a well-organised parish ; to act in a body, in which the work of each unit tells perceptibly on the rest ; or to aid in working out the great problem of the union of the newly formed Churches with the rest of Christendom ; he may find ample scope for the most devoted and useful labours in the colonies.

Of the other class of minds, of which I have met with specimens, I cannot speak with the same respect ; and would distinctly discourage them from offering themselves for colonial work. We want none of them.

They are such as wish to go out to a colonial cure because they think that so far from England they may do more as they like, and find themselves less tied to the work of souls. They have a notion that in the bush they will have more opportunities of indulging in a *semi-secular* life than if they remained in England. There are some who hope that in a new country they may combine a good measure of agricultural or sheep-farming pursuits with the work of the ministry : and show pretty plainly, as might be expected, that on the more secular object a very large share of their interest is fixed, and that Christ's ministry would be their second, not their first care.

These men, who are really unfit for Christ's service any-where, are especially mischievous in the colonial Church, where clergymen are so few and far between, and where the scarcity of the workmen needs to be compensated by

their fervent zeal and single-minded devotion to their
work. As in the large cities of England a man's whole
soul needs concentrating upon the spiritual welfare of the
multitudes in alleys and crowded streets; so in the wide
extent of a colonial district, including perhaps several
scattered townships, God's servant must be continually
intent upon his work, that he may penetrate the nooks
and distant corners, pick up stray sheep anywhere, and be
ready to show to all, according to their needs, how, under
difficult circumstances, they may maintain their union
with Christ's Holy Church.

It should be branded on the heart of every man who
aspires to be a colonial clergyman : "*No man that warreth
entangleth himself with the affairs of this life, that he may
please Him Who hath chosen him to be a soldier.*"* A
faithful worker will find many a pleasure by the way, besides those deeper comforts which Christ gives to all who
honestly make sacrifices for Him. He will find on his
rides many an object of interest, many a little adventure
—if he likes such things; he will find those who become
warm and firm friends; he will find some who welcome
his ministry, and some who learn to do so after a time.
But his duty cannot be done without casting aside thoughts
of ease, and throwing his whole heart and energies into it.
There may be few such severe privations in New South
Wales as fall to the lot of Bishops and clergy in Newfoundland and the Labrador; but those who fancy that
they will never have to rough it, or that they can take
their work easily, are greatly mistaken.

For some time after I had become, as I thought,
acquainted with the district, outlying places kept opening
upon me, claiming thought and attention when head and
hands were already more than full. To meet the new
claims it was necessary to abridge times of rest, and to
encroach as much as possible on the mornings and

* 2 Tim. ii. 4.

evenings: generally arriving at a station long enough
before bedtime to have service that night, and starting
for the next place early the following morning; or, if I
arrived too late, owing to the distance, or the amount of
work I had found to do before, we had an early service
the next day, before those at the station dispersed for their
work.

On one occasion I saw some strange faces among the
congregation assembled at the Cassilis Court-House; and
found a settler and his wife, named Nevill, who had
driven through the bush in a cart, bringing their child to
be baptized. When the service was over I had some conversation with them, and found them steady Church
people, natives of the colony, born of English parents,
who were living many miles off in the Sydney diocese.
They had come in from their place at Deridgery, a
station on the south of Cassilis, not far from the upper
part of the Goulbourn; and they were very glad when I
promised to visit them.

The next month Nevill came by appointment to meet
me at Cassilis, and after the second service escorted me
to his home. We had ridden nearly sixteen miles, touching once or twice upon the Munmurra Creek, and only
passing one shepherd's hut on our way. During the last
few miles the iron-bark forest, the change from the black
to the sandy soil, and the thinner grasses, showed that
we were approaching the Goulbourn ranges, when, on
emerging upon a small clearing, we saw the little bush
settlement a short distance before us.

On our left was a small watercourse, the Deridgery
Creek, not flowing—those small creeks hardly ever flow—
but containing a water-hole or two, which after rains were
well filled. On the other side of the creek was a railed
paddock, where was grown wheat for the household, and
oats or barley for cutting as hay; and there stood also the
barn and outhouse, made of the roughest slabs, split from

trees which had once grown on the spot, and roofed with bark. One or two small huts were before us on the right, and just beyond them Nevill's own dwelling, built of slabs, not more pretentious, but a little larger. As the eye looked on beyond these primitive dwellings, it saw, on a little rise some fifty yards further, that universal accompaniment of a settler's homestead, the stock-yard, with the gallows at one corner.

A stock-yard is an enclosure varying in size according to the size of the settler's herd of cattle or horses. It is strongly made with the stoutest poles and rails, six or seven feet high, and divided into two or more compartments, so that part of the herd may be drafted off from one to another, if necessary, for the purposes of taming, branding, or killing. The gallows is made of two young trees let firmly into the ground, with a fork at the top of each. Across these a round log is placed, like the windlass of a well, having a strong rope, usually of plaited bullock-hide, attached to it. By this the bullock or sheep that has been killed at sundown is hoisted out of the reach of native or other dogs till the next morning to cool, when it is taken down and cut up, and the greater part salted for future use. Fresh meat is rarely used at the stations.

The arrival of horsemen at a station is always a signal for getting some tea, with its accompaniments, salt beef and *damper;* and after the first words of welcome, while my good host was taking care of my horse, and his wife putting on the kettle, I got a few minutes of rest and quiet thought.

It was always with me a matter of anxious consideration how to spend these visits to the best advantage. Owing to the many other calls on my time, I could seldom visit such outlying places as Deridgery more than two or three times in the year. To carry on any regular and complete system of teaching at such long intervals was impossible. Written sermons were, of course, not to be thought of.

I usually chose some striking part of Holy Scripture, and endeavoured to point out its bearing upon reconciliation with God, the daily struggles and progressive holiness of Christian life, and on future hopes and fears ; and I used portions of the morning and evening prayers or the Litany, with some of the Collects that seemed most suitable. The Psalms for the day were almost invariably used, unless those for the day before or after seemed better adapted to my small congregation.

In conversation many little points were drawn out, and such advice and encouragement given as might recur to their minds afterwards. Just before going to bed I not unfrequently read some of the admirable "Hymns for Little Children," which the grown members of the party, as well as the younger ones, always appreciated. And whenever there were children, and sometimes when there were not, I tried to find half-an-hour for the Catechism and its explanation, in order to leave some systematic doctrine for after use. From time to time, while endeavouring to supply food for their use during their long privation of service, I pointed out the order of the Church's seasons, and the great doctrines which they taught ; and so I was obliged to commit them to His love and care Who had sent me to them.

The most serious difficulty in the way of genuine improvement was the inability to bring the poor outliers to Holy Communion. Many were too far off to come in to the regular administrations at Muswell Brook, Merton, Merriwa, and Cassilis ; and I was only able to administer it at five out-stations. At the rest various causes prevented my offering it, or the offer being embraced. In many cases, long years of sin, not sufficiently repented of, prevented anything but exhortations to repentance and preparation for better things. In others, long absence from all services and my own unfrequent ministrations had not overcome the grievously wide-spread idea, too

common even in England, where the church bell can be
heard all over the parish, that the Holy Eucharist is only
intended for some advanced Christians, and that others,
if they neglect it, may safely content themselves with a
lower Christianity.

I can hardly see the way out of this difficulty in a bush
district, on any sufficient scale, except by providing more
clergy, and thereby enabling them to see the people more
frequently, and thus raise their faith and practice to the
standard of the Church.

One of the bush huts where I was enabled to celebrate
the Holy Communion was Rainbow Station, situated in the
midst of abrupt hills and narrow valleys, about twelve
miles from Muswell Brook. I found there a shepherd and
his wife, lately come from Scotland—Episcopalians, from
the neighbourhood of Glencoe. They were unable to
come into church at the township, and having been com-
municants at home, embraced gladly the offer which I
made of administering to them at their own hut.

The Rev. J. Blackwood, then a deacon, who had been
fixed by himself at Singleton after Mr. Irwin's removal to
Moreton Bay, was glad of the opportunity, and rode up to
me at Muswell Brook. The next day we rode out together
to the sheep-station. It was a rough hut, roofed with
bark, consisting of one room only, and the floor of earth.
But, humble though the place was, all preparations had
been made which reverence could have dictated to simple
minds.

The very earth before the door—for the ground round
a hut is usually bare of grass—had been swept for some
distance; and no spade, broom, or iron pot, or any of
the untidiness usually seen outside a shepherd's hut, was
visible. Inside all was neat, and looked as well as the
poor materials allowed. Some clean curtains screened off
the bed. Everything was arranged with scrupulous care,
and the table, covered with a snowy cloth, was placed at

the end of the room. M'Coll and his wife, who appeared to be some forty-five years old, were in the Sunday clothes they had used at home; and during the whole service their appearance was that of Christians worshipping with the deepest reverence of Him in Whose presence they were.

When all was over, and we were thinking of getting our horses and finding our way back, good Mrs. M'Coll begged us to stay and take some refreshment; and taking down a shawl which hung in one corner across a string, showed us a table with a simple dinner ready prepared for us. A few years later they removed to a place about four miles from the township, and were enabled to come in to the service on Sundays. I believe they have now bought a piece of land some miles further away, and have settled upon it.

The Nevills, of whom I spoke just now, were always attentive; and, I believe, made good use of the very little which I could do for them. She has, since I left the diocese, been called from this world and from her young family; but I can quite remember her thoughtful look when I was speaking to her little ones, then very small, or showing her what she might do for them as a Christian mother, without any school to aid them.

At most of the small stations I visited, we used to separate for the night at ten o'clock. I usually remained in the sitting-room for an hour or two more, or, if I had the luxury of a table in my bedroom, sat there, to get some quiet time for reading and writing. I had another reason in many places for not going early to bed, though generally very tired with the riding and work of the day. Insect life of all kinds is very abundant; and, on sandy soils especially, fleas swarmed, not unattended by their broader cousins. Happy are they whose skins are thick. I have stayed out of bed till I could hardly keep my eyes open, in hope that on lying down I might fall asleep

before my persecutors found me out. But the hope was
often vain. No sooner was the candle out, and the first
forgetfulness coming on, than I felt, what Cicero tells us is
a noble sentiment, that I was "never less alone than when
alone." Several times in a night have I struck a light,
rubbed my eyes, and killed all I could find, and put out
my candle, only to light it again in a short time. Once at
Deridgery, when goaded beyond endurance, I dressed
myself at two o'clock in the morning, went out of the hut,
and, though there was a slight frost, for. it was winter, lay
down in my macintosh by the stock-yard fence until
daybreak, at about half-past six. Such nights were not
the best restoratives after a day's labour; but a good
wash in the morning, the pure air, and the bright blue
sky, set one up again for another day's work.

A case occurred about half-a-mile from the little township of Cockrabel, mentioned in the last chapter, which
made me long for additional clergy, to visit the stations
more frequently than it was possible for me to do.

There was an overseer's station on a rising hill above
the bank of the Krui Creek; and calling one day on my
way to Cassilis, I found a poor shepherd there far gone in
heart disease. His master had kindly brought him from
his station at the Liverpool Plains, where he could get no
nursing, to be looked after as well as possible for what
seemed likely to be the last few weeks of his life. He
was unable to move from his bed, which was placed on the
floor of a spare room, and the overseer's wife tended him
carefully.

His pains were often very severe; and she told me that
during the paroxysms, or whenever she did not attend to
him as soon as he knocked on the floor with his stick, his
language was fearfully blasphemous. I visited him, and
returned two days after from Cassilis, on my way home,
to minister to him again. The next month he was still
living, and seemed glad to see me; and the overseer's wife

said that after the last visit he was for some days more patient, and more watchful over his words. This visit also seemed to have left a temporary effect upon him.

But the next month I found the room empty, and the poor man buried. About a week before, when he had hardly strength to move, and seemed to have but a day or two to live, he lost all patience ; and, putting his stick into the handkerchief which was about his neck, twisted it round and round until he choked himself. Had he, in his misery, enjoyed the benefit of constant ministerial visits, the thoughts which seemed to have been awakened in him might have been deepened into repentance, and his end have been very different.

Had Sodom enjoyed the opportunities which were lavished in vain upon Capernaum, it would not have perished.

Surely it is not too much to hope that some at least who have read of these wants of their brethren in the bush will make it a part of their fervent daily prayers, if they do not so already, that the "Lord of the harvest would send forth more labourers into His harvest;" and that others, *who are fitted* for the work, will feel called upon to leave, for Christ's sake, home, friends, and country, and to devote themselves heart and soul to carrying His Gospel to the distant corners of the earth, where His scattered people are so much in need of help.

Many Englishmen are led out by the hope of *gain:* will not *Churchmen* be led out to help to gather in fruit for their Lord, and look for a lasting home, friends among the blessed, and "*a better country, that is, a heavenly?*" *

* Heb. xi. 16.

CHAPTER VIII.

DESTITUTION OF THE SICK IN THE BUSH.

THOSE who realise the inevitable conditions of a young colony will readily understand that many a want and many a difficulty must be occasionally experienced in the *bush*.

More especially is this the case in a country where the few aboriginal natives have been so entirely neglectful of the first command of their Maker, to "*subdue*" the earth, as those of New South Wales. It must not be forgotten that no civilised man had lived on any part of Australasia, or thought of beginning to turn to account its abundant resources, before the year 1788. On the 28th January in that year, Captain Phillip, at the head of 279 free persons and 751 convicts, having found the sandy and waterless shores of Botany Bay, which the English Government had destined for the settlement, unsuited for the purpose, landed on the site of the present city of Sydney; and the first tents were pitched, and the iron axe rung among the trees of the dense forest which then surrounded Port Jackson, and which had hitherto heard nothing but the blows of the *stone tomahawk*, with which the natives had cut out for their food opossums or the tree grubs.

The colony was, therefore, only between sixty and seventy years old at the time to which these recollections refer. And it is rather a cause of wonder that so much had been effected within that time at a distance of 16,000 miles from the mother country, than that many things still remained to be done to meet the wants of the settlers. It must be remembered, too, that nearly all supplies had to be sent from the coast, so that the further the settlers pushed inwards to the west in search of grazing country, the longer was the line of conveyance from the port. And professional men or mechanics had to be brought out from England, and forwarded by degrees further and further from Sydney.

For several years after our arrival, there was no medical man to the west of Muswell Brook. On one occasion, when I arrived at Cassilis, I found the blacksmith, a tall, sturdy fellow, suffering from dislocation of the shoulder. The day before, he had been trying to shoe a half-broken colt for the first time, and had been kicked across the smithy. No bone was broken, but the poor fellow was much bruised, and his shoulder put out. His neighbours had already been doing their very best by pulling at his arm till they were tired. At last, finding that all their well-meant endeavours had only succeeded in putting the poor man to much pain, and increasing the swelling of the upper part of the limb, they had sent a man off on horseback for the *nearest* doctor, seventy miles distant.

On entering the hut, I was asked to try my hand at the case. But as the doctor had been sent for, and I had never been present when a dislocated joint was reduced, I would not make the attempt, for fear of giving more useless pain. The doctor might have been away twenty or thirty miles in another direction; but, fortunately, he was at home, and lost no time in setting off. On his arrival, he soon put the shoulder in its right place; but owing to the first delay in sending to Muswell Brook, and the 140 miles which had to be ridden by the messenger and the doctor, the patient had been forty-eight hours without surgical aid.

A few years later, a medical man was settled at Cassilis; and, as the mounted police were no longer wanted, owing

to the more settled state of the country, the police barracks
on the bank of the Munmurra were converted into his
house.

In 1851, when on a long journey to the Castlereagh
River, far to the west of Cassilis, of which I will speak
hereafter, I found a settler who had broken his collar-bone
a week or two previously. He had been galloping with
his dogs after a kangaroo, and his horse getting his foot
into one of those large deep cracks which, in the volcanic
soil, open during long droughts, had fallen and thrown
his rider heavily. No doctor could be procured, and those
about him set the bone as well as they could, bandaged
the man firmly; and, without the aid of a licentiate of any
college of medicine or surgery, the bone united, and a
cure was effected.

If a man has self-restraint enough to avoid interfering
in serious cases when a regular medical man can be procured, and to abstain from an endless quackery of himself
or others for slight ailments, it is most useful for him to
gain some acquaintance both with medicine and surgery
before going out to a colony. My own knowledge of
either was very small, yet I often found the little I knew
useful to those who were suffering, and would have found
it impossible to get to a doctor.

Among all the valuable training which St. Augustine's
College gives its pupils, their medical instruction, and
their access to the practice in the hospital at Canterbury,
are not least in importance. Had not my time been too
fully occupied with the discharge of my last duties to my
English parish, and the preparation for leaving England,
after I had accepted the call of the good Bishop of Newcastle to accompany him, I should have put myself under
some medical man, or gained admission to some hospital
for a while before sailing. I might then have relieved
much misery, which I saw at outlying stations, more
effectually, at least, than I was able to do.

At the small township of Cockrabol I certainly gained
a credit which I did not deserve. One day, as I was returning by that route from Cassilis, after calling at the
other huts, I went to that which, in the sixth chapter, I
mentioned that the owner afterwards packed on his dray
and removed to Merriwa. He was, as usual, away with
his drays, but his wife was in bed suffering great pain
from a bad leg. I visited her simply as her clergyman,
and, after reading to and praying with her, was leaving
her with such comfort as I could give, when she said,
imploringly, "Please, sir, will you look at my leg?"

I begged her not to unfasten the bandages. But I
could not persuade her; and with much care she un-
bandaged the swollen and discoloured limb. It showed
so much inflammation that I gently touched it with the
palm of my hand, and, finding the heat quite as great as I
had expected, commiserated the poor woman and proceeded
on my journey. Two months afterwards, when I dismounted at her door, she met me with tears in her eyes,
and abundant invocation of blessings. "O sir!" she
said, "from the time you touched my leg it began to get
better, and is now quite well."

It was in vain that I disclaimed the efficacy which she
attributed to the touch, and bade her thank God for His
mercies to her, reminding her how we had prayed for such
relief as His love and wisdom saw fit to grant. For
years after, when I visited her, she would still recur to
her old idea that the recovery dated from the touch.

In one emergency I was really enabled to be of some
use to a little sufferer. I had started from home for
Merriwa in order to select the ground on which the church
was afterwards built; and wishing to visit some stations
on the lower part of the Wybong, I altered my usual
route a little. It was a delicious spring morning, about
the third week in October, 1849, one of those bright, calm
Australian days, neither hot nor cool, with a gentle air

breathing from the east, when existence itself seems a
delight.

After a ride of sixteen miles, and having passed round
the base of a fine upstanding mass of rock on my right,
studded to its summit with flowering shrubs and patches
of the yellow *dendrobium*, I had entered the Wybong
Valley through a low gap in the sandstone ridge, which
bounds its eastern side. Turning to the left down the
valley, I soon fell in with a shepherd following his flock.
As usual, I dismounted, and remained with him for a
time, and then proceeded towards his station, rather more
than a mile off, to visit his wife.

I had not gone more than half the distance, when I met
a child six years old, running in evident terror, crying,
and calling for his father with all the breath he had left.
His fright and haste were so great, that I could get no
further into the cause of his trouble than that something
had happened to his little brother. On galloping up to
the hut, I found the poor mother wailing over her little
two-year-old boy who had just been severely burnt.

She had been washing, and, as is a common practice in
the bush, had lighted her fire of dead branches in the
open air, near the bank of the creek, that she might have
a shorter distance to carry the water. Of course, while
she was at her tub the child played, as children always
will play, with the fire. His only article of dress was a
calico night-shirt. This caught fire; and, before his mother
could do anything to help him, he was severely burnt from
the knees to the throat. When I rode up she had him in
her lap, and was sluicing him and herself too with soap-
suds. The poor little boy was screaming violently with
the pain; and the mother kept up a despairing wail,
alternately trying to soothe him, and saying, "Oh, my
pretty, pretty boy; oh, what shall I do? My pretty boy!
Sure, and he 'll die." Those who know how an Irish
mother laments can guess that I had some difficulty in

I

checking the flow of words, which ran on to the father's going out in the morning, and his pictured sorrow at coming back, and seeing his little one dying.

Seeing the state of the child, I said immediately, "Those half-warm suds are no good; where's your flour-bag? Flour is far the best thing to put to the poor little fellow." "It's all gone, your reverence; I made up the last into a damper last night." "When shall you have more?" "Not till to-night, your reverence; the ration-cart will be here this evening." "Why, the poor child will be dead before it comes. Where's the nearest station?" "There's a *gunyeh** over that hill, your reverence, about half-a-mile off, where a shepherd of Captain Pike's is lambing down." "Well, where shall I find a bag?" She told me; and, snatching the bag from the hut, I galloped as fast as my good horse could carry me to the *gunyeh*. You are always sure to find the shepherd where lambing is going on; so I got the flour at once, and hastened back with my bag.

From the bed in the hut I pulled a sheet, which we put under the little sufferer; and as the mother wetted the different parts of the body, I sprinkled flour over them. By degrees the screams became less violent; and after about twenty minutes, just as we had finished our work, the little one fell asleep. I charged the mother to keep

---

* *Gunyeh* is the name given by the aborigines to the slight shelter which they extemporise in a high cold wind or driving rain. To protect them from the former they stick a few boughs into the earth to the windward, sloping slightly to leeward. Against the rain, when it is of long continuance, they use sheets of the eucalyptus bark, sloped in the same way, and propped to leeward by sticks. They never *enclose* themselves. The name has been applied by the settlers to the temporary shelter made for shepherds, when they are sent for a short time to any place where there is no hut. It is something like a gipsy tent, and is made of saplings stuck into the ground, and meeting at the top like the rafters of a high-pitched roof. Over this framework are fastened sheets of bark, tied on with bullock-hide. A sheet of bark is laid on the ground to keep the hay bed from the damp, and the fire is made outside.

the body covered with flour, and to send her husband
to Muswell Brook for the doctor: and then, thankful to
have dropped in just at the time of need, rode on to
Merriwa, about twenty-five miles further.

The doctor came the next day, and applied lime-water
and oil, and in due time the child recovered from the
effects of his burn.

In severe sickness the condition of a shepherd far in the
bush is very miserable.   There is no medical attendance,
no nursing, none of those little comforts which relieve
pain—nothing but salt beef, and damper, and tea; and
these nauseate a weak and sick man.   There is no doubt
that pure air and God's blessing on nature work a cure in
not a few cases, which with so little assistance would sink
in the crowded alleys of London; but I have often seen
suffering in a hut which a very few of the appliances
which are easily obtained in a town or village would have
relieved.

At Maitland there was a hospital, to which many a sick
man or woman was sent from the bush, if able to bear the
journey.   But a distance of 100 or 200 miles, in a horse
or bullock dray, often under a burning sun, was more
than some patients could bear, and I have known some
die on the road.

CHAPTER IX.

RANDOM RECOLLECTIONS.

ONE hot summer morning, as I was leaving Mr. Perry's house at Terragong, near Merriwa, for the upper part of the Wybong, I heard that S—, a shepherd, whom I had often visited near Robert Baird's,* on Coulson's Creek, was supposed to be in a dying state. I had lost sight of him for some time, as he had been removed to a sheep-station of which I had never heard, two miles from his former hut, high up among the broken volcanic ranges towards Hall's Creek.

No track led past it; but having heard in what direction it lay, bush instinct guided me to it; and, after climbing some steep ascents, I found it perched on one of those steps which abound in ranges of trap formation. Abrupt hills rose behind it, ridge above ridge; beside it a stony gully descended rapidly from the higher ridges, and was soon lost among the lower hills, as it went down towards the creek below. In heavy rains this was a brawling watercourse, but in ordinary times it was quite dry. I cannot now remember how the station was watered—no water or well was to be seen when I visited it. Probably what was retained by a dam thrown across the gully lasted for some time after rains; but in a long drought it would be necessary to drive the sheep down to the creek for water two or three times in a week; and the supply for drinking would be sent up to the hut. Some such stations are only used when the season gives water in the

---

* The shepherd mentioned in Chapter V.

dams or gullies. Wells are not always serviceable. I have known several in which the water, when reached, held a strong solution of alum. One, sunk at a sheep-station, two miles from Collaroy, was as salt as sea-water —utterly useless, unless salt-works were to be established there; and a cask of water was sent on a dray for the men once or twice a-week.

The hut where poor S— was lying was a very wretched one. Originally made of the roughest slabs, put up green, the gaps which the shrinking wood had left had never been plastered up with mud or mortar, and you could see in or out all round it at will. A storm had blown off one large sheet of the roofing bark, which had not been replaced, and a gap was left more than two feet by four feet over-head. Fastening my horse's bridle round a neighbouring "box" tree, I pushed the door open, and walked in.

The inside of the hut was very saddening indeed. On his hay bed, on the floor of the hut, with everything in disorder around him, lay the poor man, unable to raise himself—so disfigured by disease, that I could not have recognised in him the strong, fine-looking man I used to visit in the valley. In spite of the free admission of air, the smell was almost sickening, and the hut was full of the restless buzz of hundreds of blow-flies—like our English bluebottle, but of a duller hue—which sometimes settled on the patient's face, and then, darting hither and thither in all directions, seemed as if they would warn off all intruders from their prey. The temperature in the shade was nearly 100° Fahr.; and the first words that my poor suffering brother uttered as he saw me enter were, "O sir, for the love of God, give me a drink of tea." Within a few feet of him were a quart pot of tea and a tin pannikin, which his son had left there for him in the morning, when he went out with his flock; but he had been too feeble to reach them.

It was now about twelve o'clock, and he had been left

quite alone since a little after eight. His wife had been dead some years; and he was living with his son, a lad of seventeen or eighteen years of age, who had the charge of a flock of sheep, while the father was supposed to be acting as hut-keeper. I stayed by that sad bedside as long as I could, giving such poor relief as the hut afforded, and endeavouring to minister to the soul which would so soon be removed from all help on earth. Oh, who shall know what the God of mercy may do with souls that have lived the greater part of their time "in a barren and dry land where no water is?"

Before I left the hut to go on my journey the son returned for a few minutes, to help his father to anything he needed, and then to leave him for some five hours more, until he brought in his flock at sunset. I crossed the gully, and rode over the steep hills beyond it, sadly thinking of that dying brother, who with the severe and increasing bodily infirmities of ebbing life, and the more awful spiritual needs of a soul which had been sadly neglected, was lying in that lonely sheep-station with none to relieve his bodily sufferings, and no man to care for his soul.

Within a day or two poor S— died; but the knowledge of such a case, and the certainty that there are always similar cases existing in the far-off corners of the earth, give a *reality* and a *wide scope* to the petitions in the Litany, for "all in necessity and tribulation," for "all sick persons," to the commendation of God's "fatherly goodness" in the prayer for all conditions of men, of "all who are in any ways afflicted and distressed in mind, body, or estate," and to the fervent supplication in the prayer for the Church militant—"We most humbly beseech Thee of Thy goodness, O Lord, to comfort and succour all them who in this transitory life are in trouble, sorrow, need, sickness, or any other adversity." If when we use these prayers we would but remember how the

Eye of our heavenly Father is over all His creation, and
would lift up our heart for those far distant brethren whom
we do not see but shall one day meet, the prayer of
charity would surely bless the heart that offers it; and
who shall say how many a prayer sent up to God in the
daily services of an English church may "*drop upon the
dwellings of the wilderness*" in blessing?

      "The course of prayer who knows?"*

The cup of suffering may not be removed, and no minister
of Christ may pass that way; yet an angel may be sent
from heaven, from Him Who knows what anguish is, to
strengthen the desolate and afflicted in ways man does not
know.

The distance from poor S——'s hut to the Wybong was
sixteen miles, without a track, and, until the last two
miles, without a hut; and hence, it may be easily inferred,
without water; for it is not long before sheep-stations are
put up where water is to be found. In all other respects
it would have been the very paradise of the sheep-farmer.
There was abundance of rich feed, the thick *kangaroo grass*
standing more than knee deep over all the hills and
valleys, the timber thin, and comparatively small, though
at a distance seeming to cover the whole country. No
large hollow logs or sandstone caves to afford shelter for
the native dogs;† and only surface-water or wells are
wanting to cover it with flocks. As it is, such country is
well suited to cattle and horses, which travel further for
water.

Oh, what a sound is that of water to an Australian in

---

* "Christian Year;" Second Sunday after Easter.

† The native dog, or *dingo*, is about the size and make of a fox: it
has a brush. Generally the colour is of a lighter shade than the fox;
but some few are of a blackish brown. They are very destructive to
sheep, and will kill very young calves, but will not touch a man,
though they will follow him, when on horseback, for miles.

such a day! Without a cloud to screen you from that
blazing sun which looks down upon you from the north;
with scarcely a breath of wind to stir those few narrow,
pointed leaves that hang dangling overhead between you
and the intensely blue sky; with a cloud of flies buzzing
round your head, and settling on your face if you intermit
for an instant the whisking of your handkerchief, or of the
little spray of gum-tree or native cherry with which you
are trying to defend yourself; with the shrill whizz of the
tettigonia all round, now making you feel as if every gum-
leaf were screaming at you—now changing for a minute or
two to a deep low " *hum, hum, hum,*" only to burst forth
with a whizz of fresh intensity, and to recall, under very
different feelings, Wordsworth's descr ption of the cuckoo's
note,—

> "That seems to fill the whole air's space,
> As loud far off as near."*

Around and on some tree, as you pass it, even the poor
black *mutton-birds*† droop their wings, and show their
white bar of feathers, as they sway unsteadily to and fro,
and gasp with open bills for the cooler air that won't
come.

Your own brow and your reeking clothes seem to have
the only moisture that exists for miles—a moisture, by
the way, which tends from its rapid evaporation to cool
the body, and thus to make the scorching heat of from

---

* Wordsworth's *Poems of the Imagination*, ii.
† The bird commonly called the " mutton-bird " is nearly the size of
a rook, with a bill curved like a honeysucker's, and a tail which wags
almost like the motacilla. It is quite black when the wings are closed;
when anything makes it open them, it shows a very marked band of
white feathers on each wing. It builds a large mud-nest, like a swallow's in material, and the shape of a large pudding-basin; this it
perches on the upper side of some large horizontal branch. The nest
answers its purpose so long as the hen is sitting; but when the brood
is hatched, and the wings no longer thatch it over, the first heavy rains
soften it, and it falls off.

100° to 114° in the shade much more endurable than 85° or 90° in a damp atmosphere.

It is well for you if, under these circumstances, the intense thirst does not come on before you are within a few miles of some creek or hut. Hunger you may forget, but not thirst, whenever from any cause it is excessive. When you have been long in want, if you cannot get a draught of tea or of pure water, you are not particular, and swallow eagerly whatever comes first, disregarding its colour and taste. I have gone down on my knees to drink from a wheel-rut water so muddy that you could not see your finger half-an-inch below the surface; and a large settler now in the colony has told me that he has taken thick mud in his handkerchief to strain off water enough to boil his pot of tea when travelling.

On one of my monthly journeys, I was nearly paying for my drink more dearly than I had intended. I had been by no means well; and hence my journey, in very hot weather, told on me more than usual. I had left Mount Warrendie in the morning; and, after a service and teaching a family on my way, was proceeding to Collaroy by a route now little used, called, from a stone building three miles from Merriwa, the "Stone-house Road." Many times I had dismounted and lain down to rest, leaving my good horse Dobbin to feed with the bridle tied to the stirrup. As I approached Bow Creek, I knew that, a little below the point where the road crossed it, there were several rocky holes in the creek-bed usually containing water. The first of these had been so fouled by cattle that I only let my horse drink; and when I had given him enough, tied the bridle to the stirrup, and turned him to feed in the long grass, while I went to a smaller hole below where the water was better, and whence my arrival scared a whole flock of bright-green and red parrots.

On returning, I found that my intemperate drinker had

returned to the water; and there, up to his girths in the pool, and with outstretched neck, he was slowly drinking on and on, as Baron Munchausen's horse is said to have done after passing the portcullis. My salutation was not friendly—"Get out, you greedy old fellow." He was not accustomed to be scolded; and with a sudden splash, which sent the water over him in a shower, out he went at a long trot.

Quiet as he was, and often as I had caught him in the grass and mounted him that very day, I had no doubt of his allowing me to come up to him. But I was mistaken. Holding up his head high, and setting out his tail, he started off with that long, high, springy trot, which seemed to say, "Catch me who can," looking back at his unfortunate master, sometimes over one shoulder, sometimes over the other. After running and calling to him until I had hardly breath or strength left, I tried another plan. I went off far to the right, walking briskly, trying to get beyond him, and drive him back; for, unfortunately, he had struck off from the road at right angles, and was making away from all huts and dwellings of man towards the Goulbourn. Seeing me go from him, he began to feed, but kept a good eye on me; and just as I had got on a line with him, though far away to the right, he started off again at that provoking long trot.

Matters began to look serious. It wanted but an hour of sundown; I was seven miles at least in each direction from the nearest stations where I could get a horse to run my truant in; he had my all on his back, and I was spent and weak, and not in condition for camping out. But in the bush you must depend on yourself, and you must never give in when one plan fails.

I had not long before heard how the natives got near enough to kangaroos to spear them; and other means having failed, I determined to try the same plan. Lying down on the ground, as if resting, I remained quiet until

Page 122.

Dobbin began feeding. When he was engaged, I crawled along towards him on my right side with both hands and the left foot. He soon looked up again uneasily; and I lay still again, moving on when he began to feed. I was a considerable distance from him, but gradually crept nearer.

As the space between us became considerably less, my stealthy hunt grew more anxious. Several times he looked at me suspiciously, and was almost starting off again. The least sudden movement on my part would have placed several hundred yards between us, and made my task hopeless. At last I was within a length of him; he took a long, doubtful look at me, and then put his head down and went on feeding. I did not venture to speak to him, but, sliding a little nearer, jumped up and caught the stirrup, and with it his bridle. Old rogue! I felt sorely tempted to give him a cut with my whip for the trouble he had given me; but more prudential, if not more kindly motives prevailed, and, looking forward to what might be my needs in any like case for the future, I only patted his neck, and made him gallop back as fast as he could to the road.

I reached Collaroy late and a good deal exhausted, but far better off than if I had been forced to walk on, with the unpleasant uncertainty whether my horse would not roll, break the saddle, and perhaps the girths, and stray off homewards, leaving my saddle and saddle-bags in the bush.

In estimating the fatigue of a colonial clergyman's work, something more must be considered than the actual length of his rides, from twenty to fifty, or sometimes sixty miles in a day, with, occasionally, exhausting heat, and at other times pouring rains and heavy soil. When a settler travels, he has nothing to think of at his stopping-places, but how to make himself most comfortable, and to prepare by rest for the journey of the next day. The clergyman travelling in his district may stop many times in the day at huts

or stations; but when he stops it is not to rest—the great
object of his journey has to be attended to; and very often,
at the end of a long day, the first thing he does after dismounting is to prepare for or begin a service, or to visit
people with different spiritual wants, prepare a confirmation
class, or try to reconcile a quarrel. He has but a short
time to do a great work, and enters upon it, very often,
wearied in body. He is making up, perhaps, for the
wants of several weeks, and preparing for a blank of
several weeks to come. He has to think for each, and
cannot afford to attend sufficiently to himself. Often he
contrives to forget his own weariness of body in attending
to the subjects which occupy his mind.

But this kind of work tells surely upon human strength
in the course of time. It is one of those ways in which,
though freed from the terrible persecutions and torments
of former ages, we must cheerfully take up our cross, and
follow whithersoever Jesus leads us, and be ready to spend
and be spent for Him Who died for us.

CHAPTER X.

A SERVANT OF CHRIST IN TRAINING.

IN the fifth chapter of these " recollections " mention was incidentally made of the little township of Jerry's Plains. I did not at that time expect to have occasion to bring forward its name again. But it has lately gained an interest in the heart of many a sorrowing brother and parishioner as the resting-place of the body of a faithful and holy-minded pastor and priest, whom we had hoped might have been spared to do many years of good service in the diocese in which he had so zealously laboured hitherto.

The dust of the old world is hallowed by hundreds of thousands of the bodies of saints : and many a village and churchyard is dear for the sake of those that sleep there. In the newly Christianised lands of the South such spots are as yet rare. The territories have been taken possession of by British sailors for the Crown of England. It is the office of the Church to consecrate the hills and valleys of those sunny lands for her Redeemer and Lord by the deeds of her children, who take up the cross for His sake, and by the bodies of those who have been nurtured into saints through the presence of Christ that resides in her.

Henceforth Jerry's Plains will be one of those spots to which the thoughts of many a brother will lovingly turn.

William Woodman Dove, who was taken to his rest on the 28rd of March, 1867, at the early age of thirty-five, was one of those many earnest spirits which the great Catholic awakening of the Church of England has drawn into her bosom from the dissenting bodies; one of those sheep whose forefathers were scattered from the true fold through our supineness or worldliness, when the "shepherds fed themselves, and fed not their flock,"* but who have heard the voice of the Good Shepherd rousing both shepherds and sheep, and calling back wanderers " out of places where they have been scattered in the cloudy and dark day."† They have known the Shepherd's voice, and have followed Him.

William Dove's father was a respected Congregationalist minister in Gloucestershire. I am unable to say by what means the son was led to feel the defects of the system in which he had been brought up, and to believe in the faith of the Church. Whatever were the means employed, the attraction of the Body divinely appointed prevailed over every earthly consideration; and the strength of his convictions decided him to emigrate to New South Wales, in the hope that he might be permitted to obtain entrance into the ministry, and devote his life to the service of Him Who had called him.

Those who knew him best will estimate the cost at which he followed the call which he had received. They know how strong the love of home was in him; how eminently domestic was his disposition; and how lovingly he thought of those old grey church towers of England, which linked his faith in the present to the hallowed past. But all that he had loved and valued, save the Church itself, he had given up to come to a land of strangers, not to seek a worldly competence, and to return; not even with the offer of that employment to which he most longed to devote himself; but in the hope that He Who had led him thus far would still lead him on.

Another point remarkable in him was his *devotional spirit*, as contrasted with the spirit of controversy. There

* Ezek. xxxiv. 8.   † Ezek. xxxiv. 12.

was in him none of the pugnacity of the neophyte, who
thinks it necessary to justify his change by arguing against
the views held by those from whom he has come. In all
my acquaintance with him—and some of it was very intimate—I never knew him bring forward unnecessarily
the errors of those among whom he had been brought up.
He was eminently positive and constructive in his religion;
yet if it were necessary to prove the wrong to be wrong,
as well as the right to be right, he did not shrink from
doing so ; and he did it clearly, with charity.

He arrived in Sydney about the middle of the year
1858, and soon put himself in communication with the
Rev. Canon Walsh, of the parish of Christ Church, by
whom he was temporarily employed in his parochial
school.

A few weeks ago I received a letter from Canon Walsh
in answer to my announcement of his death. He says,
" I never can forget those days when he used to come to
me from the neighbouring police-barracks to consult me
about taking holy orders, I was then so much struck
with both the depth and the simplicity of his character."

At that time the See of Sydney was vacant, owing to
the death of good Bishop Broughton in England, and the
Bishop of Newcastle had gone to Sydney for a few weeks,
and was endeavouring to prevent the newly projected
university from being as much without religious teaching
as its chief promoters desired. To him Canon Walsh
recommended Dove, then about twenty-two years of age, and
the Bishop at once resolved to take him into his diocese.

It was the Bishop's practice, when any man offered himself for holy orders who was not a graduate of one of our
universities, or who had not been sent out from St.
Augustine's, to test him- by offering him the mastership
of some parish school. If he failed, or showed any un-
worthiness, of course all idea of ordination was at an end.
But if he bore the trial well, and showed that he was able

to influence the young minds for good, he was then sent
to one of the clergy to read with him, or in some cases
taken by the Bishop himself to be prepared, and to aid as
far as he could in parish work. The ordeal of the school
was a searching one in many ways, and those who have
stood it well have proved some of our useful men.

The plan was also of service as a means of providing
masters temporarily for schools in need, which was often
a sore difficulty. Drunkards and idlers might have been
procured in abundance from that class of men who were
sent out from England by their friends because they could
do little with them at home. But steady, painstaking
men, who might be trusted in some township far from
their clergyman, were not so easily found.

Our first master at Cassilis, who had been thus sent on
probation, and had proved to be a useful man, was removed about the time that Dove arrived at Sydney.

On the Bishop's return to Morpeth he wrote to me promising to send Dove up by the next mail to Cassilis, and
telling me of the high character he had gained during his
short sojourn in Sydney.

My first interview with him was by the roadside on the
top of a hill about a mile and a-half from Cassilis. Heavy
rains, and consequently the heavy black soil, which you
cannot avoid either on the grass or on the road, had
delayed him ; and, as it was Saturday, I had been obliged
to leave Cassilis before his arrival, to be in readiness for
the duties of the next day at Merriwa.

He was riding up on one of the mail horses—a very
common way of reaching Cassilis from Merriwa—and
while the mailman proceeded on his way with the bags,
dismounted ; seating ourselves on a fallen box-tree, we had
a long conversation about the duties which awaited him,
and the people among whom he would have to live and
work.

There are persons whose genuineness impresses you at

once—not because they are very demonstrative and forthcoming, for they are rather the reverse, but their quiet
manner carries a reality with it; their few thoughtful
questions show that they appreciate the difficulties which
they are prepared to meet, and you feel that they are only
anxious to know their duty and to do it.   Dove was one of
these; and I was thankful to have him provided as my
fellow-worker, where true and steady work was greatly
wanted.

In addition to his school work, the Bishop had authorised him to read prayers on those Sundays on which I
was not there, and sermons, which I should give him for
the purpose; and I have still the sermons which I lent
him to read to the people, marked with the dates at which
he read them.

After my first bush interview with him, I rode on my
way to Merriwa, feeling confident of one thing, which
cheered me—that whatever he had to do with things
sacred, whether in giving religious instruction to the children, or in joining with the people in prayers on Sunday,
he would do it with *reverence*.   It required a very short
acquaintance with him to show that his habit of mind was
essentially reverential.

He arrived at Cassilis on the 13th of August, 1853;
and until he could be settled, Mr. Denison kindly invited
him to his house at Llangollen.   We had been obliged
to give up the cottage, where the school was originally
opened; and the only place we could get was a large slab
hut, roofed in with bark.   It was a rough place enough
to live in.   The greatest luxury about it was its being
papered all round with sheets of the "Sydney Morning
Herald," interspersed with some prints from the "Illustrated London News."   Here Dove taught; and here he
lived alone for five months, preparing his own meals, and
only having a woman to come in once a-day to sweep and
clean the place for him.

K

Fresh as he was from England, and from his relations, and with feelings wounded by the breaking of old ties, which the better light and the dictates of his conscience had caused, this lonely life was a sore trial to him.   He often wrote to me for advice and comfort; and when I paid my regular visits, he used to pour out without reserve all his pent-up feelings, and rejoiced in the opportunity of free Christian intercourse.   But there was no complaining, no shrinking from any cross which was laid upon him; and no regret—nothing but thankfulness for the step which God had enabled him to take.

He was especially fond of and beloved by children, for the one love nearly always begets the other ; and he set himself with right good will to his task as schoolmaster.   Even in the short time that he was at Cassilis I found the school improved in knowledge, in discipline, and reverent behaviour.   He was especially careful in teaching the children their prayers, and guiding them in the use of them.

He also made the care of the children a reason for calling often on the parents.   And though he called on all, whether they had children or not, the parents of his scholars were especially made to feel that he and they had deep Christian interests in common—the example to be set, and the training to be given to their little ones.

In whatever I did for the teaching or training of the lambs of my flock he heartily co-operated.   What I wished to be prepared for me I always found ready ; and he would carry on any instruction I had given in my short visits.   We both pulled the same way.

He was a valuable helper to me in gaining a knowledge of my people, and meeting any particular evil which might have been going on during my absence.   To have listened to what neighbours might be disposed to tell of each other would not have elicited the truth, and would have fostered a spirit of tale-telling, with all the evils which it implies.   From him I learned all that it was needful to

know; and he directed me at once to any especial case of
sickness and trouble. He was himself a most useful
visitor among the sick, helping sometimes to nurse, as
well as to read to them.

In January, 1854, my school at Muswell Brook needed
a master; and a successor having been provided at Cassilis, Dove came down to reside with me, read more
regularly for holy orders, and managed a mixed school of
about 100 boys and girls; a mistress, who resided at the
schoolhouse, taking charge of the infants and needlework.

He left Cassilis with the regret of all. The parents and
children had become attached to him; and Mr. Busby
wrote expressing his regret at losing so " exemplary "
and useful a man from his neighbourhood. Poor fellow!
he brought away an unpleasant reminiscence of his last
days there. A large centipede—a giant in size, strength,
and venom, compared with its puny English namesake—
had found its way between his sheets; and as he was
turning into bed one night gave him a very severe bite on
the foot. The pain was excessive, and the subsequent inflammation very great. After his arrival at our house
many weeks passed before he recovered from the effects
of it.

From that time till his ordination as deacon in September, 1855, I was in close communication with him, and
had every opportunity of observing his character and
work.

In the school he was most painstaking; and while firm
and judicious in enforcing discipline, he was gentle and
forbearing under very trying circumstances, both with
children and with unreasonable parents; and colonial
parents are often very unreasonable, from having no such
control over them as lingers in many country parishes in
England. I remember his coming to me in a state of
comical perplexity, one day when I had gone down to help
him in the teaching, to consult me about the treatment of

K 2

a boy, the very pickle of the school, who was always in disgrace, and whose ingenuity in wrong-doing was out of the common way. "What *shall* I do with this boy? He has been catching bees; and, while avoiding being stung himself, has contrived to pull off their wings, and to drop them down the backs of the little children." The culprit did not look one bit ashamed, and had quite the expression of one who would have enjoyed devising some practical joke for us if he could. Of course we visited the boy with condign punishment. But, by perseverance, Dove succeeded in taming this wild spirit; and this very boy became his mother's greatest help and comfort, when a few years later his poor father was thrown from his horse and killed on the spot, leaving his widow with six or seven young children. This little fellow seemed to have imbibed some of Dove's gentleness to ballast his own vigour; and he would watch his mother's wishes, and give up his time to help his little brothers and sisters, with a thoughtfulness which surprised all who knew his earlier character, and fancied that he could turn out nothing but a bushranger.

Out of school, as well as in it, Dove won the heart of the children; and on the annual school feast-day he was always the contriver of some popular amusement. With children of higher education he was also a universal favourite. His self-forgetfulness and love of children very soon drew them to him.

But he never forgot his higher calling. He was a thoughtful student, and read early and late, and turned gladly from copies, slates, and school routine, to Pearson, Butler, Hooker, and his Greek Testament. In our lectures he always showed a readiness in catching the point of an argument, and was never satisfied with conclusions without taking pains to master the steps by which they were reached.

He took great delight in the ancients, wisely seeing how needful it is to balance modern views by those which prevailed nearer the fountain-head. He frequently borrowed the Oxford translation of the Fathers; and as I had not the originals, nor would he have had time to master them, he gladly availed himself of this accessible form, to learn how St. Chrysostom or St. Augustine explained the Gospels, or the Acts of the Apostles, or the Epistles of St. Paul.

The devotional element in his character was strong and deep. And he felt a great happiness to come from the rare services at Cassilis to the opportunity of daily morning service. We were not able to have daily evensong.

He made a conscientious use of the fasts of the Church as seasons of humiliation and self-discipline; and her festivals were to him seasons of holy joy. So surely in this point, as in others, is the Lord's promise fulfilled, "Blessed are they that mourn, for they shall be comforted."

He was very active, and most useful in church decorations. There were not among us, as may be found in most well-worked English parishes, a body of willing and intelligent helpers. The taste and the ability had to be formed; and there were no examples around us to stimulate or guide us. Year by year we found more help, and the helpers understood their work better; but the supply was less than the demand, and the work fell heavily upon those who undertook it. Among these, Dove was one of the most energetic and successful. That it was for God's house and service was enough to make him throw all his heart into it.

CHAPTER XI.

WILLIAM DOVE was admitted to the Diaconate, at Morpeth, in September, 1855. During the examination, and until the day following the ordination, we were both staying under the roof of the Bishop of Newcastle. And thus, in many ways, all of us who were concerned in the ordination were thrown together, both familiarly at meals, and in the solemn heart-searchings of examination and converse, as well as in the holy services of the Church. Under such circumstances much of the inner man shows itself in the demeanour, in answer to questions, in casual remarks dropped, and in expressive silence.

Dove's manner had in it nothing over-wrought or excited. There was not a trace of what one has sometimes seen with anxiety—the forward, self-satisfied manner of one who only awaits the reception of his commission to begin setting everything right by his confident inexperience. There was in him a calm, reverent thoughtfulness, a swiftness to hear and a slowness to speak, as in one who felt great difficulties and responsibilities—great above human power—which were opening b ˈˈre him ; and yet had humble confidence in the guidance provided for him, and in the presence of the Lord, Who was sending him forth to the work. Ready to go and devote himself to Christ's service, he yet looked, after having been pronounced " apt and meet " for the work, to receive, by " laying on of hands " and prayer, that grace which would onable him to go forth in his Saviour's name, and to discharge effectually the duties of the ministry.

The latter part of that ordination day was one of those calm, peaceful evenings in the Australian springtide so exquisite in their temperature, before the heat of the year has set in. The heavy rains which had fallen early in the preceding week had made everything on earth green ; and there was that intensely blue sky above, which, if it did not bring heaven nearer earth, at least lifted up the heart with the eye to that place, whither Jesus had ascended, and whence He sent the Holy Spirit on His Church. It was to that young labourer in Christ's vineyard a restful pause, before he was sent to bear " the burden and heat of the day."

On that evening, whatever were the thankful feelings of his heart for the gifts which had been given him, whatever were the steadfast resolutions to use them faithfully unto the end, a colouring must have been given to them by those words of our Divine Master to Peter—" *Lovest tho Me more than these ? Feed My sheep, feed My lambs.*" For on these words the striking and heart-stirring words of the Bishop to the candidates had been founded. At all events, we who tarry behind him a while in our work can feel convinced, as we think of his ministry, that he did indeed love the Lord Jesus fervently, and endeavoured to the last to feed His sheep and His lambs.

Dove was first appointed to assist the Rev. B. Glennie in the distant and almost unlimited district of the Darling Downs. That district is *now* in the colony of Queensland, and in the diocese of Brisbane, but was *then* a portion of the diocese of Newcastle, and in the colony of New South Wales.

One of the most dangerous modes of employing the services of a young deacon is to place him *by himself* in one of the large bush districts. He is thus cut off from the support of the Holy Communion when he especially needs it. He is removed from the example, advice, and influence of clerical brethren ; and, while the clerical life and duties are new to him, he has to itinerate for weeks together among settlers, stockmen and shepherds ; among the greater number of whom, to say the least, the tone of religion is very low. It requires some knowledge of men, as well as deep habitual piety and soundness of doctrine, to enable him to maintain his clerical character wherever he goes, and at the same time to lead on the minds of those among whom he ministers. Some young men have failed grievously under the trial ; and have sunk down to the level of those to whom they have been sent, instead of raising them up to a higher standard of faith and practice. A colonial Bishop is in continual danger of giving way to the temptation of filling up some large destitute bush district with a freshly-ordained man, because he sees the people standing in such exceeding need ; and it is not easy to get a man of experience to go out so far from civilisation.

This evil was mitigated in Dove's case by the Bishop considerately placing him with a priest, from whom he could obtain the Holy Communion, and take counsel on his return from his long journeyings. It would be well if in every outlying station a priest and deacon were located together. To do this there are two difficulties which must be faced : one is the paucity of men, which, alas ! we are everywhere feeling ; the other, the insufficiency of funds. But, serious as these difficulties are, I believe they are not insuperable ; and the gain to the *workers* of sending two together, after the pattern of our Lord's Mission of the Seventy, and, I believe, the gain to the *Church*, would be very great.

The day following Dove's ordination he started with me ; and we rode up together in two days to Muswell Brook. He rested with me one day, and then, with the very hearty good wishes of all who had known him there,

proceeded on his long journey of some 400 miles to the
north. His route lay over the Liverpool range, by Murrurundi, through Tamworth, and New England ; and, after
the late rains, it was not an easy one. But he reached his
destination safely, to the great joy of Mr. Glennie, who
cordially welcomed his fellow-labourer.

The small township of Drayton was Mr. Glennie's head-
quarters. With him Dove lived, and found it a great
comfort to get a day or two of his society occasionally,
and as much reading—little enough—as he could find
time to secure. Their joint district extended over the
Darling Downs, which lie high on the westward slopes of
the dividing range, and far away down the course of the
Condamine River and its tributary creeks, as they wind
towards the Darling.

Drayton is about eighty miles from the coast at Moreton
Bay, and so is within reach of the sea-breeze, which generally reaches it two or three hours before sundown, and
makes it more pleasant as a residence. But the farther
you go in towards the lower country round the Condamine, the more intense and unrelieved is the heat.

I have unfortunately lost all the letters which I received
from him during the early years of his ministry, and have
only a general recollection that they evidenced hard and
laborious work, conscientiously done, among widely-scattered sheep and cattle stations. He often wrote to me for
advice ; and all his difficulties and questions showed his
anxiety to do his best for those among whom he laboured.
His work as a deacon, as indeed is the case with the
greater part of even a priest's work in the early stages of
such a mission, was *preparatory.* Much simple teaching
had to be given, which had never been heard, or had been
forgotten, since the days of childhood. There were many
places which he could visit but eight or twelve times in
the year, and many not so frequently. He had chiefly to
break up ground for sowing seed, or to sow that which

others might reap ; but whether he taught repentance, faith, or holiness, he did it in the spirit of the Church's teaching, and with a genuine reverence and love of souls, which no want of the externals and aids to devotion could quench.

He served in the diaconate about two years and a quarter, and was ordained to the priesthood on the 20th of December, 1857. In consequence of a break-down of my health from over-work, the Bishop had most kindly urged me to leave Muswell Brook in the August preceding, and to take the parish of Morpeth, as being less in area, and putting me in the way of his help. We were therefore delighted to be able to have Dove under our roof for five weeks before the ordination, and found him not only not in the least deteriorated by his bush work, but improved by all the discipline he had gone through, and more matured in all his views. He stayed with us nearly a week after his ordination, and actively aided us in our Christmas decorations. Let no one think of frost and snow, and warm clothing without, and holly berries within, as necessary accompaniments of Christmas. All things are reversed on the other side of the line.

Our decorations on that occasion were rather a fight against the difficulties of the climate ; our native cherry and the bright foliage of the scarlet Bignonia, on which we relied for our green, were safe enough : and so, at sunrise on Christmas Eve, were our Oleanders, which were in the full beauty of their rose-coloured blossoms. But a hot west wind sprang up early, and soon reached a temperature of 104° in the shade, and, aided by a scorching sun, quickly reduced all the blossoms which were exposed to their united force to the colour of brown paper. The only ones which escaped were a few on the larger bushes in the Bishop's garden ; which, growing in the middle of the shrubs, had been in some degree protected from the heat.

Dove left us on the feast of St. Stephen, under a blazing

sky, which would make it hard for your English carollers
to realise the favourite carol of "Good King Wenceslas."
He went, not overland but by steamer, up the coast to
Brisbane ; and thence rode through Ipswich up to Drayton.   There he remained about a year more.   But as the
northern part of the diocese had been apportioned to the
see of Brisbane, he requested to be moved, before the new
Bishop's arrival, in order that he might remain still
under the Bishop of Newcastle.

The Richmond River district needed a clergyman, and
to that post the Bishop appointed him, fixing him at Lismore.   The scenery of this district is very different from
that of the Darling Downs.   It lies on the eastern side of
the dividing range, not more than thirty miles from the coast.

The country is less open, and more broken by picturesque hills and abrupt valleys than the interior.   There is
much rich pasture-land ; but there are also large forests
of valuable trees, and scrubs, from which large quantities
of red cedar and other timber are sent down to the coast
for shipment.   Here he only remained till July in 1859,
but carried with him, on leaving, the kind regards of the
settlers, rich and poor, among whom he had ministered.
This move was not his own seeking, but was owing to the
Bishop's kind consideration of him.

On the 8th of September in that year he married in
Sydney one whom he had long known in England : and
the Bishop offered him the cure of Jerry's Plains, on the
Hunter River, as being better suited than the remote
Richmond to the circumstances of a married man.   He
brought his young bride up to Morpeth, and left her to
our care for six weeks, while he went to Lismore to take
leave of his parishioners, and remove his furniture and
books.   He stayed with us but a few days after his return,
and then went up with his wife to the new cure, which
was to have the labours of the last seven years of his life.

Jerry's Plains is a small straggling township, about fifty

miles north-west of Morpeth, on the most direct line to
Merton and Merriwa.   There is nothing remarkable in
the scenery.   As you emerge from the monotonous gum-
tree forest on the Morpeth side, you look down to the
right across the alluvial flat which gives its name to the
place ; and by the line of the Casuarinas you trace the
course of the Hunter in its deep-sunk bed.   From the
opposite bank of the river rise low hills ; beyond which,
twenty miles off to the north, lies Muswell Brook.   About
half-a-mile before you, upon a rising ground, on the left
of the road, stands a small wood-built house with its
verandah, with a garden sloping down in front of it.   This
was the house rented as the parsonage.   A little beyond
it, by the side of the road, two room. of a cottage thrown
into one made the school and church : a few houses follow ; and on an abrupt rise, about a quarter of a mile
farther, are the foundations of a stone church, begun in
Bishop Broughton's time, but checked, almost at the
beginning, from want of funds, which, in so small and
poor a place, it has never as yet been possible to raise.

The area of the whole district attached to Jerry's Plains
is 1,200 square miles, and in it there are two fairly built
churches—one of brick, in the Norman style, at Wark-
worth, about seven miles on the road towards Morpeth ;
the other of stone, at Fall Brook, about twelve miles off,
between Singleton and Muswell Brook, which was consecrated in 1855.

In his first letter, written from an inn in Jerry's Plains,
where he and his wife were awaiting their furniture, he
says, "I am pleased with my new parish ; and, from the
little intercourse I have been able to have with my people,
I think I shall, with God's blessing, get on tolerably well.
They all seem very kind and glad to see me, and to have
a clergyman again with them."

He soon began to set himself steadily to his work, and
found much to do in the outskirts of his parish, under

Mount Popong on the south, and round the spurs of Mount Royal to the north, so that a second horse was necessary to enable him to accomplish his parochial visitings. In February, 1860, he wrote:

"I am, as you may suppose, very busy, this parish having got into a sad state. The approaching confirmation gives me additional work. The amount of ignorance is quite wonderful. Every one is very kind, but many think me a sad innovator for doing even the commonest parts of a pastor's duty. For instance, the candidates for confirmation had never been instructed in any other way than by being heard say the Catechism; and my classes have excited some wonder, though the work in them is the merest rudimentary instruction, such as at Muswell Brook would hardly have been needful, even in the Sunday-school. But in time, by keeping a standing upper class, and by care in the school for the younger ones, I do hope to break through the barriers of gross ignorance and deadness of heart which seem to hedge round so many of our young people. The work is certainly hard; but, after all, I do not know what I should do without hard work. Sometimes, when I think of all the trials of our Church at home, the riots in churches " (we had then been hearing much of the profane disturbances at St. George-in-the-East), " the controversies on the Holy Eucharist and other high and holy doctrines and practices, paraded, as such controversies are, in the newspapers, I often feel that, if I were not a man, I could almost shed tears at the dangers and difficulties of so much that I love with all my heart. And then I feel how valuable a remedy I have in my work. I jump on horseback, and take a long round, and then come back with the bright side uppermost; more ready to give thanks to God for what He has done, and to hope in His Name, than to look forward to evil before it comes. I often find a good round of visiting or a long ride like a tonic to the mind."

This extract is characteristic ; the same kind of history of acts and feelings is ever recurring in the many letters he wrote to me after this. There is the same evidence of careful pastoral labour in many different ways ; the same earnest sympathy with the stirrings of the Divine life in the Church ; the same genuine feeling of distress at any seeming or temporary triumph of unbelief or misbelief over the faith of the Church. It must be remembered that this young clergyman was sixteen miles from his nearest clerical brother, or from any one with whom he could discuss the deep subjects which were of such vital concern to him. In January, 1863, referring to the on-slaught of unbelief made in and after the publication of "Essays and Reviews," he said : — "Through God's mercy we shall, I trust, meet once more ; in a better world, if the course of our work and duties keeps us apart all our lives here. Meanwhile, let me tell you how great a help and comfort your letters are. . . . Anything which strengthens us against the incoming tide of faithlessness, which already beats against our ancient landmarks, is of the greatest importance. I hope I do not doubt concern-ing His care for the Church, Who has promised that the gates of hell shall never prevail against her : but one is saddened from day to day by the great want on all sides, and even in oneself, of practical faith, a realising and living upon the great verities of our Holy Religion." Nor did the difficulties of misbelief meet him merely as tho distant sound of what was going on in other parts of the world : he had to cope with them among his people. In January, 1864, he wrote : "We are not altogether free from scepticism even in this remote diocese. Unfor-tunately many have grown up in this country without opportunities of instruction in Catholic truth, having only very vague ideas of the Christian faith ; and yet often with sharp intellects, uncultivated, yet still shrewd and thoughtful. Such persons are sadly injured when such books as Colenso's, or 'Essays and Reviews,' get into their hands. They cannot see beyond the circle of doubts and difficulties, which such as Colenso raise; and they take all they read as true and unanswerable. Too often they do not like to speak of their difficulties to their clergyman, who would at least pray for them, and direct their reading towards a solution of that which has perplexed them."

While he was thus anxious about the maintenance of the integrity of the faith against assault, he was indefatigable in building up the *devotion* which is essential to the growth of Christ's people in holiness. It has been mentioned that there was no church at the township of Jerry's Plains; and in a letter already quoted, written a little more than three months after his arrival, he thus refers to the place used for Divine service: "When I came here I found everything dirty and wretched, and quite unfit for God's service. The desk was a tower-like erection, very shabby, and so high, that in the low hut, which is our only church here, my head was nearly against the shingles, and the heat made me quite faint." He says, "I got the whole affair removed, and from the material a neat and rather more church-like prayer-desk and pulpit (in one) made."

Little as this may seem to those who have more money or more assistance, it was all that could be done at first; and was a simple first move towards doing all things decently and in order. To carry out the design of the original stone church was out of the question for a long time. But he very soon began to prepare for getting up a more suitable school-church of wood, and early in 1862 he began the building. He says in February: "You will be pleased to hear that our new school-church is begun. It will be a large wooden building, and is to be finished in about three months. It will consist of chancel, nave, vestry, and porch." As to his own residence, owing to the difficulties thrown in the way by the freeholder, it had not been made over to the Church. "I am sorry to say," he adds, "that we shall not be able to buy the parsonage after all." And so it continued till his death. The owner, a few months before he was taken to a better home, sold the house over his head; and had he lived a few months longer his lease would have been out. Like Abraham, who "sojourned in the land of promise as in a strange country," he had no place which he could call his own, except the "possession of a burying-place." He very truly felt himself a "stranger and pilgrim upon earth." Yet in the country which he loved *far less* than the land of his birth, he expended every energy of mind and body, till he sank under the strain, and rests where he toiled for Christ and His Church.

The spring from which this faithful labour issued peeps out in a letter written June, 1862: "I have received more than most other men—pardon, guidance, strength, especially the first, and nothing I can do should be too great an exertion to show my thankfulness." His sense also of the blessing of being in, and ministering in, Christ's Church was very deep. In September, 1864, he says, after mentioning both troubles and successes: "I do hope that I am willing to stay here, or anywhere, all my life, if Our Blessed Lord wills it. I do feel most deeply the great joy and honour of being a priest in Christ's Holy Church." He was also deeply sensible of the blessing and aid of *intercessory prayer*. There is scarcely a letter of his that does not witness to this. "I know you kindly remember me and my work in your prayers. It is such a comfort and help to remember this; and thus to realise the tie, which no distance nor length of absence can ever break." He particularly remembered others, and asked that himself and his work should be especially laid before the Lord, in the Holy Communion.

He found great comfort in the occasional clerical meetings which were held in the houses of himself and some three or four others of his brethren ; and in one letter speaks with satisfaction on the *increase of devotional tone* which pervaded those meetings, and that several of the members had joined an "English Association for Intercessory Prayer."

Owing to some of those troubles which try the constancy and patience of all church builders, his school-church was not opened till July, 1863. But when finished he fitted up the church, which was kept entirely for holy services, with much care. After this, the congregations steadily increased ; and the singing, to which he paid much attention, improved. "You will be glad," he writes in January, 1864, "to hear that our congregations have increased nicely since the new church has been opened. We have now a really good number of regular attendants, and often a very fair week-day congregation. I am *unable, through absence from home,* to have the daily service ; but I say the Litany every Wednesday and Friday, and have full service on all saints' days, and other holy days. On Christmas, Easter, and Ascension Days we have Holy Communion over and above the regular times, which are once in four weeks. Otherwise we have not yet increased the celebrations." After thinking much about a Hymnal, he introduced "Hymns, Ancient and Modern."

The northern railroad which was being made between Singleton and Muswell Brook, added much to his work, as many navvies were for some time in that portion of his district near and above Fallbrook ; but he laid himself out for these strangers, as well as for his own permanent flock, and ministered to them in no perfunctory way, but, as he did everything for Christ's service, with thought and care and love.

He, in common with most of his brethren, long felt the want of some good reading, of a sound Church tendency,

to put into the hands of his people. A paper was started
called the "Christian Volunteer," but all the clergy were
too incessantly working to have time to do it justice, and
its life was short. After a short interval he joined several
of his brethren, and sent for Erskine Clarke's "Parish
Magazine," which they "localised," Dove becoming editor
of the few added pages.

Space does not allow me to mention many things which
I fain would add. In August, 1855, after many endeavours after synodical action, the first regular synod of the
diocese of Newcastle was held at Morpeth : it consisted of
clerical and lay members, and Dove was elected honorary
secretary for the clergy. In all matters connected with the
establishment and working of the synod he took a warm
interest ; and, in common with his Bishop and the rest of
his brethren, was strongly opposed to asking any legisla-
tion from the secular power *in such form* as would throw
any doubt upon the *spiritual independence* of the Church.
The Bishop of Sydney and Goulbourn on the other side,
most unhappily, took another view. But the diocese of
Newcastle maintained its ground effectually.

In the midst of all Dove's work an hereditary disease
developed itself. In June, 1865, he wrote : " I broke
down after Easter, and thought it necessary to consult
Dr. B—, who attributed my ill-health to overwork on
Sundays, and the excessive amount of riding needful in
this parish. He told me also, which I had suspected,
that I had heart disease, which required care to prevent
its immediate growth. I am giving up the third service
on Sunday, and my kind people have enabled me to buy a
buggy, so I shall now drive to many duties. . . . .
It is a trial at my age to feel oneself less useful than here-
tofore."

That he did not take his work even now very easily is
clear from a letter written six months later. " My symp-
toms do not leave me, and I do not think my strength

increases. I am quite knocked up for two or three days by a *moderately* heavy Sunday's work, such as that of last Sunday : two services, two baptisms, and churchings, and *forty-two miles*. However, I must not complain, for I can keep on steadily, if not very actively." Others would think that he worked *actively* still. His last letter, written October, 1866, speaks of his being "just in the thick of confirmation work;" which, where candidates are so widely scattered, implies very heavy fatigue. He says : "Our good Bishop visited us on the 8th, and stayed until the 10th. Nothing could exceed his genial kindness and pleasantness. On the 9th he had a confirmation here, nineteen receiving the holy rite." The Bishop then went on to some parishes farther up the country, and a week or two later was to return for a confirmation in another part of Dove's district. He says : "My work is increasing much at the head of Fallbrook, and round Mount Royal. I have very nice congregations and encouraging work in that direction. Once or twice lately a 'bush missionary,' a kind of ranter, has been round warning the people against me and my teachings. And it has been quite cheering to find how generally they have refused to have anything to do with him. He has made a point of elaborately shaking off the dust of his feet against them, or rather cleaning it off with a cloth he carries for the purpose. Such things really cure themselves.

Referring to an offer the Bishop had made him of removing to some other cure, he says : "One's life is too short and uncertain to throw aside all the confidence and affection and readiness to be taught, which I may have succeeded in gaining during my seven years' residence here. I would rather work here till I die or return to England. God is very good in giving me so much sympathy and kindness from my dear parishioners, and in leading them to make such kind allowances for my neglect, when strength will not hold out for all the work I should like to do."

The work he did at that time prostrated him severely, and for some time he was obliged to take a rest. The Bishop of Newcastle asked him down to stay with him and get advice; and, after about a fortnight's stay at Morpeth, he returned home, about the middle of January, apparently better. He, however, soon fell back again; and, in spite of all that could be done for him, faded away towards that land where the saints are made perfect. Through February, and the first three weeks of March, his prostration daily increased. His clerical brethren came from many miles to comfort and to aid in nursing him. The Bishop says of his dear friend at Muswell Brook: "William White has been nursing him day and night, like a brother, and all the neighbouring clergy have been very kind. In fact, our dear brother is a general favourite, and we shall all feel his loss very much."

Mr. White, who was with him to the last, wrote about the last steps of his earthly pilgrimage. " He never lost his consciousness to the last. He was quite powerless to move or turn in his bed, and I remained with him constantly for more than a fortnight, Wilson kindly taking my Sunday duty. The kindness of the parishioners could not be surpassed. His mind was most active, almost too active, during his illness. He would discuss the most difficult Church questions. The difficulty was to keep him from thinking too much. He was very fond of being read to. Neale's Poems, and the 'Christian Year'—' Safe Home' in the former, and the piece for the Wednesday before Easter in the latter—were his favourites."

Mr. White was obliged to go away to the Wybong and Mount Dangar, parts of his district, on the 19th, 20th, and 21st of March, but the Rev. James Blackwood, of Singleton, remained with him. Mr. White says: "When I returned, on Thursday, the 21st, to Muswell Brook, I

was grieved to hear a bad account of him. I hurried over
on Friday morning, not knowing whether I should find the
dear fellow living; dear old Blackwood had remained all
the week. At three that afternoon we all expected his
death, and Blackwood read the commendatory prayer; but
he rallied again for a little while. He never murmured
through the whole. About two hours before his death he
asked me to read him the last chapter of the Revelation.
He said, 'I cannot say much.' I answered, 'You mean
that those words express what you feel?' and he said,
'Yes, *even so, come, Lord Jesus.*' He held out his hand
to feel for poor Mrs. Dove just before he breathed his
last. I had gone out of the room for a few minutes at a
quarter past two on the morning of the 23rd, when
Blackwood ran to call me. Dove's spirit passed away just
as I came in. His end was as calm and peaceful as a
sleep. I was so thankful that Blackwood was there; we
were able to assist poor old Mrs. A— to lay out the
remains of our dear brother in his robes, as he expressly
wished himself."

Two days after, on the Feast of the Annunciation, he
was buried.

The Rev. James Blackwood and the Rev. W. E. White
were two of the pall-bearers, and the Rev. Canon Child,
of Scone, read the Burial Service. All had in their
time, though not together, been reading with me at
Muswell Brook.

Mr. Child says: "At two P.M. we walked down from
the house, I leading the way, White and Blackwood
following as pall-bearers, and the churchwardens behind
them; then the people—a large train. The body was
borne by very willing bearers all the way to church and
grave. On entering the church the coffin was placed in
front of the communion rails, within the chancel. . . .
The church was quite full. After leaving the church
Mrs. Dove and the children follow. 1 the coffin in the

carriage, and got out at the bottom of the steep bank to walk up to the grave, which was made in the north-east angle of the chancel foundation of the Jerry's Plain church, and was built up of stone; so that if ever the church is built, the pastor will lie within its sacred precincts. Here, amid a crowd of anxious parishioners, we laid him in his grave. . . . There were probably 200 people present, and the coffin, therefore, was not immediately covered, as they seemed so desirous of taking the last look of the coffin which held their pastor's remains. The coffin was very plain, of brown cedar varnished; on the name-plate was 'Rev. W. W. Dove, 85.' Mr. White says, 'It was a touching sight; I don't think there was a dry eye there. . . . I feel I have lost more than a brother in dear Dove. He was always with us in every good work; and such a gentle, humble spirit! We did not appreciate him fully whilst he was among us. We need not grieve, however, for him; he died a martyr's death—a martyr to overwork.' "

Such was that dear brother in life and death, leaving, now he has passed from our sight, a train of blessed memories behind him. Will no young man, with the health and strength which God has given him, devote himself, in his Saviour's service, to take up the pastoral staff which William Dove has laid down ?

> " Mortal! if life smile on thee, and thou find
>   All to thy mind;
> Think, Who did once from Heaven to Hell descend
>   Thee to befriend:
> So shalt thou dare forego, at His dear call,
>   Thy best, thine all."
>
> KEBLE'S *Christian Year.* Wednesday before Easter.

CHAPTER XII.

THE ABORIGINES.

I CANNOT put on paper my few recollections of the aborigines of New South Wales without a feeling of sadness. As an Englishman and a Churchman, I am bitterly ashamed, nay, I am *afraid*, of the account to be rendered at the Judgment-day, when I reflect how the arrival of my fellow-countrymen, bearing the name of Christian, and having the habits and appliances of civilisation, brought a curse upon those wild children of the forest, debased a large part of them by fresh sins, instead of raising them towards the God Who made them, and has been the cause of their rapid diminution in numbers, if not of their complete extinction.

Some persons speak very complacently about the *law*, as they call it, by which the savage fades away before a civilised race. But unhappily the working of this law is to be traced only too evidently to the human agents. It is not so much to the white man's musket or rifle, used in self-defence or in protection of property, that the destruction of the aboriginal inhabitants is to be traced, as to the white man's drunkenness and the white man's lust, which have imported deadly diseases into the native veins, and have not only caused many premature deaths, but have checked the birth of native children, who might at least have filled up the gaps made in their ranks by death. W are accustomed to see in the returns of the Registrar-General of England a large annual *increase* of population. In New South Wales and other Australian colonies, there has been a considerable annual *decrease* in those tribes which have been brought into connection with the white man, the decrease being in proportion to the intercourse between the two races.

Collins, the historian of the early years of the colony, makes mention of several native tribes which he saw on both sides of the Sydney harbour. "When I landed in Sydney in January, 1848, *not one individual* of those tribes remained alive. I saw one wretched, drunken native in the suburbs, who belonged to a distant tribe ; but those men, women, and children, who used to fish in the waters of the north and south shores of the harbour, were simply wiped out, and, except in God's book of remembrance, and in the future resurrection, were as though they had never existed. *There* the Englishman had first set his foot and multiplied, and *there* the natives were not driven away, but *simply extinct.*"

The same result has followed in different degrees in most other parts of Australia. In a report on the Australian aborigines ordered to be printed by the House of Commons in 1844, there is a letter from a missionary at Port Phillip to Mr. La Trobe, the Government Superintendent, dated 1842 ; in which it is stated that the population of four tribes immediately round the station had, since the beginning of the mission, a period of *four years*, *decreased one-half;* and the writer adds, " Should the present state of things continue, but a very few years will suffice to complete the annihilation of the aborigines of Australia Felix."

Where my lot was cast, on the Hunter River, the extermination was far advanced, though not quite complete. It must be remembered that before 1831 the white man had not settled on the Hunter Valley from Morpeth upwards. Only twenty-seven years later, when I first saw it, the sight of two or three natives about Morpeth and Maitland was of rare occurrence, and they were, in nearly all cases, those who would hang about public-houses for drink. As you advanced farther from the places which had been longest settled, you might now and then see small knots of natives. In the district intrusted to me, measuring roughly, from Muswell Brook to some few miles beyond Cassilis, about 8,000 square miles, there were, of men, women, and children, about sixty remaining: the small fragments of several independent tribes, who, like partridges in the winter, when the sportsman's gun has thinned the coveys, had amalgamated; and at certain times would assemble from various parts of the bush to hold a *corroberee*, or native festival, which was but the shadow of such meetings in former times.

Further to the west and to the north, in the districts of the Castlereagh, New England, the Clarence and Richmond Rivers, and Moreton Bay, the tribes were more populous. Mr. Oliver Fry, Commissioner of Crown lands on the Clarence River, made a report in 1848 to the Hon. E. Deas Thompson, the Colonial Secretary in Sydney; in which he says that on the Clarence River were seven tribes, containing from fifty to one hundred men in each, and on the smaller river, the Richmond, four tribes, numbering about one hundred in each. The aggregate of the district under his charge, including some other tribes besides those mentioned, was about 2,000. I am unable to say to what extent the present census of that part of the colony would differ from that which he furnished more than twenty-four years ago; but he mentions, quite as an independent fact, a distinction between the tribes of those parts and others, which I cannot but consider one chief cause of the larger native population of that neighbourhood, that they have "evinced a *disinclination to almost any intercourse with the settlers*, manifested by the exceeding infrequency and short duration of their visits to the stations; nor can they," he continues, "be prevailed on to allow a white man to approach their camps, and in no instance have they ever become domesticated, or attached themselves to any establishment on the river."*

Neither the home Government of those days, nor the authorities in the colonies, are chargeable with indifference to the preservation of the natives. On every occasion they showed their anxiety for their welfare, and had the same spirit prevailed among the convict population and free settlers, the efforts made for their civilisation and conversion would have had some prospect of success. In a despatch from Downing Street to Sir George Gipps, Governor of New South Wales, dated December 20th, 1842, Lord Stanley, after commenting upon the unfavourable reports both of the missionaries and of the "native protectors," concludes, "I should not, without the most extreme reluctance, admit that nothing can be done; that with them alone the doctrines of Christianity must be inoperative, and the advantages of civilisation incommunicable. I cannot acquiesce in the theory that they are incapable of improvement, and that their extinction before the advance of the white settler is a necessity which it is impossible to control. I recommend them to your protection and favourable consideration with the greatest earnestness, but at the same time with perfect confidence, and I assure you that I shall be willing and anxious to co-operate with you in any arrangement for their civilisation which may hold out a fair prospect of success."

The colonial authorities on their part endeavoured to protect the natives from injury, and to promote their civilisation. Laws were made and penalties enforced for their good. It was made penal to sell spirits to them, and the police were charged to prevent the white men drawing the native women away. Considerable sums were expended out of the proceeds of the lands sold to settlers by Government for the support of native " protectors," whose duties were not only to protect the aborigines against

* "Report," p. 252.

wrong, but to endeavour to teach them the arts and habits of civilised life. Lands were set apart for them in different districts, tools were provided, blankets and food given, and encouragements held out to them to betake themselves to agriculture and pastoral pursuits.

Among the settlers there were some few who interested themselves in the welfare of the natives around them, treated them with kindness, and taught them, as well as made use of their services. But the example of the majority of white men in the bush was so unchristian, and their treatment of the blacks so demoralising, that the missionaries desired to be removed as far as possible from them. And as the sheep and cattle stations were gradually pushed farther into the interior and surrounded them, they asked to be removed still farther into the unsettled parts. Sir George Gipps, in a letter to Lord Stanley in January, 1848, endorses the statement of a missionary, that one of the *chief causes* of the failure of a mission, of which he is speaking, is " *the deadly influence of ungodly Europeans.*" Mr. La Trobe also, in an official paper referring to the bad practice and influence of European settlers, says: " I think it my duty to state that the evil effects of that influence *can scarcely be exaggerated.*" *

The attempts that were made to bring them to Jesus Christ were, from various causes, very disheartening in their results. And yet, on looking back upon them, one is not surprised at their almost entire failure. Within that part of Australia extending from Moreton Bay on the eastern coast to Geelong on the south, comprising, at the present time, the colonies of Queensland, New South Wales, and Victoria, four missions were established, and received pecuniary aid from the Government in addition to the land granted to them. No doubt many earnest men were interested in each of them, but the very

* " Report of House of Commons on Australian Aborigines," p. 243.

enumeration of them is suggestive of disunion, and therefore of weak and desultory attempts at the great work of
bringing wild, uncultivated heathen tribes to the faith of
Jesus Christ.

The earliest mission was that of the Church Missionary
Society, at Wellington Valley, about 160 miles north-west
of Sydney, founded in the year 1832. Within a few
years the London Missionary Society had fixed a mission
near Lake Macquarie, on the coast, sixty miles north of
Sydney. A Lutheran mission was planted at Moreton
Bay, and a Wesleyan mission near Melbourne, in 1838.

Within ten years from the foundation of the first of
these, two of them were entirely broken up, and the
others were in a state of collapse. A few children had
been taught to read, and read fairly. They could say
prayers, and had some knowledge of religious truth. A
very small number of adults received instruction, and
some of them became useful in various kinds of work.
But the impressions made on them were in very few
instances lasting, the partially-formed habits were soon
discarded; and those who had hoped to see their plans
for them succeed lost heart, and gave up the work.

Sir George Gipps, who passed four days at the mission
station at Wellington Valley, makes particular mention of
a native, named George, who could both read and write,
and was superior in every point to any native he had ever
seen. As a proof of his civilisation, the Governor states
that a gentleman, with whom he was dining, caused
George to dine at the table with him, and that on this
occasion he "behaved with perfect propriety; so much so,
indeed, that, but for his colour and his modesty in speaking only when spoken to, he might have passed for an
ordinary guest." But two years after this, in 1843, the
clergyman in charge of the mission writes in a desponding
tone about the whole mission, and adds, "a young man,
the same who was prominently introduced to his Excellency

the Governor, on his visit two years ago, as one far advanced in civilisation, has almost entirely returned to wild habits," *i.e.*, the habits of the natives. "He has been more unsettled for these eighteen months than I have ever known him before."

This is only a specimen of the way in which, in nearly all cases, the work, which seemed to be progressing for a while, was stopped, and soon undone. And the consequence was that the Government declined to continue the aid it had, for a few years, given to the missions; and the missions themselves were discontinued. I believe I am right in saying that the Roman Catholics, of whom there was a considerable number, never attempted a mission in New South Wales. And it must be sadly confessed that the want of vigour, and the disunion, which prevailed in the Church Missionary establishment at Wellington Valley, were ill-suited to cope with the many and serious difficulties which were found in the natives themselves, and with the evils of European influence.

But it is impossible to accept the ill-success which has attended former missions to the aborigines as sufficient to absolve the Church from the duty of renewing her labours for their conversion.

Wiser, more zealous, and more *patient* efforts may, we trust, receive that blessing from the Lord, which seems in great measure to have been withheld hitherto. British energy is not usually repelled by a few early failures in some important worldly object. Shall men of the same race and blood lose all their energy when the cause is their Saviour's, and the price is the rescue of souls for which He died?

At the present time the state of the white population of the colony, though very far from showing to the heathen a pattern of the effect which the faith should have on the lives of those who embrace it, is less grossly and actively antagonistic to Christian teaching than it was thirty years ago. And if one or two sound and earnest Churchmen, with a large-hearted and energetic priest to lead them, were appointed to this work—if they would seek out and follow the natives, study their character, and give them *such teaching as they can take in*, I believe the seeds sown would, in God's good time, spring and grow up man "knoweth not how." It would be very important that one of the party should be always at the centre; and, according to the plan sketched by the Bishop of Newcastle, should give more regular instruction and training to any adults or children who might be persuaded to come to him; but visitation of the wanderers should, I firmly believe, be an essential feature of the mission. This, of course, could only be done by an exercise of self-denial of no common sort: but self-denial is no strange idea to those who have tried in earnest to obey the Lord's words, " If any man will come after Me let him deny himself, and take up his cross daily, and follow Me."

I have no doubt, from what I have seen and heard of the natives, that there are among them intellects more capable of understanding the truths of the Gospel than we may find among some of our baptized labourers in the parishes of Christian England, and hearts and consciences ɩ. .ich the call to repentance and holy living will not fall in vain.

It would be, I think, most unwise to make fixed residence and regular manual labour necessary conditions of discipleship, but there are always individuals among the tribes who will, with more or less regularity, join themselves to the white man, tend or wash sheep, act as stockmen (for they are very fond of riding), work about a house or garden, reap, or take part in many of the other occupations of civilised life; and these men would acquire useful habits while they were being taught Christian principles.

It must be borne in mind that, independently of natural indolence or inferiority of intellect, the circumstances of

the aborigines had for ages been most unfavourable to improvement. Cut off by oceans from all the world besides,
for generations unknown, destitute of the example or teachings of their more advanced fellow-men, they had not
been led by opportunities to those pursuits, nor forced by
necessity to those inventions, which insensibly elevate and
civilise men. They had no grain to encourage them to
till the ground, no sheep, oxen, or other useful animals, to
train them to the comparative regularity of pastoral pursuits. The warmth of their climate enabled them generally
to live without shelter. There were no beasts of prey to
oblige them to seek the protection of a dwelling at night;
and their mode of procuring subsistence by hunting, fishing, cutting from the hollow trees the honeycomb of the
small native bee,* or the opossum as he slept through the
day, made a fixed dwelling inconvenient. When the wind
blew cold from the south, it was warded off by a few
boughs stuck into the ground to windward; and a sheet
or two of bark stripped from a gum-tree, and propped by
sticks, formed a temporary shelter to these black children
of the forest when the rain was more heavy or of longer
continuance than usual. After (at the utmost) a few
nights' sojourn on the same spot of ground, they would
walk away almost as unencumbered as the kangaroo,
leaving *no home* behind them; and, having procured their
food for the day, they would lie down in any fresh place
where water was procurable.

Their manufactures were of the simplest kind, consisting
of wooden weapons for war and hunting; the spear simply
pointed or barbed; the *nulla nulla*, or knobbed war-club;
the *waddy*, a sort of elongated policeman's truncheon
drawn to a point at the end; a small hand shield for

---

* The native bee is no more than one-sixth of an inch in length. It
has a sting, which, when caught, it attempts to use in its defence, but
is so weak that it is unable to penetrate the thinnest skin. Hence the
natives cut out their nests with impunity.

parrying an enemy's spear; and the *boomerang*, which, if it missed its mark, returned through the air to the thrower. The women made some well-twisted string (of different degrees of fineness) from the fibres of the currajong bark, which they sometimes netted, sometimes linked together without knots, into girdles or headbands for the men, or bags for the women to carry roots, fish, or other eatables; they plaited, also, very neatly, bags of rush and grass; and then there was the blanket-shaped opossum rug made of skins, not badly sewn together with fine string, or with the sinews of the kangaroo.

Their mode of life called for no forethought, exercised little skill. They lived from hand to mouth; nothing could be laid up, for they had *no home* in which to store it. In a thousand years the children were no farther advanced than their ancestors.

Among such a people the arrival of the white man has poured a flood of civilisation and complicated social relations, the aggregate of the experience of ages. And however we, who have been nurtured in them, may appreciate these advantages, we can far less reasonably expect that the free wanderers of the forest will, at our exhortation, fix themselves in any large numbers to regular labour, than we could hope to induce the English country lad, who has from his childhood ridden his master's horses to water or followed the plough, to consent at once to sit for long hours at a compositor's desk in a close room in the city, and to work long after midnight setting up the type of a parliamentary speech; though he might thereby eat meat more frequently than before, or dress in smoother cloth and a better shirt on Sunday.

We must not push the natives on too fast, but *lead them gently forward* as they are able to bear it.

I have before stated that when I arrived at Muswell Brook, I found but sixty individuals alive out of the five tribes that once roamed over the large area comprised in my clerical district. Very rarely did any considerable number even of those meet in one place; they generally wandered in parties of from two or three to twenty: sometimes camping for a few days near a township, and then scattering among the hills, or by the rivers, and disappearing for months. Occasionally, in a long bush ride, a few might be overtaken (with their hatchet, boomerang, and waddy stuck in their girdle), with a lump or two of fat twisted among the curls of their hair, and perhaps their *gins*, or wives, following, carrying by the tail the newly killed opossums. The clothing of the men was sometimes a striped shirt, sometimes a blanket given by Government, sometimes nothing but their girdle. The women usually wore a blanket or opossum rug, unless some white woman had given them a gown.

I saw at once how little I could hope to effect with those whom I could so seldom see, and whom I had not time to search out; but it was a plain duty to seize every possible opportunity of conversing with them. My first attempt was to learn the language; but it was not very successful. I found one of the survivors of the Merton tribe, King Jerry, who, from intercourse with the white man, had picked up a fair stock of broken English; and I agreed with him that he should teach me, and I was to give him a dinner each time. The first lesson was short, and Jerry was well satisfied; the second time I kept him about an hour, which proved altogether too much for his patience. As we sat in the verandah he continually stopped me to ask, "When you give me what you promise me?" He looked wistfully towards the kitchen to see if the cook was coming; and showed every symptom of weariness. When his dinner arrived he did full justice to it; but he avoided me for the future, and I had no more teaching from King Jerry.

Finding that I could get so few opportunities of learning the language, but that many of the natives could talk

M

and understand broken English, I devoted my endeavours, when I could meet with them, to winning their confidence and teaching what I could. And I found that some of the teaching, at least, was remembered.

One afternoon in 1849, as I was on my monthly journey to Merriwa, I overtook a party of about fifteen returning to their camp, which was then at the township; some women and children were among them. One *gin* had her infant, where they usually carry them, at her back, sitting in a fold of her opossum rug, and looking over his mother's shoulder. Two or three little boys, fat little fellows, full of fun and merriment, were running about by the side of their elders, clothed only in their own black skins, and throwing with exuberant glee some toy boomerangs, which, I suppose, their fathers had made for them.

We were more than a mile from the township; so I dismounted, and, after a few ordinary observations, determined to teach what I could. I had made up my mind that my first teaching must be the existence of God, His omnipresence, and His moral government. The sun was towards the west; so, pointing to it, I said, " See big sun! You know Who made him?" The only answer was a laugh and a look of inquiry. I took off my hat and bowed my head as I said, pointing to the sky, "Great God make sun." The same question was asked in reference to many different objects—the ground on which we were walking, the trees around us, the river, the hills, the beasts and birds; and, pausing for a few seconds after each question, I gave the same answer as before, with the same gestures of reverence; and then said, " Great God make me white fellow, great God make you black fellow," and then, spreading out my hands, "Great God make 'em all."

By this time we were on a ridge, and twenty miles to the north rose clear and distinct the bold Liverpool range.

Pointing to it, I asked, "You see black follow up on big range? Black follow on big range see you, me? You see Muswell Brook?" (forty-five miles over the hills to the east). "You see Cassilis?" (twenty-five miles to the west). And then, as the half-inquiring laugh followed each question, I said, uncovering my head, "Great God see black fellow on big range—see you, me—see Muswell Brook—see Cassilis—see all place. Dark night—no star, no moon, no camp fire—all dark; you no see, great God see; see in dark, see in light—see you, me, now—see you, me, all time." In similar broken language, and referring to the white man's gardens and fruit, with which the natives were well acquainted, I spoke of Eden as a mark of God's love; the prohibition, the sin, and the punishment. We had now reached Merriwa and each went our way, with a mental prayer on my part that God would bless the seed I had been attempting to sow in those poor untaught hearts.

Several months later some blacks came to me at Muswell Brook, offering to get me some native honey; for which (when brought) I paid them in flour and meat. I asked them to come into the verandah, as I wished to speak to them. I did not know them, for to an un-practised eye one black is not very easily distinguished from another. When I began to say much that I had on the last occasion, one who appeared to be listening attentively said, "That what you tell me up at Merriwa." It was evident that, if I had forgotten his features, he had not forgotten my words. "Have I seen you before?" "Oh! you not know me?—I Peter." "Well, Peter," said I, looking full into his face, which, though certainly not good-looking, had an expression far from unpleasant, "I not know you now, I know you after. Glad you think what I told you." He said he had thought of it much, and had talked of it to other natives, so that to a certain extent poor Peter was becoming, like St. Andrew, a missionary to his brethren of some portion of the truth.

It was but seldom, and usually at considerable intervals, that I could see my poor black friend. The jealousy of his tribe, which feared the influence of the white man, kept him much away. From him I learnt a little of their native vocabulary; and when I had the opportunity of seeing him, carried on his teaching. He told me that he and his people had no prayer or worship of any kind. He said that when he was a boy he used to hear the voice of the spirit of the woods in the dark stormy nights, but he had heard nothing of him since.

Into that chaos dark and void I tried to infuse something of the knowledge of God. By degrees I pointed out to him that God sent His own Son for us sinners; and told him that, upon repentance and faith (though I put it in a less technical form), he could be made by baptism a partaker of God's blessings. And I taught him almost at the outset a short prayer, which I taught to every native to whom I was able to give any instruction: "O Lord, make me to know Thee, and to know Jesus Christ, Thy Son." I took care to guard him not unfrequently against the idea, which he would naturally imbibe from seeing the evil lives of too many white men, that becoming a Christian need not bind him to holy living. I said, "You no do what bad white fellow do. Bad white fellow get drunk, swear, tell lies, steal. Great God angry." Peter's was a mild, kindly-disposed, and trustful disposition, and I was beginning to have great hope that ere long I might have had the privilege of baptizing him unto Christ, but it was not granted to me.

Some time in the winter of 1850, on my return from Cassilis, my servant told me that a native woman had been to the parsonage during my absence to ask for some tea and sugar for Peter, who was ill, and some had been given. The next morning I started with Mr. Kemp (who was reading with me for Holy Orders) to see what else poor Peter might want. The native camp was a mile out of the

township towards St. Helier's, a station then the property
of the widow of the late Colonel Dumaresq. The rain was
falling in a heavy, determined, business-like way, without
wind; and on reaching the camp we found poor Peter
lying on the ground under the partial shelter of a sheet of
bark, with a log fire burning before him, and suffering
from intense headache. He had been ill for some time;
and his face had a ghastly look, as if half the blackness
had been washed out of it. I persuaded him to walk
home with us, had a bed made for him on the kitchen
floor by the fire, and gave him some medicine and
some gruel. Next morning he told me, "*Cobborn* house
make him go round, round, round," *i.e.*, the big house
made him feel giddy. And before midday two of the men
of his tribe, jealous of my keeping him away from them,
came for him, and took him back to the camp. The party
soon moved; and some time after I heard that Peter was
better, and had taken a job of shepherding at a station in
another clerical district.

Not long after this I heard that a native at the gate
wanted to speak to me. I had never seen him before, but
saw he was oppressed with some great grief. He burst
into tears as I went up to him, and said, bitterly, "Poor
Peter dead! poor Peter, your black fellow, dead! he my
brother." He told me that he was far away in the interior
when Peter died; and, having just returned, he had been
sent by his uncle to inform me of his death, and to bring
me Peter's dying message.

The poor fellow had again been very ill; and one day
said to his uncle, "I *murry* bad; take me to Misser Boodle,
Muswell Brook." He walked a short distance with great
difficulty, leaning on his uncle; and then, finding his end
approaching, said, "I no go further; I die. You bury me.
Go to Misser Boodle; say to him, I going to Almighty
God."

I mentioned this the next day to my schoolmistress, who

told me the following story, which I believe she had heard
from her husband, the chief constable. Peter, with other
natives, had at one time been employed by a publican to
strip some bark for the roof of an out-building, and the
payment was to be made in tobacco. The job being
finished, a good many blacks were crowding into the tap-
room, some to be paid for the bark, others for mere
companionship ; and some of those who were being paid
were trying to get as much as they could. Peter had
received his tobacco in the crowd ; but afterwards came in
again, and held out his hand for payment. G——, the
publican's son, said, "No, Peter, go away, I paid you."
" No, massa," was the ready reply ; " you pay another
black fellow." G——, not feeling sure, paid him again.
He went out with his prize, and nothing more would have
been thought of the matter ; but in a few minutes back
came poor Peter, looking very much ashamed, and held
out his hand with the tobacco, saying, "Massa say musn't
tell lies ; you did give me 'bacca," and restored the ill-
gotten treasure.

I thanked God for this evidence of his denying himself
and confessing his fault for conscience sake. Though my
poor friend Peter had not been baptized, who shall say
that Christ's truth had not wrought in him *some* fruit,
which, through His precious blood, He may accept ?
Who shall say what he might have become with less than
half the blessings lavished on the barren heart of many a
Christian man and woman ?

In my limited experience I found several more of the
aborigines (with less steadiness than Peter, but yet with
sufficient willingness to be taught) to convince me that
persevering labour on such a soil, rightly directed, would,
with God's blessing, produce fruit. But little can be
expected from the desultory efforts of those who are over-
burdened with the charge of a Christian population, which,
if not overwhelmingly *numerous*, is scattered ever so wide

an area as to leave no time or strength for due attention to the peculiar wants of the heathen.

Men are wanted, able to bear fatigue and hardship, sound in the doctrines of the Church, and zealous in heart, and especially gifted with a power of adapting their manner of teaching to the peculiarities of their disciples. To such men a mission to the aborigines should be given as *their one great work*, to which they must devote their full energies for the love of Christ.

I would only add that what is done should be *at once* undertaken by those who have authority; or, while we are delaying, these poor souls may have passed away to the presence of the God Whom they have not known on earth, Who seems to have committed them to the care of our branch of His Church, that we may impart to them that blessed faith which He has committed as a talent to us.

CHAPTER XIII.

THE FORMATION OF THE CHURCH SOCIETY.

For the first three years from the foundation of the See of Newcastle, the Bishop and his clergy found themselves far more than occupied in endeavouring to minister to the people as widely as possible. They increased the services, sought out those who were scattered in the far-away corners of the bush, among hills and valleys, where no minister of Christ had before been seen. Fresh schools were set on foot, and some much-needed churches were built.

Many very urgent wants had to be supplied, though in a most imperfect way, in order to arouse anything like Christian life among our flocks. Over the wide area assigned to each clergyman it was no small labour, especially during the heats of summer, even to find out all Christ's wandering sheep, still more to minister to them regularly. And then we had to learn the character and habits of the people, and to gain their confidence before we could prudently lay down, or ask them to join in, any plans of united diocesan action.

But from the first we saw that in order to make any progress in the great work which was opening before us, a *society must be organised* to collect and manage funds for various diocesan purposes. Even in the mother country, where there are tithes for the support of the clergy, and where old grey churches and parsonages, within short distances of each other, attest the rich inheritance, for which the present generation is indebted to the piety of

those long since with God, societies are indispensable for
the maintenance or advance of Church work. Far more
are they needed in a young and growing colony, whose
birth is in the recollection of some few who are still
living.

We did not find old churches and church-buildings
dotted over and hallowing the land. There was the vast
stretch of unfenced forest country, with here and there
a town or little village on the banks of a river, and many
a settler's establishment or shepherd's hut in the bush:
showing the energy of our countrymen, who had left home
and friends sixteen thousand miles away, to gain a livelihood or to make a fortune. But there was no provision
by tithes or endowments which could place Christ's ministers among them, to remind them, as God's children, that
they were destined for a better world.

Some measure of assistance was given by the Colonial
Legislature; but the principle of Sir R. Bourke's Act,
passed in 1836, by which grants were annually made to
the Church of England, with other religious bodies, was
one which contained the elements of decay within itself.
There was no chance of its being allowed to provide in
any *adequate* degree for the growing needs of the population; and attempts were made from time to time by the
various sects which did not share in the grant, and by
politicians who sympathised with their aim, to abolish all
State aid to religion—attempts which, at length, have
unhappily succeeded, reservation being made of the
interests of those individuals who have hitherto received
salaries as long as they shall hold their present posts.

By the exertions of the Bishop of Newcastle before he
left England, subscriptions had been promised to the
young diocese from members of the Mother Church for
five years. The cessation of this aid could, of course,
easily be calculated. And the excellent Society for the
Propagation of the Gospel, which " hath been a succourer

of many," and had, during the seven years from 1840 to
1846, given to the Church in the whole Australian continent, then under Bishop Broughton, £4,000 per annum,
gave diminished sums to each of the newly-formed sees,
and *by degrees lessened the amounts* given to them, as they
might be expected to become better able to provide for
themselves.

It was, therefore, quite evident to those who would not
obstinately close their eyes to the present needs—and
still more those that were impending—that funds must
be raised in the diocese itself, if the growth of the Church
was not to be stunted.

For the first public introduction of this subject, the
Bishop took advantage of the presence of some of his
episcopal brethren in the colony.

The year 1850 was memorable in the annals of our
Southern Church for the "meeting" of the six Bishops
of the province of Australasia. That meeting was held at
Sydney, and its objects, as stated in its minutes, afterwards published, were—1st. "To consult together upon
the various difficulties in which we are at present placed
by the doubtful application to the Church in this province
of the ecclesiastical laws which are now in force in England." 2nd. "To suggest such measures as may seem
to be most suitable for removing our present embarrass-
ments." 3rd. "To consider such questions as affect the
progress of true religion, and the preservation of ecclesiastical order, in the several dioceses of this province; and
finally, in reliance on Divine providence, to adopt plans
for the propagation of the Gospel among the heathen races
of Australasia and the adjacent islands of the Western
Pacific."

The session began on the 1st of October, 1850, and
ended on the 1st of November. Those present at it were,
Bishop Broughton, of Sydney, the revered Metropolitan,
and the Bishops of New Zealand, Tasmania, Adelaide,

Melbourne, and Newcastle—the only Bishops then consecrated in Australia and the islands of the Pacific.

At the close of the session, the Bishop of Newcastle
invited his old college friend, Bishop Selwyn, and Bishop
Nixon, of Tasmania, to visit Morpeth; and in order to
make full use of our episcopal visitors, the 14th of November was fixed for the meeting, at which the general
wants of the Church in the diocese were to be put before
the people.

Bishop Selwyn had already been for some days under
the Bishop's roof, had visited with him several of the districts near Morpeth, and had stirred up the hearts of a
congregation assembled in Christ Church, Newcastle, by
his burning words, in a sermon upon the first part of Joel
ii. 28.

On the morning of the 14th of November, Bishop Nixon
arrived by the Sydney steamer. I was appointed to meet
him, and to escort him to the service at St. James' Church,
Morpeth, with which we were to begin our day. The
steamer had stuck on the " flats," some miles down the
river—no uncommon event; and while I was waiting
impatiently on the wharf, the church-bell ceased. I quite
despaired of our reaching the church before the congregation left it; but at last the steamer came in sight, and, as
our walk was only five minutes long, we were in time for
the celebration of the Holy Communion.

The meeting was held in the afternoon at the Court-
house, East Maitland, two miles distant; and there, to a
large number of attentive Churchmen and women, the three
Bishops, and some of the clergy present, explained how
much, and in how many branches of its work, the extension
and prosperity of Christ's Church in that newly-settled
land depended upon their zeal and steady co-operation.

An outline was given of the constitution and objects of
the proposed society. It was intended that during the
next five months the clergy should speak of it in their

several districts; that the Bishop should take every
opportunity of preparing the way for it wherever he might
go ; and that in the meantime rules should be prepared,
in order to be submitted to a meeting to be called for the
formation of the society.

Before the meeting separated an address of hearty and
respectful welcome was presented to the Bishops who had
come among us ; in which, among other things, it was
said : " We feel assured that your Lordships' visit is not
to be considered as one of mere friendship to our respected
Diocesan, but as one made by Bishops of Christ's Church,
coming, in the spirit of Christian brotherhood, to aid and
cheer a brother Bishop and the flock entrusted to his
charge. . . . . On the departure of your Lordships
for your respective dioceses, permit us to express the
earnest hope that you will continually remember us in
your prayers, and be pleased to convey to our brethren
committed to your charge the assurance of our love in
Christ, and of our prayers for their spiritual and temporal
welfare. . . . . We would desire, above all, to render
our humble thanks to our merciful Father, that while sin
and infidelity are arousing themselves through the world,
He has graciously stirred up to now life our branch of the
Church. We consider it no small sign of His goodness
towards us, that six Bishops of the Church of England
have been allowed to meet and take counsel in the diocese
of Sydney ; and three to assemble in this diocese, where,
within the memory of man, the Word of God and the
Name of Jesus were unknown."

At the conclusion of the meeting a collection was made,
and £22 14s. was collected ; which, as the first-fruits of
the united action of the diocese of Newcastle, was given to
the Bishop of New Zealand for his mission to the heathen
in the islands of the Pacific. The clergy present returned
to Morpeth, and spent the rest of the day with the three
Bishops—a day not to be forgotten by those who shared

in its proceedings, and especially refreshing to those who
for three years had spent most of their time in labouring
in the bush, cut off from personal intercourse with their
brethren in other places.

The seed thus happily sown sprang up into life in the
Easter week of the following year. On Sunday, April 14,
1851, after service in Morpeth church, and a very excellent
sermon by the Bishop, a meeting was held in the school-
room, at which the Newcastle Church Society was called
into being, the rules which had been drawn up for it
adopted, and its officers appointed.

The names of the six different funds, into any or all of
which subscriptions might be paid, show how extensive
was the ground which the Church Society covered.   They
were called—1. Education Fund; 2. Book Fund; 3. Building Fund; 4. Clergy Fund; 5. Mission Fund; 6. General
Fund.   The young diocese desired to keep before its
members the duty of—1st. Training up Christ's little ones
entrusted to her care, whether in primary or in more
advanced schools; 2nd. Of aiding in the supply of God's
Holy Word, books of sacred reading, and secular literature
of a sound and improving character; 3rd. Of encouraging
Church buildings, whether churches, schools, or parsonages;
4th. Of providing for an increase of clergy, either by
collecting money for salaries where none existed, or by
adding something to those that were insufficient; 5th. Of
helping missions to the heathen according to their power,
in fulfilment of the Lord's last command, " Go ye into all
the world, and preach the gospel to *every* creature;" and,
lastly, there being many needs which arise, when the Church
is engaged in its work, which can hardly be foreseen or
specified, and, perhaps, are temporary; and yet, if there
is no fund to meet them, the Church suffers : for these the
" General Fund" was intended to provide.

Thus six distinct purses were provided *under one management*, enlisting the different sympathies and supplying the

different needs of the Church, yet without the rivalry, and perhaps the jealousy, of different societies.

It was also at the option of each subscriber either to make his offering a *special* one to any particular local or diocesan object, or to pay it, without further limitation, into any of the funds.

Another feature of the society was that it was intended to be rather an aggregate of *Parochial* Associations, called "District Associations," than an aggregate of individuals. Any one might pay his subscription to the treasurer of the society, and some few subscriptions were always so paid, especially those of subscribers not residing in the diocese; but the bulk of the subscriptions was paid to the district committees in the several parishes or districts of the diocese.

Two-thirds of these local contributions to the "Education," "Book," and "Building Funds" might, if desired, be retained in the district in which they were contributed; and the remaining third, with the *total* of the "Clergy," "Mission," and "General Funds," were to be remitted to the Diocesan Society.

These provisions gave the widely-scattered members of the Church a greater interest in the society; and made it more easy to bring its claims before them, and to look up and collect subscriptions, than if all had depended upon one central committee. The principles of local interest and extended Christian brotherhood were both represented.

The first years of the existence of the society, beginning in the middle of April, contained the subscriptions of less than nine months. That year was also one of great change and excitement in the colony, for it was in May, 1851, that the discovery of gold at Sofala, near Bathurst, startled us all, and for a while threatened to turn everything upside down. We were, therefore, well pleased and thankful to find that our first year's total amounted to £531, out of which the sum given for additional clergy was £276.

There were two items which pleasantly marked the time—one contribution of £20, and another of £5, from *successful gold-diggers*, who thus sanctified their gains by rendering a tribute to the Lord.

The funds of the Newcastle Church Society afterwards increased far beyond our expectations; and in many ways it became a great blessing to the diocese.

CHAPTER XIV.

GROWTH AND PROGRESS OF THE CHURCH SOCIETY.

It was an important day for the Diocese of Newcastle when the Church Society was formed. It was a day of hopes and fears : of hopes that, by God's blessing, it might be the means of drawing out the energy of the laity to aid in the great work that was before us, and of refreshing the thirsty places of the land ; of fears, lest worldly selfishness, prejudices, and jealousies might close the hearts and hands which should open to help forward Christ's work.

The formation of the Church Society was the first steady effort towards making the young diocese self-reliant.

The Church at home is rightly called upon to provide for *planting missions* in heathen lands, and aiding the *first struggles* of a colonial Church, where the shoot newly planted needs watering from without until it has taken root and begun to draw its moisture from the new soil. And there are some colonies, like Newfoundland, where the battle for life is so hard that greater and longer-continued assistance is required than in others. To supply those great and increasing needs, the Churchmen of England are in Christian charity bound—and are well able—to offer far more largely than they have yet done. Many still give nothing ; and of those who do give, many do not make offerings in a fair proportion to their means. But, however much a colonial Church requires and has a right to look for the help of the Mother Church during the early years of its existence, nothing could be more enervating to it than to continue year after year trusting to external sources for support, and making no call upon its own members to supply their spiritual wants.

The effort was made in the Diocese of Newcastle after the first three years of its existence, and two years before the cessation of the special subscriptions which had been promised in England to meet its first necessities.

There were some real difficulties which threatened us at the outset; for the most important object of the Church Society was the support of additional clergy—not to speak of the increase of existing salaries—and the approaching need of providing for the *whole* number, when the State aid should cease.

Churchmen who had come from England were unprepared for this. They had been accustomed to see their clergyman provided for by tithes secured by law, and the greater number of the parishioners, who profited by his ministrations, were not called to contribute anything to his support. The old associations of the emigrant Churchman were, therefore, against the Apostolic precept, " Let him that is taught communicate unto him that teacheth in all good things." To the Church of England layman it was, for the most part, a new idea, and new ideas do not generally spring into vigorous action at once.

Then there was the positive irreligion of many of the settlers and convicts—especially in the bush, where more clergymen were wanted. Those whose daily lives were a denial of all religion were little likely to contribute to its support.

There were many, also, who had come to the colony, not to make it their home, but to realise a sum of money and return to England. Many of these took no interest in improving things around them, and especially grudged spending money upon things so unremunerative as clergy, and churches, and religious schools.

The miserable divisions, which prevail wherever our

N

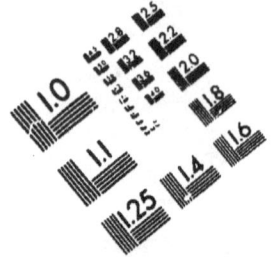

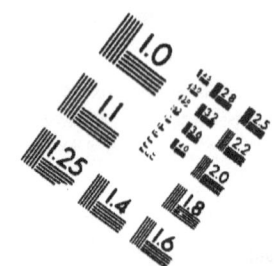

IMAGE EVALUATION
TEST TARGET (MT-3)

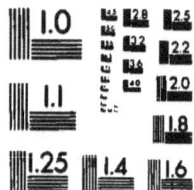

countrymen are settled, had their effect in dissipating energies which, if united in Christ's Church, would have economised money and men, and have been able to act with vigour. In each little township, if it had but two or three hundred inhabitants, were found representatives of three or four different sects. Roman Catholics, Presbyterians, Wesleyans, and Baptists or Independents, would divide the little community with the Church. And a flock, which might have been efficiently tended by one pastor, residing among or near them, was scantily fed at irregular times by the occasional visits of ministers who lived at a distance, and performed similar desultory work in other places.

From these and other causes there was, among the majority of the colonists, an unwillingness to contribute to the pressing needs of the Church, up to the time when the Church Society was formed. As an illustration of this, the Bishop of Newcastle has mentioned, that when Bishop Broughton was on the point of sailing to England for the last time, he was anxious to send a clergyman to a district in the south of his diocese. The full stipend was available, but there was no parsonage. The Bishop, therefore, asked a settler, who was a member of Council, and had an income of £5,000 or £6,000 per annum, to guarantee the collection in the district of twenty pounds per annum for the rent of a house. The settler replied that he had consulted with his neighbours, and that they were willing to guarantee ten pounds per annum, but would not undertake to promise so much as twenty pounds, and this wealthy settler pledged himself to *one pound.*

This is a sample of the spirit against which the Church Society had to win its way, and against which it *did* win its way year by year, with a success that astonished the workers as well as the bystanders.

From its first establishment in 1851, until the separation of the northern portion of the diocese in 1860, and

its erection into the see of Brisbane, the numbers of con-
tributors, and the total contributed, not only never fell off,
but increased considerably each year.   The amounts contributed in these nine years, and their increase, were as
follows :—

		Total Amount of Collections.		Increase on Preceding Year.
1851	...	£531	...	—
1852	...	£1,412	...	£881
1853	...	£2,247	...	£835
1854	...	£3,362	...	£1,115
1855	...	£4,627	...	£1,265
1856	...	£5,323	...	£696
1857	...	£6,028	...	£705
1858	...	£6,849	...	£821
1859	...	£7,400	...	£551

When in 1860 the receipts from what had then become
the new Diocese of Brisbane were cut off from the Newcastle Church Society, the receipts were diminished to
£5,361; but the responsibilities of the society were also
largely diminished.   And a comparison of the receipts for
the *reduced* diocese with those of the *same portion*, before
its division in the preceding year, shows an *increase* of
£453.

It ought to be added that on May 12th, 1868, after
seventeen years of valuable labour, the Church Society was
merged in the then established Diocesan Synod, under
the direction of which the same important work of raising
and administering the funds of the diocese was then
carried on.   In each of the years, between the reduction
of the diocese and the transmigration of the spirit of the
Church Society into the Diocesan Synod, the funds steadily
increased; and the concluding year, so far from showing
any diminution of the zeal of the members of the Church,
shows an *increase* of £1,640 upon the year preceding,
making a sum of £8,546, or £1,146 more than was contributed in the last year of the undivided diocese in 1859.

It has not been during a period of uninterrupted pros-

N 2

perity that the offerings of the Churchmen in the diocese have continued to increase. There have been several years since the foundation of the society, when troubles and losses affecting the colony would have fully accounted for a falling off of subscriptions; but the steady rise was maintained, notwithstanding all difficulties. An extract from the Report for 1857 will give one instance of this. It says, "The circumstances of the year 1857 will long be remembered among us. Agricultural produce swept away by three devastating floods, each more disastrous than the preceding; growing crops destroyed, houses submerged, merchandise and stores injured or carried away by the rising waters, rents generously forgiven or lowered, from want of ability in the tenants to pay, traffic for several months almost stopped, and trade at a standstill; then the commercial panic in England and America, which for a time affected even this distant member of the great Anglo-Saxon body; and, in the midst of these trials, contributions freely made by those who suffered much, to lighten the burdens of those who suffered more; and more recently, the calls of charity responded to in the colony for the overwhelming afflictions of our Indian brethren. All these circumstances, which impress the past year indelibly upon our memories, ought to be taken into consideration, if we would rightly estimate the amount of the funds raised for our Church Society." These words prefaced an announcement of an *increase* of £705 on the previous year's subscriptions. The Report went on to add, "With this increase in the funds of the society, there has also been a steady advance in the great work which we are labouring to promote. There are more ministers' dwellings built, or in progress, more schools, more churches, and, we may thank God, more ministers labouring in this diocese than when we last met together."

The means which, under God's blessing, produced such satisfactory results, were, in the first place, plain statements

of the needs which existed in the diocese, and of the use-
lessness of looking to external sources for their supply.
It was frequently and widely impressed upon the members
of the Church, that they must themselves provide that
pecuniary support which could not be looked for elsewhere.
When a clergyman was required for any place *which had
not a Government stipend*, the Bishop impressed upon the
Churchmen in the district, that, if they desired one to be
sent to them, they must contribute to his support.   In
order to secure the income, the principal laymen were
asked to guarantee a certain sum—part of which was their
own subscription, and part was raised from the contributions of the smaller settlers and poorer members of the
Church.   Many shepherds in the bush gave willingly,
some of them 5s., 10s., or £1 a-year.

Those districts *which received Government aid* for their
clergyman were appealed to, as a matter of *justice*, to
contribute towards those who had none; and the duty was
generally acknowledged when laid clearly before them.
In several of the districts *half of the offertory* was paid to
the Clergy Fund, in accordance with the Bishop's expressed
desire.   The Bishop urged upon all the districts that had
£200 a-year from Government for their clergyman, that
they should each contribute £100 a-year towards those
who had no Government aid.   Any sum which a district
contributed to the Clergy Fund above this £100, was paid
to its own clergyman in augmentation of his income.

None of these sums were paid to the clergy *directly*, but
to the Church Society itself: and were distributed in quarterly payments by the committee to the clergy who were
entitled to them.

The work was much helped forward in those districts
where the parochial meetings were regularly held, and
information given on Church subjects in general.   In these
there was greater steadiness in the contributions, and a
growing interest was felt in the progress of the Church.

Much good also resulted, where, through the influence of the clergy, some of the more earnest laymen undertook to collect from the scattered settlers.

There were some districts in which the clergy did not understand how to make a beginning, or shrank from enlisting their better-minded parishioners in the cause. Here the Bishop's visits were invaluable. Always ready for any work, he sometimes aided the clergyman in a meeting; or he would call on the laity and set them in motion ; and in some parishes, where nothing had been effected, and the clergyman was disheartened, the Bishop's visit drew out willing workers ; and the result showed itself in the increased funds of the society.

It must not be supposed that when success is mentioned, a whole spiritual desert is represented as brought into fertility ; nor that it was as easy to effect what was really done, as it is to write or read of it. Very much remained and still remains to be done. But that an actual and considerable success was granted to the Church Society, even in its early days, is evident, when it is said that in the beginning of the third year of its existence it was found that the colonial resources, partly derived from the Government aid, and partly from the funds of the Church Society, provided all the stipends for the clergy, and that the Bishop announced to the Society for the Propagation of the Gospel, and to his English friends, that henceforth their aid would not be required for the *current expenses*, but for the most important object of investments for its permanent good. The Bishop says in a letter appended to the Society's Report, and dated May 9th, 1853: "Two thousand pounds will be available this year for these purposes, and, I trust, a similar sum during each of the next four years."

That plan of endowment was, that, as far as there were funds available for the purpose, any donation up to £500 should be met by a similar sum from the investment fund, and the amount invested as a *permanent endowment* for the object fixed upon.

Several schools were partially endowed in this way; three canonries were endowed with £20 a-year each, half of the principal for endowment being contributed by the Bishop and his English friends.   Some parishes received a small endowment for their clergy; the endowment of the bishopric was completed; and to enable the Church Society to pay the clergy their quarterly salaries, when due, before all the subscriptions had been paid in, the society itself was endowed with £1,000 as a *permanent balance;* out of which the sums required were *advanced,* and into which they were repaid again as soon as the subscriptions of the districts were sent in.

These and other endowments are of the greatest possible benefit where the large bulk of Church funds arises from voluntary subscriptions, and the prudent management and forethought of the Bishop have enabled him to raise them as an off-growth of the Church Society.

The Diocesan Depôt, which is most useful, and has been most successful in its working, is a nursling of the society, which, for the first eight or nine years of its existence, voted a sum annually to aid the payment of its original debt.   But it would never have succeeded at first, nor have maintained its efficiency as it has done, had it not been for the wise care of the Bishop.

It has now a stock of £1,600 worth of books, free from debt, replenished by orders from England to the value of £200 each quarter.   It is so managed that the Bibles and the Book of Common Prayer are sold in the colony at prices charged by the Society for Promoting Christian Knowledge to its *subscribers;* and other publications of all kinds are sold at English retail prices; the expense of carriage, packing, &c., from England, being borne by the Depôt.   To meet the wants and tastes of various persons, any one is allowed to send, through the manager of the

Depôt, any list of books which he may desire to have, provided they are unobjectionable ; and his list is included in the quarterly order, so that in about eight months' time he may obtain his books at the Morpeth Depôt, for the same price he would have given for them in Paternoster Row.

Such are some of the instances of progress which the Newcastle Church Society has exhibited during the seventeen years of its separate existence. We may well hope that, as a department of the Synod which has taken it to itself, it will be, as before, increasingly a blessing to the Church in the Diocese of Newcastle.

Mission Work in British Columbia.

CHIEFLY FROM THE JOURNALS OF THE REV. R. J. DUNDAS.

CHAPTER I.

NOTES FROM THE BISHOP'S JOURNAL.

YALE, *Wednesday, June* 14, 1866.—Left New Westminster in the *Lilloet* for Hope and Yale at three o'clock. Rained all the morning and the whole day incessantly. 212 passengers, many Chinese. There was a row in the evening, and a white man stabbed a Chinaman, and was secured. At night we lay to ; there was much noise, and I could get but broken rest.

SERVICES—YALE AND HOPE, *Sunday, June* 18.—Held service at Yale. The attendance was forty. The harmonium was played very fairly by the daughter of the schoolmaster. I had the morning prayer and litany. The collection was 13 dollars. In the afternoon I went by canoe to Hope, where at six o'clock in the pretty church of that lovely spot I held service. Hope is now all but deserted. Still we had eighteen persons, besides a few Indians.

CANOE VOYAGE TO HOPE.—The river at this time is at its height, some twenty feet above the common level, through the melting of the snow. It is a tremendous torrent, rushing onwards, carrying in its vast breadth and depth the waters of many great tributary rivers gathered in its course of nearly 1,000 miles ; at times, whirling and upheaving surges seemed enough to overset and swallow up in an instant our tiny bark, but with quick,

cool, and unerring eye, our Indian guided us safely
through.   At other times there were rapids and canyons,
or gorges, along which the contracted waters rushed more
fiercely, as if enraged.   The famous and dangerous Em-
mory rapid and " Hell's Gate " warned us long before by
their roar and din ; at the latter there was but one passage
safe at this time for the canoe.   It was on the opposite
side of the stream, here about a quarter of a mile wide.
The current was sweeping us down at the rate of seven
miles an hour.   It was necessary to begin to cross in sufficient time to prevent our being cast upon the rocks in
mid-stream.   As we were coming down it seemed as if
nothing could prevent our being smashed to pieces, and
we seemed only just to escape destruction.   With our
three Indians, however, there really was no danger.   They
knew the water and the ground so well that they could
make the exact calculation necessary to avoid a catastrophe.
It was exciting, however, even to those who had confidence
in the Indian canoemen ; to others it would certainly be
alarming.   There is no mode of transit so pleasant on a
fine day as the canoe ; there is no concussion, as in a boat
with oars, but you glide noiselessly and rapidly along.
We did the fifteen miles in an hour and a-half.   The
scenery was magnificent, as one set of mountains after
another, with a variety of new beauties, opened up to
view.   The lofty heights, the vast and rapid stream, the
blue vault of heaven, were calculated to impress the soul
with reverential fear, while the flowering shrubs, the dog-
wood, and the rose, smiling upon us and perfuming the
air, together with the graceful dress and manner of our
Indians, made the scene more picturesque.

VISIT TO THE LEECH RIVER MINES—*Saturday, July* 8.
—We started about one, my wife, Mr. Alston, and myself
on horseback, with our saddle-bags, for the Leech River
Mines.   The road as far as Goldstream, twelve miles, was
pretty good.   We rested there an hour, at a wayside

house kept by two English gentlemen, and then entered upon a more difficult path of nine miles, chiefly through forest, but over swamps, and up and down steep heights, the trail being such as is common to new and unopened countries—the first path roughly hewn, precursor to a road. It rained a good deal. We reached our destination at Leech River Mines just before dark, having accomplished twenty miles, of which the latter nine could not be traversed at more than a walking pace.

SERVICES AT THE MINES—*Sunday, July 9.*—This morning we rode to the North Forks of the Leech, where I held an open-air service. In the afternoon I held service at Kennedy Flat. It rained in torrents, but the attendance of miners was good.

"LONG JIM."—I was told I had a great friend in a miner who went by the name of "Long Jim." Miners are seldom known except by their nick-names. He had spoken with indignation at some evil-speaking and slandering which had been indulged in on the subject of Christ Church Trust property. He thought the Church ought to have the reserve. So talked Long Jim. I called upon the same individual to-day in his log cabin. The storekeeper who was with me discoursed eloquently upon the excellence of his character. "He was greatly respected on the creek, was a steady and very industrious man, always ready to serve others." Jim was very glad to see me, and not only came himself, but did all he could to induce others to attend the service. Jim was no stranger to me, for he had been a patient in the Victoria Hospital. I thought him then a rough and uncouth miner; he did not attend at first particularly to the exhortations, but did so latterly, and I had a conversation with him. He got well and left the hospital. I never knew his name, and until I saw his face to-day was not aware that Long Jim was the patient of the hospital. This is one of those instances where the work of the minister of Christ is more effectual and blessed than he supposes at the time. We may be encouraged, by the cases which thus show results, to believe thankfully in good effects in other instances, though hidden from us. We are of course encouraged by promises that God's Word shall not go forth and return unto Him void. This poor man found blessing in the ministrations at the hospital, and now shows the result in friendly feeling towards the humble instrument of his good, in zeal for God's service, and in doing kind acts for others, letting his light shine before men, even amidst the excitement and exceeding worldliness of a gold-mining community. I asked his name; the storekeeper said he really did not know, the man was always called Long Jim.

BREAK-DOWN OF A STEAMER—*Saturday, August* 19.— Embarked to-day on board the *Emily Harris* for the consecration of Nanaimo Church, accompanied by Archdeacon Gilson. We ought to have sailed at seven o'clock, but did not get away till eleven. When off the bay beyond Cadboro' Point, our steamer's head was suddenly pointed direct in to the shore. Something was amiss; presently the firemen and others were rapidly drawing out the fire. The lead pipe had failed at its connection with the boiler. The fires were therefore put out, and the vessel brought to anchor. As it might be some time before the necessary repairs could be effected, I thought it better to come on shore and return to Victoria, which we did, thankful to have. escaped from what was nearly being a disastrous explosion.

INDIAN FIGHT—*Sunday, October* 1.—After visiting the Indian school this afternoon, I went, accompanied by the Rev. A. C. Garrett, to visit the Indian village. We heard a disturbance going on at the Hydah Camp. As we approached, we perceived groups of Indians on the surrounding heights in a state of excitement. These were songees and others looking on at a fight between rival tribes of Hydahs. The scene was truly savage. Naked men, wild and distorted, were raging about and hurling large stones, some with fearful precision, at each other. There were women wild with fury and screaming, urging on the fight. We went into the midst of them, and with some difficulty got them to desist. It was an exciting scene as we stood between the combatants, who continued to gesticulate to each other, their blood freely flowing from wounds, and their countenances showing passion and revenge to reign supreme. Mr. Garrett showed great courage and coolness; many huge stones were dropped at his bidding, and maniacs became calm at his words. Poor creatures! it was pitiable to see them, as they sobered, realising their wounds and showing them to us. A woman brought her husband to me, whose face, breast, back, and arms, were bedaubed with blood from many wounds and bruises; his face was excited with anger, and in his two hands were firmly grasped heavy stones as large as he could hold. At length we quieted them, and there were many voices to be heard as we came away, saying, "Good! good!" A chief cause of this excitement, in which probably lives were lost, was drink.

CHAPTER II.

WE had had a long and hard day's tramp under a hot sun, and were beginning to weary for the first glimpse of the wayside "ranch" (known as Alkali Lake House, from the piece of water near it), by which we intended to camp. I had been separated from my companion, Sheepshanks, for the best part of the day. After getting over the first six miles of our journey in the morning, he discovered that he had left his watch at our last camping-ground. Of course he had to return, and this added twelve miles to his travel that day. Late in the afternoon I turned up from the great benches and valley of the Fraser River, along which our route had lain for some days, into a smaller valley running up from it to the high wide plateaus that separate this part of the Fraser from the basin of Williams Lake. I had begun to doubt whether Sheepshanks would catch me up at all that evening, when, on looking back, I could see his tall figure striding along, and soon he overtook me, rejoicing in the recovery of his watch, but, in miners' parlance, "pretty well played out."

Another half-hour brought us to where the trail wound round the shore of the little Alkali Lake, which gives its name to the valley. The settler's house and land, where we purposed to make our camp, lay, we believed, at no great distance from the lake. Tired of the frugal fare of beans, bacon, and damper of previous days, we began to anticipate with feelings of satisfaction the "good square meal" for which the ranch was famous—including, we had heard, even such delicacies as milk, vegetables, and fresh beef. We were not, however, to reach this Goshen. Three figures now appeared on the trail in front, coming towards us. They proved to be Indians, two men and a woman. Their tribe (I think an offset from the Shaswap, or some other further east in the interior) was in summer quarters hard by, on a small plateau above the lake. A Lilloet Indian, lately come among them, had seen and heard us 150 miles down the country, and had told these people that two "King George"* priests were on their way up. They had watched for us, and now this party was deputed to pray that we would "turn aside and tarry with them." We could not refuse such an invitation; and very soon, guided by the three natives, we and our tired packhorse had made our way up the bank to the little plain on which the Indian camp was located. There was no need for us to do much ourselves in the way of arrangement; plenty of willing hands were soon hard at work. The horse was unpacked and led to water, the tent was pitched, and in front of it a blazing fire of pine-logs was quickly provided, at which to bake the bread and cook the beans and bacon. While supper was preparing and daylight lasted, Sheepshanks was busily engaged in vaccinating.

The small-pox raged that summer in Vancouver's Island and parts of British Columbia, proving, as usual, especially fatal among the native tribes. When we started from New Westminster, the surgeon of the R. E. Corps supplied us with lancets and vaccine, and wherever we stopped on our way up country near an Indian village or camp, Sheepshanks was ready to operate on all comers. On this occasion, men, women, and children crowded round, all anxious to obtain the white man's "little medicine," in which they put unbounded faith. Fading daylight put a stop to our

* The invariable Indian expression for everything English, as Boston is for everything American.

surgical operations ; then we had supper—beans and bacon,
tea, and damper.   We always carried on our horse a three
or four days' supply, in case we might have to camp where
nothing could be had.   After supper, all the Indians assembled in front of the chief's lodge.   Sheepshanks and I
occupied places of honour upon two scarlet blankets just
at the entrance.   The chief was on one side of us ; his wife,
the woman who had met us, on the other.   He was a short,
squat man, with a good-humoured face ; she was tall and
elegant, with a fine face and well-dressed ; over her other
garments she had a white linen robe, something like a
short sleeveless surplice.   This, and a large chain and
crucifix worn round the neck, gave her a priestly look.
In the recesses of the lodge behind us were the family of
the chief and others.   In front of us a huge fire had been .
kindled, which threw its ruddy light over the scene, and
round it in a huge semicircle the rest of the Indians were
clustered, squatting on the ground.   Sheepshanks was the
speaker, for he understood Chinook.   This barbarous jargon, a mixture of English, Canadian French, Spanish, and
Indian, is universally spoken by the natives of Vancouver,
but only to a limited extent by the northern and inland
tribes of British Columbia.   On the present occasion,
Sheepshanks's Chinook had to be translated into their
tongue by the Lilloet native, who fortunately understood
it.   So far as anything could be made of so poor and
uncouth a dialect, speaker and interpreter did their best ;
and, all things considered, Sheepshanks's address was a
fair sketch of the great leading truths of Christianity.   The
natives were wonderfully attentive ; and now and then, as
some fact or truth not unfamiliar struck their attention,
a half-suppressed " agh" burst from them.   When the
Crucifixion and Death of our Lord were spoken of, one of
them instantly drew forth a crucifix and held it up.   I
could not but think, if so necessarily imperfect a statement,
simply of leading heads and facts, through the medium of

a rude jargon, could thus rivet their whole attention, what a mighty effect would be produced by the full, free utterance of the glad tidings *in their own language,* where all the consolations, the persuasions, the encouragements of the Gospel could be brought to bear. To them it would be as life from the dead. Many of them, in the interior of the country, had heard something of the facts of Christianity from Roman Catholic missionaries. While we condemn the false, soul-destroying system of Rome, let us give all honour to the self-denying labours of many a Roman Catholic missionary in heathen lands. There are few parts of America—North or South—in which these men have not left some mark among the native tribes. As in many other cases, the men are often far better than their system.

When Sheepshanks had finished his address, he dictated, through the interpreter, a short prayer to be used by them all. We closed a most deeply interesting hour and a-half by singing in English the Doxology, and offering up the Lord's Prayer. Truly it was but little we had been able to do for these poor natives, and yet their gratitude was very great. What I have described was a very common incident in the journeyings of the Bishop and his clergy to and fro through the mining districts. We had at this time only two or three permanent mission stations amongst the natives of the two colonies, but we did what we could to scatter seed on our way up and down through the interior. Let us hope that even a few grains have fructified in that great human field, where " the harvest is plenteous, but the labourers are few." And if any are disposed to think that such *fugitive* teachings were profitless, and that we might as well have spared ourselves the labour for any good result that was to come of it, I can only say that, doing what little we could, we remembered the admonition, " Have faith in God."

Our tent was pitched some hundred yards or so from the

o

Indian lodges on the open plain. At about three o'clock in the morning, I was awoke by a feeling of suffocation, and became conscious that, in a tremendous squall of wind and rain, the tent had been blown down, and that we were enveloped in folds of dripping canvas. As soon as we could disentangle ourselves, we set to work to remedy the disaster. It was no easy work to get the tent up again in the face of the wind; and, being but lightly clad in a flannel shirt, we were well washed by the down-pour of rain. Some of our things, too, got loose, and almost in a state of nature we had to chase them over the plain. The absurdity of our position and appearance made us shout with laughter; though the discomfort was not slight of having to creep in under the dripping canvas, and lie down in wet blankets to soak till the morning. Luckily, the rain cleared off, and so we spent the forenoon (which ought to have seen us many miles on our journey to Williams Lake, where we hoped to meet the Bishop) in drying our packs; and in the afternoon, as it was then too late to make a start for the next good camping-ground, we remained by the Alkali Lake House, and gathered together as many as we could for an evening service.

The heavy rain did one good thing for us; it regularly beat down the mosquitoes for the next twenty-four hours, so that we were but little plagued with them during our stay. The place, however, had an evil name for the pest. As a Yankee said, when I asked before we got there, "Yes, sir-ee, guess they do bark at you, some."

CHAPTER III.

A SUNDAY ON A MINING CREEK.

THE following may serve as an instance of the rough itinerant kind of work done amongst the miners and settlers in British Columbia.

. . . . The last 100 miles had indeed been enough to try the endurance of the stoutest traveller. We felt completely "played out." As to our poor pack-horse, it gave out completely before our journey's end, and we had to leave it on the high ridges of the Bald Mountains, over which the trail passes between the forks of the Quesnelles River and Antler Creek, to take care of itself, while we sought shelter for the night at a filthy cabin kept by a black man, and known to travellers as "the Nigger's," the only house of refuge within many miles. This was on Friday night, and we were most anxious not to lose the Sunday on the creek, as already, from various delays, and difficulty in getting along, we were a week later than the Bishop had expected we should be. We accordingly resolved that one of us should push on next morning alone for Antler Creek (it was seventeen miles distant, and a good stiff walk), so as to be there the next day and secure the holding of Divine service upon Sunday, while the other stayed upon the mountain to find the strayed horse, and make terms, if possible, with some packer or muleteer, to bring it on with his train, if it should survive, which we thought doubtful. A man at the cabin, who happened to be going to Antler Creek with two or three unloaded animals, consented to take the heaviest part of

our pack, the tent, blankets, and flour-bag; for which
little service he only charged twelve dollars (about two
guineas and a-half) for sixteen or seventeen miles!

The day might have been worse for Cariboo. Not infrequently, however, there came sharp, cold squalls of wind
and driving rain, which soon reduced me to the normal
condition of those who travel through these parts before
the settled weather of autumn. Still, with the exception
of the last seven miles, the ground was very different
from our experience of several previous days. No longer
dense swampy forests, nor tracts of doleful burnt timber,
nor the stifling heat and insects of deep valleys. I was
now at an elevation of some 6,000 or 7,000 feet, going
upon nearly level ground in places, over the glorious
pasture of these lofty mountain ridges, which are called
the Bald Mountains, because devoid of timber, not because
they were without verdure. On all sides, especially to
north and east, there was an extended prospect: in the
latter direction over the grand sky line of the Peaked
Mountains to the still higher line of the Rocky Mountains.
Frequently we passed over beds of unmelted snow. At
length we began to descend. The last six miles down
through the forest was enough to *break a mule's heart*, and
never did sounds seem more grateful to me than the
creaking of the great water-wheels and other appliances of
mining, which told me I was nearing the point at which I
was bound to deliver my testimony. A small stream of
water ran through the valley, thick and turbid from the
operations of the mining gangs. The valley at the bottom
was a narrow flat, from which on either side rose the steep
densely-wooded hills. The flat had once been thickly
timbered, but was now quite bare, every stick having been
cut down for lumber. The settlement, or, as it would be
called here, the "City" of Antler, consisted of some sixty
or seventy houses, stores, saloons, &c.; the drinking and
feeding saloons being most numerous. There were not

above half-a-dozen two-storied buildings; all of course were of wood. They stood in two rows facing each other, so as to form a *street*, not more than twelve feet wide, and of course unpaved and filthily dirty, though there was an attempt at a wide walk of plank. There were two slaughter-yards at each end of the street, which did not smell sweet. The trade in bullocks has been a fortune to a few enterprising men. They purchase for ten dollars a-head in Oregon, south of the boundary line, poor thin beasts, which they bring up through stretches of grass country by the Okanagan and Shaswap district to the Cariboo. They feed themselves as they travel, stay for a few weeks upon the rich pasture of the Bald Mountains, and are driven down to the different mining creeks to be slaughtered at fifty cents. per lb. (two shillings). The meat is cheaper and more nutritious than salt bacon at six shillings a pound. Such was the market price in all the early part of the mining season in 1862; provisions (except beef) consisting mainly of bacon, beans, and flour, were six shillings a pound. No wonder men without rich paying claims (and the fortunate ones were few) broke down completely.

As I entered the *street* of Antler, I was hailed by a certain Mr. C——, whom I knew in Victoria, a publican and restaurant keeper, a man of not the most respectable character. He welcomed me, however, in a friendly way, expressing great astonishment at seeing me, and offering me quarters in his establishment, which proved to be the crack hotel of Antler City. I was thankful to find rest anywhere, for I was thoroughly beat. The house into which I was brought consisted of a large entrance-room, the bar-room, and lounge of customers, an inner apartment, which served as the eating-room, and up a ladder a great loft, guiltless of windows, which was the general sleeping-room for all comers. Behind, as a kind of lean-to, was a kitchen and two small rooms, used by Mr. and

Mrs. C——, and her mother and sister. I looked at the sleeping-loft for a corner on which to lay my blankets; but oh, it was dirty, and alive with worse things than fleas! Mr. C—— good-naturedly promised to let me sleep on the floor of the eating-room, which at least was clean, and told me that supper would be ready in a few minutes. I was nearly famished, and did full justice to Mrs. C——'s cookery, which for Cariboo was extremely fair—good bread, fresh beef-steaks, beans, dried apples, tea and coffee. After supper, I thought it well to make some inquiries about a place for holding service on the following day. On going outside the house to look for Mr. C——, to my astonishment and delight I saw Sheep-shanks entering the row of houses. He had found our horse, committed it to the care of a packer to come on the next day (it never did turn up), and then by a forced march had got in just before dark. His arrival that night was quite unlooked-for, and a source of unbounded satis-faction to me. Two men can do much more than one on such an occasion. After his wants had been attended to, we got hold of Mr. C——, and first of all tried to get his consent to having service in his bar-room, the largest and most convenient room in the place. But his good-nature did not extend so far as to forego trade for an hour on the best pay-day of the week. So we had to go and look about us, but that evening could find no place. Tired with our hard day's work, we were not sorry to unroll our blankets, and soon slept soundly on our bed of boards.

Breakfast over next morning, we still had to fix on a place for service. We looked into several stores, but could find no owner willing to aid us. At length a man said there was a capital new room alongside the Express office. We went, and as I stood outside the door I could hear the sound of many rough voices, and the "clink, clink" of money. I looked in. What a sight! what bold, hard, and in some instances ruffian faces! There were some

ɪ me
ɪt was
a few
ice to
emely
pples,
make
ɪ the
k for
heep-
l our
ɪe on
ɔreed
night
satis-
ɪe on
d to,
t his
; and
iture
ɪ the
look
ʔired
l our

.

ɔn a
ould
said

thirty round a table with a green cloth, on which lay twenty-dollar pieces, nuggets, gold dust, &c. It was a gambling saloon. "No," thought I, "Satan is master here, it is of no use making terms with him." Place after place we tried, but to no purpose. I was nearly giving it up in despair. At length we were told that nearly opposite Mr. C——'s a German had a liquor saloon with a room inside it which, perhaps, he would "loan" for the purpose. He was willing to do so, though he declined to stop his trade during service. The room was small: it could not hold more than forty people, or fifty with a cram. However, it was an only chance, and we were thankful for it. This being arranged, Sheepshanks started for a walk up and down the creek to give notice of service at eleven o'clock and seven o'clock P.M., while I set to work to try and extemporise some sitting accommodation. I was helped by a young fellow against whom I stumbled, a young watchmaker from Norfolk, whom I had known in Victoria, a regular member of my congregation, and a communicant. Him I at once appointed church-warden, sexton, and clerk, and with his aid got the room "fixed." Mr. C—— lent a small table for the parson, and a green cloth to put over it. To what unhallowed purposes, I wonder, was that green cloth put at other times! By-and-by Sheepshanks returned, having seen not a few whom he knew, some of whom thought they might "give us a look." About a quarter before eleven we rang the bell for church. I stood outside the door with Mr. C——'s triangle, making a horrible din and receiving a fire of chaff from all sides. Several promised to come in if we would "stand drinks" all round. All, however, were good-humoured enough. At length it was time to begin. Some forty persons assembled. We distributed among them printed cards, two to each: on one was the litany and selected prayers and collects, on the other, some thirty hymns. Thus each man had prayer-book and hymn-book, and was able to join in worship, which very many did. Sheepshanks said prayers, I preached from 1 Cor. i. 18. I stood just in the entrance-way to the outer bar-room, so that those who came in might hear.

Several, seeing what was going on, kept still, and listened attentively enough. Our notice had been rather short, so we looked for an improvement in the evening. After a midday meal we strolled down the creek, telling all whom we met of an evening service, pressing them to attend, and holding conversation with many, especially any of our own Victoria or New Westminster people we came across. A few well-disposed ones can do a great deal in a place like this, if a clergyman comes among the miners and they back up his efforts. Again, at a quarter to seven, we rang the church bell, and this time our presence being more generally known, we had more than twice the number of the morning. They filled up half the outer bar-room as well as the inner one. The singing led by me was most hearty. I said prayers, and Sheepshanks preached a most excellent sermon upon Felix and St. Paul. Several after service thanked us heartily, and said it was the first real Sunday they had had upon the creek. Sheepshanks was to remain here, so we bade them avail themselves regularly of his ministrations.

On the same day, another of our body was fifty miles to the westward on Lightning Creek, and the Bishop halfway between the two on Williams Creek; thus the three chief centres were all supplied. I was to proceed to Williams Creek as my post, the Bishop taking a turn at each successively.

At supper, there being present some dozen persons, we were waited upon mainly by Mrs. C——'s sister, a girl of about fifteen. She had been in my Sunday-school at Victoria, and it was painful to see how sadly this rough life had told upon her as regards manner and tone. She, her mother, and her sister (I except three women of in-famous character), were the only females in Antler Creek, amid a population of perhaps 1,000 men, and these many of them the roughest and most reckless characters. How could any young girl fail of receiving hurt in such an atmosphere? Sadly indeed do these gold countries need the elevating and sanctifying influences of family life. The families already there being too few to tell upon the surrounding mass for good, are too often themselves infected with evil. By everything he sees as he passes through mining districts, the conviction is forced upon the missionary that " it is not good for man to be alone."

CHAPTER IV.

A MINER'S FUNERAL.

THERE is no more healthy climate anywhere than that of
British Columbia and Vancouver Island. During the many
years I was in the colony I do not recollect any serious
instance of epidemic sickness, except a year of smallpox
among the Indians. Cariboo in the summer months, such
time at least as I knew it, was splendid. The nights were
never hot, and the air upon the mountains is the finest in
the world. The miners on Williams Creek worked at an
elevation of some 8,000 feet—about the height of Chamouni
—in a very favourable temperature. There was comparatively little sickness, except what arose in the earlier days
from want of proper food, especially fresh meat and vegetables. Rheumatism, arising from exposure to cold and
working in the wet, was the most common, and in weakly
constitutions the seeds of consumption were apt to be
developed. One, out of the two deaths which happened
on the creek while I was there, was from this cause. The
other case came from a drunken row in a liquor saloon.
A man was pitched violently out of the door down the
bank while intoxicated; he fell on his head and broke
the spinal cord. He only lived a few hours, insensible
the whole time. In poor E——'s case the Bishop visited
him regularly during his stay on the creek; I only occasionally, except for the two days after the Bishop left.
He did not survive longer. He was a native originally of
our own country, I think, but had been in Canada or the
United States most of his life. He lay in a miserable

hovel, waited on by his brother, who though a rude, yet proved himself an attentive nurse. The poor man had lived a careless enough life, and did not know much, but he expressed great contrition for mis-spent time. I spoke much to him of God's love, and was thankful to find his heart responded to the message. He said the strongest proof of it to his mind was that he was not left to die in that remotest and most inhospitable corner of the earth, without the consolation of the Gospel tidings of pardon and peace. He sank very rapidly at the last.

The afternoon of the day he died, some of his "mates" called on me to speak about his funeral. He had expressed a wish to be buried at "Maloney's Ranch," across the mountains on the upper part of Antler Creek. It was arranged that the interment should be next day. They thought that starting in the early morning by 7 o'clock they could get the coffin over by noon—eleven miles of stiff ascent and descent. Thinking that the Bishop, who had seen so much of him, might like to be present (the spot in question being only five miles from the mining settlement where he was then camped), I got a packer who was starting that afternoon to take a note, telling him the hour.

Next morning I called at the cabin where the poor man lay, and finding the cortége was not likely to start before 8 o'clock, I set off alone. I followed the ordinary pack-mule trail. The first few miles was a fearful ascent through the forest. I sank nearly to the knee sometimes in mud. Then I reached more open ground, and followed along the ridge above the valley, the division between Williams Creek and Grouse Creek. Another ascent for a mile or more over grassy slopes brought me to the highest part of the Bald Mountain that was crossed by the Williams and Antler Creek trail. Near this point was a rough cabin, inside some rough fencing, known as the "Milk Ranch." (In British Columbia, be it remembered,

every location or farm up country is spoken of as a
"ranch.") Here lived a man who, in the early part of
the season, drove a dozen cows into the Cariboo district.
They found abundance of feed on the bold summits and
ridges of these green mountains, and every morning their
enterprising owner took his milk down to the settlement
below, and vended it at three dollars (12s. 6d.) a gallon.
I had started without breakfast, and was glad now to
expend a dollar in the purchase of a pannikin of milk and
a lump of "damper." In the crisp bracing air of the
morning I thought it as delightful a meal as I had ever
tasted. I then ascended to a little knoll above the trail,
and sat down to enjoy the magnificent prospect. It was
shut off to the west and south by the higher parts of the
oblong mountain mass on which I was. To the north,
the eye ranged over a great chopping sea of forest-clad
mountains, with grassy summits and deep valleys that for
the most part trended away towards the northerly bend of
the great Fraser River. The grandest view was to the
east, distant some thirty or forty miles, high above the
lower ridges of the green Cariboo hills; from north to
south there ran a splendid range, with peaks thrown up
in every fantastic shape, many of them recalling to mind
the obelisk of the Matterhorn. They were streaked in
places with bands and wreaths of snow, but for the most
part they seemed too precipitous for the snow to rest upon
them. Between two of these peaks, but at a much greater
distance, probably some hundred miles, I could discern a
snowy mass, grander than any of them, which for a short
time puzzled me—till it flashed upon me that I was looking
full at the giant of the Rocky Mountains, Mount Hooker,
16,000 feet in height. The day was cloudless, and the
air was delightful: seldom have I looked upon a grander
scene.

After an hour's delay I proceeded across the mountain,
and then by another tremendous descent of mud, through

the forest, I reached the upper waters of Antler Creek.
On the trail, not far from Maloney's Ranch, I met the
Bishop and Sheepshanks. They were waiting for me, and
the Bishop explained the order of service he proposed.
He had brought with him his printed cards of hymns
which we used in our Mission services. Soon the funeral
train appeared in sight. The coffin had been borne by
relays ; there were some forty or fifty following it. We
headed the procession when it drew near the place of interment, and having first distributed hymn cards to the party,
we proceeded, singing the ninetieth Psalm, to the spot
where the grave was dug. It was on a grassy flat, up a
bank by which the trail ran, and some little way in the
rear of the settler's log house. Coming in sight of the
grave, the Bishop read the opening sentences. The friends
clustered round, the Bishop, Sheepshanks, and myself,
stood together at the head. I read the Lesson, the Bishop
taking the rest of the service, and after the prayers were
ended he made a short and seasonable address to those
assembled. Not a few were listening to a preacher for
the first time since their childhood ! All seemed impressed
with what, in that wild region, was a striking sight, and the
brother of the deceased stood forward and thanked the
Bishop heartily for his great kindness. The attendance of
so many of poor Emory's "mates" was a good instance
of the great sympathy and cordiality that exists even among
these rough men. Many of them were working for wages,
on others' claims—the rate at the time ten dollars (two
guineas) a day—but simply to show respect for one
whose only connection with them was that he had been a
comrade in distress, they were ready to forego a day's
work and pay, and take a rough fatiguing tramp in order
to do honour to his memory, and aid his brother in per-
forming his last wish.

The Bishop suggested that I should go on to Antler
Creek with him and Sheepshanks, and spend the evening,

in place of returning to my own tent on Williams Creek.
Glad of their society, I assented, and a smart walk of an
hour and a quarter brought us to the camp the Bishop
had formed some quarter of a mile from the settlement.
We enjoyed an open-air supper together, and after dark I
started with Sheepshanks to take up my night's quarters
in his "rectory." He had appropriated a deserted hut
about half-a-mile down the valley, where it narrowed
almost to a gorge, and the stream fell in a roaring cataract
over a steep ledge of rock. It stood alone; one other
cabin near him was the only sign of human abode. He
soon kindled a fire of pine logs on the mud floor, by which
we sat and chatted, and smoked our pipes; and in an
hour or so I was glad to roll myself in a spare blanket,
and stretch myself on a rude shelf or bunk of boards, soon
to fall asleep.

I returned to Williams Creek next morning. At
Maloney's Ranch I stopped for half-an-hour to rest and
get some food. I was joined at the table by a man who
would say little, but who ate voraciously. We had nearly
finished our unsociable meal of fried beef and coffee, when
an ill-looking rowdy bolted into the log hut, with a warning
cry of "Look out, boy!" Before the words were well
uttered, my silent friend made a spring at the door, shot
out, and springing up the bank, was soon hid in the forest.
Wondering at what it all meant, I proceeded to the door,
and saw coming along the trail, from Williams Creek, the
magistrate's head constable and another man; evidently
they "wanted" some one, and the object of their search
was my silent companion at dinner. It appeared that he
was a noted gambler; that the night before he had shot
and dangerously wounded a man on Williams Creek, and
that a warrant for his apprehension had been issued by
Mr. E——, the magistrate, in the early morning, but not
in time to prevent his escape from the creek. His chum
had kept watch on the constable's movements, and, starting

out in advance, had kept ahead to give warning, if he should sight his friend, that he was being followed. He was just in time. Had the constable been 100 yards nearer, his revolver would have been brought into play, and perhaps answered by Hill's, for he was armed for resistance. However, he got clean off and out of the country, and, as the man whom he shot recovered, perhaps the country was cheaply rid of the notorious gambler and ruffian. It formed a staple of jest afterwards on Williams Creek, that the parson was found in close and familiar intercourse with a man flying from justice—an attempted murderer. "Noscitur a sociis" is a good rule. Let us hope it has its exceptions.

CHAPTER V.

LIFE ON A MINING CREEK.[*]

August 11*th.*—An express came over to-day from Antler Creek, with letters and papers for the magistrate. The Government profess to have established a regular mail service this season between the lower country and Cariboo; that is to say, they have given an express man several thousand dollars to convey letters from New Westminster to Antler Creek, at the rate of one dollar per letter! They forgot, however, to include Williams Creek in the contract, and so the contractor charges half-a-dollar more for the sixteen miles between this and Antler—six shillings a letter, not including the extra colonial postage! Last year one of our brethren had to pay ten shillings a letter for some which were carelessly sent up country to him contrary to his instructions.

I walked a mile or two down the creek this afternoon, notifying to miners the fact of there being Sunday services. Returning again to the "town," as I passed a drinking saloon I was told that a man lay badly hurt in a back room. I asked if I could see him. He had been engaged in a drunken row the night before, and, falling out of the door in a state of intoxication, he was rolled over the plank side-walks, with others at the top of him, and received fatal injury. They think the spine is dislocated. He was paralysed and unconscious. Shortly afterwards he died. I was afraid they would ask me to bury him.

[*] The incidents contained in the accompanying paper are chiefly notes taken from the writer's private journal for 1862.

However, as he was professedly a Romanist, some of his own creed took the matter in hand without application to me.

August 12th.—There is no flour to be had; the supply is exhausted. A man has been offering 10s. a pound for it, but cannot get any even at that price. We are told there is none at Antler Creek either. When plentiful, it has been selling for 4s. to 4s. 6d. per pound, other provisions in proportion, beans and bacon. Beef fresh slaughtered is the cheapest food; this can be had for about 3s. per pound, and sometimes as low as 2s. A half-pound loaf, just such a small twist as an English baker sells for a penny or twopence, costs me a dollar. A box of matches, 2s. It is easy to understand how men get "broke" with such prices as these. And it is also easy to see at how heavy a cost the Church's Missions are sustained in mining districts imperfectly opened up.

Coming out of the principal restaurant, my eye caught an announcement which at first puzzled me. It was a notice, over the bar, to the effect that jawbone was played out. In mining parlance, a thing or a person is "played out" when good-for-nothing men are used up, &c. But "jawbone," what did that signify? It appeared that when a man had no money, and went about living on credit, and putting off with promises to "pay next week," or with assurances that he was certain to "strike it rich" in a mining claim in a few days, he was said to be living by jawbone, *i.e.*, by a free exercise of that portion of his physiological structure. The notice, therefore, done into Queen's English, was simply an announcement of no credit given.

Sunday, August 17th.—There was a considerable falling off to-day in the attendance at service, morning and afternoon. Some pack trains came in, and all was bustle and excitement.

P

The order of service we use (printed on cards, which are distributed) is as follows :—

1. A hymn is sung. (These, some thirty in number, are on another card.)

2. A short address from the clergyman, explaining the nature of Common Prayer and worship, and the duty of the people in bearing their parts.

3. General Confession ; prayer, "O Lord, we beseech Thee," from the Communion Service ; Lord's Prayer ; and Versicles.

4. Venite, and Psalm ciii.

5. A lesson from Old or New Testament.

6. Various collects and prayers from the Morning and Evening Service.

7. Special prayers, compiled by the Bishop for use in mission and mining districts.

8. Prayer for all conditions of men ; General Thanksgiving ; Prayer of St. Chrysostom ; and Benediction.

9. A hymn.

10. The sermon.

11. A hymn.

This is our usual morning service. The afternoon (printed on a third card) consists of the Litany, other selected or compiled prayers, with a lesson, hymns, and sermon. It will be seen that the service is varied, the breaks are frequent, and we endeavour to confine it to an hour, if possible. Very often I find it impossible to have the closing hymn. My voice is all used up, and of course we have to lead, sometimes wholly to sustain the singing. The plan of service and hymn cards is a most useful one, and might be adopted with success, I think, in mission services at home. Here they are absolutely necessary, as often there are not three Prayer-books to be found amongst hundreds of men. As an American told the Bishop one day after service, they are "a great institooshun."

A very great deal of unnecessary work is done on the claims upon Sundays, though, as a rule, the miner observes it, so far as striking off work is concerned, for his own interest. He rests, washes his clothes, divides with his mates the yield of the week, does his marketing at the stores, and hangs about the gambling and liquor saloons. The drunkenness on a Sunday is appalling.

Sunday, August 24th.—To-day I changed the place of service, and also the hour of the second service, from afternoon to evening. The store we formerly used was let last week, and is now full of goods. I tried in vain in several quarters for a place under cover, and at last was driven to choose the open air. I took up my position on the planked footway just outside the bar of the principal eating saloon. A tub hauled out and inverted served for my pulpit. I borrowed the eating-house triangle, and stood beating it for some ten minutes by the door, as a call to church. Then I mounted my extemporised pulpit, and began service for some twelve persons who had boldly seated themselves before me on a bench. As usual we began with a hymn, and the singing quickly attracted others. Before it was ended I had some forty persons round me. They came out in numbers from the adjoining doorway, the principal gambling-hell on the creek, which was always crowded on on Sundays. Seeing that my congregation consisted of *hearers* far more than *worshippers*, I inverted the usual order of service, and proceeded to read a chapter, from which I preached at great length. I am bound to say I had a very attentive congregation. On such an occasion, however, preaching seemed more fitly to precede worship, and though many moved away when, after my sermon, I knelt down and offered up the Church's beautiful prayers, yet some thirty remained to the close, not, I trust, without profit to themselves. The strain to the voice of this open-air service, with singing, is, however, very great, and I never could get through more than two such in the same

day, with difficulty even so much. In the evening the
proprietors of the restaurant let me use the bar-room,
and took some trouble to help me extemporise plank seats.
I got some sixty persons together, and standing myself
just in the open doorway, I had a supplementary congregation of many more upon the plank pathway outside.

Both services were an immense improvement upon those
of the former Sunday, and I rejoiced that necessity had
driven me from the store we previously occupied.

Thursday, August 28th.—A great part of the magistrate's
time is occupied daily in trying mining suits. These may
be brought before him any day, after twenty-four hours'
notice, except when he has given previous notice of a
criminal court. The laws which regulate the proceedings
of free miners are simple enough on the whole, and, save
in exceptional cases, suits call out the exercise of common
sense rather than any extended knowledge of law. Mr.
E——, in fact, is no lawyer at all, and yet is considered
an excellent magistrate and gold commissioner.

We may stroll in and listen to a case, a sample of the
ordinary suits that come before the magistrate. It is a
dispute between two companies on the creek respecting
water privilege. Company A, requiring extra water for
washing up the "pay-dirt," had brought in last year a
small run of water from a gulch or ravine that comes
down behind my tent and the court-house. They had
constructed a ditch and built a high flume spanning the
valley, at a cost of some four thousand dollars. To
enable them to do all this, they had proved before the
magistrate that by bringing this ditch and lead of water to
their "claim," they would injure no one possessing a prior
right to the water. Thus they had obtained the sanction
of Mr. E——'s predecessor, and, on completion of their
costly work, they had "recorded" their claim to the
water, which record, by mining law, became their title-
deed. Company B lately took up ground in the ravine,

just below the spot whence the ditch was led off, and, needing more water, they quietly broke down the dam, on the plea that the waters of that stream could not be diverted from its proper channel to the detriment of the miners below. Company B were plaintiffs, Company A defendants in the suit. Company A produced their title, formerly recorded. The gold commissioner called upon Company B to prove that they had occupied their claims before the ditch was made, the water diverted, and the title granted to A. B thereupon asserted a prior claim. They had worked the ground last year, and when the ditch water was drawn off had protested, and Commissioner N—— (Mr. E——'s predecessor) had shown gross partiality, and refused to entertain their protest. So, for want of water, they had been forced to abandon their " claim," but they had now determined to go in and contest it again before Mr. E——, " whom they knew to be a gentleman," &c. &c. All this looked rather " fishy " for Company B, the attempt to blacken the character of Mr. N——, and then to curry favour with Mr. E—— at his predecessor's expense. However, Company A proceeded to argue that, admitting Company B had had any prior claim (which they disbelieved), they had forfeited it by leaving their ground for an entire season, whereas the law only allows " a claim " to be unoccupied for seventy-two hours. To this B pleaded that they had been forced to leave the ground, and could obtain no redress from the then gold commissioner; that this, therefore, was not such a voluntary abandonment as the law supposed to bar a mining company's right. Here the magistrate put in a question to Company B. " When you sued before Mr. N——, of course you held Government licences as free miners ?" To this an evasive answer was returned, and a reference to the roll of licensed miners for the previous year did not show their names to have been upon it. This of course ended the suit. Mr. N—— in the previous

year could not have entertained any suit or protest of
Company B, as the law declares that without a licence,
renewed each year, no man can hold or work a claim,
enter a suit, or enjoy any mining privilege whatsoever.
So Company B were ignominiously put out of court, and
Company A continued in possession of their ditch.

Sunday, August 31st.—Service, as on previous Sundays,
in the open air in front of the restaurant at 10 A.M., and
again at 7 P.M. in the bar-room. Crowded attendance,
especially in the evening. The singing to-day was excellent, thanks to two splendid bass voices, the best in the
colony, those of Mr. Begbie, the Chief Justice of B. C.,
and Mr. Mathew, his registrar, who had arrived during the
preceding week on circuit. They are frequent helpers of my
choir at St. John's, in Victoria, during the winter months.

My evening sermon was from 1 Cor. vi. 19, 20. After
a few explanatory remarks on the illustration the Apostle
uses here, and the idea of a *Temple*, I went on to speak of
the heinousness of sin in redeemed, baptized, professing
Christians—how it is sin against our redeemed nature—a
nature which is raised and ennobled by being worn by
God the Son, and dwelt in by God the Holy Ghost. I
urged the great practical lesson to be carried out by all of
us, as redeemed at such a cost, the lesson of the text,
" Glorify God in your *body* and in your *spirit*," dwelling
on the nature of practical religion, as being just this living
to God's glory, whatever our calling or business might be.

Several friends came round me after service to say good-
bye, as I had announced my departure next morning, and
my hope that Sheepshanks, who was remaining a few
weeks longer, would come over from Antler Creek on
alternate Sundays to hold service.

I was to start early next morning across the mountains
to Lightning Creek, where I should find the Bishop, to
travel down country with him. I made up my pack over
night and gave it to a man who was to start at 2 A.M. ;

my own departure I postponed till the more timely hour of 6 A.M. I had to borrow a blanket for the night, and slept for the last time in my corner on the floor of the court-house. The building was a plain rough shell of split logs, some 25 ft. by 15 ft. with a small room built on at one end, which was Mr. Elwyn's office, sitting-room, bedroom, and kitchen, and in which slept, besides himself, his clerk, two constables, and a friend who was mining ! We formed a curious company that night on the floor of the big room. In one corner lay Charles Hankin and my-self under a pair of blankets, with our coats rolled round our boots for pillows. In another corner lay Mr. Elwyn's man-of-all work ; near him Mr. Bogbie's Indian boy. On the side of the room opposite me lay together Mr. O'Reilly (magistrate and gold commissioner on Lightning Creek and high sheriff of the colony) and Lieutenant Palmer, R.E. ; in a corner near them a constable and a manacled prisoner ! He had been arrested and brought up about eight o'clock for drawing a revolver and firing at a man in a drinking-saloon. They chained him to the tall flagstaff outside the door at first, this being the ordinary jail ! But about midnight it began to rain, and he made such a row that, in self-defence, we were glad to allow him to come under our shelter in the court-room, which made him quiet. Such was my last night on Williams Creek.

In bidding farewell to Cariboo, I could not but feel that a clergyman must submit to a great deal of forced inac-tivity in these young mining districts, so far as regards ministerial or missionary work. In fact he is able to do little more than hold his Sunday services, and visit the sick where there are any. Often I used to feel, between Sunday and Sunday, that I might as well be 500 or 600 miles away, at my own regular post. Week-day services it was very difficult to hold. Directly the men were off work they had their suppers to prepare, and found them-selves fit only to turn in and sleep after the meal was over.

And while they were at work during the day they did not much care to have a parson interrupting them. For days together I would rove up and down the Creek for two or three miles, as far as "claims" were "located," trying to effect something in the way of pastoral and religious conversation with the rough gangs dotted along the little stream. Occasionally I might succeed; but still the general feeling was, "I have not done much to-day." But yet, in an indirect way, I cannot but believe more was done than I could measure or estimate. The very presence, in the three principal mining districts, of three clergymen and their Bishop, was a testimony borne to higher truth, and could not be without some effect on the complex mass of beings. Our mingling, as we did, with miners of all sorts tended much to disabuse their minds of prejudice against the Church of England and ministers of religion. Sometimes, at least, we were able, during our daily wanderings up and down the creeks, or as we sat in the evening by a miner's fire outside his tent, to speak " a word in season to him that is weary;" and how many such are to be found in that strange region! Sometimes we have been able to touch deep springs of feeling by allusions to *home* and *parents*, when the heart seemed callous to other influences. No; I believe that our work, small as it might seem to people at a distance, was not unimportant or superfluous, or wasted. It was the work of preparation for others to build upon; of breaking up ground where others might plant seed. Above all, it was work for Him with Whom nothing is lost, not even the poor fragments which others who are richly blessed with privileges might have thought valueless. I believe that in it all our good Bishop's prayer was simply this—" Show Thy servants Thy work, and their children Thy glory." He sowed in faith in this journey with his clergy, and I cannot think the seed scattered by these trails and way-sides will bear no fruit in days to come.

CHAPTER VI.

JOURNEY BACK FROM THE MINES, 1862.

AT the mining town of Lilloet, the consecration of the new church had been fixed for Sunday, the 14th of September. We calculated that a fortnight would suffice for our journey down country, and accordingly on Monday, the 1st, the Bishop and I were to start, leaving Sheepshanks and Knipe to carry on the work for a few weeks longer on the principal Cariboo Creeks. As it happened, we did not get away from Lightning Creek until the Tuesday; the Bishop's horses strayed, and the packer did not get them in till daylight on the Tuesday morning. The magistrate, Mr. O'R——, and Knipe were waiting to see us start from camp about ten o'clock. Our train was reduced from ten horses to six, there being comparatively little in the way of provisions to carry down country. On my way up some three months before, in company with Sheepshanks, I had gone along painfully and ingloriously on foot. I felt now the dignity, and still more the comfort, of a "horseback ride," and held my head high as we started from the little mining town of Lightning or Van Winkle. "You came up like a pauper, but you go down like a king," was my reverend brother's comment as we parted. Before many minutes I "went down," whether most like a pauper or king I cannot say—but there is no royal method of tumbling in this country. Every one looks like a pauper whose horse rolls with him, as mine did, into a liquid bath of Cariboo mud, and so, at the outset, I learned that riding, like everything else, may prove dear in this country.

Our road for the whole day was down the valley of the
Lightning Creek, through forest and swamp, trying to man
and beast alike.   At night we camped by the side of the
trail, in a small clearing, hearing that below, near the
river, there was coarse grass for our animals.   Three or
four young men, camping near, came up to our tents.
One of them was a young Englishman, newly arrived in
the country.   He come from Great Yarmouth.   It was the
old story.   He had come out with one idea, viz., gold
mining—the most uncertain, the most costly, the least
satisfactory, *as a rule*, of colonial pursuits.   He and his
chums had been at it during the summer season on
Lightning—made nothing, and spent all their little stock
of cash.   I gave him all I could, which was—advice.
They gladly joined us at our little evening service, held
by the camp fire under the shade of the great pine-trees.

September 3rd.—I was pleased with the appearance of
Cottonwood, which settlement we came to about midday.
The situation is very well chosen, just at the confluence of
the Lightning and Cottonwood rivers, which eventually reach
the Fraser.   There are great tracts of beautiful grassy
plains and meadows, and plenty of hard-wood trees—a
relief to the eye that has grown weary of the monotonous
pine forest.   As yet there are few houses, the land where
a town would naturally stand having been pre-empted by
one Yankee settler.   Lieutenant Palmer, R.E., during his
summer surveys through this region, has marked the spot
as a suitable one for a town site, and probably, therefore,
the settler's pre-emption claim will not be allowed, and a
town will spring up which will be a point of depôt and
supply for a large mining district more into the mountains.
Thus it is that fresh centres of population are continually
forming themselves, and as yet all we can do is to make
an occasional visit in these missionary towns, and gather
as many as we can for worship and teaching.   A resident
missionary in each such locality is a hopeless expectation ;

he would find, for a long time, little support in his district; and no home fund could supply the number that would thus be needed.

While the Bishop was buying some beef and potatoes, for which he probably paid gold, I rode on a few hundred yards, over beautiful natural lawn, to a small wigwam of posts and bark, lightly put together, standing within a roughly enclosed paddock. Chief Justice Begbie had described to me, before I left Williams Creek, the position of his newly pre-empted estate, and magnificent residence at Cottonwood. This seemed to answer the description. It was a decidedly judicial abode. I suppose he had no fear of dishonest visitors during his absence on circuit through the mines, for the door stood open. There was not much to take—a wooden table and stools, and two sleeping shelves or bunks, formed the entire furnishing of the one-roomed domicile, and law books were scattered about in various corners.

We had to camp again in the forest, a most weird, dismal spot. Fires had swept through and destroyed everything. There was no feed of any kind. Before us was an unhealthy swamp, and except in the swamp there was no water. Our animals tried to eat the swamp grass round the edges; but, getting engulfed nearly up to their bellies, they gave it up; nor did we encourage them to try, for we could see the decayed remains of various mules and horses, to which, incautiously venturing in, the morass had proved a grave. So the horses had to go pretty well supperless, and we had to forego our " wash," a privation which none can fully estimate who are not on the tramp as we were.

September 7th.—The Bishop and I reached Williams Lake late yesterday afternoon, after a hard ride of forty-one miles from our camp, three miles beyond Alexandria. We had to leave our man and the packers with four horses to come on alone part of the way, and make a

Sabbath day's journey this forenoon of some fifteen miles, in order to join us here. They could not have come the whole distance, and we could not well stop short of this place, there being no settlement between Alexandria and Williams Lake at which we could have spent our Sunday: while this is one of the principal centres of population in the upper country. We could not afford to miss the Sunday here, at the same time we were unwilling to encourage, by an example, the usual custom with traders and packers of Sunday travelling. But there seemed no help for it as regarded our men. They must have joined us to-day to start to-morrow, as it will be all we can manage to reach Lilloet by Saturday next, leaving early to-morrow.

The "Government house," as usual, was our hotel, on getting in tired and hungry; and no praise is too great for the *cuisine* at Woodward's restaurant — about the only thing one *can* praise, for the proprietors are worldly men and gamblers. However, we got a good supper, made arrangements for holding service on the following day, and returned to our quarters for the night, where we found some copies of the *Times*—a rare sight in the interior of British Columbia. They were several months old, but contained *news* to us. Taking up the latest, the first thing my eye lit upon was the notice of dear Charles Mackenzie's death in Central Africa. So soon! and yet not too soon for one whose faith had borne him to the end of the course appointed for him. Men will say it was a "waste of life." So Calvary and its sacrifice must have seemed to some!

A great staring placard announces "races" to come off here on "the Mission Racecourse," two weeks hence. (Williams Lake was till not many years back one of the principal Roman Catholic Missions for Indians.) Of course the object is to get up a grand saturnalia, and put money in the pockets of the restaurant proprietors. The first proof of the notice appeared, about nine or ten o'clock, in the shape of a large party of professional gamblers, rowdies, &c., from higher up the country, who came to "make arrangements" for the forthcoming meeting. In a short time Woodward's establishment was a perfect Pandemonium. On my going there to make preparations for service, one of the three proprietors came to me and advised that we should "quit preaching" to-day, there were so many "loafers" and drunken men about, that we should certainly be interrupted, perhaps insulted. I said I was quite sure the Bishop would not consent to forego the service. We had ridden over forty miles the day before, simply to spend the Sunday here, where there were plenty of people to whom a chance of joining in worship and of hearing God's message was rarely offered ; that for ourselves we could stand the risk of interruption, which, in fact, I did not believe in. But the man was obstinate. He raised objection after objection, and I saw clearly enough his sole object was to prevent the service—partly because its being held in or outside his house would to a certain extent interfere with what promised to be a paying morning for business, and partly because he did not wish to be identified too closely with parsons or their doings. At length I asked him plainly, "Will you help us, or will you not?" and I offered to be satisfied with simply the loan of his benches to sit upon the ground for open-air service in the front of his establishment. But even this he refused. So I told him that never yet, from end to end of British Columbia, had a clergyman been compelled to forego service on Sunday for fear of inter- ruption—not even among the gambling saloons of Cariboo ; and that I should take care his refusal was known as the one refusal we had met with. He expressed himself very sorry he should have to refuse, which I told him plainly I did not believe a word of.

The Bishop, on my return to the house, was greatly

annoyed; but there was no help for it. We held our
service at another house, in an inconvenient place, and
had for congregation five persons, to whom the Bishop
preached. Last time I held service at Williams Lake we
had not less than seventy at each, morning and evening.
Our afternoon service was held on the grass, close to the
Government building, when we got about ten, including
our two men, who arrived with the horses at midday.

Rarely has it happened in my experience to be refused
in British Columbia, as we were to-day. Even the wildest
and roughest are generally willing to hear what the preacher
has to say. To-day there could not have been less than
from 100 to 140 men stopping at or about Woodward's
house on their way up or down country.

Saturday, September 13th.—We reached Lillooet this
afternoon, after a glorious week of weather, and a very
enjoyable journey from Williams. After the first day or
so, the country we passed through was entirely new to
me, as it was to the Bishop also. He had travelled up
country to the east of our route; I had come to the west
of it. We travelled for the most part over stretches of
grassy plain land, studded with beautiful lakes, and belted
with forest. To the west, about thirty miles, were the
mountains which shut in the Fraser River Valley, while
to the east all seemed level, alternately plain and wood.
It seemed only to need farmers to make it a great grain-
producing country for Cariboo. So I thought, till the
Bishop ascertained the altitude of these plains along
which he travelled to be some 2,000 feet, while sharp
frost at night, after the balmy sunshine of the day—frosts
which are not uncommon here, I believe, in July—boded
no good assurance for the farmer. We, however, enjoyed
our journey immensely. The great plague of British
Columbia in the summer months, the insect plague,
troubled us not; the cold nights were too much for them.
Our packer had a gun, and not a day passed that he did

not secure a brace or two of duck and grouse, so that our camp kettles in the evening were well supplied. This route, however, the shortest and easiest to Lilloet, carried us by no settlements for the greater part of the way, so that we were unable to minister to the spiritual necessities of our brethren scattered through these remote regions.

One evening my life was for a few moments in jeopardy. We had made our camp on the edge of a fine prairie, near a stream of water, which was almost hidden by the thick shrubs that lined its banks. After putting my tent to rights, I started to have a good wash while supper was preparing. The Bishop had preceded me and was in the water, when I came upon him unawares, and without his having perceived me, I beat a retreat through the thick bush, and struck the stream about fifty yards lower down. I was quickly in the water splashing about. In a few minutes I heard the Bishop calling loudly to the men at the camp fire, " King, where's the gun? Load it; make haste!" and then I could hear King working away and ramming down his charge of buckshot and old nails. An idea occurred to me, and I thought it well to call out to the Bishop, who was hidden by a bend in the stream, "What do you see?" "Oh, is that you? I thought you were a bear!" was the assuring answer. It was well I spoke in time, or there might have been cold missionary for supper. I fancy my excellent diocesan rather enjoyed the joke afterwards, though I doubted if it would popularise the mission in England were it to be known that the clergy were apt to be bagged by their Bishop as game.

The last two days we had again to part from our animals and kits, and ride on alone, in order to reach Lilloet. We did not get there till late this afternoon, and found that Mr. Brown, the resident clergyman, had given us up in despair. He was greatly relieved at seeing us, and for the rest of the evening we were occupied in various preliminary arrangements, and making out papers.

September 14th.—Consecration of St. Mary's Church. The work here, as in all other mining towns and districts, is simply the work of pioneering; but Mr. Brown, amidst evil report and good report, has proved a most devoted pioneer; and while he has faithfully borne the Church's testimony to her Master to them that will not receive it, he can also show some real work of outward Church extension, which can hardly fail of proving a means of real spiritual grace to those who will use it, of whom there are some at least even in this wild district. The new church is about completed. There only needs some finishing work. It stands at one end of the settlement, on a plot of its own. It will hold about 150 persons. His own rectory (?), a log cabin, of one room, stands in the centre of the village. Its situation for business is good, and two men have accordingly offered to build a proper parsonage, after approved plans, upon the church lot, in exchange for the cabin and lot on which it stands—an offer which the Bishop has accepted. So, before another summer, Brown will be more comfortably lodged, and the gain to the Church property will be considerable.

Morning service was at eleven o'clock. The Bishop, with his chaplain (myself), was met at the entrance by the Rev. R. L. Brown, Mr. E——, the resident magistrate, and gold commissioner for Lilloet district, and one or two other chief traders in the place, who presented the petition, praying him to consecrate. This was read by the chaplain; and the Bishop, having signified his assent, proceeded to the east end, attended by the clergy, saying the appointed psalm. The preliminary forms were gone through, and the service continued. Brown said prayers, I read the lessons, the Bishop preached an earnest, loving sermon, and administered the Holy Communion to five persons, besides the clergy—a small beginning. The church was well filled, and the singing, helped by Mrs. E——'s harmonium and voice, extremely creditable.

Evening service was at seven o'clock. Again the church was quite full. Brown said the prayers, the Bishop read the lesson, and I preached from Matt. viii. 34. The offertory for the day amounted to over 100 dollars. The church, at Brown's especial desire, is dedicated to St. Mary. One would not willingly offend any reasonable scruples in a Christian brother, least of all in a land and a place where even professing Christians are but few. Still, it was a very unreasonable scruple that took exception to the name, as savouring of superstition. The objection, however, was never pressed. It was discovered by the people of the place, perhaps by the objector himself, that the church was so called in honour of the excellent magistrate's wife, whose name was Mary, and she being extremely popular, as the only English lady in the place, they "concluded" it would do very well!

The prospects of Lilloet have greatly improved this year. The place has not grown much, but what there is has improved in appearance. Buildings are becoming more substantial; trade is looking up. It was quite necessary, if the Church's work was to be done, that a church should be built. Of course there is, and must be in such cases, a great risk. No one can say that trade will continue here, that travel will go by this route, that population will remain. Two years hence the place may have "gone in," and houses be left to fall to ruin—the church included. Well, these are parts of the trials of faith which a man in the Bishop's position must be prepared to encounter. There must, in the early years of the work in such countries, be a certain proportion of loss, in hard cash, money expended and *sunk* in places which at last "go in" when all reasonable anticipations pointed the other way. That mistakes will never be made by our excellent chief pastor, I shall not pretend to assert. Even

Q

our far-seeing Governor, in matters of colonial expenditure
which brought no return, has made mistakes.   That the
Bishop makes fewer mistakes than almost any other man
would do in his position will, I think, be allowed readily
by all who have had the high privilege of working under
that most self-denying and unwearied servant of his
Master.

Monday, September 22nd.—We arrived to-day at Yale,
the head of navigation on Fraser River.   We had expected
to reach it on Saturday in time to share Mr. Reeve's
duties, but Saturday forenoon only found us entering the
great Cañon of the Fraser, below Boston Bar ; and coming
upon the gangs of men who were making the new waggon
road from Yale to Lytton, we determined to remain among
them for Sunday services.   The work in question is being
carried out by the brothers T——, two of our best colonial
Churchmen.   The elder is one of Mr. Cridge's churchwardens at Christ Church, in Victoria ; the younger is one
of my church committee at St. John's.   We camped by
their huts near Chapman's Bar, amidst the magnificent
scenery of this great gorge, which extends for some sixteen
miles or more.

Two unexpected arrivals took place just after we got to
our quarters.   Mrs. T—— arrived at her husband's camp
with Mrs. C——, the wife of the Attorney-General.   They
had come up 120 miles from New Westminster to see the
new road through the mountains, and of course brought
us all the latest Victoria and home news.   Amongst other
things we heard of the arrival of the Tynemouth steamer
from England, with forty young women on board, con-
signed to the Bishop.   Let us hope that, as domestic
servants, they may form a valuable and useful addition to
the female population of the colony.   There is room for
hundreds, and, if respectable and industrious, they cannot
fail to get along well.   All, we learned from Mrs. T——,
had got places, a committee of Churchmen having been

formed under Mr. Cridge, the Rector of Christ Church. The wages given were from fifteen to thirty dollars a-month! This for girls, who in England would have had factory wages of a few shillings a-week!

We held forenoon service in the open air at our camp yesterday, having got together all who would attend from the gangs of workers within reach. The ladies helped out our singing, and the Bishop preached a most appropriate sermon from Isaiah xl. 3, 4, 5. The scene gave a wondrous reality to the words. In the afternoon we had another service at the tents of the nearest road party, with a fair attendance, though many, mistaking the hour fixed, had gone up the pass, and came back just in time to be too late. A pleasant ride of nineteen miles down the valley, and through the Lesser Cañon, brought us to-day to Yale. Mr. Pringle came up in a canoe from Hope and spent the night.

September 23rd.—Towards evening I got my traps together, and started in a canoe with Pringle to go down sixteen miles to Hope, leaving the Bishop to follow to-morrow with Mrs. T—— and Mrs. C——, who were glad to avail themselves of our escort again down the river. We passed the dreaded "Emay's Bar" (only to be dreaded in the high stage of the water at "freshets"), and reached our destination in an hour and a-half. It took Pringle seven hours yesterday to come up. I found the place materially changed for the worse since I was here a year ago. The people have almost all deserted it. It is a town of shut-up stores and houses going to ruin. There are not thirty people in it. Yet here we have an active, zealous clergyman, and the prettiest church in the colony out of New Westminster. The Bishop, too, owns a considerable amount of land in and near the town, bought for purposes of diocesan endowment. Three years ago no town promised better throughout the colony than this. The Governor had faith in it; the Chief Justice and Chief Commissioner of Lands and Works had faith in it; and the Bishop was considered very fortunate in making the investments he did. It may yet become an important place, as the depôt and starting-place for the whole of the country eastward, through the Similkomeen and Rock Creek districts, on towards the Kootaine River and passes of the Rocky Mountains. In all these western countries towns repeatedly " go ahead" for a time, then " cave in" for some years, and perhaps end by becoming important places; and such may be the future of Hope, whose situation, for beauty and for other advantages of position and surroundings, is unrivalled. But meantime it has ceased to be a fitting post for a clergyman, and that Mr. Pringle feels most keenly. It is an instance of the difficulty the Bishop finds in determining what shall be mere temporary mission posts, and what shall be constituted regular parishes with consecrated churches.

We remained here for some days waiting for a steamer from below, and reached New Westminster on the Saturday. Here we spent the Sunday, the Bishop at the Archdeacon's house, and I in the hospitable quarters of the R. E. camp. We returned to Victoria the following week. I found that my one-roomed shanty, which had been the rectory house of St. John's for some three years, had been added to and improved by certain members of the congregation. They had built on a small kitchen, plastered the domicile inside, built a fireplace and a chimney, put in a grate, and built a porch to the door. It looked quite grand.

So ended our Cariboo Mission tour for 1862.

CHAPTER VII.

TWO YEARS AMONGST THE INDIANS OF QUEEN CHARLOTTE'S
ISLAND.

Turning my back upon many sincere friends in Canada, I
hastened to catch the first steamer from New York to
Aspinwall, not without considerable difficulty, owing to the
great rush of gold-hunters for Cariboo. I secured a berth
by paying a premium. The steamer was an old one,
of about 1,500 tons register, and carried over 2,000
passengers. Under British laws, I may mention, such a
steamer would not have been allowed to carry more than
800. With this great crowd on board we obtained very
slight comfort or accommodation; huddled together for
eight days and twenty hours, we at last reached Aspinwall
(2,838 miles).

Glad we were indeed to get on shore for a few hours.
At Aspinwall we had now to pass over to the Pacific by
crossing the isthmus to Panama by railway, a distance of
about forty-seven miles. When this railway was constructed some years ago, ague and other fevers raged
terribly; it is reported that every yard of rail laid was at
the cost or sacrifice of a human being; even now the
bones of the victims may be seen jutting out from under
the railway sleepers and bleaching in the sun. Fortunately
for travellers, in the present day those malignant fevers are
in a manner unknown, or have wholly ceased. It is well
it is so, for this is the most delightful and interesting part
of the whole voyage.

The chief characteristic which a stranger observes on

landing here is the deep green foliage of the cocoanut-tree and palm. Pine-apples were selling at ninepence each, such beauties! All the tavern or storekeepers have monkeys at their doors. Turkey-buzzards are as common here as crows are in Britain. A good supply of delicious fruit is always to be had from the natives in this wonderful vegetable kingdom, where at every stoppage of the train the women and children crowd into the carriages, crying, "Bananas, my dear? Oranges or pine-apples, my dear?" &c.

What a wonderful contrast is here presented to the eye of a stranger from more northern latitudes—every point of the compass discloses magnificent vistas of leaf, bough, and blossom, while all outline of landscape is lost under a perfect deluge of vegetation. No trace of the soil is to be seen. Lowland and highland are the same. Mountain rises upon mountain in graceful majesty, covered to their very crests with every variety of vegetation and floral beauty. The loveliness of Nature here is indescribable ; she seems decked out in her richest and most costly garb to welcome the adventurous pioneer to that Eden of the world and the Eldorado beyond. You simply gaze upon the scene before you with delight.

I would strongly recommend all those who are lovers of matchless scenery and fond of botanical research, to spend a few weeks in the vicinity of the railway which crosses the Isthmus of Panama, and divides the Pacific from the Atlantic. Here all the gorgeous growths of an eternal summer are mingled in one impenetrable mass, whilst from the rank jungle of canes and gigantic lilies, and the thickets of strange shrubs that line the water, rise the trunks of the mango, the cocoa, the sycamore, and the superb palm.

Arriving at Panama, we went immediately on board the steamer's tender, and were conveyed out to the California steamer, anchored about two miles from the

shore in the Bay of Panama. She was a magnificent-
four-decker, and American built, with much less crowding
on board, though we had 200 more passengers *direct* from
Britain, by West Indian steamer, which is *much the best
route* from Europe.

We kept close in towards the Mexican shore, stopping
only once (at Acapulco) before we entered the " Golden
Gate," which protects the harbour of San Francisco.
This being the end of the second steamer's voyage
(thirteen days and eighteen hours), all the passengers
landed to re-ship by another steamer for Vancouver Island.
We had a very pleasant passage from Panama to San
Francisco, there being only one thing that I regretted
much, namely, the want of Divine service, especially on
Sundays, on board ship, such not being the custom under
the American flag.   However, a few Canadians and myself
took possession of the bow of the steamer, and here we
joined in reading and singing Psalms morning and evening
during each Sunday.   There was a great difference in the
social habits and national characteristics of the passengers,
many of whom, like myself, were in the pursuit of health
or the acquisition of knowledge ; but the majority of them
were braving the dangers of the deep and enduring the
privations of the passage for the sole purpose of amassing
wealth at the gold-fields of California or British Columbia.
A large majority intending for the latter place were
Canadians (with the exception of the 200 before mentioned) ; and a more steady, hard-working looking set of
men I have never seen together in such numbers.   They
were all Protestants, and spent much of their leisure time
on board in reading religious books and in singing sacred
music.

Those Canadians are the very class of men wanted in
such a country as British Columbia, and who are certain
to prosper there ; in fact, I have good reason to know that
nearly all those Canadians have since secured good

*

positions, while a few of them have amassed large fortunes. The contrast, I may say, between the Americans and Canadians on board ship was very striking ; the former, seemingly, were without religious sentiment or devout impressions upon their mind, displaying much discontent about some trifle day after day, while the Canadians were of an agreeable and sociable disposition, cheerful and humorous, gay and grave by turns, or like men who could be brotherly to their race and mindful of and dutiful towards their God. Committed to the mercy of a kind Providence, in spite of capricious elements, and such regrets as the sensitive mind cannot fail to indulge in, for all that had been left behind in the land of our birth, I am confident a happier and more joyful company never pursued the trackless path of the deep.

We had four days to wait for the steamer in that bustling go-ahead city, San Francisco, with its gold-loving population, and another five days took us the remainder of the voyage, landing us in the convenient little harbour of Esquimalt, distant about three miles from the capital, Victoria.

The day we arrived at San Francisco was the anniversary of the fire-brigades ; there was a magnificent turn-out of all the firemen and engines in Portsmouth Square, the brilliant silver and brass mountings of the engines, with their profusion of gay flags and wreaths of natural flowers, looking very dazzling and imposing to a stranger ; added to this the reflection of the sun's hot rays upon the many different glittering uniforms of the men, at once gave a good idea of the wealth and prosperity of San Francisco. " Frisco " is most decidedly a flourishing city, and well worth a visit, or the delay in stopping for a few days before proceeding by steamer to British Columbia.

On reaching Queen Charlotte's Island, I went to visit the " racecourse," one of the great and many attractions of the place. The afternoon was calm and clear while I lounged on the crest of the hill that forms the centre of the " course," gazing on the picturesque scenes around. Southward, washing the base of the hill, are the Straits of St. Juan-de-Fuca, with the wide white pebble shores, bounded on the north side by Vancouver Island, and on the south by long high mountain chains that form the northern boundary of Oregon Territory. It was a sight which, once seen, can never be forgotten ! I felt amply repaid for the little hardships attending the long voyage to this beautiful spot. I paid the course a second visit ; indeed it is worth a dozen visits, just to stand on the top of that elevated grassy slope in the centre of the course, and get a commanding view of the city and " strait," with the snow-capped hills of Oregon towering high above the highest clouds. The climate is delightful, resembling the south of Scotland, but with a much purer atmosphere ; and it is easy to predict that at no distant date this beautiful island will become a perfect Eden ! The soil in general abounds with inexhaustible forests of fine timber, rich undulating small prairies, extensive fisheries, and large deposits of coal, copper, and other minerals. The island is about 250 miles long and from fifty to seventy miles wide. The chief timbers are the pine, spruce, red and white oak, cedar, arbutus, poplar, maple, willow, and yew, particularly the first, many of which I have measured and found five feet in diameter by 300 feet high, perfectly straight, and without joints. There are many lofty hills and mountain peaks in different parts of the island, some of them beautifully wooded to their very summits, and others craggy, barren, precipitous, and full of dark caverns and frightful ravines, which add to the marvellous beauty and solemnity of the grand scenery around.

Eight times have I been *round, in,* and *at* every accessible point of this island ; and I can truly say, without hesitation, here is a site, a beautiful and profitable home for the surplus labour of the British Isles, where

more than 100,000 men could find immediate homes and
live by the gun and fishing-net, and by cultivating its
marvellous productive soil.   There is only one thing
which this island lacks, namely, convenient and safe
harbours for large *sailing* ships; there are, in fact, only
two; but with an enterprising population and assistance
from the mother country this *only difficulty* could be
easily overcome.

I must pass over the rest of the journey to Queen
Charlotte's Island.   The first thing is to colonise this
island.   It is, as I have said, teeming with the richest and
most valuable mineral ores, wooded throughout with the
stateliest pines and cedars of the world—an island which
is, as to extent of surface, as large as Scotland, but the
habitation at present wholly of Indian tribes.

The Bellacoola Indians now number about 500; they
are a very industrious people, and encourage the "whites"
to live among them.   This is an advantage, as these
Indians are remarkably successful fishermen, and can be
always employed in catching any quantity of fish in the
river for the supply of the settlers.   They are a hardy
race of people, but rather dirty in their habits.   Their
houses are very substantially built, and many of them are
entered by an opening of a circular form about two feet in
diameter, which is made in the building *after* it has been
erected; others are constructed with doors, after the
white man's system.   These houses vary in size, from
thirty to eighty feet in length, and from twenty to forty
feet in breadth, are one storey high, with nearly flat roofs.
The whole building is constructed of wood (cedar), the
boards generally two inches thick, and averaging from six
to eighteen feet in length by eighteen inches in breadth,
remarkably regular and smoothly cut.   When I first
examined them I was under the impression they were
sawn and planed by white mechanics, but such was not
the case, as I shortly afterwards saw the mode by which

the natives manufactured the timber into boards previous
to their erecting a house for a newly-created chief. The
tool which they use for planing is a simple piece of iron
fastened to a round wooden handle by a piece of cord
manufactured from the inner bark of the cedar; this tool
is shaped and worked like an "adze," and is their
principal working implement. Their next tool of importance is an awl-shaped knife : the point of the blade is bent
up in the form of a half-circle ; this instrument they hold
like the tool held by English blacksmiths when cutting
horses' hoofs, that is, with the back of the hand down
and drawing the blade towards the body. It is really
remarkable the number of articles for general purposes
and for ornament which they make with this last simple
implement, all beautifully and artistically finished. I was
shown a perfect facsimile of a sovereign carved on a piece
of ivory of the same size as the gold coin.

But to complete my description of their houses. The
frame is supported by posts driven into the ground, an
open space of about eight feet in depth being left between
the floor and the ground. This space is used for *general
purposes*, all filth, refuse, &c., being dropped through the
openings in the floor ; and when, in course of time, this
space gets filled up, the house or "frame" is removed
to another spot, and placed again on the top of new posts,
and there it remains till the space is again filled up. Thus
they continue from time to time to remove their abode.
The roofs of these houses generally consist of two great
logs or trees, the full length of the building and about
three feet in diameter. Each of these requires at least a
hundred Indians to hoist it up to its place. On these
huge logs rest the boards, *unfastened*, so that when the
house inside is full of smoke, or the weather is fine, they
can be pushed aside. This, however, is seldom done,
owing to the lazy habits of the people.

On the centre of the floor is spread a quantity of gravel

to protect the wood from catching fire; on this is placed the fire, before which is placed or spread the mats, which serve as seats for squatting on during the day, and are used as mattresses at night, the sleepers lying with their feet towards the fire. Overhead, amidst the dense smoke, hang their uncured fish; while at the far corner of the room are piled up in large boxes their winter stock of dried and cured fish, berries, and their various articles of merchandise.

The Indians are very superstitious. They will not allow the whites to wash, or throw any water or rubbish into the river, under the impression that it will cause the fish to leave it. The fish when caught are strung on a rope and moored to a pole stuck into the bed of the river, while on the top of the pole are fastened bunches of feathers to charm them, and after they have remained in the water for several hours they are taken on shore, one at a time, and as they are being landed a crowd of children keep crying at the top of their voices, but in a solemn strain, "Vil-o-o-o." They generally banish one of their tribe to the mountains during the fishing season, there to exist on berries and what he can find. He is not allowed to have a fire, and none of his tribe may hold any communication with him "while the spell lasts," it being their belief that if the banished Indian once sees any part of the river the fish will depart from it for ever. This is a cruel fate, even for an Indian, and I shall never forget the first time I heard one of those poor Indians' heartrending and most piercing wails as they came echoing from cliff to cliff. Once heard they are never to be forgotten.

On reaching Queen Charlotte's Island, I built a log house, in which I resided about twelve months, which was a most comfortable house to live in, and could be quickly and cheaply built after the Canadian bush style. The trees, *growing in the morning*, are cut down and converted into a comfortable house *by sundown*. It generally takes about fifty men to build one, every man giving a day's labour free, while you give him his food and pay for a fiddler, to wind up with a merry dance, this being called a "house-warming." Of course, in the event of your neighbour requiring a house, a barn, or stable built, ten acres of bush cleared for crop, or fifty acres of potatoes dug up and put in pits in one day, you have to reciprocate, and in this way you may have to give your *services free* two or three days in the course of a year. But if the section in which you are located becomes thickly settled, your services are not required. In a few years, say five or six, you are neither called upon to give nor take, but become perfectly independent, and pay for your own labourers.

Of the climate I may say that it is much milder here than at the capital (Victoria), and milder than in any part of Scotland, the summer being not quite so hot during the hottest days, while the winter is much warmer, and the atmosphere always clearer and more pure.

Fish are perhaps more plentiful than in any other part of the world. The quantity of game is really marvellous.

The natives have been justly considered the finest, most savage, and warlike Indians on the Pacific, but they are well disposed towards the whites, and wish us to settle amongst them. The chief, Kitguna, believing that he had the right to do as he liked with his own islands, actually made me a present of them, on condition that I lived amongst them and induced all my friends, the "English," to settle with me—not a very small gift, considering that the island is nearly 200 miles long, and averages about thirty miles wide!

The population (*all natives*) is about 4,500; they are exceedingly industrious; they make very creditable ear-rings, nicely carved, besides pipes and flutes, cut out of wood, ivory, and slates. The majority of them, male and female, wear only a small-sized half-blanket loosely thrown over their shoulders, more for the purpose of warmth than

any sense of decency. They live for the most part on
bears, ducks, geese, and such shell-fish as they find near
their camps.

Some of the women are exceedingly handsome and
symmetrical in shape, but unfortunately they are in the
habit of disfiguring their breasts, arms, ears, and under
lip. One particularly fine woman, the daughter of the
little chief "Skilleyguts," had her arms tattooed with
figures representing chiefs and fish.

When they have resigned their husbands (who take to
another wife), and gone into widowhood, their under lips
are put between two pieces of ivory, each the size of a
halfpenny piece, and these are riveted together; sometimes it will be one solid piece, and this is let into the
hole, which has been gradually enlarging during her
younger lifetime, causing the lip to project straight out
at least two inches from the under jaw.

Among these simple and primitive tribes marriage is unknown, nor is polygamy one of their institutions. Woman
is a creature purely of purchase, to be had connubially
for a month's trial, and if the man is dissatisfied with her
(which is too often the case), he returns her to her parents,
and receives back what he gave for her—a trinket or a
blanket. I may add that there are no ceremonies whatever performed such as are customary among many savage
tribes on the occasion of a man and woman undertaking to
live together for a short or a long period. It is a simple
matter on the man's part of purchase and possession.
The beautiful attachment and heroic constancy of affection
ending only in death, amongst civilised or Christian nations,
is to them unknown.

The men are in general a fine race of men, and only
look hideous when they blacken their faces with charred
wood. Many of them are notoriously lazy and given to
gambling; and I have always observed that this gambling
class were the most troublesome to the whites (we are

called "whites" to make a distinction, yet it is a well-known fact on the American continent that the natives in Canada and British Columbia are nearly as white as we are; the "dusky Indians" stain their skins with the bark of trees, and those in our colonies on the North Pacific paint themselves black with charred wood).

It is painful to be reminded of those unfortunate and benighted creatures, with no religious faith, no elevated principle of duty; and in bringing these cursory remarks to a close, I may perhaps state the mode which I would suggest should be adopted for the colonisation or early settlement of Queen Charlotte's Island.

After the emigrants had arrived at the island, all hands would be set to work to build a large one-roomed log house, in which all could lodge temporarily, and which could be used afterwards as a Mission station or school-house. When this is accomplished, positions for fifty houses might be staked out, and then all hands could be employed in building log-house No. 1. When No. 1 is completed, No. 2 could be commenced and completed, and so on till the completion of the whole number required; and thus, within two or three months after landing on the island, every family would be comfortably housed. Thus domiciled in substantial wooden erections, the attention of the emigrants would be directed to the cultivation of the soil, which is most rich and fertile.

Each family could begin farming operations on a small or extended scale, seeds and implements being provided from the general stock, and my impression is that at the end of the first year they would find themselves not only with every comfort, but on the road to independence. Of course the Government would require to grant 200 acres free to each family emigrating, or more land, if wished by them, under stipulated conditions. I will merely add that I have every confidence in the success of such an emigration scheme under Government authority.

All that I crave is the sympathy of my countrymen and countrywomen on behalf of those poor "Hydah" Indians on that isolated island, discovered by Captain Cook nearly a hundred years ago, and explored so recently by me; and I do trust that I may be the means through the present channel of awakening a public interest in their fate.

Sketches from New Zealand.

CHAPTER I.

SWAMPLANDS.

FAR, far away on the Canterbury Plains, in the land of the wéka and the booming bittern, and about twenty miles north of the city of Christchurch, lies Swamplands, our rural district.

A huge morass to the westward borders off all direct communication with Eliotville, a rising locality and laid-out township, where blankets and "corduroys," sardines and grog, figure behind the panes of an ambitious store; and a zealous blacksmith, splendid in gold ring earned at "the diggings," acknowledges to be driving, to use a colonial phrase, a "slap-up" trade. To the eastward flows the Wainia, incursive, devastating, ever-shifting, and unreliable, as is the custom of New Zealand rivers to be.

This forms the ostensible Rubicon between Swamplands and its neighbours *de l'autre côté*. The latter are one and all in a better position as to worldly means and rank of life, holding large runs, or extensive freeholds; inhabiting fine houses, and having time as well as means for enjoyment—representatives, in fact, of the yeomen or squirearchy of English counties. With these, however, we have at present nothing to do. Our subject is the working

B

freeholder of from twenty to fifty or a hundred acres ;
one who is practically versed in the science of cross
ploughing, dibbling, and harrowing ; who is familiar with
tents, and conversant with shanties—a simple " Arcadian
farmer."

Ten years ago Swamplands did not exist in the maps of
City draughtsmen and among the reports of surveyors.
It was one of the many hundreds of unlaid-out regions
far back in the swamps. Such are constantly uprising,
habitations seemingly of a night's growth, with populations
springing into existence as spontaneously as themselves.
Now, near the spots where Maories camped, to fish and
doze away a miserable existence, and where, at a remote
period, their forefathers had held their savage carnivals,
as the remains of ancient ovens constructed with stones
against the sides of the sandhills may to this day testify,
there oats, and *green* grass, and waving corn, have
displaced indigenous tussucks* and bunches of flax,
which formerly constituted the sole vegetation of the
dreary spot ; a vegetation that, like the features of an
expressionless face, overspread the surface, without
stamping it with any character. Here too, but at
intervals few and far between, rises the smoke from
wooden homesteads into the most pure and bright of
atmospheres ; the thriving hedge of broom or gorse
encircling the low walls, with the saplings and plants of
English origin, sufficiently attest the nationality and
persevering industry of the inmates. Sweetly from over
the sandhills comes the scent of the potatoe and the
bean-field, and the traveller on the distant track, whilst
" pricking o'er the plain," may hear the sound of craning
kine and bleating sheep, commanded by the shepherd's
voice or urged by resounding whips of strong-lunged
stockmen. In the gullies of the shingly river-bed also,

* The native grass, growing to a height of two feet, is of a dull
yellow colour, very monotonous to the eye.

where erst the "noble savage," in his stark nakedness, was wont to spear his daily food ("ki, ki"), now wander the hardy flocks of divers owners, intent on securing for themselves a meagre and difficult subsistence; but despite the frugality of their fare, varied, by way of an occasional luxury, with a mouthful of English grass, they mostly present a decent and respectable appearance.

So much for the scene; now for the people. What sort of being is a Swamplandite? what kind of life does he lead? and what are his pursuits, aims, and occupations? The Ultima Thule of his ambition, the subject of his nightly prayers, is to gain independence, to leave an inheritance to his children. With this view he emigrated; for this he begins life over again, willing to struggle onwards though his task be futile as that of Sisyphus, and his efforts as vain as those of the unhappy Tantalus. Toil is the necessity of his life; no time has he to contemplate aught that may entrench upon his labours. Amusements he has none. The difficulties of communication between the few houses there are, and the fact of every one being unexceptionally wrapt up and incrusted in his own affairs, render all interchange of the courtesies of social life and all freedom of intercourse extremely difficult. And the encroachment of a dreaded river on one side, and the obstinacy of an irreclaimable swamp on the other, are matters of too deep moment to allow much entertainment or diversion of spirit. Yet the Swamplandite is by no means an unhappy or a discontented mortal. He is rather apt to pride himself upon having turned his back on the pollutions, the follies, and conventionalities and restraints of a great city. He is a strict conservative in theory and practice, carrying out as well as is in his power the time-honoured institutions and prejudices of the old country. And dearly he loves a social evening, when he can get it, about three times a year; when he can afford to be profusely hospitable and genial beyond measure.

When thus doing the honours of his own roof, he can seldom refrain from extolling the benefits of his peculiar mode of life and place of abode—the pure air he enjoys, salubrious water, and free and easy style of living. So far from bewailing the scarcity of congenial spirits, he is inclined to say, with the poet,

"How sweet, how passing sweet is solitude!"

Concerning the education of the young in these parts, we may say that it is not a rule as binding as the law of the Medes and Persians that they be initiated into mysteries which are not immediately connected with the advancement of their success in that particular mode of life for which they may be destined. The spade, the plough, and the stock-whip, take precedence, in fact, over all other subjects of education.

Our sturdy youth languish under no terrors of the cane and the imposition, nor under any over-excitement of the brain and over-development of the nervous system; unabashed, precocious beyond measure are they. Lusty and strong as young eagles; strangers to more than half the ills that infant flesh is heir to, they believe in no other land than their own Arcadia.

Swamplands possesses one blessing, of which many an up-country district of equal cultivation still mourns the want. A church—a *very* modest wooden structure—a tabernacle in the wilderness of treeless plain—has within the last few years been erected. *Once in six weeks* the services are conducted by clergymen from a distance, riding fifteen or twenty miles in the course of a day. As yet there is no resident minister. If we may judge from appearances, making allowance for the scattered and sparse population of the district, the number of horses tied to posts, and the vehicles of all description seen on "church Sundays," might shame the lukewarmness of

many an English congregation labouring under no obstacle
as to route and conveyance. Many of these good people
have emerged from nearly uninhabitable wilds of the
swamp and river-bed. Some have come in drays or
ponderous waggons drawn by six or eight fat bullocks;
others in "traps," on horseback, or on foot; over miles
of tangled grass and "nigger head," and ground made
horrible by wild pigs—those over-pleasing mementoes of
Captain Cook's legacy. Then we may sometimes see a
smart "buggy" or two, the springs of which have been
jeopardised to humour the vanity of the proprietor.
Especially we must not forget to notice those very
fashionable-looking horsemen, with white-covered hats
and veils dependent, who are talking and flirting with the
fair equestrians by their side; which same buxom damsels
later in the day may be surprised hard-taxed with milking
and skimming operations, or actively superintending the
preparation of a substantial supper.

In New Zealand you come upon both people and places
in the most unexpected manner. Society, like the climate,*
is formed of a hundred mingling varieties. It is a land
of eccentricities, variabilities, and inconsistencies.

At Swamplands people make their appearance at church,
whose manner of life and place of abode, though known to
exist, are involved in mystery even to their near neighbours. With such remotely situated families the journey
to church occupies the whole day, entailing a veritable
pilgrimage. And we cannot be surprised that friends and
scattered relations should look forward to the service
Sunday as a time for the exchange of mutual greetings
and kindly salutations, which the difficulties of communication so effectually interrupt. The effects of extreme
isolation are always more or less visible in both large and
small families.

Picture to yourselves (which is a very common case) a
number of boys and girls ranging from the age of six to

sixteen, all rampant in Swamplands! Of the boys, nearly
all of them are great adepts in fishing, shooting, and, of
course, riding; even the little one of six born up there,
and never having set foot beyond his paternal acres, wins
and merits the reputation of being able to ride "any
horse." He can "*tail the sheep*," "*head a mob*" (of
cattle), and help "*cut out a beast*," with the ease of a
growing Hercules! But this little boy, infallible though
he be in the eyes of parents and admiring kinsfolk, has
never seen a boat, a bridge, a mill, or a stone building.
Of these things, and many others equally familiar to our
eyes, he knows only by hearsay and by illustrations. He
has never wandered in a lane, nor gathered flowers from a
hedge-row, nor scrambled over the ruins of an old stone
wall. His highest notion of a tree is embodied in the
blue and red gum saplings, the poplars and willows of but
few years' growth, that are rapidly springing up in his
father's garden. He has never listened to the sound of
bells, nor heard the song of blackbird or of thrush, or
"Philomel's soft lay!" The glories of bird's-nesting, of
climbing, or rambling in shady groves, delightful copses,
and "watery glades," are Eleusinian mysteries to this
child of matter-of-fact and unromance. The eggs of the
lark, the dotted and gorgeous "swamp hen," he stumbles
upon midst the tussucks of the plain; but the real English
enjoyment of bird's-nesting, with its attendant excitements
and spice of adventure, is unknown, impracticable, to the
dweller in swamps and treeless wastes.

We frequently see in the elder boys and girls of a family
dispositions to study and improve their minds; they wish
to "get up" what they did know or were beginning to
know when they left school in England or elsewhere. In
the winter evenings, when the blaze of roots or flax stalks
from the open hearth gleams cheerily upon the wooden or
the clay-washed walls, they endeavour to study; they bring
out the old books. But now, alas! the task is harder;

the eyes are sore and heavy from exposure to the wind and sun of a more tropical clime; the hands are grown stiff and stubborn from daily toil; and, with so "few appliances and means to boot," how can the tired stockman, the fencer, the shepherd, control and subjugate those too powerful thoughts which, despite his best efforts, will wander on "bullocks?"

That very equivocal personage "the tutor," whom one occasionally meets in the houses of thriving or *superior* people, is by no means a reliable source of intellectual superiority or special mental endowments. To some degree he does answer the purpose of a useful walking dictionary, or Bibliotheca domestica; and is, therefore, a convenient and proper person to have in an ambitious household. But his position is certainly ambiguous, and differs very widely from our English and European notions of a dominie. His real vocation may be summed up in the words of his own advertisement, wherein he styles himself "a person willing to make himself *generally useful and agreeable.*" With regard to his pupils, he must have entire control over them, *i.e.*, take the little ones entirely off the hands of other people, teach them when willing, and cram into the heads of the elder ones as much as it is possible within a very short compass of time. That his duties may be pleasingly diversified, in his spare time let him take up the spade or the rake, and thus learn to be colonial, as it is every one's duty to be. He need not be strict, neither too quiet, nor given to lecturing or commentating; but in all things let him be the cheerful, active, accommodating, *colonial* tutor.

In the education of girls, also, the tutor often plays an important part. In very remote places, where the procuring of a governess is impracticable, "the tutor" officiates *pro tem.* as a sort of masculine "bonne," or male duenna. He accompanies the young ladies to church on horseback, carrying books or parcels, sits near them, that

he may kindly find out their places for them during service, and otherwise conducts himself as a pious guardian.
In all long and hazardous rides he is their attendant
cavalier to guide them through swampy quagmires or
troublesome rivers.   In short, so complaisant and so kind
a being as a "harmless, necessary" tutor, is universally
esteemed a great gain to a household of growing sons and
daughters.   Stories *have* been told (cruelly) of runaway
tutors, dishonest tutors, and sentimental tutors; but, on
the whole, the scheme is decidedly successful, and has
been pretty generally adopted whenever practicable.

Genteel people view an appendage of this sort as the
Chinese do their long nails.   It is so respectable to have a
tutor! so very colonial! and, withal, so thoroughly convenient!

But in extremely isolated households, where neither
governess nor tutor are likely to find their much-desired
way, the condition of the young people is truly deplorable.
We know one family immersed in the innermost recesses
of Swamplands, who for five years lived in a state of compulsory estrangement.   Now, by means of drains and
cleared lands, matters are daily getting better and better;
but in the early days to which I allude, this side of the
swamp was entirely isolated, both ingress and egress being
impracticable on foot.   Once a-year the master of the
house, with a servant, brought up their store of provisions
from town, after having first carted and sold his crop of
oats, wheat, turnips, &c.   It were vain to attempt to describe the difficulties of his circuitous route, the labours,
the hardships, and disappointments that too frequently
awaited him.   All I can say is, that he still performs that
journey, and thus the family live on.   About twice during
the lingering summer, when the parching winds have
created dry paths and temporary tracks in the season of
grasshoppers and lizards; and when the screams of swamp
hens, and wèkas, and ducks, with the boom of the bittern,

seem lulled by a transitory spell, then do the ladies of
this secluded mansion venture forth on exploring expedi-
tions and visiting excursions. But as soon as the winter
rains set in, when the snow on the distant Alps is bril-
liantly visible in the exquisite sunshine of a June day;
when river and lake, and dismal lagoon, and every solitary and insignificant building that dots the plain is trans-
formed by the mirage into objects of the wildest signifi-
cance; then do these ladies feel that their time of imprisonment is come, and that at least for three months to
come must they be confined to the precincts, if not the
walls, of their homes, like the inhabitants of some be-
leaguered fortress. Now, what constitutes the routine of
this family's life from day to week, from month to year?
Hard work of almost any kind both in-doors and out, and
plenty of it. There are three daughters and four sons.
The mother and eldest daughter, a stout girl of eighteen,
do all the important work of the house, including washing,
and the management of a dairy. They keep no maid-
servant—a common occurrence in small houses, especially
up the country. Notwithstanding their incessant occupations, and their often tired bodies, the mother and grown-up
daughter sedulously devote two afternoons in the week to
slates and copy-books. They gather the children around
them, and endeavour by every possible means to concen-
trate their attention. Alas! here again is up-hill work;
a weary, one-sided struggle. The children have been out
in the (almost tropical) sun all day; the nor'-wester has
blistered their eyes and worried their minds; they are
restless and high-spirited, as only colonial children can be.
They *don't believe in* this humbug; " *no fear*," they are
not going to be crammed with a lot of bosh. Then in
comes the father, or big elder brother, stock-whip in hand,
to say it is high time to be seeing after the cows. A loud
" *too-à* " is heard from distant quarters, instantly claiming
and rivetting universal attention, and ultimately giving

warning of the delightful fact that the horses are all in amongst the new oats in the far paddock; the sheep have all crossed the rice and must be instantly headed back. The pigs have found out the door of the dairy, are enjoying themselves, and taking it thoroughly easy; and the calves, having first broken their tether ropes, are with gusto demolishing the newly-washed linen and bleaching collars upon the lawn. So away fly the urchins in all the glee of emancipation, and away are put the lessons, as they have been so many times before. And then the poor mother bewails her lot. She is really a well-informed, educated person—a lady of birth once familiar with comfort and luxury; and she willingly consented to come to New Zealand. But she never realised the impediments that were to obstruct her pathway and perplex her career —if only this education question did not worry her so much!—if her husband would but take the boys in hand himself!

The evils of isolation are painfully exhibited in bachelors! Swamplands, like all newly settled places, of course contains many bachelors. We have every variety of them: from the gay, young, would-be " swell," delighting in " larks " and "sprees" whenever obtainable, who travels to distant races to see and to be seen, and whose saddle and spurs seem part of himself, to the grave, aristocratic gentleman of middle age, who abandoned England in grief or disgust, *blasé* and sick of a world whose pleasures he had exhausted; and there is the old Australian or Californian digger, perhaps an old " lag," or turned-off convict, who knows a " thing or two," is up to many a clever " dodge," and heeds little what passes around him, except it be work. Some of these bachelors are remarkable for their neatness in person and attire, the method of their arrangements, and the prim order of their abodes; others, we grieve to say, are terribly the reverse! Many young men (especially among gentlemen's sons we notice it) of good birth and education, thoroughly reared in etiquette and the requirements of polite society, appear to take delight in living in a state of barbaric dirtiness, and savage disregard of appearances. We can mention one case in particular,* that of four young men, calling themselves mates or partners in a large block of land adjoining the river-bed, who live in a style that we cannot describe as colonial, but truly *piggish!* The hut which they inhabit, and which they built themselves, is about twelve feet long by twelve. It is made of cob, or native clay (often used for building, and which *may* be made to look very presentable), and through the interstices of the rude sods may be seen many a tuft of native grass or weed, proving highly alluring to grasshoppers, lizards, and other insignificant and innocuous reptiles that may choose to enter. Inside the hut an extremity is partitioned off to form a receptacle for milk, butter, cheese, &c. This is called " the dairy," and not only forms a sleeping apartment for one of the " mates," but into it a strange medley of rags, boots, old bottles, clothes, books, tools, and every kind of miscellaneous lumber is tossed as into a common dusthole. The larger or " living-room " — also replete with miscellaneous furniture, such as saddles, guns, boxes, and sacks, in picturesque attitudes—is principally devoted to huge " salting-down " tubs, or crocks, filled with meat often in a higher state of putrefaction than preservation. The young lords of the manor spend their days out of doors, sometimes really working, most times riding long and furiously after their cattle—an employment far more congenial to their taste ! In the evenings they come in to cook their supper, to wash, and, when positively compulsory, to mend their clothes ; then they " turn in," or retire on couches formed of boxes, in " bunks," or on the tops of the very odoriferous meat tubs before mentioned. One of the " mates " who possesses on a yet more enlarged

* A notorious but perfectly *true* case ; but one not often equalled.

scale than his companions the delightful quality of accommodating himself to circumstances, and of not being *at all
particular*, generally retires to rest in an outside building
formed and planned after the original model, and connected with it by means of an enormous puddle that from
time immemorial has been known to exist.   This apartment is entitled the " harness room," and is therefore unreservedly dedicated to all species of horse and cattle gear,
and moreover serves as an additional reserve for lumber,
rags, &c.

These young men are all sons of gentlemen living at home
at ease, who are quite satisfied with the assurance that
their boys are roughing it in the colony, and *therefore*,
they believe, certain to do well.

CHAPTER II.

HOKITIKA, *Oct. 20th*, 1867.—We are in the midst of rather bad weather—rain and storms—which seems to be the proper commencement of spring in these latitudes. However, I have got a little done to my garden before it began, and I can already see some blades of grass growing up.

I have been hard at work lately at my school, endeavouring to get it into better shape than before. West Coast children are like unbroken colts, and will take a long time to learn ordinary habits of discipline.

Last week I had to go to Ross under peculiar circumstances, which will give you an insight into the ways and customs of our digging population. Mr. Beaumont had just returned from Ross, and was away at Greymouth, when a letter came to me telling me of a terrible accident which had happened at Ross. A drive, or tunnel, in a mine had fallen in on some men, and had crushed one and wounded another. They wanted me or Mr. Beaumont to come to bury him; but, unfortunately, the letter coming up the coast had been mislaid, and only reached me two hours before the time appointed for the funeral, after the inquest. However, I made a push for it. Ross is about eighteen miles away, south of Hokitika, but there are several rivers to cross, one takes half-an-hour in a boat; you get a horse at the other side, and then your road lies along the sea-beach, over several streams that can be forded, and, at last, in and out of a river called the Totara, some fifteen times, until you arrive at the township,

which is four miles back from the sea. This road up the
river is very beautiful, as the river runs down through the
forest, and trees shut you in on each side. When I got
over the Hokitika, I had just an hour and a-half to do
about seventeen miles of this broken riding; but, by help
of my own spurs and a hired horse, and no delays, I did
it just in the time. I had not been at Ross for some time,
as Mr. Beaumont takes charge of it. The town is situated
on a large cleared space in the heart of the forest, not all
flat, but rising in terraces, and shut in on all sides by the
mountains, which are completely clothed with timber. I
found preparations for the funeral going on, the greater
part of the township, which is full of all manner of
"diggings," machinery for pumping, and a few steam-
engines, was more or less hushed and quiet. The church
stands right at the end of the main street, broadside to
the street, on the highest terrace, with the porch-door
looking down the street. I went up there, and, standing at
the door in my surplice, waited for the procession. It was
very striking; at least 300 men, all diggers, many of them
Danes and Swedes, with light blue eyes and yellow hair,
dressed with neatness in darkish clothes, came in line up
the street. The foremost carried the coffin, about which
there was no symptom of undertaker's art. They had
made it themselves. It was neatly studded with bright
brass nails, and on it three wreaths of beautiful ferns and
the white flowering creeper which is to be seen in the
forest here in spring; it had also two white satin ribbons
arranged cross-wise on it; it was carried by means of
white bands, as you may have seen a child's coffin carried.
The procession came slowly up to the church, and then I
went out to meet it. We entered the church (it holds
200), which was soon crammed, and crowds stood outside at the open windows: you could not find a more
attentive congregation in all England. After this part of
the service we went in procession up the terrace above the

church to the grave-yard, which is seen over the church roof, and there he was buried. As we stood round the grave on the steep hillside the scene was wonderfully impressive. Some 500 people were there, all silent; below us, the diggings and the town, a few flags half-mast high, and work at a standstill; all around, hills and terraces covered with the interminable forest, and, over the tree-tops, the sea stretching out into far distance. A beautiful sunshine lit up everything with a bright glow; you would hardly have expected such a scene in these wild places, where gold-diggers are supposed to be semi-heathen, and utterly careless of the future. The man who was buried was a Dane,—a sober, hard-working man. After the funeral, his "mates" came to offer £10 to the church. I was much struck with the evident fruits of Mr. Beaumont's work amongst them. Of course he has not come into close personal contact with one-fifth of them, yet he is known and recognised as the pastor to whom they have recourse in time of trouble. No Roman Catholic priest, or Wesleyan itinerant, or local minister, has this position. It was very pleasant to hear their spokesman say, "We were afraid, sir, that the letter had miscarried; but we waited as long as possible, for we knew that either Mr. Beaumont or you would come."

The funeral was hardly over when news was spread about of a second equally fatal accident, another man had just been killed—this time through carelessness. He was working in a deep shaft with a mate, and "sending up," in a bucket hooked to a rope with an iron hook, slabs of wood to those who were at the windlass overhead; diggers are very careless about their buckets and hooks, and by some accident, when the bucket and heavy slabs were nearly at the top of the shaft, down they fell, crushing one man to death, and knocking the other senseless. The man was a Cornishman.

The next day we held the funeral; there must have

been more present even than the day before, and this
funeral had its own peculiar features. The long procession of men came up the street singing in beautiful
harmony one of Wesley's hymns. It was very striking.
They continued to sing until I met them and led the way
into the church. They carried the coffin, as yesterday,
in their hands; after the service round the grave, they
began another hymn—words by Wesley, but the tune
was a sort of chorale rather than an ordinary hymn tune.
It was sung with great expression, at times. rising loud
and full, and then dying away with really exquisite soft-
ness. I stood above the great crowd on the upper side
of the hill, and, as yesterday, looked down on them.
Many of them were standing with tears in their eyes, and
their faces fixed on the distant sea, as if their thoughts
were far away from gold and gold-fields, and wandering to
old scenes and perhaps holy associations. I suppose the
crowd stood thus for nearly a quarter of an hour. Some
one had on the previous evening suggested to me that I
should speak to them, but I doubt whether any spoken
words could have done more to penetrate the hard crust
of a digger's indifference to religion than the simple
strains which arrested every one's attention.

I spent one or two days in the place, chiefly amongst
the diggers. There is here, as elsewhere, a great mixture
of people—Germans, Danes, Swedes, English, and Irish;
but it is a mistake to think that they are as bad and
reckless as they are generally supposed to be. Many do
spend their earnings as quickly as they get them in public-houses, and all are thoroughly possessed with the
spirit of speculation; but the larger population in this
field are hard-working men, who save something. They
are all intelligent, many well educated, and with scarcely
an exception, in spite of their neglect of religion, men who
have known what it is to attend church or school; consequently, although the good soil is overlaid with much

débris of careless, godless living, yet it is there down below, and can be got at now and then: at least we may be sure that the digger's idea of what religion ought to be, and what a clergyman should be, is very much the same as that which any ordinary Englishman would entertain. So that the work which an English clergyman brings to bear on them is not thrown away, however little can be seen of its immediate effect.

When I come down to Ross, or when Mr. Beaumont does, we live in a somewhat colonial style. The "warden" of the gold fields, who entertains us, has nothing but the roughest accommodation to offer. He seems to like primitive simplicity, and lives in a sort of "lean-to," which is part of the Court-house. I was sleeping last night in a shed on a bed formed of two bits of timber and a strip of canvas, just two feet wide, plenty of blankets, but no sheets; the door is full of holes and cracks; the shed contains a basin and jug, a looking-glass, and one small towel—no chairs, table, or furniture. In the morning I go out to get water at a tank, and to get my boots cleaned at another shed partly built of canvas, in which the servants of the establishment live. It is raining a little, but we don't mind doing part of our toilette out of doors in this region. I see two policemen saddling their horses, preparing to go off with a heavy gold consignment; they are breeched and booted, with sabre and revolver, and they have just announced that they are in a great fright lest the river be too high for them to cross without swimming. These well-dressed gentlemen who carry the gold seem to fear a ducking ten times more than a possible bushranger, who is altogether an unknown animal in these parts now.

The town is astir; diggers are beginning to work. I hear the "warden" having his bath in the Court-house; he always uses that as his bath-room, and puts his soap on "his worship's seat." Presently we get breakfast.

s

There is no meat in the place, and has not been for a
week, so we eat eggs and bacon; and a talkative servant,
a Devonshire woman, insists on expatiating on the terrible
price of meat, 1s. 6d. a pound, and the number of rats
which ran under her bed last night.   I have just now met
an old friend, an Oxford man, and we are going to ride
back together.

With the Bishop of Gu...na.

The Demerara River, though scarcely known by name to the majority even of well-educated people, is yet a river, with a trade of its own, and a history not without interest. This will appear from the following narrative of a missionary journey on its waters, quite recently undertaken.

Georgetown, the capital of the colony of British Guiana, is situated at the mouth of the Demerara. About 150 miles up are the first rapids, and fifty miles higher the Great Falls; here is the limit of civilisation, there being no settlement, except of pure Indians, above these falls. Up to the foot of these falls, however, the European and Creole population have advanced their wood-cutting operations; the country for hundreds of square miles being one mass of primeval forest, drained by mighty rivers and their tributaries, commonly called creeks. The wood-cutters, as far as they have gone, have carried with them the doctrines, and, to some extent, the system and discipline of the Church. Hitherto the Indians, or Bucks, as they are called by the settlers, have shown little disposition on this river to embrace the Gospel; the Arawaks, who are, of all the tribes, the most open to the influences of civilisation, being the only ones gathered into the Church in any number. During the last few years, however, there has been a continually increasing desire among the Acawoios to listen to the Gospel; and on the occasion at present under consideration, we shall see them flocking in by hundreds, to obtain a share of the same precious privileges as we enjoy.

Of the aboriginal tribes in general, it may be well to

s 2

promise here, that they are of all barbarous people the
least barbarous and most gentle, shy and reserved to a
fault, harmless and inoffensive in every way, with no
vices but what they learn from their Christian masters.
They have wonderfully few wants, and know wonderfully
well how to supply them. So they are utterly independent, feeling themselves quite self-sufficient. They
are adverse, not to hard labour, so much as to continuous
work; most loving and peaceable among themselves,
never quarrelling, except tribe with tribe. The great bar
in the way of their civilisation is their roving disposition.
They appear to be incapable of remaining more than three
or four months in the same spot. They mix sparingly
with the whites, still more sparingly with the blacks
(Africans), with whom they seem to have little in common.
Their ideas of the Deity, and of the next life, seem to be
very few and vague. They have no religious rites or observances, no priesthood, no temples, no prayers. They
live in the bush, along the banks, principally, of the rivers
and creeks, in settlements called Buck-towns, consisting
of three or four families, in as many huts, constructed in
the rudest way of the rudest materials—a few spars and
palm-leaves tied and sewn together with common vine or
bush-rope. Their entire suite of furniture consists of the
hammock and barbra-cut; the former serving the purpose
of bed, sofa, and chair, the latter of meat-safe, dresser,
and plate-rack. Their occupations are cutting and planting
"fields," or provision-grounds, hunting, fishing, making
bows and arrows, hammocks, goglets, buck-pots, packalls,
and cutting timber either to sell to merchants, or for wages
from the licensed woodcutters. The rivers and creeks
are their principal roads, their only crafts the woodskin
and corial: the former made of the bark of a particular
tree, the latter of the trunk of a tree, shaped and hollowed
out. Neither for these, nor for their houses, do they want
any nail or bolt whatever. They are almost amphibious,

and therefore hardly able to exist away from the water-
side. They keep no stock of any kind, but are very
clever at taming the wild animals and birds of the forest.

Such are the people whom the Bishop met in greatest
numbers on his late missionary tour. Starting from
Georgetown on the evening of Thursday, the 27th August,
with a former curate of the Upper Demerara River as his
chaplain, in a tent-boat manned with four oars—all river
hands—and provisioned for a fortnight, the Bishop arrived
about midnight, on the top of the tide, at the first missionary station, in the village of Hyde Park. Across the
river, and nearly opposite the chapel-school here, is the
mouth of the Camouni Creek, up which is the flourishing Chinese settlement of Hopetown. Here is stationed
Mr. Bispham, superintendent of the Chinese settlement,
and catechist of Hyde Park. He has living near him a
good old Chinaman, a Christian, who is always ready to
act as interpreter, and assists Mr. Bispham in the study
of the Chinese language. To the chapel-school at Hyde
Park, Mr. Bispham brought on Friday morning twenty-
five Chinese, nearly all adults, to be baptized; and forty-
seven, including these adult Chinese, to be confirmed.
All of these partook also of Holy Communion with their
Creole brethren—seventy in all. The services, as may be
imagined, were very impressive; and one felt that a great
work was being carried on well. On his way down, twelve
days later, the Bishop stopped at this chapel-school, and
examined the Creole children, to the number of thirty: they
seem to be well taught and managed. As this station has but
lately been established, and is in the midst of a considerable
population, it is confidently hoped that both the congregation
of the chapel and the number of scholars will increase rapidly.

The services on Friday lasted till about three P.M. A
violent thunderstorm was raging, and as the weather
looked ugly, it was arranged that the Bishop's visit to the
Chinese settlement in the Camouni should not be made

that afternoon, as originally intended, but early next morning. As the tide would begin to flow about eleven o'clock on Saturday morning, it was necessary to be at the settlement by eight. At this time only a few Chinese had assembled; others, however, kept arriving in driblets, and at half-past eight o'clock, when no further delay could be made, the Bishop addressed some sixty or seventy in the school-room through their interpreter; pointing out to them the necessity of being industrious, of getting their children taught, and of trying to learn themselves as fast as they could. After hearing a few of their grievances, and saying what he could to soften them down, and giving some further good advice, the Bishop left them, evidently delighted with his visit. About half-past ten, the little *bâteau* that had carried the party up the creek reached the tent-boat; and, after breakfasting, the Bishop started again at eleven for the next station, Dalgyn, where he was to spend the Sunday. The day was very hot, and the stage a long one; but, by keeping the oars well at it, Dalgyn was reached at seven. This is the oldest outpost occupied by our Church on the river. The chapel is a substantial building, raised to a great extent by the people themselves, materially assisted by Mr. George Alleyne, an African, the patriarch of the village—who, amongst other things, gave the site. Here the Bishop and chaplain were quite at home, and had a little leisure to talk over matters with the warden, inspect the chapel and school accounts, &c. The chapel is served every Sunday by a catechist, Mr. Bowrey, living in the neighbourhood: an earnest, good man, who has brought many Indians into the fold, and otherwise shown himself a faithful and valuable servant to the Church. Every alternate month, a clergyman in full orders is sent for twelve or thirteen days into the district, to administer the Sacrament on Sundays, marry, inspect the schools, visit the sick, and perform other functions of the pastoral office.

There were no candidates for confirmation here, as the Bishop had confirmed in this same chapel last year. There was a good congregation at the eleven o'clock service; two children were baptized, of which one was an Indian; and the number attending Holy Communion was fifty-seven, several of these being Indians. Soon after five in the afternoon—the tide still flowing—the Bishop started for Christianburgh, about eight miles higher up, and reached it a little before seven. Here is a large saw-mill, with a capital dwelling-house, always open for the accommodation of travellers. The family were in town; but hospitality was given all the same. This, however, was not the object of the Bishop's visit: his plan had been to spend Sunday night at Dalgyn; but Mr. Newton, the catechist from above, had come to meet the Bishop at Dalgyn, and the report he gave of his work induced him to visit the station in Ducoura Creek on Monday. The best way to manage this seemed to be to walk from Christianburgh through the bush, the path being a fair one of about six miles. Time was valuable, so Christianburgh was reached on Sunday night, and the boat sent up early on Monday morning to Ducoura mouth, there to wait for the Bishop and chaplain, who reckoned upon being sent down the creek in a canoe or *bâteau*. As soon as the boat had started from Christianburgh, early on Monday morning, the Bishop and chaplain set off too, with Mr. Newton, to trudge through the bush. The walk, for the most part, was pleasant enough, through the cool forest in the early morning; but towards the end, the path was a little troublesome in the valley of the creek, owing to swampy ground, fallen trees, rough timber. aths, &c., and the travellers were a little fatigued when they reached their destination. They were not expected; but the good lady of the establishment soon got ready a capital breakfast, to which they did ample justice. While break-fast was cooking, the catechist went out to beat up his

school children ; but the day being Monday, and nothing
of the kind anticipated, this could not be done in a hurry.
The few whom he succeeded in getting together were
examined by the Bishop, and acquitted themselves well.

But now, when the day was more than half gone, and it
was time for the travellers to be getting to their boat at
Ducoura mouth, a most unexpected difficulty presented
itself. From an accumulation of adverse causes (as events
do sometimes conspire together to cheat honest men of
their reasonable expectations), no boat could be found
capable of conveying the Bishop to the creek mouth. A
leaky old canoe was put afloat and an attempt made to caulk
her, but it would not do ; she could hardly carry a couple
of boys. Well, they sent up the creek to borrow a craft,
and they sent down the creek ; but nothing but unfavourable
answers came from above, and nothing at all in the shape
of an answer from below. Meanwhile, the weather had
set in wet, with thunder and heavy showers. The only
thing seemed to be to spend the night where they were ;
but not a hammock or change of garment of any kind had
they with them, so there was no alternative but to set
out and walk through the wet bush another five or six
miles, to a place called Luckie Spot, about a mile from the
creek mouth, where the boat was waiting.

Off they set, therefore, with the giant trees pouring down
upon them such great and copious drops that it mattered
little whether it rained or not. The path was anything but
smooth, and required a good deal of clambering ; this,
combined with the slipperiness of the soil and timber
occasioned by the rain, added immensely to the fatigue of
the journey. Luckily there was no sun, but the afternoon
was extremely close. After a depressing and tiresome
walk, the travellers arrived at last, wet and weary, at
Luckie Spot, on the river-side. Whatever this may have
been in former days, certainly "there 's nae luck about
the house" now. To be sure "the gudeman's awa',"

and his widow, much reduced and aged herself, was fain
to ask an alms of the Bishop—not for herself, but for one
of her dependants, who has five fatherless children under
eleven years of age to provide for. What this poor woman
could give, however, she did give most willingly—a room
for the Bishop to change his clothes in; for the boat was
soon fetched on from the creek mouth. This operation
over, the travellers started again, as the tide was running
up and no more time could be lost. No dinner that day
after their wanderings through the wilderness, but they
nibbled bread and cheese by the kindly light of the moon,
and agreed that they might very easily fare worse, and
that there was no fear of their dinner interfering with
their slumbers that night. They arrived between nine
and ten o'clock at a woodcutter's house, where they got
comfortable lodgings for the night, and started next morning, about seven o'clock, upwards again.

Houses and settlements on the river now become fewer and
fewer, and the tide felt is less and less. A day and a-half
more brought them to the Rapids (Malùli), where stands
the little chapel of St. Saviour. This is usually the end
of the route of the visiting clergy, who are sent up every
alternate month to officiate at the several chapels. For
lack of men, it is found impracticable to station a clergyman permanently as curate of the district, though there is
a good salary provided, and a residence might easily be
obtained. The writer of this paper can recommend the
post as by no means unenviable to any one in Holy Orders,
who is young and active, and has a liking for missionary
work. Here first, at Malùli, the Bishop became aware, to
his great delight, of the wonderful increase that had been
vouchsafed to the good seed sown sixteen months before,
when he visited the district with the Rev. W. H. Brett.*
Mr. Brett, the Apostle to the Indians, as the Bishop

* Author of " The Indian Tribes," several books of the Bible in
Arawak, Acawoio, &c.

delights to call him, brought with him on that occasion
his Indian catechist, Philip. As both of them are perfect masters of the Arawāk and Acawoio languages, the
impression made by their visit was amazing.

From the Rapids upwards to the Great Falls, and over
them again to old Kanaimapo's place (the captain of the
Acawoios of the Demerara); the good Bishop and his staff
had pushed their way on that memorable occasion. And
all night long, after the work of the day was over, the
Indians would beset Mr. Brett and his catechist for
instruction, and hardly give them time for sleep. "So
mightily grew the Word of God, and prevailed." And now
was seen the fruits of this zeal on the part of the teachers
and the taught. As the Mission-boat began to round the
last point that opens the view of the pond at the foot of
the Rapids, the banks were seen to be alive with Indians.
On right, on left, every tree of the forest seemed to be
tenanted. Fires were gleaming in the shade, and buck-
pots were hanging over them. Groups of Buckines and
their children ran and peered from their covert at the
advance of the boat; and, as she came in view of the
pond, the water was alive with redskins—men in crafts
and men in the water—all hard at work loading timber, to
send to town.

Captain Kanaimapo had come down with his people to
see the Bishop, and beg to be baptized. On the largest
punt (barge) stood Mr. George Couchman, the principal
woodcutter of the Upper River, and friend of the Indians.
He was superintending the work for them. From him the
Bishop learnt that all the children of the forest now about
him, and many more awaiting him at his (Mr. Couchman's)
place above—for there the Bishop had arranged to go—
were anxiously looking to be baptized and confirmed, as
many of them as were ready. They had been trying
for months to make plenty of timber, to send to town for
the purchase of cloth, that they might be clad as Christians

should be. The Bishop's plan had been to pass the Rapids that evening in Mr. Couchman's boat, that was lighter than his, and manned by Indians used to the falls. But he now altered his purpose, that he might assemble the Indians to evening service in the chapel. The afternoon, however, which had been extremely hot, closed with a tremendous thunder-storm. The wind was so violent, that it forced the spray of the pelting thunder-drops through every crevice of the little chapel; and the poor Indians, bivouacking in the bush, suffered sadly. After this, it was out of the question summoning them to evening prayer. This was a great disappointment, and determined the Bishop to press on next day quite up to Mr. Couchman's place, that he might see the Indians there, and get back to Malùli by Friday evening, so as to have all Saturday to give to the Indians there. Accordingly, by starting at early dawn and stopping only once, for breakfast, they reached their destination at seven o'clock. The Indians pulled nobly the whole day against a strong current, and under a terrific sun.

At the little settlement where the party stopped for breakfast, they found a poor Creole woman, who had long been a communicant at Malùli, but was now, from age and sickness, unable to travel so far. To her they administered the Holy Communion : an old Buckino, wife of the principal man of the place, herself a communicant, partaking with them. Next morning the Indians were mustered at seven, to the number of one hundred and forty, in and around Mr. Couchman's house. The chaplain read Pss. xix. and xx., two of the Psalms for that morning; Mr. Couchman interpreting, verse by verse. After that, St. Matt. v. 1—12, part of the 2nd Lesson, was read, and interpreted by Mr. Couchman. Then the Indians all repeated together the Apostles' Creed, in their own tongue. So soft and sweet is their voice, and so distinctly and intelligently did they repeat the several articles of the

Creed, that, as the good Bishop observed, no one could have desired anything more musical, or more reverent. Next, all knelt, and the Indians said the Lord's Prayer in their own tongue, and with the same exquisite effect. It was, indeed, most affecting to hear them. Then, after a few Collects, the Bishop addressed them through Mr. Couchman, telling them how his heart, indeed, yearned to them, and how glad he was to see them so in earnest; and how he hoped and prayed that they might continue good Christians after they were baptized; and how they must try and learn their prayers and Catechism in the English tongue, as that seemed destined by Providence to be the one language in which all nations should praise God, when the confusion of Babel should be done away. Mr. Couchman then heard them some of the Catechism in Acawoio. They answered most readily and accurately. Then the Bishop dismissed them, with his blessing. Mr. Couchman told him that these people had been at him continually day and night, since Mr. Brett's visit, to teach them; and that they would have learned four times as much, had they been able to get more books. What they have done since Mr. Brett's visit (with the few books he left in their own language), is truly marvellous. Most of them can read the books perfectly, and all appear to know them through by heart. Unfortunately, the supply is at present unequal to the demand, but it is likely that this will soon be remedied.

After breakfast, the Bishop and his party started again at eleven o'clock, and reached Malùli at six; for it is easy work going down stream. Next day, Saturday, was devoted to the work of baptizing the adult Indians; and pretty hard work it was, 177 being baptized. On Sunday, again, there were 64 adults to be baptized, besides 152 children; there were candidates for confirmation; there was an Indian couple to be married; and Holy Communion to be administered. How the work was to be got through decently seemed a puzzle. . At first peep of day, Mr. Couchman was at work, paper and pencil in hand, arranging with the Indians the order in which they should come up to the font, and the names they should there receive. At half-past ten this necessary work was hardly accomplished. The congregation had by this time assembled in the chapel, and Divine service began with the Office for the Baptism of Adults; it was absolutely necessary to dispense with the Morning Prayer and Litany; even then the Bishop and his chaplain were occupied four hours and forty minutes, uninterruptedly, about the several services; the heat of the over-crowded chapel was scarcely bearable.

There were five young persons confirmed, of whom two were newly-baptized Indians. The Bishop thought it good to let the others, that had just been baptized, have a few months more of instruction and probation, promising to visit them again early next year.

Engagements below compelled the Bishop to start downwards that same evening. Accordingly, at six o'clock the boat left Malúli, with the best wishes of all the Indians: many of whom ran alongside as far as the path extended, waving their hands, and cheering as they had never done before—for they are a most taciturn and undemonstrative race. A melancholy event happened to cast something of gloom over these happy doings, as though to admonish, that the very purest of earthly delights are liable to a touch, at least, of sorrow. Kanaimapo's eldest son had gone from Malúli on the Tuesday, leaving behind him his wife and family, and intending to be back on the Saturday; but he was detained below, and did not get back till midday on Sunday. Meantime, his wife had been confined on the Wednesday, and was very ill in the bush. The poor Indians did all they could for her, walling-in her hut as well as they were able; and the Bishop sent her chlorodyne, which appeared to relieve her. On his return to

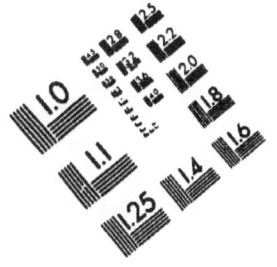

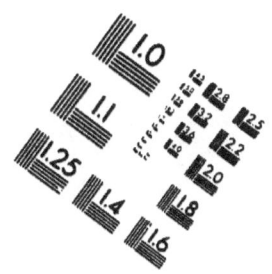

**IMAGE EVALUATION
TEST TARGET (MT-3)**

Malùli, on Friday evening, she was better; and it was arranged that she should be baptized in her own hut, as the Bishop passed down after service on Sunday. After the adult baptisms were over on Sunday morning, and while the infants were being baptized, a message was brought to the chapel, praying the Bishop to wait for her, as she was dressing to come and be baptized in church. But presently after came another message, saying that she was unable to cross the river; for her hut was a little way down on the other shore. When the services were over, news came that she was dead. This is a sample of the earnestness of these poor people to become Christians. Old Kanaimapo himself had been suffering so much from fever all Thursday and Friday, that he fainted in church early in the service, and had to be baptized in his hammock, which was brought in and slung for him in one corner. Two good doses of quinine had been given him, and he was better when he shook hands with the Bishop, to bid him good-bye on Sunday evening. Three poor lads, out of nearly 400 Indians, had to be refused the coveted privilege of Holy Baptism. From the Macousie country, far, far away in the interior, they had come—a six weeks' journey, probably, according to their manner of travelling—not perhaps in the first instance to hear the Gospel; but they were evidently sorry, and every one was sorry for them, when they were told they were hardly ready to be baptized, and had better wait a little longer.

It is impossible to over-estimate the importance of this gathering-in of the Acawoios, which is going on in the other rivers of the country more extensively even than in the Demerara. They are the pedlars of the Caribbean tribes in general; and so mix constantly with the other tribes, and can make themselves understood by most of them. By them, doubtless, the whole lump will in due time become leavened—" Hoc erit in votis."

Sketches from India.

CHAPTER I.

CASTE.

AT some meetings of the Committee of the Society for the Propagation of the Gospel, the question of caste was brought under consideration, and, after discussion, a resolution was passed to the effect that missionaries in India were "not to select any converts to Christianity for catechists who had not renounced caste." The word "entirely," with which the resolution as first proposed concluded, it was thought, on second consideration, advisable to omit. This may be regarded as an intimation that the war against caste in India is not yet over; that missionaries are unable or unwilling to demand the renunciation of it by *all* their converts, but are satisfied at present that at least the paid agents of the Society, the native catechists and schoolmasters, should not be the upholders or retainers of the system.

We propose to give our readers some account of caste. Not indeed a learned disquisition on it, with theoretical suggestions of how its evils may be met, but simply a familiar and practical account of how it at present exists, and how it is brought in contact with Christianity.

The young missionary in India (supposing him to be one who is unacquainted with the practical effects of caste) will very soon begin to perceive that there is some latent feeling of disunion and exclusiveness among the people with whom he has cast his lot. He finds that they

mix, yet do not mingle; that there is some strong lack
of sympathy and common fellowship even in the ordinary
concerns of life which he cannot understand, and to which
he has hitherto been a stranger.   Thus, for instance, he
will perceive that the native moonshee (almost always a
Brahmin and a heathen) whom he has engaged to give
him his first lessons in an Indian tongue, is polite, attentive, even obsequious, yet strangely reserved and repel-
lent; he continually draws himself back like a snail
into its shell, shrinks from your touch or close approach,
and has an anxious " noli me tangere " written on every
line of his countenance.   He sits indeed in the same room,
and not far from you, on a chair or mat, but he gathers
his loose flowing drapery together, so that it shall not
touch your person; he will not take the book you are
reading from your hand, and thus be in momentary contact with you : politely he waits till you lay it on the table
before he will take it up to examine or explain.   Should
one of your native servants (who are principally of the
lower castes) enter the room, unmistakable signs of un-
easiness and repugnance are expressed, and probably he
will ask you before many days are over to give orders that
your conferences may not be so interrupted ; prepared
food of any kind brought into the room would produce
horror, the sight of flesh would fill him with loathing,
and he would not hesitate to leave the room precipitately,
and beg to be excused, perhaps, from entering it again.

   This man, the young missionary soon learns, prides
himself on his birth as a Brahmin, and as belonging to
the highest of the four great castes.   He would indignantly deny " that all men are brethren."   God, according to his belief, has *not* made of one blood all the nations
of the earth, but has created them differently, and enjoined
that they should ever remain separate and distinct.   Very
soon he will turn the conversation to this very subject,
and explain to the missionary the existence and the divine

origin of the institution which gives him his superiority; the reason why, though he is too polite to say so, he still considers himself immeasurably your superior and also the superior of millions of his fellow Hindus. He will say that "throughout India there prevails the marvellous system which the English call caste, and the origin of caste is this: We Hindus are all born out of our great god Brahma, but we sprang from different portions of the deity, and it is because the birth and source of origin of each caste is different that we hold it to be the design of the Creator that the members of each division should all through life remain distinct and unconnected. First, out of the head of the god, the Brahmin was born, and as he derives his origin from the highest member, the seat of the more noble and intellectual faculties, his is therefore the highest caste. To pray, to read the sacred books, to study religion and science, to instruct the people, is his duty; born from the mouth, the wisdom that proceeds out of the mouth is his province. Next in order was born the Chatrya, or warrior, from the shoulders and arms of the deity; and as he issued from the seat of strength and vigour, the arms of the warrior, the controlling power of government, are entrusted to him. In peace, the land finds her kings and rulers and magistrates in the members of this class; in war, her soldiers and generals were to be supplied by the second or kingly caste. The third is the merchant caste, born from the belly and thighs of Brahma, to whom is entrusted the duty of providing for the support and nourishment of a state. And last of all is the lowest caste, because born from the lowest member, the Sudra or farmer caste, which sprang from the feet of the god, and the duties of which are of the earth, earthy—to till the ground, to labour, to serve. In this last division is included the great mass of the agricultural and labouring classes in India. The burly ryot, as we have seen him ploughing with six yoke of oxen, the slim

T

women weeding the rice fields, the coolies in our tea and coffee plantations, those who have died like rotten sheep in Orissa, and the troublesome individuals with whom the indigo factor is ever at variance."

Our Indian moonshee, from whom we have supposed this account to proceed, will be ready to quote from the sacred books in proof of his account of the divine origin of caste. He will argue, it is not a temporary distinction to be assumed or dropped at pleasure ; it does not consist in some trifling difference of food or dress ; but it is a *distinct birth*, as is expressed in the very word " caste," which is a corruption of the Portuguese *casta*, a breed or birth. Hence it is that, as among many nations, the intermixture of different species is regarded with horror, so the mingling of the different castes is opposed to the command and the design of God. God has willed that they should be distinct ; he has appointed to each the duties of their province ; given each a rule of life stated in laws as explicit as the Levitical code—the dress, the food, the custom of each. It is pious to obey ; the well-being of each caste, and the general prosperity of the whole state is ensured thereby. It is the height of folly and iniquity to omit, to oppose, to innovate. " I am a Brahmin," he will say ; " but if I am born to high position, high and arduous duties are also assigned me ; restrictions of various kinds are imposed, and I am a Brahmin *only* so long as I comply with those exactions and act up to those requirements. A simple and pure life is required of me. I live on fruit, and grain, and milk : flesh and spirits of all kinds are forbidden to me. I must perform frequent ablutions ; I must fast continually. When I go home, after our lesson, I may not partake of food till I have changed my garments, bathed from head to foot, and thus washed off the ceremonial defilement which I have incurred by my connection with yourself. The hindrances which hedge me about, the various enactments to which I and the order to which I

belong are subject, may be considered vexatious and un-
meaning to others; but to me they are a birthright and
inheritance, and I am content to observe them, because
they have come down to me as the necessary conditions of
the high lot to which I was born. I declined to sit on
that chair, because it was covered with leather, to me an
impure substance. I would rather tread on a mat than on
a carpet, because the latter more easily contracts and retains impurity. I cannot receive food or drink at your
hands, and when your servants, Pariahs and outcasts as I
have been accustomed to regard them, approach me, their
presence is polluting and disgusting; but all these are the
necessary conditions of my life. I should not be a Brahmin
at all unless thus separated and hedged about. Again, I
have not the power which attaches to the kingly or Chatrya
caste. I am far poorer than the wealthy merchants who
form the third caste. I know nothing of the self-gratifica-
tions and bodily pleasures which are permitted to the hard-
working farmer caste; but all this is compensated for by
the high position I hold, by the respect which all other
classes are *bound* to pay me. We are the councillors of
kings, the conscience-keepers of princes; we read the
stars, we foretell the eclipses, we declare the propitious
time at which a king may be crowned, or a journey undertaken. Observe the salute and obeisances which all will
pay me as I walk down the street. Once, your Pariah
servant would have incurred death for his heedless approach; and even now, among those who are uninfluenced
by your teaching, the Pariah will get off the high-road
and crouch in the paddy fields till I pass. Well may we
Brahmins view with sorrowful indignation the spread of
Christianity, for with its growth we are every day losing
our position, our *prestige*, and our privileges."

Supposing a colloquy such as the above to have served
in introducing the subject to the young missionary, it will
not be long before the workings of the vast system are

still further unfolded to him, and he will become gradually
conscious of the many-headed hydra, the mighty coils, the
far-reaching circlings and windings of the python that
holds India in its embrace.   He learns that caste is not so
simple a division as his moonshee has led him to suppose;
that it has, like every evil, "increased and multiplied
exceedingly;" that, in the first place, not comprised in
any of the four great castes, is a vast mixed multitude who
still boast of their caste; that, secondly, each of the four
first-mentioned castes is split up and divided in itself to
an inconceivable extent, so that there are wheels within
wheels—Brahmins who will not eat with Brahmins, and
Sudras who will not intermarry with Sudras; and, thirdly,
he will soon observe that so much does this system of
division and exclusiveness pervade all classes of Hindu
society, that the very lowest are not free from it, so that
when you have come to the lowest depth there is still a
lower; the very Pariahs or outcasts have several divisions
and castes among themselves, each member of which is as
exclusive towards the others as the Brahmin is to himself.
There may at first have been but four castes; there are
now four thousand, the divine origin of which our Brahmin
moonshee would find it very hard indeed to prove.

Let us take, for instance, the great *artizan* caste, comprising five classes, the white and the black smith, carpenters,
masons, and weavers—a body composing within itself so
much of the skill, the wealth, and especially the intelligence
of the middle classes.   What is to be said of them?   From
what member of Brahma do they spring?   They are the
offspring of illicit intercourse, and of irregular intermarriage, say the Brahmins: an aspersion which the five
castes themselves (for thus are they known) indignantly
deny, and, moreover, systematically oppose the rights and
pretensions of the priestly order.   Whatever their origin,
there they are as a caste, or rather as five more castes,
all boasting of it, wearing even the sacred Brahminical

cord over the shoulders as a sign of equality, abstaining from meat, clinging to little self-imposed ordinances and restrictions, as jealous of the intrusion of others into their body, as they are jealous to encroach on the rights of others. So also every trade has now become a caste—the barber, the washerwoman, the fisherman, the petty retailer, the wandering story-teller, tumbler, and juggler, the musician, and the dancing-girl, each and all cling to their caste, cook their food separately, and will not share it, assume some little mark or peculiarity which is considered distinctive and of more value than wealth or even life itself. A spot or streak of paint on the forehead, a fold of cloth thrown over one shoulder or another, a peculiarity in the tie of a turban; any of these suffice, and are retained and clung to from father to son with more than religious pertinacity.

And if there are *additional* castes, there are also *divisional* ones. Not merely are there countless castes not included in the four great ones, but there are also countless subdivisions in each of the first four great divisions. It would be a great mistake to suppose that all Brahmins are the same: there are Brahmins and Brahmins, and each keep to their own little clique, marrying only within their own little circle, declining not merely to eat with others of the same great tribe, but even, in some cases, refusing to let others look on while they partake of their meals. The Brahmin of the north looks down with contempt on one born in a more southerly province, and therefore farther from the holy cities, the ancient homes of learning and piety. A missionary once succeeded in obtaining the services as moonshee of a Brahmin from a territory some 200 miles north of his own district. This man, when he came to his employer, could find among the Brahmins of the place none of the same clan as himself, therefore none whose house he might enter, whose food he might partake of. He was obliged to have a house for

himself, a man of his own family to cook his food; he
drew a curtain around him when he ate; and every year,
when he was obliged to perform some religious observances,
at which the presence of two or three of his own particular
sect were necessary, he was obliged to incur a long and
expensive journey till he had found a Brahmin family of
just that particular caste, to aid in his religious rites.

Nor must this be regarded as at all an extreme case.
There are clerical Brahmins devoted to the service of
religion, and lay Brahmins, who may become writers,
Government officials, lawyers, and even soldiers; there are
Vishnavites, or the followers of Vishnu; and Shivites, or
the worshippers of Shiva; there are Vedantists or Pan-
theists, and Smarthas or Eclectics; and all these may be
considered, to all intents and purposes, different castes,
some not eating, others not marrying, with their fellow
Brahmins.   As to the subdivisions of the Sudra or farmer
caste, they are so numerous that, according to a common
proverb, there are as many castes among the farmers as
there are species of fishes in the sea.

But it is when we consider the case of those tens of
thousands who are considered beyond the pale of caste,
and in the eyes of their fellow Hindus are destitute of all
caste, that we can understand and appreciate the hold
which caste has obtained upon the Hindu mind—the com-
pleteness as well as the complications of its working. What
will our readers say when they learn that even the Pariah
has his caste, and not merely does he keep himself apart
from the Chandala (the common sweeper and the worker
in leather), but even in his degraded community there is
division and subdivision, and Pariah will not mingle with
Pariah, but parades his little rag of distinction, and says
to his fellows, " I am better than thou."   Among these
outcasts, whom others esteem so wretched and despise, are
at least four distinct classes or clans; and among those who
have no right to caste at all, caste disputes are perhaps more

frequent and virulent than among the higher and by all
acknowledged castes.

Very soon, indeed, will this fact obtrude itself upon the
attention of the missionary, and be to him a fruitful source
of anxiety. Let him be in Tinnevelly, in Tanjore, in Travancore, or in Bengal, caste is still a stumbling-block in
his way; let his flock be the representatives of high or low,
or even no caste people, still the manifestations of this all-
pervading spirit are the same; be they the Pariah servants
of the English, the bond-slaves of Travancore, poor palmyra
climbers, or intelligent Brahmins, artizans, and well-to-do
farmers, still caste disputes crop up eternally, and each
little clique will endeavour to gain over the missionary to
espouse their cause, to permit them to retain their little
privileges and distinctions, to shut out those below, to
make themselves equal with those above. We have heard
the Brahmin moonshee boasting of his high order and
privileges; but we could also show the Pariah declaring
how he is superior to the Madiga; and if the Brahmin
keeps himself at a distance from others, the Pariah, too,
builds his hut away from the scavenger and street-cleaner,
and, exiled from others himself, will by no means associate
with his fellow in misfortune. Bloody strife has taken place
between Mala or Pariah and Madiga because the latter has
presumed to wear a red turban, to carry a sword or dagger,
to mount a horse, to have more than the prescribed number
of water-vessels before his door at a marriage feast, all of
which are encroachments upon the *quasi* caste privileges of
the former. Endless litigation also takes place; sums of
money, very considerable in proportion to their means,
are freely spent in order that it may be decided which
of these miserable classes of *outcasts* is still the higher
caste!

It is in the midst of such a scene of division and strife
and arrogant self-assertion, among low as well as high, that
the missionary finds himself placed, the teacher of that

blessed religion whose end and object is "that they all
may be one."

We have now endeavoured to show how widely spread
and how deeply seated was the spirit of caste in all classes
of Hindu society. We placed much stress, moreover, on
the fact that not the Brahmin alone or the members of the
four legitimate castes were the upholders of the system,
but that even the Pariah or outcast maintained pseudo-
caste distinctions and differences, with as much pertinacity
as those who had a right to do so. It will be seen from
this that from whatever class or grade our converts to
Christianity in India may have been drawn, they are all
to a certain extent the upholders of caste; and therefore
troubles and disputes concerning caste take place quite as
much among the low caste converts of Tinnevelly, as among
those of a higher caste in Bengal. "From the very outset
I felt persuaded," writes Dr. Caldwell, "that the Shanars
(a class but little above the Pariahs or outcasts), who form
the large proportion of our Tinnevelly Christians, were as
much influenced by caste feelings as the people of any
caste in India;" and we ourselves can bear testimony that
the Malas of the Telugu country, who are regarded as
immeasurably inferior to any of the other castes, have still
the spirit of caste as strongly developed as in the Brahmin
or the Rajpoot. The missionary in India, then, must be
prepared for disputes concerning caste in whatever part of
the country he may be stationed, and whatever may be the
social position of his people. In our previous article we
supposed the case of a young missionary made aware for
the first time of this feeling of exclusion by the conduct
and explanations of his Brahmin moonshee. Let us complete the picture, and describe the circumstances under
which the strong caste feeling among his own people will
very probably be brought to his notice. His moonshee (a
heathen in most cases) has described to him the hold which
caste retains on those who have not yet been brought into

the glorious liberty of the Gospel; and the missionary will
naturally suppose that, in the case of the converts under
his charge, such distinctions and prejudices have long since
been abandoned. But very quickly will he be undeceived.
It is not too much to say that the first disputes which he
will be called upon to decide—the first quarrels he will
find it necessary to quell—will have reference to this vexed
question of caste. Occasionally the ability of the young
missionary to govern is tested at the very outset by the
village elders raking up some long-standing caste feud,
and appealing to him for a decision which will serve to
show them whether he intends to keep aloof from such
matters, or will lend himself unwittingly to be made the
tool of the stronger party. Let us see the nature of some
of these disputes and caste troubles as they crop up more
or less in every community of converted Hindus. The
missionary perceives that occasionally in the same Christian
village various castes live apart. By some tacit consent or
agreement among themselves, the higher castes have their
quarter and the lower theirs, and any attempt of the latter
to encroach—of a Pariah, for instance, to build a house in
the street of the Sudras—would be resented and resisted
to the last. Again, in church all do not sit promiscuously,
but certain parties arrogate to themselves certain portions
of the sacred edifice. This attempt, indeed, of classifi-
cation and of each caste sitting apart is opposed by
missionaries of our Church (the Romish and Lutheran
missionaries allow it) to the utmost; but if this matter is
a little lost sight of—if for a few months it escapes the
missionary's notice—things return to their old course; the
higher castes are found occupying the "chief places," the
lower shrink back, and are found farthest from the altar
and nearest the door. But it is, sad to say, at the Holy
Communion, and in the order of approach to the altar to
partake of the blessed elements, that the greatest difficulties
occur. There is no difficulty about the bread; that is

delivered by the priest into the hand of each communicant, and therefore the order of precedence is a matter of indifference. With the cup it is different, and the object of the higher caste is to partake before it has been contaminated by the touch and taste of the lower. The missionary, therefore, is forced to be most particular and most observant on this head, to see that all classes are well mixed together, high and low approaching together, and the latter partaking in the first instance, more commonly than the former. The battle against caste has now so long been fought that the case stands thus: converts of the higher caste will not absolutely refuse the cup because one of a lower caste has already participated, but they will strive perseveringly and unceasingly to be admitted first; and if this be permitted in a few instances by a young and inexperienced missionary, they will come ultimately to claim it as a right. In thus insisting on the exclusion of all caste distinctions in the house and at the services of God, the missionaries have, indeed, gained a step; but it still requires unceasing vigilance to keep the advantage thus gained; and the same may be said of all the devices and schemes which the missionaries have put in effect against caste. They succeed, but only for the time, and only in particular instances; they succeed in the letter, but fail in the spirit. Many caste customs have successfully been opposed, many prejudices almost eradicated; but let the least carelessness on this subject prevail—let the vigilance of the missionary cease—let the systematic opposition to caste be withdrawn under the idea that the victory has been won, that the feeling is now extinct—and the old leaven once more begins to work, old customs creep in, and we find that we have only annulled the *letter* of caste in a few particular cases, but that the *spirit* of caste is still unquenched. Village wells, and the exclusive right to them of certain castes, is another fertile source of dispute. None but the higher castes may draw from these wells. The lower castes have their own wells, occasionally at some distance off, and in cases where they have not they are obliged to *beg* water from their more fortunate companions. We have ourselves seen in one of the hottest regions of India unfortunates of this class with their water-pots ranged a few yards distant from the well, standing patiently by till one of the more good-natured or kindly disposed of their high-caste brethren empties the pot he has just filled into the vessel eagerly held forth, and returns for a second supply for himself. Even when a river is the source from which all parties in a village draw their supplies of water, caste distinctions are still observed, and all may not draw water in the same spot. The higher castes, like the wolf in the fable, choose a spot *up* the stream, which flows down from them to poor Pariah lambs, who are glad thus to escape from the charge of fouling the stream. When a village adopts Christianity it is not an easy matter for members of the higher caste to give up the privileges to which they have been so long accustomed ; and on no matter are they more sensitive than on this, viz., the exclusive right to their own wells. Here there is a source of perpetual discord. One fine morning it is rumoured about that Kulla, the Pariah convert, presuming on his position as gardener to the new missionary, has determined to try again the question of his right to draw water in the village well. What a hubbub is raised—children roar, women scream, men gesticulate. In earlier days a great row would have been the result, and Kulla would probably have been beaten within an inch of his life. Now a deputation waits upon the missionary, to protest against the act of the innovating Kulla. He, on the other hand, pleads the new *régime*— are not all now Christians—are not all one—and was not the water for the *iyer's* (priest's) garden ? It will be very difficult indeed for the missionary to know what step to take, without on the one hand offending prejudices, or, on the other, permitting the lower castes to take the initiative in acts known to be offensive to their high-caste brethren. The difficulty is met in many villages by digging a new well, and insisting that all parties shall have common access to this, without infringing on the ancient rights of each party to the wells formerly in use.

Let us now proceed to consider the various steps taken by missionaries to eradicate the spirit of caste, and to overcome each manifestation of it, and consider to what extent they have succeeded in so doing. It is one misfortune that missionaries themselves are not agreed in the view they take of caste, and that there is no combined plan of action against it. Indeed there are a few who uphold caste, on the plea that it is a national custom or a social distinction, which need not interfere with religion; but these are for the most part connected with the German Lutheran missions. Again, there are others who disapprove of it in theory, but who do nothing in opposition to it; who wink at its evils, and conceive themselves not called upon to discountenance it. There are others, also, who as yet have nothing to do with caste, whose converts belong entirely to one and the same caste, and who are not yet called upon to assert their separateness by the admission of other denominations into their body. To such communities caste troubles have not yet come, and the battle of caste will have to be fought by their missionaries when converts of some lower grade are brought for the first time in connection with them. Lastly, there are some missionaries who, in opposing caste, make the mistake of denouncing usages that have nothing to do with caste, but are simply national customs of the Hindus. We remember the ill-feeling created when in one mission the *top-knot* was ordered to be cut off, as savouring of caste. It would, indeed, be well if there could be one plan of combined action; but in the absence of this, let us state the several steps which the most advanced reformers have taken, and estimate the success with which these have been attended.

Everything like priority of position in church or of access to the holy table is steadily discountenanced and opposed ; and we believe it is coming to be taken for granted by all Hindus, that in the presence of God and in His house all are equal. Love-feasts are held, not merely at the head-quarters of the missionary, but in the out-stations (where caste is more apt to lurk secure), at which all partake of food cooked by a man of the lowest caste. In some missions, prayer-meetings from house to house, irrespective of caste, are carried out by those who wish to declare against the system. High and low sit toge'her in all schools without discrimination, and in boarding-schools children of all castes eat promiscuously food that has been cooked by a man of the lowest caste. A great advance this since the time when, as described by a missionary of the S. P. G. in the Tanjore district, a young child of about six or seven years of age, in one of the boarding-schools, burst into passionate tears because *the platter which contained his rice had touched that of a boy of lower caste.* Lastly, all paid agents of the societies, the native catechists and schoolmasters, who have so important a share in the work of missions in India, are required to give up caste *in toto*, and, moreover, to give some proof of their having abandoned it. With reference to these native agents, the missionary is bound to take up a higher and more decisive tone and to demand the utter abandonment of caste. If they are to be the teachers of others—if they are to work hand in hand with the missionary—if they are to labour freely and unreservedly among all classes, entering into the houses of high and low caste alike, praying at the bedside of the Brahmin, if need be, or tending the couch of the cholera-stricken Pariah—no vestige of the proud, cold, exclusive systems in which they have been brought up can be permitted to still cling to them. And here will be perceived the different line which the missionary is compelled to take in dealing with

the teachers from what he adopted in working among the
people. The former we have a right to command—tho
latter we can but exhort, and advise, by patient deed and
loving counsel, to abandon what is so incon...stent with
their Christian profession.

And now, in conclusion, let us draw tho attention of our
readers to the point whereunto we have desired that all
that has been here written should tend, viz., a just idea of
the hold and influence which caste still has upon the Hindu
mind. We have seen that it pervades all classes of Hindus
—that four original ca...es have now become four thousand
—that there are divisions and sub-divisions—and tho
tendency to exclusiveness which it engenders has led the
Brahmin to separate from the Brahmin, as well as tho
Pariah to set up divisions in his own despised class, and
to shrink from contact with those whom he esteems still
lower than himself. We have seen that all the efforts of
Christian missionaries during upwards of a quarter of a
century have attained but partial success; that caste disputes are almost as rife now as when good Daniel Wilson
went down into the south to set in order the things that
were wanting, and vehemently opposed this unchristian
"devilish" practice; that at recent committee meetings
of the S.P.G. the question of what steps were to be taken
against it in the diocese of Madras came under consideration, and in the resolution passed the Society ex-
presses itself as awaiting with interest the account of farther
steps taken by missionaries in this matter. All this is
sufficient to show how ingrained in the mind of the Hindu
is the idea of caste, how difficult it is for him to shake
himself free of its thraldom, and how patiently and perseveringly the fight against caste should still be maintained.
Let the friends of missions in England also endeavour to
appreciate the marvellous elasticity and pliancy of the
whole system—the way in which caste recovers itself from
every blow which was to have laid it prostrate, and con-

forms and adapts itself to even the most adverse circumstances. We cannot do better here than quote from a report of Dr. Caldwell, published in 1860, in which this subject is considered. He writes—

"Every arrangement that ignores caste, or that has the effect of bringing the different castes together, is protested and contended against as if it were foreknown to be a fatal injury; and yet when the arrangement has actually been carried into effect, instead of admitting itself to be beaten, it pretends that what has been done was merely a matter of course or of official routine, which goes for nothing, and that it retains all that it really cares for as firmly as ever. Whenever convenience or gain is at stake it lays aside its scruples, to be resumed again at a more favourable season. It adapts itself to the new state of things, whatever that new state may be, with wonderful elasticity, forms new alliances instead of those that failed it in the hour of need, shifts its front, changes its mode of warfare, bends to the blast like the reed, and as soon as the storm is over raises its head as vauntingly as ever. It was once supposed that caste would be destroyed if pupils of all castes learned together in the same school; but this arrangement is now almost universal, and yet caste survives. It was then supposed that it would be a fatal blow to caste if native Christians of all castes received the Communion at the same time, and especially if they all partook of one and the same cup; but this arrangement goes for nothing now; it is done in church, only it does not count. It was believed that if boys were brought up promiscuously in a boarding-school or seminary in which food was prepared by low-caste cooks, caste would be destroyed—caste could never survive such an arrangement as that; but that arrangement has been made, and caste survives. 'It was an unavoidable inconvenience;' 'It was done merely for the sake of a situation;' 'They were boys only that did it, and boys can submit to anything.' It did not count. It was then said, 'Women are the real upholders of caste. Educate girls on anti-caste principles, and caste will be at an end.' Multitudes of girls have now received a boarding-school education, in the course of which caste has been set at naught daily. Many of them have been married also to young men who had been brought up in a similar manner. In many respects it is unquestionable that girls brought up in our boarding-schools have been very greatly improved, and yet no sooner are they married and settled in life than caste reappears in all their domestic arrangements. What they did in school does not count. Those who truly, honestly, and voluntarily carry out in their homes the anti-caste principles on which they were educated are but the fraction of a fraction."

We may add to these instances of the vitality of caste; and it does not want much foresight to be able to say that it will outlive even the innovations which the *railway in India* have rendered necessary. We have heard a hope expressed by many that the railway would do more to abolish caste than anything else that had been attempted by the missionaries. But how stands the case? Brahmin and Pariah sit side by side in a railway carriage without the caste of the former being injured thereby. "It is a matter of necessity," they say; "it is altogether a new circumstance, an unforeseen emergency; it does not count." Those who in the carriage sat side by side, when they come to their native villages will not approach within twenty yards of each other.

It is the continual occurrence of anomalies and inconsistencies and new developments such as these that render the struggle against caste so difficult. What is to be said of an enemy that, Protean-like, continually changes its form; that, like a Mahratta army, when scattered in one quarter, only appears in greater array in another; that makes each successive defeat but the prelude to a victory? What Napoleon said of an English army is true of caste—

"It does not know when it is beaten." It is marvellous to see how like the deadly cobra, or some cold-blooded monster of the deep, after several successive blows has laid it prostrate, it is still tenacious of life, and after a time rears its crest as powerful and triumphant as ever.

Let not the missionary abroad or the friends of missions at home be too sanguine of immediate success, and look forward with impatience for some well-devised scheme that may be expected to overcome the subtle spirit of caste. Rather let patient persevering opposition to each successive development of caste in a mission be their aim, and let this be supplemented by endeavours to alter and raise the whole tone of feeling on this point. No system that *forces* a renunciation of caste is likely to succeed, except for a time and in particular cases; it may succeed in opposing the letter, but it will fail to overcome the spirit of caste. To obtain a *voluntary* relinquishment of caste is what they should strive for, and this can best be done by raising the tone of Christian society, and insisting on the incompatibility of the divisions and distinctions with the "mind of Christ." One other proposition remains, and that can best be stated in the words of one of the ablest missionaries of the Indian Church: "The one arrangement by which caste can be extinguished is intermarriage. This unquestionably is the final battle; but before that battle can be fought with a prospect of success, a hundred preparatory battles must be fought and won. Intermarriage cannot be urged with any prospect of the alliance proving a happy one so long as there is no social intercourse between the different castes, so long as the touch of a low-caste person is supposed to communicate pollution, and so long as there is so great a disparity between the higher and lower castes with respect to modes of life and habits. When all ideas of caste defilement have been eradicated, when social intercourse by eating and drinking has become common, when the lower castes have risen in cleanliness at least to

U

the level of the higher, intermarriage will follow as a matter of course."

This is one of the "things that are before" which are to be realised; and in attempting to bring it about, the workers in India may well take for their motto the words, "In quietness and confidence shall be your strength."

CHAPTER II.

CHRISTMAS IN AN INDIAN MISSION.

I HAVE always been particularly susceptible on the subject of Christmas and its due observance. It was, I suppose, because my own Christmases as a boy at home were such happy ones, that I have always been anxious to make the day as bright and cheerful as possible to those with whom I have been brought in contact. And the result has been that happier even than the Christmases of boyhood have been those spent in the solitude of an Indian Mission, and among converts but just acquainted with the hallowed rejoicing of the day. To each of us, the older we grow, it is the light of the past that sheds a glow upon the present, and he enjoys most the return of that day who can go back in spirit and conjure up most vividly the happy hours it brought, and the pleasure with which it was anticipated and greeted.

Such reminiscences have always been very sweet in my own case. How well I remember our anticipations of its coming, our reckonings and calculations as to its approach, and the almost impossibility of believing that at last it had come. I can recall how we woke at midnight to go, a long string of little ones in our white night dresses, falling for that one occasion into due order of precedence, the eldest first, the youngest, whom no stratagem could keep asleep, last, to our mother's bedside to wish her a happy Christmas, and then to wake my father with the same filial but untimely gratulation. I can feel once more my mother's hands about the chubby cheeks that are now considerably weatherbeaten, and then from under her

pillow came forth little parcels—a Christmas present for
each. We were supposed to know nothing of these tiny
rewards till the moment of reception, but it was a make-
believe of ignorance—for had we not heard distinctly
over-night the locking of the press where such treasures
were kept, the wrapping of them in tissue-paper, and had
we not speculated during the livelong night as to what
would fall to the lot of each? And then having obtained
each his toy or reward, what degenerate soul could think
any longer of sleep! We sat up in our cribs holding
what might be called a *bed* of justice, and waited as ship-
wrecked mariners wait for the dawn, and longed as only
children can long for the morning that is to bring new joys.

But I shall picture no more of these early scenes. I
have but alluded to them, because long years after, and
under far different circumstances, it was the thought of
what Christmas had been to myself as a child that impelled
and guided me in the endeavour to make it indeed a day
of rejoicing to those who stood to me in the relation of
disciples and children.

And now let me endeavour to describe a Christmas very
different from those early ones I have just mentioned. It
is Christmas-eve, and has been indeed a busy day to all at
the mission-station. The missionary's little house, which
is to be the place of common rendezvous, has assumed
quite a holiday aspect. It has been thoroughly cleaned
and whitewashed, a great space in front has been swept
out and kept clean, and a temporary verandah has been
erected with poles and mats, which are so bewreathed and
garlanded that the rough material and the ruder workmanship is concealed. I myself have had a great deal to
occupy me, for by nightfall I expect hundreds of guests,
and all my preparations for their reception, for our
Christmas to-morrow, and for the feast which is to succeed
it, must be completed before they arrive. At least a
hundred measures of rice have been purchased, half a

dozen or more fat sheep have been selected, a row of
temporary fire-places have been prepared in the open air,
and by them stand great earthen pots and vessels for
boiling the rice and preparing the curry—the beginning
and the ending of an Indian feast.

Wearied with these many cares, I am glad that they are
coming to a close. As it is now the cool of the evening,
I place my easy-chair under the shade of the verandah,
and before my guests begin to arrive, before the spot now
so quiet and almost deserted becomes full of life and
bustle, let me occupy a few moments in recording the
suggestions which the circumstances under which I find
myself naturally give rise to.

The due observance of Christian festivals in a heathen
country has always appeared to me a matter of great
importance. A judgment is formed of the religion itself
by the festivals which adorn it, and it is not too much to
say that many a heathen will take his deepest and most
vivid impressions of Christianity from what he has seen of
the observance of its feasts. And so also with catechumens
and recent converts. How important a matter is it that
Christian festivals should be placed before them in an
interesting and attractive guise, so that the great doctrines
they are intended to teach may be prominently brought
forth and leave deep and lasting impressions on the mind.

Let it be remembered that the Hindus, to whatever sect
they belong, are not without their own great feasts and
fasts, and that these are enjoyed by high and low; that
even among those separated by caste observances and
difference of worship, they are regarded as national opportunities for common rejoicing, as seasons when it is
incumbent to make merry, to eat and to drink, and to
send portions to those who have not, and at least as
seasons when *expense* in entertainment, in charity,. or
simply in display, must be incurred. Not to mention
countless minor ones, the feast of the Hindu New Year,

and in the country the feast of ingathering at the end of the year, when the Great Mother-earth is worshipped, are most commonly and generally observed—in anticipation of which the poorest farmer keeps a lamb, and fattens it up carefully to be slaughtered on the great day (to tens of thousands the only occasion when flesh is partaken of) for the use of his family and that of his friends and dependents. The lesser festivals and what may be termed the movable feasts are countless. Each god of any note in the calendar has his day; each temple or fane has its anniversary or fête, when its votaries gather together, and contributions are made, and the regalia of the idol is brought forth, and torch-light processions are arranged; each little village has its gala day, when the village-potter is engaged to mould a form of the rural deity, and a house-to-house collection is made to defray the expense of the sacrifices and offerings. So numerous are the festivals of the Hindu calendar that they are a serious hindrance to the progress of the public business; and English officials in nearly every department are obliged to complain that public work of all kinds is thrown back and delayed by the oft-recurring and continued absence of their native subordinates, on account of the feasts and fasts they have to observe.

And here, too, we should state, that these occasions are indeed what they profess to be, intervals of rest and amusement, highly congenial to the habits of an Eastern people, and very necessary among those whom a burning climate makes peculiarly susceptible of that *dolce far niente,* which elsewhere also is appreciated. A gala-day in the country is not marked with even as much of riot and drunkenness as disgraces the green of an English village on a fair or market-day. There is a quiet, lazy, sensuous enjoyment—a little noise of drum or horn—an attempt at a procession—a great display of finery—partial cessation from labour—a somewhat better meal at nightfall—and the feast is over. Not very much harm it will be seen, even if there has not been much good. Thus in the agricultural districts, and among the ryots or farmers : in towns or cities the display is far greater. Any one who has seen the tens of thousands of both sexes and of all ranks, lining the railway stations for a quarter of a mile, and waiting to be conveyed by special train to the great temple of Tripathy on the feast of the new moon, will not quickly forget the sight—he will see in them living evidence to the fact that the Hindus are a holiday-making and pleasure-seeking nation.

Now Christianity does away with all this at one fell sweep, and the question presents itself—what does it give in return ? Nothing, I answer unhesitatingly, nothing at all commensurate with the necessities of the case ; nothing to compensate for the loss of all this, to fill up the void that must necessarily take place in the minds of those accustomed to a trivial and showy but chastened and innocent gaiety. We require of our converts that they abandon all heathen (I had almost said all Hindu) observances, that they forsake all heathen enjoyments ; we insist that they no longer observe heathen festivals or frequent heathen temples. At one blow the new convert is cut off from the great mass of his fellows—the village-fête is nothing to him any more—he may no more be seen in the idol's temple—he is brought to task for it if any more he joins himself to his heathen relatives, in the new moons and feasts and solemn assemblies, and takes part with the multitude that keep holiday. And let us see what is given to him by way of compensation for the utter annulling of old feasts and observances. Little more in most cases than a dismal Christmas, an Easter but little observed and less understood, a love-feast,* a school-

* In some missions Christians of all castes meet to partake of a common meal, in defiance of caste prejudice. These assemblies are termed love-feasts.

examination or two, and last, not least, that favourite in
England but in India novel form of dissipation—a
missionary meeting! Little or no pains is taken in many
cases to make these great days occasions of marked though
innocent rejoicing; little endeavour is used to cull out
from the mass of Hindu observances what is simply
national and therefore optional to be retained—what is
clearly religious and therefore to be undoubtedly rejected.
As Christmas or Easter approaches the missionary will
naturally endeavour to inform his people of the great
truths which those days are intended to commemorate;
they will be told that these are the two greatest festivals
of the Christian Church, and therefore days to be much
observed; but *how* they are to be observed he takes little
pains to inform them; too often concluding that the same
quiet, cold, spiritual rejoicing which it is to be taken for
granted will welcome the day to his own soul, will suffice
to mark the occasions as Christian festivals in the minds
of his people. And so when the day is come there is a
larger congregation it may be than usual; the people are
expectant to hear when the note of rejoicing will be
struck; they hear the same service as on Sunday—they
are told in the sermon to welcome the day as that whereon
the Saviour of the world was born, and then they are bidden
to depart with the congratulation that that day may be to
them a merry and a happy one. Vain wish indeed if no
personal, no persistent endeavours have been taken to
render that day happy; to instil a new vein of Christian
and quiet joy: vain wish indeed if it is supposed that the
cold, puritanical spirit which has marked our festival
observances for the last three hundred years can ever be
successfully infused into the Hindu mind, and such tame
rejoicings ever sufficiently satisfy the ardent nature of an
Eastern people.

But instead of finding fault with the system adopted by
others, it will be better if I describe the steps I was

accustomed to take, in order to make the great festivals of
the Church more thoroughly observed by my people. It
will be found, I doubt not (indeed I should be the first to
confess it), that many blunders were perpetrated—that
many attempts were failures; but at least I have the
satisfaction of thinking that I was groping in the right
direction, and that the recollection of some of the Christmases in the mission bring with them remembrances of
earnest efforts in myself and of happy enjoyment to my
people.

Weeks beforehand the preparations for the great feast
would begin; in fact, with the first Sunday in Advent is
sounded the first note of preparation, in the repetition and
practising of Christmas carols. As our people are unable
to read or write, they learn these hymns by word of mouth,
repeating line after line, as the catechist or schoolmaster
pronounces it. One hymn especially I remember was a
favourite one—it was on the subject of the Second Advent,
contrasting its glories with the humility of the Saviour's
first appearance, and was sung to the slow, solemn notes
of an Indian air, not unlike some grand old Gregorian
chant. There was something in its beauty and simplicity
that rendered it very attractive and very suggestive, and
when year by year upon Advent Sunday it was pealed
forth in the heartiest manner at our services, people knew
that Christmas was drawing near, and that it was time to
think of preparing for it. These preparations were not
confined to head-quarters, or to the principal station
where the missionary resided—much was to be done in
every little village where there was a Christian community.
The school-rooms and chapels had to be repaired and put
in thorough order; and whatever amount of thatch and
whitewash and plaster was ever expended on the little
huts of our people, was applied for purposes of repair
and ornament in anticipation of the feast. The houses of
the natives are plastered over with mud, and on Hindu

festivals are painted with broad stripes of red and white
alternately, which give them a gay aspect; but I perceived
that the houses of the Christians were, at first, allowed to
remain neglected from one year's end to another, simply
because there was no *fixed occasion* on which renovation
and adornment was incumbent. When they abandoned
idolatry and were required to refrain from the observance
of heathen festivals, no opportunity whatever (except
perhaps the occasional one of a marriage) presented itself
to them for putting in practice the old custom of brighten-
ing up the mud walls from which the heavy monsoons
had washed away every trace of adornment; and the result
was that in outward appearance the Christian villages
contrasted unfavourably with the heathen ones around.
For be it remembered, a Hindu will not whitewash his
house save at such time as he and his neighbours have
been accustomed to do so; and when, owing to some
great social revolution, that stated time does not return to
him, or its obligations are no longer binding, then he is
glad of the excuse to save himself time, and trouble, and
expense. Christmas brought with it an opportunity for
introducing each year more and more of that cleanliness
which is next to godliness; then there was a general
prevalence of whitewash, sweeping, and painting, and
furbishing was the order of the day. Then was the time
for the missionary to introduce some design for widening
the streets, for enlarging the houses, for removing some
obstructions, and generally to improve the beauty and the
sanitary condition of his villages. "Will you spend
another Christmas in that wigwam instead of building a
decent house?" he will say to one. "I cannot allow
that heap of manure to remain any longer so near the
church," to another. "How your relations and Christmas visitors would be astonished if you were to beautify
your village, by rebuilding this street and planting a row
of trees on either side," to a third. Of course, where so

much is done for private dwelling-houses, the little church or chapel in the centre of the village cannot be neglected. I can assert that as much time and trouble is occasionally expended in repairing and decorating the little huts in which our native converts assemble together for prayer, as is devoted to the adornment of our beautiful churches at home, at the blessed seasons of Christmas or Easter. And if Christmas presents an occasion for repairing and cleansing the houses and churches of the converts, it also brings an opportunity for insisting on improvement in dress and in personal cleanliness. The Hindus are, as a nation, scrupulously clean, and naturally fond of bright colours and gay clothing; but some of the converts to Christianity are among the lowest of the low, degraded in person, squalid in appearance, and filthy in their dress. If the country parson at home delights to have his choir-boys, his Sunday scholars, his school-teachers, looking fresh and clean on Christmas morning in holiday attire, tenfold greater is the longing of the missionary to exorcise the demon of dirt, and raise his degraded flock to habits of cleanliness and to outward comeliness that may more assimilate them to the higher castes of the country, and lessen in some respects the wide abyss between the Brahmin and the Pariah. And Christmas is the season, when, without making the people too dependent, help may be afforded; without introducing a love of finery, cleanliness and decency may be encouraged; without detracting from the dignity of his position, the missionary may condescend even to matters of dress—and by satire, by approval, by hint and inuendo, by rewards of clothing to deserving children, by improving the appearance of those immediately connected with himself, introduce a general desire for outward and personal improvement. The gift of a bright red turban to a school-boy, with strict injunctions that it is to be worn for the first time on Christmas-day, may be considered by some a trivial act, unworthy of second thought to the missionary—but if it draws the attention of the boy's relatives and friends to the importance of the approaching occasion, if half-a-dozen grown-up persons feel it incumbent on themselves to discard their greasy head-dresses for new jackets and turbans, the ' price of the red *roomal* will have been well spent, and the deed deemed not unworthy of careful repetition.

These thoughts have occupied the mind of the missionary while seated in his easy-chair in front of his bungalow —he awaits the arrival of his anticipated guests who have been invited to attend the Christmas service and the Christmas feast at head-quarters. A few days before Christmas I was accustomed to publish a kind of encyclical letter, which the master in charge of each village and out-station read aloud to the assembled congregation, inviting all who were able to do so to attend the morning service on Christmas-day at K——, and to accept for that one day of the missionary's hospitality. This, I must observe, was the only occasion on which I permitted myself to make some return for the countless hospitable and kind deeds which I received at the hands of my people. A missionary has to be circumspect and self-denying, even in his charities and benefactions, lest on the one hand he encourage pauperism and too great dependence on himself, or, on the other hand, give cause for the objection that considerations of temporal gain have attracted followers to his teaching. I can only say in answer to the common taunt that Christian converts in India "have everything to gain and nothing to lose," by their adoption of the religion, and in deprecation of the phrase "rice Christians" as insultingly and unjustly applied to our people—that I have received in the way of personal kindness and temporal advantage a hundred-fold more from my people than I was ever able to give them. How many a kind and self-denying deed can I not remember! how many an act of delicate attention and hospitality! the general entertain-

ment offered in my Christmas dinner was but a tithe of the
return due to unwearying attention and habitual hospitality.
And thus it is that on this Christmas-eve I expect to see
the faces of those who have done me kindnesses in stealth
and shamefacedness; the man who wrung the neck of his
solitary hen, that I might not go supperless; the woman
who appeared one day before me and with timid bashfulness
produced a little pot of curds, saying that her "cow had
yeaned, and would I honour her by sharing the abundance
God had given her?" If to-morrow I can send them away
after having enjoyed the rare luxury of curry and rice, will
any carp at or deny my right or privilege to do so? And
that it is which imparts increased satisfaction to the due
observance of this sacred season.

But now my guests are beginning to arrive. As I look
across the plains, now flooded with the rosy light of an
Indian sunset, I can perceive from various points of the
compass processions of men, women, and children, all
dressed in their gayest and best attire, tending to one
common centre—the grove where stands the mission
bungalow. Those from the more distant villages arrive
over-night, in order to recover the fatigue of a walk of
seven or ten miles, by a night's rest before the services
of the next day commence: the Christians of the nearer
villages (for there are some half-dozen hamlets within two
or three miles of head-quarters) will not make their
appearance till an early hour on Christmas-day. The
greeting between missionary and people, as each group
comes up and makes its salutation, is at once graceful and
grotesque. There is the beautiful Oriental form of salutation,—raising the folded hands to the forehead and the
breast, and repeating the Christian formula, "Praise to
the Lord;" and yet one can hardly refrain from a smile
to see how some officious head man *will* insist on arranging
his following in due order, and at a given signal firing off a
very volley of salutes. And then come kind inquiries:

"Have you all been well since my last visit? and the women and children? any more babies?" "All are well, thank God and the efficacy of your prayers. Star of Beauty has been safely delivered of twins." "And how are your crops?" "By the grace of God and your favour, we have had the rice harvest earlier this year than ever before." "Have your houses and the chapel been put in good order? Do you intend, when you return, to have a village feast among yourselves? Whose son is that little boy, whose red kerchief shows that he won the first prize at school?" Then to a head man: "Why is it that your wife has not accompanied you? it is only once a-year that you come to visit me, and she would have been pleased to see some of the wonders I possess?" to which the usual answer is, "Your servants have many buffaloes, and some one must stay at home—*all* the women wanted to come, and many wept at being left behind—but can we not tell them what we have seen?" It will be observed that curiosity as well as kindly feeling attracts many—and as the groups disperse, it is amusing to see how the exterior and interior of the missionary's house is scanned; how an excited crowd is gathered to hear the clock strike;* how the furniture, the few pictures, and especially the laden book-shelves, formed the subjects of warm debate. Natives living in the interior and removed from any considerable town or city, see but little or nothing of English life, and so even those relics of European art and civilisation, which an itinerant missionary clings to, are quite sufficient to create the highest wonder and admiration. But night is closing over us. By this time several hundreds have come together. They find shelter in the verandah, in the out-houses, or for the most part under the trees. They do

---

* A telescope and microscope, large mirror and burning-glass, my photographic camera and galvanic battery, powerful magnet and magic lantern, were, on these occasions, subjects of intense admiration and amusement.

not mingle to any great extent: the inhabitants of each village, unless united by ties of relationship with those of other villages, sitting apart or reclining on the ground in somewhat quiet and unsocial groups. Presently the sound of a hand-bell summons all to take part in the usual evening service of our Church. This arrangement is not by any means an exceptional one, or necessitated by the occasion; on the other hand, the daily morning and evening service is conducted, as a rule, in all our little stations and villages. But there is something striking in the scene now represented. The service is held in the open air; the congregation has increased to several hundreds, the gathering gloom is partially dispelled by candlesticks almost as novel as the blazing pine-torches of Allan McGregor in the "Legend of Montrose"—earthen saucers are filled with cotton-seed saturated with oil, and these placed at intervals on split bamboos, throw a wild, fitful light over the little thatched cottage, the tall tamarind trees which surround it, the white draped table at which the missionary stands in his surplice, and the dark-faced assemblage that, seated on the ground in long, receding rows, listens to the few words that fall from his lips. It is a sight sufficiently strange to attract considerable numbers of heathens of the higher castes; they stand at a little distance viewing a scene so different from all previous experience—a foreign teacher speaking in their own tongue; a religious gathering, though not in a temple made with hands; worship and adoration, but not to image or idol. And as the missionary himself looks down on the attentive, orderly gathering before him, can he repress a little sorrow and a little exultation?—exultation, that God has permitted him to see some of the labour of his hands—sorrow, that what has been achieved is but a tithe of what might be done, and what ought to have been accomplished. In my discourse on these occasions, as also on Christmas-day, I was accustomed merely to repeat again and again the

angel messages of peace and good-will—to describe the
Saviour's birth in a stable and the appearance of the
heavenly host to the poor shepherds of Bethlehem, and
then lead my hearers to think of the birth of Christianity
among themselves, and the duties and obligations of the
blessed day so near to us. And well do I remember the
deep and all-absorbing attention with which I was listened
to. It was the speaking of heart to heart. I could but
preach in a foreign language with faltering looks and
uncertain accents. I doubt not there may have been
many a blunder, many an ungainly mistake; but there is
an earnestness to understand, and an innate politeness in
all classes of Hindus, which renders them lenient critics of
any who address them in a religious capacity, and so I am
able to recall the quiet attention, the almost solemn silence,
the glittering eye, the outstretched neck, the appreciative
gesture, which more than satisfied, encouraged, and cheered
me. When the few short collects of our order of evening
prayer had been recited and responded to by hearty
amens, one or two of the hymns so long and sedulously
practised are sung to original Hindu tunes. The effect,
though somewhat monotonous, is still very sweet and
striking; and as almost every individual joins, and
occasionally cymbals are struck to mark the time, there
rises upon the still night air a volume of harmonious
sound, that may be heard far and wide, and in its soft
solemnity contrasts most favourably with the wild music and
the discordant cries that mark a Hindu idolatrous feast.
The assembled congregation is then permitted quietly to
disperse. A certain amount of shelter from the night air
and heavy dew is afforded to the women, but the men are
obliged to rough it. They light fires and sit around; they
produce the jonna-cakes and cold rice and curds, tied up
in a cloth, for their supper, and then lie down to snatch a
few hours of sleep before Christmas morning and its new
rejoicings dawn upon them.

Occasionally on Christmas eve an entertainment was afforded to the assembled people, which never failed to fill them with the utmost wonder and intense gratification. This was an exhibition of the magic lantern. A passage in Dr. Livingstone's travels had attracted my attention, in which he asserts that this was the only means of instruction that he was ever desired to repeat; and the effect of the repeated exhibitions to the African chiefs was such as to induce me to try the efficacy of this toy in conveying information in India. I had procured, at considerable expense, a lantern capable of throwing a clear disc of light ten feet in diameter, and an assortment of slides on all subjects — scriptural, astronomical, topographical, and simply comic. A display of the "light pictures," as they were called, was attended by thousands : not the Christians alone, but the surrounding heathen of all classes and denominations thronged to the spectacle. I was accustomed also to invite such of my heathen friends as I had been brought into close intimacy with, and there were not a few who came quite uninvited, but whose presence in the midst of a body of low caste Christians I was fain to regard as a compliment. In the grove before my little house two tall poles would be set up, and a great white sheet stretched between them, upon which would appear successively bright and well-painted representations on various subjects, calculated to instruct as well as amuse. Unfortunately, from the great price demanded for thoroughly good Scripture slides, I was obliged to content myself with those of inferior workmanship, some of which were pleasing, but others too roughly executed to produce any very elevating impression. My natural history slides were very good, one in especial of a tiger's head with moving eyes and opening mouth, produced a most ludicrous impression of terror; another of a wild boar, life size, elicited year by year the same joke. One of my people was a great pig-sticker, passionately fond of sport;

x

and the general cry to him would be, " Now, then, here is one of your friends." Diagrams that explained the geography of the earth, the phenomena of the eclipses, the revolutions of the planets, &c., were explained as well as I was able, and whatever was said was most attentively listened to; but it was when the slides representing the " Tiger and Tub " were shown that the " roars of laughter," so conventional in an English gathering, but exceptional in the case of all Indian assemblies, prevailed. The question has often presented itself to my mind, may not the magic lantern be made more use of for the purposes of instructing a 'semi-civilised people ? Lectures on Scripture history thus illustrated for our converts, and on general subjects for the heathen around, would, I think, leave an almost indelible impression on the mind, and convey instruction by sight as well as by hearing. This reminds me of another arrangement prepared for the Christmas gratification of my assembled people. My mother had presented the mission with a series of highly-coloured Scripture illustrations, and these were hung round the walls of the little chapels or school-rooms, and never failed to attract each a curious and amused group. It was encouraging, too, to see the self-appointed *cicerones* on these occasions ; some boy of the school, some young man of the *preparandi* class, was proud to distinguish himself, and to explain as well as he could the incident represented. All these preparations were the more interesting because they were strictly exceptional. What is common becomes but little regarded : and in India especially, what is easily obtained or gratuitously conferred is very likely to be but lightly esteemed. I confess that I was chary in my gifts and entertainments of this nature, and doled out, so to speak, the yearly amount of pleasurable excitement ; but upon the sacred feasts of our Church there was nothing calculated to afford innocent enjoyment that I scrupled to introduce or permit. Some may think that I went too far (and men

are ever prone to extremes) in permitting the use of fireworks, of Indian music, of procession, and song and dance;
but I would beg such to remember that an eastern Church
cannot be moulded on strict western principles; that
"ceremonies," as Disraeli, says, "are the salt of life;"
that, if these requirements of Oriental life be not permitted
to a certain extent within authorised limits, the probability
is that the Indian Church will in time break through the
barriers of restraint so commonly imposed, and indulge
in a license on these matters far greater than has ever
previously been permitted.

The stillness of the night would, in the very first hour
of the "great day," be broken by a short interlude, which
announced to the still slumbering crowds that the feast
had begun. I had introduced and encouraged the custom
of singing Christmas carols from house to house, and our
book of hymns in the vernacular furnished some very
suitable to the occasion; accordingly the village choirs
then present, headed by their masters, would, at the untimely hour of one in the morning, break forth into strains
loud enough to wake me from my first sleep, yet sweetly
mellowed by distance. How vividly at this moment I
recall the feeling of lying awake in my little room, listening
to the sound as it rose and fell in the still night; now it
would come near as the singers passed round my house,
and again it would die away to the softest notes as they
passed up and down the streets of the village; and then
would ensue a lull and an interval of profound quiet. A
Hindu sleeps comfortably, though the hard ground be his
bed and the star-lit heavens his canopy, till the morning
dawns for which all this has been the preparation, and
for the cheerful rejoicing of which this has been but the
earnest.

Christmas in India falls during what is called the cold
season; and in the district where I was stationed the
mornings at that time were chilly,   the days bright,

x 2

but by no means oppressive. Near by my house ran a
river, and on its banks the holiday toilet of numbers of
men and women would, at early morning, be scrupulously
arranged. The dress of the Hindu is graceful and becoming, that of the men consisting of two pieces of cloth
of considerable size, the one bound round the waist and
tucked up between the legs, the other thrown over the
shoulder, a turban and occasionally a jacket of the brightest
hue completing his attire; and that of the women comprising a short-sleeved and very tight bodice, and a long
piece of native cloth, generally white, but relieved by a
broad streak of colour along the border, which is tied
round the waist fold upon fold, and one end of it brought
over the shoulder. The hair of the women is worn à la
chignon, after a much simpler fashion; it is so arranged
as to lie, not directly at the back of the head, but either
drawn somewhat to one side or the other; on festival occasions it is filled, not with a padding fearfully and wonderfully arranged, but with a handful of sweet-smelling flowers
of the Indian jessamine, or of the more brilliant buds of
the chrysanthemum. Flowers were rare in the district,
the people being too busily engaged in the struggles for
the necessaries of life to have time to seek for its luxuries;
and in that sterile soil and parched climate flowering
shrubs are reared with difficulty; but I was accustomed to
send a hurkarah or a porter to the principal town, upwards
of fifty miles distant, and he returned laden, among other
articles, with garlands of flowers, which were distributed
among the women and girls, and otherwise made use of
for ornamenting the draped table that served as our altar.

At the early hour of eight, or at latest nine a.m., our
Christmas service began. By this time the Christians
from the nearer villages would have arrived, and it was of
importance that the services of the day should be over
before the sun's rays became too powerful to admit of our
sitting in the open air. Once more, then, the bell would

give the signal for assembling—once more in front of the
missionary's house a congregation would be gathered, still
larger than that assembled on the previous evening; and
on the little table, covered with its white sheet and garlanded with flowers, would now be exhibited the plain cup
and platter of glass and earthenware,* to be made use of
in administering the sacramental mysteries of our faith.
It was with mingled feelings of shame and satisfaction that
I looked on the scene,—on the simple altar, on the duly
ordered ranks of the worshippers; with satisfaction at the
abundant evidence of the spread of truth in the midst of
a heathen land, and yet with a tinge of shame and sorrow
at the poor and meagre development of the externals of
that holy faith.   How often on such occasions, when a
demonstration, so to speak, was made of the power and
spread of the Gospel, did I long for those outward
accompaniments of Christianity which in England serve to
strengthen the hold and to endear the associations of the
Church.   Oh, for some temple, however plain, I have
wished—some small aisle or chancel worthy of the name
and service of God, where decency and order may be
enforced—where the beauty of holiness may be exhibited,
and the Sacraments at all times and in all seasons duly
administered !

The service began with the ancient greeting, " Christ
is born to-day," and the response, " May He be born in
thine heart ; " and surely for that one moment, when the
missionary looks down on the well-ordered congregation,
stretching rank after rank to the farthest limits of his poor
accommodation, a body of five or seven hundred persons;
when he sees the reverential posture, the orderly conduct
—all sitting, standing, or kneeling as the rubric directs;

* The missionary in charge will feel no longer a twinge of shame
and sorrow as he takes in hand the glass tumbler and the willow-
pattern plate once used ; the earnestness and self-denial of a young
lady in England has furnished the mission with small, but beautiful,
sacramental vessels of silver.

above all, when the voice of that multitude is heard in the responses, like the voice of many waters—for one moment the missionary may be pardoned the happy, exulting thought, "Under God's good providence I have been instrumental in the accomplishment of so great a work."

The usual service for the day proceeded just as it would in any church in England, except that the Lessons were read by two of the catechists, or schoolmasters—young natives, who are being trained up to labour among their brethren—and the Te Deum was sung antiphonally, the men singing one verse, the women another. A short sermon was delivered, and the Holy Sacrament administered to a few of the most advanced Christians, and with this the sacred services of the day concluded.

Before, however, the people dispersed to return to their own villages, there took place a little exchange of kindness and good feeling between priest and people. They bring him small offerings as tokens of congratulation, respect, and affection—he, in return, entertains them all at one single meal before he dismisses them to their homes. Seated at the door of his hut, and assuming for the occasion a certain amount of state, it is the missionary's privilege to receive at the hands of his people some trivial offering, such as each is disposed to bring. A packet of sugar, a few flowers, fruits, or vegetables— the "little balm, and a little honey, spices, and myrrh, nuts, and almonds," which Jacob bade his sons to bear to the Governor of Egypt—these are still the offerings with which an Eastern people are accustomed to present themselves before those they love or respect. The entertainment which the missionary offers to his numerous guests is of a far simpler character, and much less expensive in itself than our English readers would suppose. To the people of the country, who principally subsist on cholum, a kind of maize, rice is considered a luxury, and if you are able to give your visitors a dish of curry and rice, you are considered to have exercised a princely hospitality. To entertain even five hundred is not, then, a matter of difficulty, and a few years ago, when grain was cheap, £5 or £6 would have been the utmost that a dinner for so many would have cost. All that the missionary has to do is to give out a certain quantity of raw grain, and, if very liberally disposed, present them with two or three sheep. Soon fires are kindled; the women prepare the food; broad leaves serve as platters; all sit down on the ground and in the open air. The missionary asks a blessing, and the savoury meal is joyfully discussed. Nor is this Christmas dinner destitute of importance in itself— it draws the people more together; will help to break down caste distinctions; unites the Christians as one great family among the heathen by whom they are surrounded, and gives an opportunity to the missionary of acknowledging and repaying the countless kindnesses which he receives at the hands of his people, the liberality and hospitality which, poor as they are, they exercise towards himself.

With the dinner the proceedings of the day came to a close, and all set out on their return to their separate villages. Soon the missionary's hut was deserted, and resumed its quiet, solitary aspect. The great event of the year was over; he must prepare to lay his plans, that next year's gathering shall outdo this year's. Would our readers have one more picture? They must try to imagine it for themselves; and if they think that the rosy hue has too much predominated in the above account, the concluding scene will supply the darker trait of missionary life. It is that of the missionary himself, left alone, after all are gone to their homes, when, weary with the excitement of the day, the re-action begins; when, perhaps, he sits down alone to his own Christmas dinner, and finds, in his solitude, that whatever it may be to others, his heart has no response for the festivity and rejoicing around. Never, perhaps, does he feel more alone; never do the difficulties of his work more press on his jaded mind; never is he more disposed to be "cast down and disquieted" within him than when the crowd has left him to himself, and joy, excitement, and enthusiasm are succeeded by weariness, and painfulness, and solitude.

Burmah.

THE great and favourable change which has taken place in the policy of the King of Burmah towards Christianity, and the successful efforts that are being made by the missionaries of our Church at Rangoon, Moulmein, and, more lately, at Mandalay, the capital of the kingdom, may give to the following sketch, compiled from various sources, an interest which otherwise it could not have possessed.

Before the wars with England, Burmah was the most considerable of the Indo-Chinese nations which inhabit the farther peninsula of India. It comprehended the whole of the extensive region lying between the latitudes 9° and 27° N. At present its limits are lat. 16° and 27° N., and long. 93° and 99° E.; its area is estimated at 195,000 square miles, and its population at about 5,000,000.

The coasts and rivers of Burmah are thickly studded with towns and villages ; the upper portion of the country is mountainous, and its scenery is described as among the most beautiful in the world.

In the maritime provinces the year has two seasons— the dry and the wet. The latter begins towards the middle of May, and lasts until October. The rainy season is the only time when the country is unhealthy for Europeans, and even then there are many places where they may reside with impunity. In the mountain districts the climate is generally healthy, and the cold sometimes approaches in severity that of our own winters.

The river Irawadi, which, like the Ganges, is regarded

as sacred, issues from the mountains, and, after passing through the whole of the empire, empties itself into the Bay of Bengal. It has a course of more than 1,200 miles to the sea, and in various parts of its course its breadth varies from one to five miles. Like the Delta of the Nile, that of the Irawadi is exceedingly fruitful; and this river, in this also like the Nile, is the commercial highway of the country. The other rivers of Burmah are of no great importance.

The fruits of Burmah are varied in their character, but inferior to those of neighbouring countries. Timber trees, however, are abundant, and the teak forests occupy no inconsiderable portion of the Burmese territory. Like the woody and uncultivated districts of Hindustan, those of Burmah are extremely pestiferous; and though the woodcutters are said to be a hardy and active race of men, on whom climate and suffering appear to have little effect, yet they are very short-lived.

The mineral riches of Burmah are great. Gold dust is procured in considerable quantities from the head waters of the various rivers; there is also much silver in the land; and rubies and other precious stones are so numerous as to form a regular portion of the commercial products. Iron, tin, lead, and many other things which form the wealth of every country, are plentiful; and coal is found in the inland provinces.

The animals of Burmah are numerous. The domestic quadrupeds are the ox, the buffalo, the horse, and the elephant. The two first are much used throughout the country, though to the Burmese the ox is an expensive animal, as their religion forbids its use as food, and they have no profitable way, therefore, of disposing of the disabled cattle. The horse is rarely used, except for the saddle, and in some parts of the country it is quite unknown. The elephant is now much more the object of royal luxury and ostentation than anything else, and is nowhere used as a beast of burden. Dogs and cats, sheep and swine, asses and goats, are but little cared for, but are allowed to pursue their own ways unmolested. Wild animals of many kinds abound in Burmah; but neither wolves, jackals, foxes, nor hyenas are to be found in the country.

Burmah is occupied by various races of people. 1. The Pegu race, or Talaim, who inhabit the delta of the Irawadi, and who were in the ascendant for many years. 2. The Karens, who live on the borders and low plains in the province of Bassein; and amongst whom, in days gone by, the Gospel found more favour than with any other of the Burmese populations. 3. The Maramas, or Burmans, who inhabit the high lands above Pegu, and who are now the imperial race. They are supposed to be of the same valiant Malay stock which has colonised so large a portion of the globe, and who probably passed by way of Polynesia to the American continent. Like the Incas of Peru, the Burmans boast a celestial origin; and the similarity of some of their institutions has led to the supposition of their being of the same original family.

The King of Burmah is probably the most despotic monarch on earth. In his titles, he asserts himself to be lord, ruler, and sole possessor of the lives, persons, and property of his subjects. Every Burman, therefore, is born the king's slave; and every Burman thinks it an honour to be the thrall of such a sovereign. It is, however, to the credit of the law-giver, and the sovereign who, though absolute, obeyed the law, to mention that no married woman can be seized on by the emissaries of the king. This naturally leads the Burmese women to contract marriages very early, either actually or fictitiously.

But, notwithstanding the King of Burmah is absolute, he, like certain absolute rulers in Europe, has two nominal councils—a public one and a cabinet. But he is not bound to follow their advice; and, his measures very frequently being predetermined, when his ministers have proved un-

willing to give an immediate and unconditional assent, he
has been known to chase them from his presence with a
drawn sword.

There is no regular Burmese army; but every man is
liable to serve. When the king requires an army, he fixes
the number of soldiers necessary for the enterprise, and
nominates the general to command them. The conduct of
the officers who levy the troops is not unlike that of
Falstaff. And persons who are able to buy themselves off
do so; and the consequence is, a rabble is assembled,
without subordination or discipline, formidable only to the
barbarian tribes of the frontier, but totally unable to cope
with the civilised forces in the service of England.

The whole country is regarded as the property of the
Crown; and the waste and uncultivated parts are at the
disposition of any one who will settle on them. The only
duty incumbent on the settler, is that he must enclose and
cultivate it. If he does not improve the land within a
certain period, it reverts to the Crown, and may be occupied by another.

In civil disputes, the parties have the right to select
their own judges; while criminal causes are tried before
the chief governor of the town or village. But notwithstanding the apparent fairness of this arrangement, the
utmost corruption appears to prevail in the administration
of justice; and "To be put to justice" is the Burman
phrase for the severest calamity that can befall any person.

The different punishments for offences are: fines, the
stocks, imprisonment, labour in chains, flogging, branding,
maiming, slavery, and death. The last is inflicted by de-
capitation, drowning, or crucifixion. The killing of slaves
is not held to be murder, and is atoned by fines.

The husband may chastise his wife for misbehaviour,
and, in the event of continued offences, may divorce her
without appeal. The wife, however, is not without her
privileges. Should her husband go away with the army,

she may marry again at the expiration of six years; if he be absent on business, she must wait seven years; and if away on any religious mission, ten years.

Changing a landmark is heavily punished. A person hurt in wrestling, or any other athletic exercise, cannot recover damages; but if he be mortally injured, he who caused the hurt must pay the price of his body. An empty vehicle must give way to a full one; and when two men laden with burdens meet, he that has the sun at his back must give place.

The flight of a debtor does not relieve his family of liability; but the wife is not obliged to pay the debts which her husband may have contracted during a former marriage. The property of insolvents is equally shared among the creditors, without preference. The eldest son inherits the arms, wardrobe, bed, and jewellery of his father; the rest of the property is divided into four equal parts, of which the widow has three, and the family, exclusive of the eldest son, take the remaining fourth.

The following is the value set upon men, women, and children:—A new-born male infant, four ticals, or 10s.; a female infant, 7s. 6d.; a boy, £1 5s.; a girl, 17s. 6d.; a young man, £3 15s.; a young woman, £4 2s. 6d. Rich persons, however, are valued in proportion to their wealth and importance.

The police are not incorruptible, or, as is the case in most places, so vigilant as they might be, and the country is infested with robbers. The fact is, personal government is not omnipotence; and among the officials responsibility is shifted from one person to another, and great ignorance and want of intelligence seems to pervade every department. The condition of the country, however, is probably no worse than that of China, where the actual amount of crime is not great in proportion to the population.

The revenue of the Burman Empire is a duty of 10 per cent. upon all merchandise coming from abroad; the produce of certain mines, export duties, a family tax, and an excise on salt, fruit-trees, rice, &c. No inconsiderable portion of the royal revenue, however, is derived from the presents which the officers of the palace receive for the granting of various favours. The sum total of the king's income, in consequence of the dishonesty of the collectors and others, is probably not more than £25,000 per annum.

The Burmese have no coined money. At every payment the money is assayed and weighed to ascertain its value. When a bargain is to be concluded, the seller very often asks to see the money the purchaser has to offer him. The circulating medium for small payments is lead; silver, however, is the standard, although gold is also in use, and is considered to be seventeen times the value of silver. A commission of two and a-half per cent. is charged for assaying money; one per cent. is lost in the operation, so that if the operation be repeated forty times, the original amount is wholly absorbed—a fact which shows the great waste which attends this rude substitute for a currency.

Burmah has a considerable foreign trade with Mergui, Chittagong, Calcutta, Penang, and Madras. The principal harbours are Rangoon and Bassein, both of which are good, though foreign vessels never go to the latter.

The exports of Burmah are teak-wood, cotton, wax, cutch, sticklac, and ivory; also lead, copper, arsenic, tin, amber, indigo, tobacco, honey, tamarinds, and gems. The most considerable article of commerce, however, is the teak-wood, of which the supply is so abundant that, though very dear in other parts of Asia, it is sold to as many ships as arrive, at a very moderate price.

The domestic architecture of the Burmese greatly resembles that of the Polynesians. The houses are constructed with timber and bamboos, fastened with lighter pieces of wood, placed transversely. Pillars made of brick or stone, supporting a frame, are never seen. The sides are usually covered with mats, but sometimes with thatch, fastened by split canes. Even in the best houses, which are never more than one storey high, the roofs are almost invariably of thatch, wrought most skilfully, and forming a perfect security against both wind and rain. The floors are elevated a few feet from the earth, which makes them more comfortable than the houses of Bengal. The doors and windows are merely of matting, in bamboo panes, which, when not closed, are propped up, so as to form a shade.

But it is in the pagodas that the architectural skill of the Burmans really displays itself, and of these extraordinary temples no mere verbal description can give an adequate idea.

The dress of the Burmese is very simple. That of the men consists of a long piece of striped cotton or silk, folded round the middle, and flowing down to the feet. When they are not at work this is loosed and is thrown partly over the shoulder, and then covers the body in no ungraceful manner. The higher classes add to this a jacket of white muslin, or occasionally of broadcloth or velvet. The turban of muslin is worn by every one. Their shoes or sandals are of wood, or cowhide covered with cloth; these are only worn abroad. The women wear a petticoat of cotton or silk. In the street they wear a jacket like that of the men, and a mantle over it.

Both sexes wear cylinders of gold, silver, horn, wood, marble, or paper in their ears. The fashionable diameter of the ear-hole is one inch. The boring of a boy's ears is the occasion of much festivity, as it is considered equal to the assumption of the *toga virilis* among the ancient Romans; yet when youth and the period of dandyism has gone by they care but little for such a decoration, and generally use the ear-hole as a cigar-rack.

The hair is always well taken care of, and is anointed

every day with sessamum oil. The men gather the hair in a bunch on the top of the head, like the North American Indians, while the women tie it in a knot behind.

Compared with our own the food of the Burmese is mean and bad, and they will eat many kinds of reptiles and insects. They have two meals a day, one about nine in the morning, and the other at sunset. Their usual beverage is water.

The bed consists of a simple mat spread on the ground, and a small pillow, or piece of wood, precisely in the manner of the Polynesians. The rich occasionally have a low wooden bedstead and mattresses.

In the treatment of the sick their practice, like that of all semi-barbarous nations, is absurd and unskilful, although some of their remedies are undoubtedly good.

At death many ceremonies are observed. While the family of the deceased give themselves up to lamentation, their friends make all the arrangements. A great store of fruits, cotton cloths, and money is prepared for distribution among the priests and the poor. This is accomplished by means of a burial club, which, strangely enough, is one of the institutions of Burmah. On the day of the burning, a procession is formed thus : first, the people carrying the presents ; secondly, female priests draped in white, bearing some of the funeral paraphernalia ; thirdly, a number of priests walking two and two ; then the musicians ; then the bier, borne by friends of the deceased ; immediately behind which come the wives, children, and nearest relatives all clad in white ; and lastly, a concourse of people more or less connected with the deceased. At the place where the body is burnt the senior priest delivers a sermon, which generally consists of reflections on the five secular commandments and the ten good works of Buddhism. The coffin is then delivered to the burners of the dead, who set fire to it, while others distribute the alms to the priests and people. Burning, however, is not invariable; persons that have been drowned or have died of infectious diseases are immediately interred. On the third day after the burning, the relatives collect the ashes, which are placed in an urn and buried. Until the ninth day after the burning the festivities are kept up, in order, it is said, to divert the minds of the relatives from the loss they have sustained.

The arts of the Burmese are very simple. Every man can build his own house, and the females of the family can manufacture all the apparel. Wood-carving has been brought by them to some perfection, though of painting they know but little. They are skilful workers in gold, and in bell-casting no Oriental nations can compete with them.

Slavery is very general among the Burmese; though the condition of slaves is not very different from that of free persons. The estimation in which they are held is also high, inasmuch as they are marked in value with " a sou, a nephew, and an ox ! "

In character the Burmese appear to differ in many points from the Hindus and other East Indians. They are more lively, active, and industrious, and, though fond of repose, are seldom idle when there is an inducement for exertion. When such inducement is offered, they exhibit not only great strength, but courage and perseverance. But these valuable traits are rendered nearly useless in consequence of the low state of civilisation and morals. The poorer classes, furnished by a happy climate with all necessaries at the price of only occasional labour, and the few who are above that necessity, find no proper pursuits to fill up their leisure. Folly and sensuality find gratification almost without an effort, and without expenditure. Sloth becomes the repose of the poor and the business of the rich ; and life is wasted in the profitless alternative of sensual ease, rude drudgery, and native sport. No institutions exist for the improvement of posterity,

Y

and successive generations pass like the crops upon their fields. Servility, the inevitable consequence of despotism, prevails amongst them to a frightful extent, overcoming, in many instances, the sense of right implanted in their bosoms as men. Servility inevitably leads to the remainder of the mean vices. One of the principal precepts of their religion forbids lying; but there is no land where truth is more disregarded. A man who tells the truth is considered a fool, and incapable of managing his own affairs. But as every rule has its exception, so there are, side by side with this dark catalogue of faults, not a few good qualities; and some travellers say, that in Burmah are found many persons whose affability and courtesy, benevolence and gratitude, and other virtues, contrast strongly with the vices of others. There are instances on record of shipwrecks on their coast, when the mariners have been relieved in the villages, and treated with a generous hospitality which they would probably not have experienced in many Christian countries.

The Burmese are probably no worse than other semi-barbarous heathen. That they have great natural capacity is certain. With Christianity, the blessings of a higher civilisation, and the peaceful arts that elevate man, as man, will obtain sway; and Burmah may then take a high position in the family of nations.

We may now glance at the religious tenets and ceremonies of the Burmese, and give some account of the work which has been and is being done for Christ in Burmah.

The reformation under Guadama, in the sixth century B.C., which led to the establishment of Buddhism in the place of the ancient Hindu creed, was important in many respects, but in none so much as in substituting the principle of the unity and indivisibility of the object of adoration for the gross polytheism of Hindustan, although it presented no clear conception of the Being to be adored.

The general principles of Buddhism have been thus summed up:—1. To take refuge only with Buddha. 2. To be steadfast in the determination of aiming at the highest pitch of excellence in order to arrive at the proper state for death. 3. To be obedient and reverent towards Buddha. 4. To make pleasing offerings. 5. To glorify and exalt Buddha by music and singing and constant praise. 6. To confess sin truly and humbly, with a fixed resolution to repent. 7. To wish well toward all. 8. To encourage the ministers of the faith in their mission.

The duty of the different classes of Buddhists has been defined in the following manner by an eminent Buddhist reformer of the fourteenth century :—

1. Men of the lowest order of mind must believe that there is a God; and that there is a future life in which they will receive the reward or punishment of their actions and conduct in this life.

2. Men of the middle degree of mental capacity must add to the above the knowledge that all things in this world are perishable; that imperfection is a pain and degradation; and that deliverance from existence is a deliverance from pain, and, consequently, a final beatitude.

3. Men of the third or highest order must believe, in further addition, that nothing exists, or will continue always, or cease absolutely, except through dependence on a casual connection or concatenation; so will they arrive at the true knowledge of God.

Such is Buddhism as recognised in Burmah; and it is not surprising that to men who have failed to realise that Christianity is a spiritual life system, it represents a creed which might be taken for Christianity, could its votaries point to Christ as its preacher and the Mosaic dispensation as its antecedent. The most perfect of the heathen systems of philosophy however can at best but improve the intellect, but Christianity in its integrity restores to man that which he lost by sin; it quickens him into spiritual life; it enables him to serve God in spirit and in truth; it makes him meet for the inheritance of saints in light. This is the grand feature of Christianity which missionaries, when dealing with Buddhists and others whose religions are systems of philosophy, should labour to make known. No mere placing of precept against precept, no simple detail of duty toward God and man will suffice; but while preaching repentance and demanding faith, the missionaries should make known that through the extension of the Incarnation by the ministrations of the Church, "We dwell in Christ, and Christ in us; we are one with Christ, and Christ with us," and that this it is which raises Christianity above every other religion in the world.

Could the disciples of Buddhism act up to its principles, oppression and injury would be known no more within their borders. Its deeds of merit are, in all cases, either really beneficial to mankind or harmless. It has no mythology of obscene and ferocious deities, no sanguinary or impure observances, no self-inflicted tortures, no confounding of right and wrong by making certain iniquities laudable in worship. In its moral code, its descriptions of the purity and peace of the first ages, of the shortening of man's life because of the sin of man, &c., it seems to have followed genuine traditions; but all this, in so far as spiritual life is concerned, profiteth nothing. The Burmese are no better than any other of the heathen: their low moral condition, and the degrading influences everywhere at work among them, prove that spiritually Buddhism does no more for man than the crude mythology and debasing superstitions of the Africans.

The priests of Burmah are named Ponghees, that is, "great example," or "great glory." Rahan, or "holy man," once much used in describing the priests, is now almost obsolete. The office of the priesthood is not hereditary, for the Burmans are unshackled by castes, and indeed a priest may become a layman again, though after re-entering society he cannot again assume the sacerdotal office. The priests' convents serve as places where an education superior to that usually obtained in the schools may be received, and the young men not being bound by vows may return to the active scenes of life, and take military or political work. The priests have but little political influence, and are only consulted in ecclesiastical and literary matters. They live on the charity of those to whom they minister, and on the whole they do not appear to be badly off. Their dress is yellow, and is composed of two cloths, which are so wrapped round them as to completely envelop them from the shoulders to the heels. Their heads are shaved, and to shade the bare poll from the sun they carry a talipot or palmyra leaf in their hands.

The priesthood is divided into regular grades. The highest functionary is called the *Tha-thena-byng;* he resides at Ava, has jurisdiction over all other priests, and appoints the president of every monastery. He stands high at court, and is considered one of the great men of the kingdom. Next to him are the *Ponghees,* strictly so called, one of whom presides in each monastery. Next are the *Oo-pe-zins,* comprising those who have passed the novitiate, sustained a regular examination, and chosen the priesthood for life. Both these orders are considered to understand religion so well as to think for themselves, and expound the law out of their own hearts, without being obliged to follow what they have read in books. Next are the *Ko-yen-ga-lay,* who have retired from the world and wear the yellow cloth, but are not all seeking to pass the examination, and become *Oo-pe-zins.* They have retired for an education or a livelihood, or to gain a divorce, or for various objects, and many such return to secular life. By courtesy all who wear the yellow cloth are called *Ponghees.*

The moral law in regard to priests is very strict in precept, but very lax in practice. Deterioration and degradation have set their seal upon all the institutions of Burmah—all are equally foul and corrupt.

The most interesting and most characteristic ceremony of the Burmese is the funeral of a priest, as it contains a mixture of solemnity and absurdity rarely to be met with. When a priest dies his body is embalmed, and the embalming process seems to be somewhat like that employed by the ancient Egyptians. The body is opened, the intestines taken out, the spaces are filled with various kinds of spices, the orifice is then closed up again and sewn together. After this the whole body is covered by a layer of wax; over the wax is placed a layer of lac, together with some bituminous compound, and the whole is then covered with leaf gold. About a year after the embalming, the body is removed from the monastery to a house built expressly for such purposes, where it is kept until the other priests order it to be burnt. The body is here placed upon a platform of bamboo and wood, and the house itself is gaily ornamented with paper and leaf gold. By the platform the coffin, overlaid with gold, and painted with various figures of death, is placed. In the courtyard two four-wheel carriages await the time fixed for the burning, one being intended for the coffin, the other for the platform and its apparatus.

The people of the place prepare rockets and other fireworks, as well as images much larger than life, which represent buffaloes, elephants, horses, and men. These images are drawn on carriages through the streets and round the town ; all the citizens, when the ceremonies are strictly observed, being compelled to assist. Flags, dancing girls and boys, singing men and women, and the principal persons of the place, carrying umbrellas as a sign of their rank, form the procession.

The following day the townspeople divide into two parties ; the carriage containing the corpse has four ropes attached to it, and the two parties pull one against the other and strive to draw away the carriage and its contents. This contest is continued till superior strength puts an end to it, or the cable breaks.

The third day is spent in discharging the rockets at the figures that were carried in procession, and in the evening there is a grand display of fireworks.

On the fourth day the corpse is burnt in a temporary house, by being made a target for rockets until the coffin and pile are set on fire and consumed. Sometimes, however, the body is blown from a cannon, in order that it may be conveyed more quickly to heaven.

Believing in a heaven, the Burmese also believe in a hell. Of heaven they conceive degrees of happiness, agreeing with the deservings of the individual, though all in heaven are supposed gradually to attain higher excellence and bliss, until that high state of eternal felicity is reached which is known by the name of Nirvân, and which consists of a perpetual ecstacy, where men are not only free from the troubles and miseries of life, from death, illness, and old age, but are abstracted from all sensation, and have no longer a thought or desire. Of hell they imagine four conditions of punishment :—1. Where men are degraded into beasts. 2. The Pieitta, a state of sorrow resembling the Tartarus of the Greeks. 3. The Assuricho, like unto the Pieitta in character but of greater degree. 4. The Niria, where the sufferings are by fire and cold, and where the worst of mankind are punished. None but infidels, however, are supposed to be condemned to an eternal punishment, though the time of confinement for believers is undecided. By good behaviour the sufferers, it is said, may gradually rise through all gradations and finally obtain Nirvân.

Such, briefly stated, is the religious system with which Christianity has to contend in Burmah. What is Christianity doing against this potent adversary?

From a pamphlet, called "God's work among the

Karens," we extract the following:—"Some who read these lines may already have heard of that glorious and blessed work among the Karens in Tennasserim and Pegu, by which the gracious Lord has animated the hearts of this waiting people, and by His wonder-working providence has confirmed that promise of His Word on which He hath caused us to hope. These noble people were never known to have a separate language or separate traditions till the first inquirers sought instruction from Dr. Judson, the heroic and devoted American missionary in Burmah. But now they appear to the eye of the Church a large distinct nation, divided into several tribes, with varying districts, but all worshipping the eternal God; all waiting for the promise of the Fathers—a true Book of Revelation, which would be brought to them by the white man over the sea." It would seem that a tradition existed among the Karens that God, the very God, had revealed His will to man, and that the "white man over the sea" had that revelation in a written word, and so when Judson and others appeared among them, hundreds upon hundreds received the word with all readiness of mind, avowed their faith and their thankfulness, and were baptized. "The facts," states the pamphlet, "are manifest and, since Apostolic days, unparalleled. These Karen people are signalising in a way most animating and most affecting the power of Divine grace. The first convert, Ko Tha Byn, 'The Karen Apostle,' was one to whom much had been forgiven, and who loved much. It was his meat and drink to do his Father's will; and he went forth warning every one night and day with tears, and proclaiming everywhere the one great truth on which his soul fed, that "Christ Jesus came into the world to save sinners." He died, and his works followed him. Men flocked in and the truth prevailed. Devoted men and women gave their lives to the service of God among these people, teaching the way of God more perfectly, but the world knew but little of their labours,

and even the Church of Christ scarcely heard of them.
Then came the last Burmese war, and Pegu was annexed
to British India. New stations were opened: the white
man went as a friend and a brother to preach salvation by
Jesus Christ, and the hearts of thousands were swayed
and softened. Native teachers who had but little human
learning, were endowed with gifts and graces which enabled
them to speak from their hearts, as dying men who had
tasted that the Lord was precious, to their dying fellow-
countrymen, beseeching them in Christ's stead to be re-
conciled to God; and their work was blessed. The wild
mountaineers who had braved the Burman despot; the
chafed survivor who mourned a family carried into slavery
by wilder tribes, or driven into exile by his cruel Burman
rulers; the savage chief who had learned no trade but war;
and the simple child, the lawless youth, even the aged
leper—all heard, received, and embraced the truth, and
then gave themselves to the Lord with all the fervour and
frankness of their simple natures."

To some this may appear to be the expression of an exaggerated feeling, but it seems a faithful summary of what
was and is being done among the Karens. We cannot
enter into the details, but letters are given from the Rev.
Dr. Mason of Tounghoo, at which place, within three years,
nearly three thousand adult believers were baptized; from
Major Phayre, the Commissioner of Pegu, and others which
testify to the truth of the above extracts. Major Phayre
in his report to the Government of India, says: "The
actual number of Christian converts among the Karens
in the province of Pegu is 10,822 persons; these, with
their families, make a probable number of 50,000 souls
under instruction and Christian influence."

During the war with England many of the converts suffered persecution, some death, on the accusation of having
called in the English to take the country; but in all things
they are said to have been faithful, and to have clung to

the Lord with all the fervour and frankness of their simple natures.

Now, if so much has been done by the exponents of an imperfect form of Christianity—for by the American Baptist missionaries this work among the Karens has been accomplished, what in God's good time, if we be but faithful, may we expect to flow from the work of the Church? Mention has been made in a number of *Mission Life* of the really wonderful way in which the work of the Church is progressing in other parts of Burmah, and the Society for the Propagation of the Gospel has given such a wide circulation to the remarkable report of the Rev. J. E. Marks, the missionary through whom this good work has been mainly brought to pass, that recapitulation here would be unnecessary. Suffice it to say, the King of Burmah has been as good as his word,—he has built and partly endowed schools at Mandalay, the capital of his kingdom, at which nearly a thousand children attend; he has given his subjects full permission to become Christians if they be moved thereto; and by the latest intelligence we learn that the foundation-stone of the first Christian church at Mandalay has just been laid on a plot of ground given by the king for that purpose. These are but promises of greater things in store, and we look and wait with faith and confidence for such things as will testify to the grace vested in the Church—will vindicate the power of redeeming love, fill our souls with gratitude and our lips with praise, and make known to all the world that the Church does wield the powers of the world to come; and that God by His ministers does act upon the souls of men, as He acts by none other.

www.ingramcontent.com/pod-product-compliance
Lightning Source LLC
Chambersburg PA
CBHW021753110726
47902CB00006B/1509